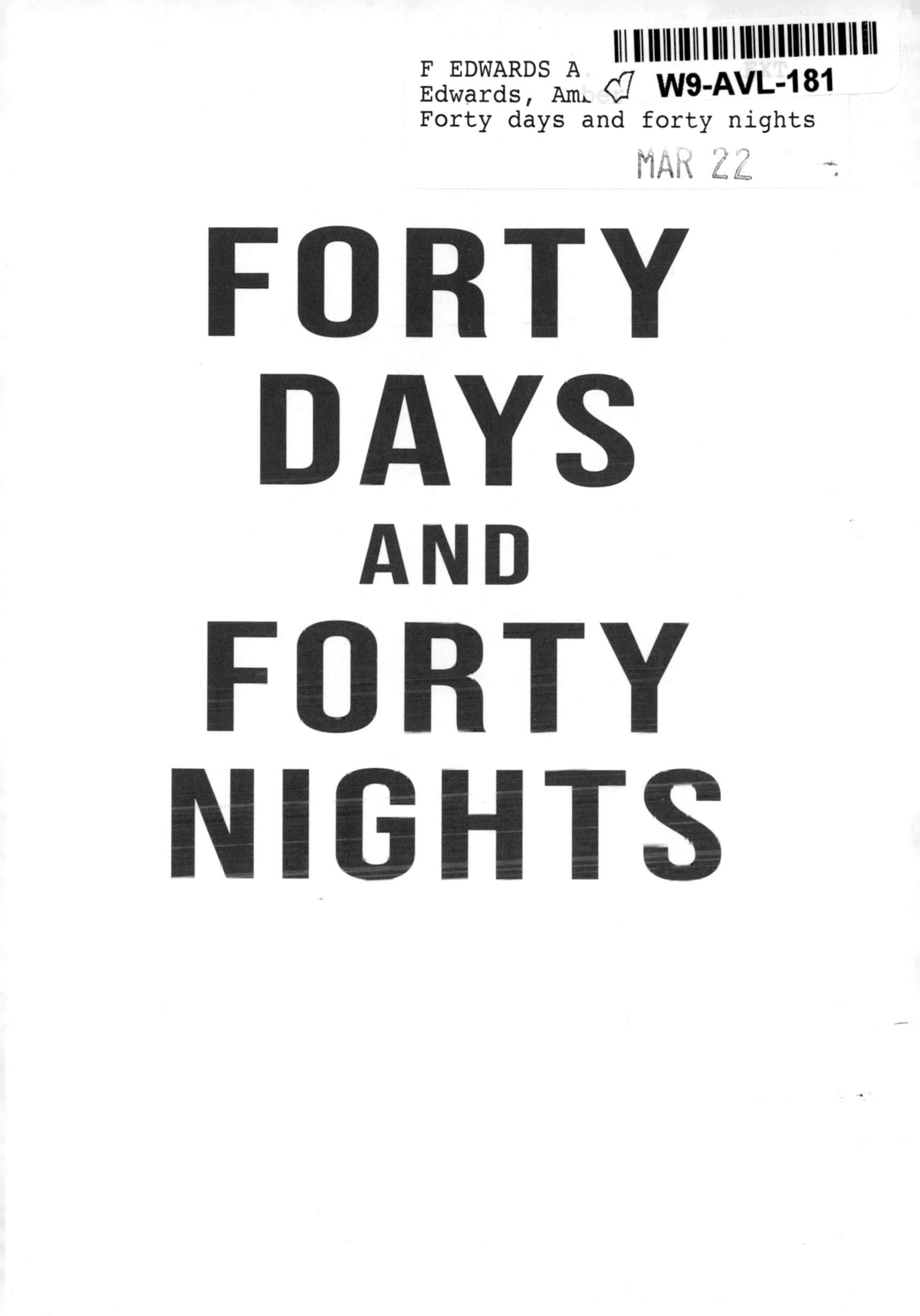

FORTY DAYS AND FORTY NIGHTS

FORTY DAYS AND FORTY NIGHTS

A Novel of the Mississippi River

Amber Edwards ▪ Justin Scott

University of Louisiana at Lafayette Press
2021

ISBN 13 (paper): 978-1-946160-76-8

cover art by Clyde Lynds

University of Louisiana at Lafayette Press
P.O. Box 43558
Lafayette, LA 70504
http://ulpress.org

Library of Congress Cataloging-in-Publication Data

Names: Edwards, Amber, 1960- author. | Scott, Justin, author.
Title: Forty days and forty nights / a novel by Amber Edwards & Justin Scott.
Description: Lafayette, LA : University of Louisiana at Lafayette Press, [2021]
Identifiers: LCCN 2021006474 | ISBN 9781946160768 (paperback)
Subjects: GSAFD: Suspense fiction.
Classification: LCC PS3605.D865 F67 2021 | DDC 813/.6--dc23
LC record available at https://lccn.loc.gov/2021006474

In memory of
Steve Stevens, at his best

ALSO BY JUSTIN SCOTT

THRILLERS by JUSTIN SCOTT
The Shipkiller
The Turning
Normandie Triangle
A Pride Of Royals
Rampage
The Widow of Desire
The Nine Dragons
The Empty Eye Of The Sea
(Published in England)
The Auction (Published in England)
Treasure Island: A Modern Novel

THRILLERS & SEA STORIES
WRITING as PAUL GARRISON
Fire And Ice
Red Sky At Morning
Buried At Sea
Sea Hunter
The Ripple Effect
The Janson Command
The Janson Option

THRILLERS
WRITING as ALEXANDER COLE
The Auction

MYSTERIES by JUSTIN SCOTT
Many Happy Returns
Treasure for Treasure

THE BEN ABBOTT MYSTERY SERIES
HardScape
StoneDust
FrostLine
McMansion
Mausoleum

MYSTERIES
WRITING as J.S. BLAZER
Deal Me Out
Lend a Hand

ISAAC BELL NOVELS
with CLIVE CUSSLER
The Wrecker
The Spy
The Race
The Thief
The Striker
The Bootlegger
The Assassin
The Gangster
The Cutthroat

"If we are to have another contest in the near future of our national existence I predict that the dividing line will not be Mason and Dixon's, but between patriotism and intelligence on the one side, and superstition, ambition, and ignorance on the other."

–Ulysses S. Grant

General Winfield Scott's Anaconda Plan
to Win the Civil War

Library of Congress, Geography and Map Division.

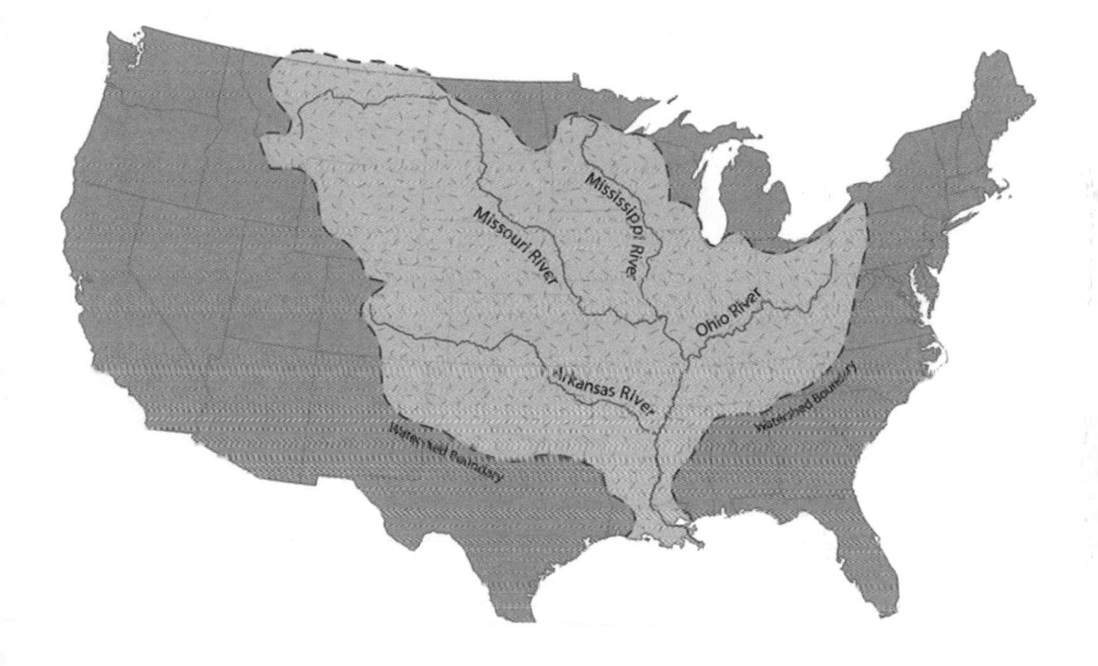

Mississippi River Drainage Basin

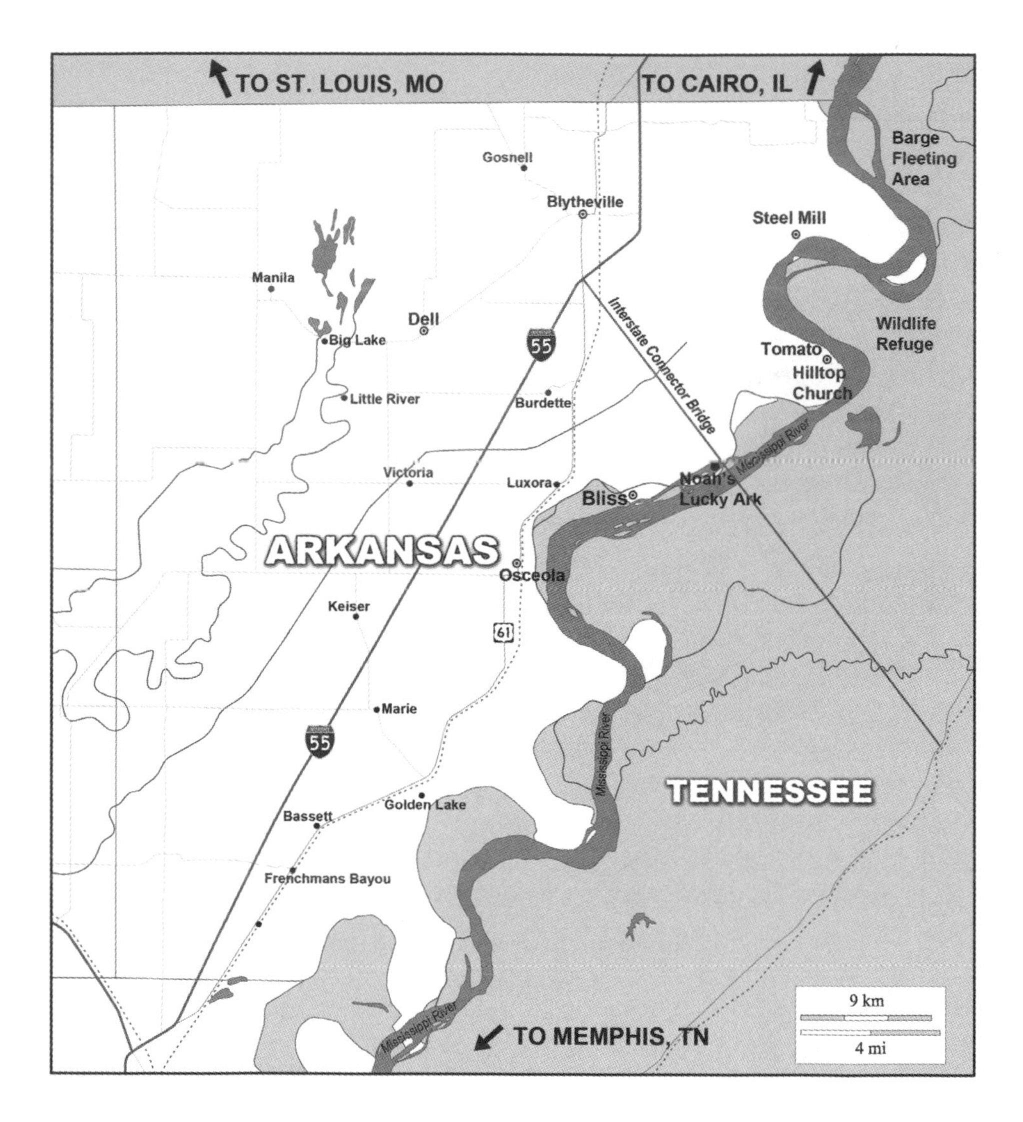
TO ST. LOUIS, MO
TO CAIRO, IL
Barge Fleeting Area
Gosnell
Blytheville
Steel Mill
Manila
Dell
Big Lake
55
Interstate Connector Bridge
Wildlife Refuge
Tomato
Hilltop Church
Little River
Burdette
Mississippi River
Victoria
Luxora
Noah's Lucky Ark
Bliss
ARKANSAS
Osceola
Keiser
61
Marie
55
Mississippi River
TENNESSEE
Bassett
Golden Lake
Frenchmans Bayou
9 km
4 mi
Mississippi River
TO MEMPHIS, TN

Map detail

Book One

And the Waters Prevailed

10 Years Ago
Tomato, Arkansas

1

Clementine's Home Place

Clementine Price, an Army Corps of Engineers first lieutenant about to make captain, could not love the Mississippi River, which coiled a mile-wide course around the Arkansas farm where she was born and reared. Who could love something you couldn't trust? But it kept a hold on her as strong as a childhood friend.

So, when she escaped to West Point, what else could she study but hydraulic engineering and river science? To her engineer's eye its mad house currents were not chaos, but complicated patterns that quantum computers might one day unravel. To her soldier's heart it was like a raw recruit who needed her help.

On leave after twelve months of restoring irrigation canals in Afghanistan, she arrived home in the middle of the night, dropped her deployment bag on the porch, and walked quickly, then broke into a long-legged run down a dirt path and climbed up onto the low embankment between the water and their farm. From that natural levee—a fragile earth barrier made of sediment heaped by centuries of floods—she checked out her river by starlight.

A front was closing in fast, stirring wind and cloud. It was almost too dark to see. But she caught a glint, the muscular heft of rain and snowmelt funneled from half of America. She smelled spring on the water. And she could hear it, a familiar heavy *thrum* that told her the Mississippi was high and bound to get higher.

Rain started falling. Clementine lifted her face to it—heaven after three days cooped up on airplanes. Before she made it back to the house, it was coming down pitchforks.

***

It rained for a week. Gravel roads washed out. Ditches overflowed. Fields turned to such sticky clay a farmer couldn't lift a boot. It kept raining. Young cotton rotted in puddles, and the Mississippi kept rising.

The Prices were used to the river spilling over its banks in the spring. They farmed on the floodplain. After a few days paddling around in rowboats, things would settle down in time to plant cotton and soybeans in alluvial soil so enriched by silt the water left behind that they didn't need fertilizer. So what if they couldn't buy insurance for love or money, and no bank in the Delta would give them a mortgage? Counting back to the Flood of 1927, it had only driven them off their ground six times.

When the radio said the sheriff was busing prisoners from the jailhouse to sandbag the mainline levee—ten miles upriver—Clementine Price prepaid for three rooms at the Motel 6 she couldn't really afford and ran a load of food and clothes over in Uncle Chance's truck. Three nights in a row, thunderstorms swept through Missouri, Kentucky, and Illinois, surprising everyone with their scope and intensity. Flash floods burst the creeks and streams that filled the Mississippi's tributaries.

Clementine tracked the water headed for Arkansas, downloading data from National Severe Storms Laboratory rain gauges, the Lightning Detection Network, and precipitation radar. She traded notes with fellow Corps officers serving in the St. Louis, Memphis, and Louisville districts. An unexpected flood crest was rampaging past Caruthersville, Missouri, only forty miles upstream. They assured her the crest was moving so fast it wouldn't be a problem.

Maybe not for folks *inside* the mainline levee—they were protected by thousand-mile-long ramparts of earth mounded three stories high and reinforced with rock and concrete. But Tomato lay *outside* the levee—right beside the raging waters. Their only protection was the natural levee—a low ridge not much taller than a dump truck. She eyeballed that embankment at first light. The earth was saturated, softening, and she discovered water scouring tree roots when she slogged up the muddy slope to see how bad the river looked.

Colored gray-brown by the flash floods and studded with whitecaps, the Mississippi rolled, high in one swath, low in another, suddenly flat, and just as suddenly spinning eddies—whirlpools that spiraled like black holes in deep space. Branches and whole trees raced by, torn from banks hundreds of miles upstream. A bright blue prefab hen house rushed along. Just as it looked like it would land beside her, the plywood coop whirled into an eddy and disappeared, sucked to the bottom.

It was clear to the young officer that she had to move her people to those motel rooms, now. Swelled by the thunderstorms, the river was fixing to attack with fast-moving floodwater that knocked houses off their footings.

***

The Arkansas Corrections Department bus stopped by a pile of sand. The monkey-brain inmate driving was too old to hump sandbags with the prison work gang. He just sat at the wheel laughing at them, shouting crazy stuff. "Y'all gonna drown out there!"

Nathan Flowers, a cold-eyed jailbird in his twenties, could hardly hear him rant. The rain pounded the roof too hard. (Later, looking back, Flowers recalled it like some sort of made-up TV show—"God-for-a-Minute"—with the demented old coot revealing to him how the world worked in a shout.)

"Gonna see wind whipping *surf* against the levee. Water seeping *under.* Sand boils ripping their guts—blowouts, blasting like *volcanos. Crevasses* busting through—mountains of river—forty feet high, ten *thousand* wide—a hundred-billion tons of water stomping the ground like crazy giants."

"What's a levee?" asked Nathan.

"You joking with me, boy?"

Born in the Arkansas hills, in a tar-paper shack three miles from the school bus stop, Nathan Flowers knew when a man reckoned he wasn't worth the time of day, which made it all right to hurt him. The driver wore the same prison-green slicker and overalls as Flowers. But give him any lip and the correctional officers would march you out of sight of the reporters gassing about "volunteers" sandbagging and kick your teeth in. Behind bars half his life, he knew to wait for a better time to hurt him back.

"No, sir. I never seen a levee." He'd never been this far from home, except to get locked up. He had never seen the river they were going to sandbag. He had only been to a city once—why go where wetbacks and welfare queens didn't have to work? He went for a Pure Dominion white pride rally. A whole bunch of them dragged a colored boy behind a pickup truck. They let Nathan drive. Nobody told him the truck was stolen. Grand theft, so the cops could hold him long enough to flip the other guys and nail him for a hate crime. Ten years.

"A levee's a heap of dirt the government piles up to hold the river. High, high heap of dirt— so damn big, sometimes they put a *road* on top. But *the river keeps scheming to get loose!*" The old coot started in on wind and boils, again. The COs rousted them into the rain before he got to the crazy giants. By then, Nathan Flowers had a fair idea of what the Mississippi was all about.

***

It took too long to get everyone in the trucks.

Clementine's father and her oldest brother were arguing they'd seen higher water all the years since she'd gone off to West Point. Her mother and her sister-in-law were struggling to herd cows into the cattle truck while kids howled to take their animals with them in the dump truck. Clementine herself ran through her parents' and her brother's houses opening doors and windows to let the floodwaters flow through instead of battering them off their footings.

What about his best tractor, her father protested. He couldn't drive it above the property onto the government levee with the transmission in pieces in his shop. If Uncle Chance—a spray pilot who'd made her his crop-dusting partner when she turned fourteen—hadn't taken Clementine's side, they'd still be milling around when the road washed out. Uncle Chance pointed at a stream of muddy water trickling through the trees. The Mississippi was topping its bank, he shouted like only he could shout. The river would wheel toward that weak spot like a hungry snake. As if to punctuate him, a boil shot up a geyser of mud in a field two-hundred meters from the bank.

Everyone slung dogs, cats, a calf, and a favorite pig in back and piled into the trucks, Aunt Rhonda's '72 Impala, and Uncle Chance's mint Ranchero—driven by Clementine's twelve-year-old brother Will, on account of Uncle Chance's torn rotator cuff.

"Clementine! Git in."

She was staring at the tin-roof open hangar where Uncle Chance parked his Air Tractor, a hard-working, sturdy yellow spray plane nearly twice her age. She'd named it Snoopy when she was little, for its long, long nose that housed the chemical hopper. But her uncle knew she wasn't staring at it sentimentally. They were about to lose the crop to a flood, and her army pay was already stretched to the limit of helping out. The spray plane would bring in cash.

"Bum shoulder won't let me fly this season."

"We'll hire a pilot when I can't get leave."

"Get in the truck, Hon. Field's too soft. That mud'll never turn her wheels loose."

"I'll take off from the driveway."

Uncle Chance would never waste breath on facts they both knew: warming the radial engine took time; rain was pounding from the sky like another river; and the gravel driveway presented a very short strip before it hooked a hard left toward the county road.

"Drive on," Clementine told her little brother.

Will blew the horn, stomped the gas, and popped the clutch. Her father and brother tore after him, spraying water and gravel, and she ran to the hangar. Rain thundered on the tin roof. She undid tie-down ropes, kicked chocks from the wheels, grabbed the big propeller with both hands and spun it three turns to expel oil from the cylinders. She folded her long legs into Snoopy's cockpit, turned on fuel, battery, and alternator, and set the brakes. She was reaching for the throttle and the starter when she heard a roar so loud it seemed to rumble out of the earth itself.

"Oh shit."

Four of the tall trees that crowned the riverbank were tumbling as if mowed down by a colossal brush hog. The earth under them appeared to melt. The ground shook the airplane. Softened by the rain, crushed by the weight of ever-rising water, the natural levee was collapsing into the field it guarded.

Clementine cranked the engine for twenty-seconds. She backed off, cranked again, got it started, and idled it at six-hundred rpms. Some things you couldn't rush, even with a river chasing you. Until the oil was warm enough to lubricate the supercharger, Snoopy was going nowhere. She used the warm-up time to check that rudder, trim controls, and flaps were moving freely, buckled in, and tugged Uncle Chance's helmet onto her head.

The river slithered into the gap between the trees. The water accelerated and scoured a channel wider than a house. More trees fell. The oil-temp gauge edged toward 40°C. Clementine let go the brakes, throttled out of the hangar into the rain, and taxied the plane across the soggy grass toward the hard gravel. The river exploded with sudden ferocity. It tore a hole a hundred feet wide. Water poured into the Price farm and snatched the ground under her wheels.

She looked back and wished she hadn't. A crest like an ocean wave rose above the water. The wave tumbled white across the field, chasing the plane straining to reach the hard gravel. It would lift the tail if it caught up and pitch the Air Tractor onto its propeller. The engine's powerful torque would finish the job, flipping the plane on its wing.

She retracted her flaps, increased fuel mixture to full rich, and advanced her throttle. Now she was rolling down the driveway, picking up speed, gravel rattling the fuselage and banging the propeller. The tail wheel rose as she passed her parents' house. The rain streamed off the windshield. She passed her father's machine shop, the smokehouse, the old mule barn, the chicken coop, the hog pen full of sows and piglets. She passed her brother Jackson's little ranch house, passed Uncle Chance's trailer. The only good news today was that Snoopy's 350-gallon hopper was empty, so the crop duster was taking off at half-weight. A thirty-foot utility pole at the sharp bend in the driveway was coming up fast. Drive on, thought Clementine Price and poured on the power.

***

They gave the fat old inmates shovels. The young ones had to hump eighty-pound canvas bags of wet sand up a steep slope and stack them in rows on top of the levee, which was already taller than a rich man's house. It was raining like a son of a bitch, and the wind blew the rain even harder. Nathan Flowers figured it wouldn't take long for the guards to be smoking cigarettes inside the bus.

What he hadn't reckoned on was how far the levee was from anywhere to run to—nothing inside the levee but miles of flat, empty fields. Outside was the river, roaring like a thousand log trucks and wide as the fields. Whatever was on the other side could be on the moon for all he could see. But all of a sudden, out of all that nothing, it brought him a present. A square shadow swooped through the rain straight at him. The other prisoners fled down the slope. But Nathan Flowers stood his ground and watched it come with eyes clearer than he had ever possessed.

He saw a huge boat, gray and rust-streaked, three stories high and a hundred feet long. The river was bringing it to him fast and furious. He watched, transfixed, picturing in his mind that when it hit the levee it would blast off the top, scatter sandbags and crash through, bust a wide hole, and slide down the slope into the field. The river would follow, mountains of river like the driver said, stomping the land like a crazy giant.

But the river had another idea. Instead of smashing the levee, it spun the boat around and brought it toward him at a shallow angle. It touched the sandbags at his feet, light as a kiss, bounced off, and kept on going. For one second it was possible to step on it like stepping onto Grandma's porch. The river snatched the boat back into the current and took Nathan Flowers for a ride.

***

Clementine Price lifted into the rain at ninety miles an hour. The farm fell beneath her wings—suddenly tiny in the storm-drenched land—lost to a wide, wild swath of river brown as a UPS truck. She followed the driveway and the county road, looking for the Price caravan. The downpour was so dense she couldn't see the tall arch of the interstate connector bridge or even the city of Bliss hugging the river six miles to the south. Finally, she saw all the vehicles were safe, speeding in tight formation on the county road that ran along the top of the mainline levee.

She banked the crop duster toward the river and flew low over the frothing torrent that marked the breach. The farm was gone under many feet of muddy water. It was up to the second-story windowsills of her parents' house. She saw chickens on the roof. The pigs were trying to swim. Her brother's house was off its foundation and smashing into Uncle Chance's trailer.

She turned away. The rain was thinning to the north and she could see for several miles, up three loops of the river to the new steel mill, guarded by the mainline levee. Beyond it, she saw a towboat, apparently adrift. Instead of looking for a place to land, she headed that way. Closer, it was definitely a runaway, a big three-decker showing no lights and spinning in circles mid-river. It was in the grip of a peculiar eddy that she recalled sometimes whirled there during highwater, kicked up by a channel-dike the Corps had installed to direct the river's flow. She saw activity on the mainline levee. Men in green slickers—the sheriff's prisoners sandbagging.

Around the bend came the Corps' own towboat, Motor Vessel *Mississippi V.* Known as "The Boat," her five-story deckhouse looked like a white wedding cake with ribbons of scarlet icing. She was enormous, the biggest on the river, but woefully underpowered, nowhere as strong as she looked. A showboat on which the Army Corps of Engineers waved the flag and entertained local dignitaries. Her timing was excellent, showing up just when needed to snag the runaway.

Clementine hailed her on the VHF. The pilot sounded like a civilian contractor, answering the radio with a laid-back drawl. "Motor Vessel *Mississippi*."

"Morning, Cap," said Clementine. "Spray plane eight hundred feet over you. Looks to me like there's a breakaway boat drifting your way."

"Morning, ma'am—Whoa, hold on, ma'am. The colonel wants to talk to you."

Colonel?

"This is Colonel Robert Garcia, U.S. Army Corps of Engineers, Memphis District. Who are you?"

"*Sir!*" Clementine sat up as straight as she could in the cockpit. She had not expected a full colonel to be onboard The Boat, much less the new commander of the Memphis District. "First Lieutenant Clementine Price, sir. Transatlantic Afghanistan District South, sir."

"What are you doing in Arkansas?"

"Home on leave, sir."

"Where'd you get the aircraft?"

"My uncle's crop duster. Sir."

"What do you see?"

"Towboat adrift at Mile 813." *Mississippi*'s pilot could locate 813—813 river miles from the Gulf of Mexico—by landmarks. So could Lieutenant Price. The newly arrived colonel could find 813, and every other river mile between the Gulf and Cairo, Illinois, on the chart.

"How do you know he's adrift, Lieutenant Price?"

"Turning lazy circles, sir."

"I don't see him on the AIS." Ordinarily, the runaway's Automatic Identification System for collision avoidance would be broadcasting its name, position, speed, and course, which the *Mississippi* would receive on its AIS.

"He could have lost power, sir. I see no lights, no smoke."

"Stand by."

She heard the colonel talking to the *Mississippi*'s pilot and the pilot answering, "The *Mary Ann* tore loose from Caruthersville last night."

Caruthersville, Missouri, was at Mile 846, the harbor at 850. With the current running at six miles an hour, five hours to get here, the breakaway was very likely her, thought Clementine. Sudden movement downriver caught her eye. She banked toward it and dove steeply until she was skimming the river, fifty feet over the water, then over the levee and across a field of mud. A powerful geyser was spraying sand and rock twenty meters in the air.

"Sir? Colonel? . . . *Sir!*"

"What is it, Lieutenant Price?"

"Liquefaction boil. Mile 812. One hundred meters inside the mainline levee."

"How big?"

"Big enough to crevasse the levee. Just above the steel mill. One mile below your position, sir." She wrestled Snoopy over the water and spotted what she was afraid she would see. "There's a big eddy in the river whirling where it wasn't earlier, opposite the boil. Looks like a column of water found itself a seepage path under the levee."

"Thank you, we'll have a look."

"There's no time for a look. You want men and machines right there now."

"What did you say to me, Lieutenant Price?"

Clementine Price had seen too much destruction in the last hour to let even West Point discipline get in the way of horse sense. "Colonel, that's a Mississippi River sand boil. They don't wait for a look. That's why I'm saying, sir, you want men and machines there *right now*."

"Lieutenant Price. Maybe the army does things differently in Afghanistan, since I served there, but in my district junior officers do not tell me what I want."

"Six hundred people work in that steel mill—six hundred jobs at risk—six hundred lives." *Ohmigod, what did I just say?* There was a long silence.

The colonel was still holding his transmit key and she heard him order, "Get men and machines there now." Then he said, "Lieutenant Price, land that airplane."

Clementine keyed her radio. "Colonel? Sir?"

"Now what?"

"May I recommend, sir?"

"What?"

"Employ the *Mary Ann* to protect the levee."

"*What?*"

"Lay her alongside the weak spot."

"—Stand by—Pilot, what is that woman talking about?"

Clementine heard the pilot drawl, "Well, shore. All we got to do is corral *Mary Ann* and shove her where it's failing before it crevasses. . . . Have I ever done it before? My great granddaddy claimed he did exactly that, back in '27. 'Course, the Old Man could spin a yarn. Any luck, she might slow the breach long enough to plug it proper. Don't suppose it'll make things much worse than they're fixing to become—there's *Mary Ann* now. . . . I imagine we'll want to get some boys on deck. Sir."

To the new district commander's credit, he made a lightning decision to bet on local expertise. Clementine saw *Mississippi V* veer into as tight a ninety as the big old boat could manage. Deckhands swarmed, dragging rigging.

"Lieutenant Price?"

"Yes, sir!"

"Find yourself a landing strip and report to me at 0900 tomorrow."

***

It was dark inside the boat, cold and strangely quiet. Nathan Flowers saw a flight of stairs dimly lit by daylight streaming from above. He climbed to the top and found himself in a room full of instruments surrounded by windows. Was this what they called a wheelhouse? Except there was no wheel. Just a big, old leather chair with a couple of sticks on either side, shiny with use. The boat lurched. The river was spinning and tossing it. He grabbed a handhold and turned a swift circle looking out the windows. Rain and river in every direction.

An engine started, suddenly, with a distant roar deep in the boat. The deck vibrated under his feet. An old man in greasy overalls came stomping up the stairs. His hair was pasted on the side of his head like he'd slept on it, his eyes were red, and he stank of whiskey. Night watchman, guessed Nathan Flowers, hired when he got too old to work on boats, fell asleep drunk, and woke up to a big surprise—floating down the river—at which point he got the motor started and now was fixing to drive the boat to dry land.

The watchman saw Nathan in his prison greens and pawed at his pistol.

Nathan Flowers sunk a fist in the watchman's eye, pounded him with both hands, grabbed him by his shirt, and slammed his head repeatedly against a steel pillar. He had been winning fights since the Arkansas Juvenile Assessment and Treatment Center, and this one-sided match was over in fifteen seconds. He dropped the body down the stairs head-first—the drunk fell down drunk—Look how bunged up his head is—and got busy learning how to drive a boat as fast as it could go into the levee, blast a hole where they were sandbagging, jump off, and get away while a stomping giant drowned every Africoon in the first city it hit.

The engine stopped as quick as it had started.

Damned fool lousy drunk hadn't started it right. And if things weren't bad enough, a huge boat was suddenly coming alongside with soldiers throwing ropes. He raced down the stairs, jumped over the drunk's body, and hid, waiting to grab the first chance that came his way. The bigger boat banged into his and started pushing it toward the levee. Nathan Flowers crouched low, ran to the other side, and jumped in the water with his alibi full-blown in his mind.

The boat knocked me in the water when it hit the levee. I was washed downstream and finally climbed out. No, sir. I was not escaping. I was knocked in the water.

He knew how to swim a little—at least better than most hill folk, thanks to the abandoned limestone quarry behind his grandma's shack that made a swimming hole—and he figured to drift out of sight, then swim to the shore. But the current was so cold he couldn't breathe, and it yanked him away from the shore and pulled him under. He fought it with all his strength, realizing too late when water stung his nose and rammed his throat that he was fighting for his life. He surfaced just long enough to see the shore racing by before it dragged him under again. Struggling to swim, he was sucked into whirlpools, tumbled and pummeled like he was a carcass they'd thrown to the hogs.

2

The Colonel

Clementine Price could fall asleep in construction sites, barracks, and war zones. A rattling Motel 6 air conditioner would never keep her awake all night. Neither would the snores of her brothers and the sobs of her nieces and nephews mourning their drowned piglets. Not even the threat of disciplinary action by Colonel Garcia; she had done what she had done and would take the consequences. But she worried, hour after hour, how would the suddenly homeless and landless Price clan keep body and soul together.

Giving up before first light, she got out of the double bed she was sharing with her sister-in-law and Aunt Rhonda and picked her way silently through littered belongings. She took her deployment bag into the bathroom. Her dress blues were packed at the top and not too wrinkled. She laid out her shoes (always shined), opened her Dopp kit, examined her tired-eyed face in the sickly fluorescent glare, and took a shower, hoping that the lukewarm drip would make her presentable.

Her Great-Aunt Martha had served in the Women's Army Corps in World War II. Aunt Martha had taught her how to make a victory roll, twirling lengths of her strawberry blond hair around her finger and pinning it just so, in the style of the black-and-white screen goddesses they watched together on Turner Classic Movies. The look was subtly glamorous yet conformed to army grooming policy. "Why look ordinary?" Aunt Martha would say. "With a little effort you can look sharp."

Aunt Martha had also taught her to sew on her 1938 electric Singer, which she left to Clementine when she passed. Clementine had used it to tailor broad-ass regulation pants and skirts to her Katherine Hepburn silhouette. She sifted through the keys heaped on the bureau and found Uncle Chance's. His Ranchero was the one vehicle sure to have enough gas to get to Bliss Marine.

The rain had stopped and the cotton fields that lined I-55 had patches of standing water, but those farmers would be able to replant their crops once the ground dried out. She pictured bits and pieces of Daddy's disassembled tractor careening down the Mississippi and wondered if he could pick up some part-time work at Bob Dickinson's John Deere dealership outside Bliss. Daddy could take just about any machine apart and put it back together with his eyes closed. She could call Bob today and persuade him to make an offer that wouldn't hurt Daddy's pride.

Driving through Bliss, she saw some streets closed and heard the din of pumps sucking water out of flooded basements, but the city looked otherwise undisturbed. Bliss Metropolitan Police manned the marina gate. Clementine joined the line of contractors' trucks and Corps Humvees and used the wait to rehearse her apology to Colonel Garcia. When it was her turn, she rolled down the fogged-up window and handed her Uniformed Services ID card to a smiling patrol woman who reached into the cab and gave her arm a strong, affectionate squeeze.

"Libby! Oh my Lord, Libby," cried Clementine, bursting into tears with the one person in the world she could let loose with.

Libby Whitcomb Winters was her best friend since first grade. They had graduated high school as co-valedictorians—the smartest black girl and the smartest white girl, both oddballs and outsiders, teaming up rather than competing for the honor—then gone their separate ways to West Point and Fisk University on full rides. Lately, Libby was emailing Clementine that she planned to enter politics. Six years on the Bliss Metropolitan Police had taught her she couldn't enforce the laws without first fixing the city itself.

The women were as physically opposite as two females could be: Libby short where Clementine was tall; compact and ample where Clementine was lanky and lean; coffee-with-cream complexioned where Clementine was peaches-with-cream and a sprinkling of freckles. This morning, Officer Winters was sporting a fishtail braid updo that Clementine couldn't have achieved if she tried. But they were two peas in a pod in every other aspect, and they liked to say that together, they were a black-eyed pea, which was good luck.

Libby commenced a very thorough examination of her friend's credentials so they could talk without interruption.

"Hon, I heard about Tomato. Thank God everybody got out safely."

"What if I hadn't been home on leave? They'd all have died! Momma and Daddy and even Uncle Chance were dithering, saying they'd seen worse floods before. It's like I'm the only responsible adult in the whole family."

"Where'd you take them?"

"We're at the Motel 6 and got some of the livestock over to the Stevenson place, but Libby—all the other animals drowned. Daddy's run out his line of credit and we don't even have a place to live." Libby handed Clementine a handkerchief and pretended to key her walkie-talkie for the benefit of the line behind the Ranchero.

"Stay with Rolly and me. We'll move the baby in with us."

"Are you sure?"

"It's no problem! Rolly just got put on night shift so practically the only time we see each other is when I'm taking my gun off and he's putting his on. And there are still some vacant apartments in our complex. You could move the family there, at least temporarily. I'm sure our landlord would extend credit to a decorated officer."

"I may not be decorated for long. I spoke out of turn to the new district commander yesterday."

"Colonel Garcia, the to-die-for-Cuban. How far out of turn?"

"Far enough to be ordered to report. I'm not sorry about it, but I'm sure he's hopping mad to have been challenged by a junior officer who's also a *woman*."

"Like you always said: we do everything the men do, backwards, in high heels. Good luck, girlfriend. Call me later. I'm off at two." Libby waved her through with a big wink. "Drive on, Lieutenant!"

Clementine reported to the Corps dock. A rigid inflatable boat with big outboard engines was waiting to ferry her upriver where *Mississippi V* was working on the weakened levee. The corporal driving and the private standing by with the bow line gave her smart salutes. She strapped into a life jacket, stepped to the helm, and laid a hand on the throttles.

"Get the stern line, Corporal. Private, stand by to let go the bow."

"Are you sure you want to drive, ma'am? We have to go pedal to the metal to get to Colonel Garcia on time and the river's going crazy."

"Seat belts, soldiers!"

Seconds after they cast off, the little RIB was roaring out of the marina and planing upriver, bouncing on whitecaps and dodging tree trunks. They passed the Old District, the new medical centers scattered along the highway, and pounded under the interstate connector bridge. The city fell behind. She noticed the corporal watching her every move. She beckoned him to lean close to hear.

"I'm not taking air unless I have no choice. Air slows you down, you want to stay on the water. Watch, we'll take that flat, skirt the eddy, flat again." She slewed around a half-submerged propane tank, slowed her engines to survive a skid turn, and gunned them to jump an eddy that looked large enough to swallow the RIB whole.

"See?"

"Yes, ma'am."

Clementine braced for what she would see at Mile 806.

From low down on the water, the Price farm looked worse than from the spray plane. It was something about the way the river just got wider and wider, as if it had always spread to the mainline levee and their home place had never existed. Houses, barns, animals, and every tree that crowned the bank were gone.

"Corporal! Take the wheel!"

She turned away, searched across the water for the Tennessee side, lost in the mist. But it was impossible not to look. Was anything left? The chimney? The shade tree? Nothing broke the surface and finality crashed down around her. All she had left in the world was packed in her deployment bag. Blinding tears would be a mercy, but it was too late to cry. She had done her weeping with Libby, and she had a boat and two young soldiers to keep afloat.

"I've got it," she said and took the helm.

She rounded a bend a few miles further up and saw *Mississippi V.*

The red and white towboat was hard at work positioning a barge carrying a hundred-foot dragline with a clamshell bucket. The derelict *Mary Ann* was moored tightly against the weakened levee. The ground was crawling with bulldozers and dump trucks—fewer than she thought were needed. A Memphis TV news helicopter hovered overhead.

"Corporal?" she said as she throttled back and it got quiet enough to talk without shouting, "How's the colonel adjusting to his new job?"

"Working at it, ma'am," said the corporal, with a wise enlisted man's neutrality. "Twenty-four-seven."

Smart, too, thought Clementine. Putting the flagship to work for the cameras was the kind of savvy PR that kept the Corps on the right side of folks. And give him credit for stationing himself on The Boat in the middle of the action instead of issuing orders from the dry comfort of Memphis headquarters, like his predecessor had.

Clementine Price had been aboard The Boat twice before: first as a child for one of the community open house meetings the Mississippi River Commission hosted; and recently, before shipping out to Afghanistan, as the guest of now-Senator Garfield, the congressman who had nominated her to West Point. Both of those times The Boat sat serenely at dockside, brightwork gleaming and decks immaculate. Today it was in constant motion, the floating command center of an emergency levee-repair site and a can-do workboat. It shuddered with effort and heeled aggressively, battling the current to help the dragline dump barge-loads of crushed stone. Winches howled, deckhands wrestled rigging, and the air stank of diesel exhaust.

Colonel Garcia's adjutant, a Captain Thomas Chow who looked a year or two older than she, escorted her through the scrum of contractors in civvies and Corps officers in camouflage to a fancy private office one deck below the wheelhouse, and told her to wait. It was hot and sticky already and she felt light-headed with nerves and hunger—she'd eaten nothing but a PowerBar since yesterday. She willed herself not to perspire and focused on the engines, which she could feel grinding far below.

"Good morning, Lieutenant Price."

Colonel Garcia glided swiftly into the room. She caught a glimpse of black, black hair and an aura of total confidence, and sensed that his elegant demeanor concealed stark, hard-driving ambition. His expression was maddeningly inscrutable.

Clementine saluted and straightened her spine to her full height of 5' 11', making her an inch taller than the colonel.

"At ease."

Colonel Garcia sat at the desk and read silently from what she suspected was a printout of her service record. His appearance was impeccable, hair sleek, his army combat camouflage fresh-pressed and trim as if a tailor had fitted him for an evening-mess uniform with gold braids. The Ranger and Sapper tabs on his left shoulder sleeve were awarded for elite combat and leadership training. Still, he'd made full colonel very young. Not much over forty, she guessed. He glanced up to study her.

Never look in need, said Aunt Martha, whose polished manners and eye for the latest fashion had vaulted her from a mud farm to a tree-shaded house in Bliss's best neighborhood. *Never let them see you sweat.*

"You've met Time-in-Service and Time-in-Grade requirements for promotion to captain."

"Yes, sir."

"What made you so sure that crevasse would breach when and where it did?"

"The boil I saw was enormous. So was the eddy feeding it. Sir."

"So sure of yourself to issue orders above your rank?"

"Crevasses love sand-filled distributary channels, sir." She glanced out the window at the earthmovers reshaping the crown. "The levee stands on the outside of this bend in the river where the force of the water is stronger going into the curve. It was likely that coarse point-bar deposits had routed seepage through organic channel fill. . . . I trained as a hydraulic engineer, sir."

"So did I, Lieutenant Price."

"Yes, sir. Also, I grew up on the river. We farmed its floodplain. I watched it from my bedroom window. And I worked *on* it since I was a child. My uncle Captain Chase Price piloted a towboat—a fair-sized, five-deck long haul boat. My brothers and I would help."

"When was this?"

"I started at twelve, sir. I was tall for my age."

"I wasn't aware children worked on towboats."

"It was family, sir. When the Coast Guard boarded, we knew to act like kids along for the ride. My brothers were older and strong. I cooked, cleaned, and stood lookout."

"What did you see?"

Clementine had seen things no one ever saw from land.

"I've seen this river swallow buildings, tractors, cattle, stands of cottonwood trees—and suddenly spit them up. I've seen it change course, run sideways and backwards. A geyser of mud shot up right beside the boat, heeled her so hard I fell in."

"How did you get out of a river that swallows buildings?"

"Sir. Uncle Chase and my brothers stuck poles in the water for me to grab, but the current was too strong, and pulling me in every direction—mostly down. The more I struggled the worse it got. I finally caught hold of a cottonwood trunk floating by."

The colonel's expression changed from inscrutable to skeptical. Clementine lowered her voice so he would have to listen more closely.

"Something told me to hang on, even when it was dragged underwater. Somehow I just gave in to the power of the river and said a prayer to it as we went down to the bottom. I was out of air. Then all of a sudden, the river just spat us out, like it wasn't ready to drown me yet. That tree shot out of the water like a cruise missile. I held tight and landed on a sand bar. Since that day on I have never been afraid of the river."

"Not to mention senior officers?"

"I apologize, sir."

"Was that your family's farm that was inundated yesterday?"

"Yes, sir."

"I'm sorry, Clementine. I'm sure that's a stressful situation to be in." He shook his head as if displeased with himself for uttering a chilly generality. "Perhaps one of the worst days of your life?"

Clementine swallowed hard. "Yes, sir. We've farmed outside the levee for four generations, and most of us still live in Tomato . . . or lived, I guess I should say. Thank you, sir, for your concern."

Captain Chow knocked on the door, which Garcia had left ajar. "Excuse me, Colonel, there's a reporter from the *Commercial Appeal* on line 2."

"Stay here, Captain, write down my answers. Adapt them for the next inquiries. Copy Public Affairs so they'll have them too. What's the reporter's name?"

"Francine Rizzo," said Chow, glancing at his clipboard, pen hovering.

Garcia picked up the phone. Whatever Cuban accent he had arrived with had been thoroughly erased. "Good morning, Ms. Rizzo. The Memphis District of the Army Corps of Engineers, Mississippi Valley Division, has activated emergency management operations to assess and repair damage from yesterday's flash flooding. Fortunately, there was no loss of life"—he turned slightly to look at Clementine—"although there was significant, regrettable damage in low-lying areas not protected by the mainline levee." He gestured for Chow to keep writing. "No ma'am, there was no crevasse at Mile 812. Corps officers did identify a weak spot in the levee at that location"—he turned back to look expressionlessly at Clementine—"but thanks to some quick thinking by the Corps' hydraulic engineers the levee was not breached. We anticipate normal barge traffic will resume within twenty-four hours. If you need additional information, my adjutant Captain Chow will be happy to assist. Thank you for calling, Ms. Rizzo."

Chow disappeared and Garcia returned his attention to Clementine. "Where did you learn to fly?"

"My Uncle Chance taught me so I could spray crops for him."

"Wait. You said your uncle was a towboat captain."

"Sir. That was Uncle *Chase*. Uncle *Chance* is a spray pilot. I know it's confusing, but similar-sounding names in one family are kind of a custom around here."

"So, your Uncle Chance took chances in the sky and your Uncle Chase chased runaway barges on the river."

"Exactly, sir. And Uncle Chance taught me to fly. During the growing season there was work from dawn to dusk if you had the manpower—or in my case, the girl power—I had just turned fourteen—so after Uncle Chance had put in eight hours I'd take over and fly until it was too dark or we ran out of chemicals."

"How did you get a pilot license at age fourteen?"

"Regs and rules are more like *suggestions* outside the levee, sir."

Garcia smiled at her for the first time and Clementine smiled back. So, there was a soul under that cool exterior after all. She was reminded of the classic lady-killing Latin Lovers in her favorite old black-and-white movies.

Captain Chow stuck his head in. His expression was grave, his tone measured. "General Penn is telephoning you, sir. *Personally*, sir. He is waiting on line 1."

Garcia stood before he picked up the phone. "Good morning, sir."

Clementine started to back out of the office. Lieutenant-General Clinton Penn was Commander of the Mississippi Valley Division and President of the Mississippi River Commission—it was as if God Himself was on the line. Garcia shook his head and gestured for her to stay.

"Yes, sir. I've ordered an inspection of every inch of levee from Mile 815 down to Bliss, which I will personally supervise as soon as we've completed this repair. . . . At this stage, sir, the best guess by one of our young hydraulic engineers with a broad overview is that the near-crevasse was caused by coarse point-bar deposits that routed seepage through organic channel fill. . . . Yes, sir, our towboat pilot, a civilian contractor, confirmed that employing a vessel to dam a breach had been done before, during the Flood of 1927. . . . Thank you, sir. You'll have that report on your desk first thing tomorrow morning."

Garcia hung up, sat back down behind his desk, and looked placidly at Clementine, who attempted the same mask of indifference, although inside she was open-mouthed and goggle-eyed at having been present while deities conferred.

"Tell me about your town, Tomato."

"It was wonderful!" *Don't babble.* "I mean, it was really different from how most people lived—or would want to live—but I loved it." *Loved. Not love. Get used to that, Clementine.* "We grew the best fruits and vegetables you ever tasted. Before I was born, there was a tiny post office that had been the postmaster's smokehouse—that's how small it was, barely enough room to hang a few hams—and there was a little grocery store too. But people kept moving away, 'til we were the last."

"Where did you go to school?"

"My Aunt Rhonda was a teacher in the Bliss consolidated district. We kids would pile into her Impala every morning and ride with her, which meant we came early and stayed late. When she was finally ready to drive us home, we'd already finished our homework. I think I read every single book in the school library by the time I graduated. That's where I discovered James Eads."

"Of the brilliant Eads Bridge in St. Louis."

"Yes, sir. And so much more! Salvage. Civil War gunboats. Diving bells. He really loved the river and understood it like no one before or since. He studied it from every angle—including the bottom! And he never gave up on himself or his ideas. 'Drive On' was his personal motto. He's my hero."

Afraid she was gushing, Clementine scanned the room for something to look at. Her eye fixed on a bowl of fresh fruit on the credenza.

"Have you had breakfast?" Garcia asked.

"Yesterday. Sir."

He telephoned for coffee and biscuits and looked out the large window facing the levee. The enormous clamshell bucket—the size of Aunt Martha's parlor—swung by and dumped its payload of rocks with a crash. Garcia picked up the phone. "Captain Chow, we need twice as many men and machines here. Ask for emergency bids ASAP. And bring me the paperwork for the borrow pit."

Breakfast arrived followed by Captain Chow carrying a sheaf of documents for Colonel Garcia to review. Clementine gorged on fruit and biscuits while he quickly read through the pile of contracts and releases. Most he signed and returned to Chow. Those judged to be inadequate he marked up aggressively with a big, manicured hand—a lefty, Clementine noticed, with a wedding ring—and consigned to a stack of shame that he handed back to Chow.

"I presume you were the first West Point cadet from Tomato?"

"Yes, sir, and the only female from Arkansas in my class. I wanted to be a civil engineer like Eads and I learned that West Point was the prime recruiting source for the Corps."

"How'd you get your nomination?"

"I didn't know anyone who'd ever been to West Point—who'd ever been back East even—and we sure didn't know any congressmen or senators to nominate me. So, I figured I'd have to do something pretty unusual to get noticed."

"Which was?"

"I decided to recreate Eads's diving bell and walk on the bottom of the river, like he did back in the 1840s."

Garcia laughed. It was a full-throated joyful sound that Clementine liked very much. "Are you serious?"

"You see, sir, my four brothers and I were pretty—um, unsupervised. Daddy worked from 'Can to Cain't' on the farm, and we worked with him whenever we were needed. Momma was pretty overwhelmed with five kids plus a passel of relatives who expected a home cooked meal whenever they showed up out of the blue. The house was flooded almost every year. Then, just as she'd dried everything out and cleaned it spic and span, a sand boil would explode and shower mud over everything, and she'd just take to her bed for a couple of days."

Why am I babbling? Why isn't the colonel barking, Dismissed?

"A sand boil? Next to your house?"

She heard her own voice get excited and couldn't stop it. "Tomato had sand boils all over town. Like Fourth of July fireworks, when the river was rising. Anyway, we kids looked after each other, so there was no adult to stop me from doing this insanely dangerous project. I found a huge iron bell rusting away in one of the old mule barns. We got the forklift and took the bell to Daddy's shop to retrofit it—me, three cousins, my brother Jackson, and my best friend Libby from school. She took all the pictures and video to document it.

"We fixed up a broken air compressor to pump air down into the bell so I could breathe underwater, and we used one of the old mule harnesses to make a seat for me—a strap across the bottom of the bell. I borrowed a wet suit from Uncle Chase's boat, but we needed to add weight to sink me. Eads used pigs of lead, and we didn't have any of that lying around. But I remembered in the gangster movies I'd watch when I stayed with my Aunt Martha in Bliss, the bad guys threatened their victims with 'cement shoes.' So, we mixed up a batch of Sakrete in two metal tubs and stuck an old work boot inside each tub. I walked like Frankenstein's monster, but I was happy to have some extra protection on my feet. So, we string a rope from the bow of the boat to hold the bell against the current, and I go down."

"To the *bottom?*"

"It was only thirty feet. James Eads worked below fifty. His bridge caissons sunk into eighty feet of mud—Any rate, I can't see anything except what's directly under my bell. And I'm holding another piece of rope that is attached to the boat as a signal cord I can yank when I need to be pulled up. I have Jackson holding the other end, on the theory that if he forgets to pull me out, he'll eventually get in trouble at home. I start walking along the bottom, breathing the air in the bell, like Eads did when he was salvaging sunken boats."

Clementine stood stock still, transfixed by the memory until she grew aware that the colonel was watching her curiously. She said, "I suppose it's strange how much a man from another century influences me."

"I feel similarly about Ulysses Grant. '*Strike hard and keep moving.*' Go on, Lieutenant."

"All sorts of things are tumbling past—parts of trees, catfish big as hound dogs, pieces of old cars and farm tools—and the currents are shifting in every direction. The most amazing thing was at the bottom, beneath my cement shoes, I could feel sand and silt and mud swirling like a living thing—like there was no bottom, just this blizzard scouring my feet and legs nearly to my waist. I even found something to salvage—evidence of my expedition—a cast-iron frying pan.

"Then came the bad part, when I tried to go back up. I jerked the signal cord, and nothing happened. I pulled it again. Nothing. I started to panic. Then I remembered when that tree dragged me underwater, and just gave myself up to the river again."

The colonel arched one black eyebrow skeptically. She tried to explain. "Like plebes learn to get past beginners' fear in boxing."

"Boxing?" Now he really looked skeptical, as if she had made up the whole story and *dismissed* was on his lips. "West Point does not include female cadets in mandatory plebe boxing. The 'art of manly defense' is not considered safe for women."

Clementine looked him in the face. "Some of us formed a female boxing society. AWD—Art of *Womanly* Defense. We trained after hours."

Garcia smiled. "Okay. How did you get out of the water?"

"When I calmed myself down, I realized the rope had snagged on one of the mule harness buckles. I untangled it and yanked again, and they brought me up. With my frying pan, which turned out to be from a gunboat that sank in the Civil War—actually one of the monitors that Eads built for the Union Army, believe it or not. I gave it to the Bliss Historical Society and got written up in the Bliss *Clarion* and the Memphis *Commercial Appeal.* I asked a family friend to send the articles to Congressman Garfield. He nominated me to West Point."

Captain Chow knocked again. "Chief Billy Bob Owen—Bliss Metro Police—is on line 1, sir. And this is a statement from Senator Garfield's office that they'd like you to approve before they broadcast it." He slipped it onto Garcia's desk like it was radioactive. "They took the liberty of composing a quote from you."

The colonel picked up the phone with his right hand and began marking up the page with his left.

"Chief Owen, thank you for the loan of your patrolmen to help us maintain law and order on our temporary base here. I've ordered a squad of MPs to cover the gate and I'll soon be able to relieve your men." Garcia was drawing a solid line through what Clementine guessed was his "composed" quotation and writing a new one in small, elegant cursive in the empty space at the bottom.

"And on line 3 is a Mr. Lester Gill," said Chow, "from Ducks Unlimited."

"What is Ducks Unlimited?" said Garcia without looking up.

"I don't know, sir," said Chow. "I'm from Chicago."

Garcia raised his eyes inquiringly to Clementine. "Sir, it's an environmental organization, devoted to hunting. In wetlands."

Garcia handed the rewritten Garfield statement to Chow and picked up the phone. Clementine had known Lester Gill since childhood and wondered how the cool, confident colonel would wrangle "The Great White Hunter" (as she and Libby had nicknamed him) who had donated a vast, tax-deductible tract of land to Ducks Unlimited for his friends and himself to hunt on, that was now crawling with bulldozers excavating a borrow pit.

"As you know, Mr. Gill, environmental stewardship, especially preserving habitat for native waterfowl, is a top priority of the Corps. Those wetlands that you and your colleagues have saved are vital to flood control and a balanced ecosystem. You have my word that as soon as we have excavated the earth we need for this emergency operation, we will fully restore those wetlands and in fact, Mr. Gill, I'd very much appreciate your input. . . . All right then. Lester. . . . I'd be delighted to hunt with you when the season opens. . . . Yes, I'll 'holler at you' next time I'm in Dell."

He placed the phone in its cradle and asked, "When do you go back, Clementine?"

"I have another ten days of leave, sir."

"I will write your commander commending your actions yesterday and forward a copy to the promotions board that will select you for captain."

"Thank you, sir. Only . . ."

"Only what?

"I've finished my tour in Afghanistan, sir. Right before I came home, I had an offer to transfer to the New York District to work on the coastal storm risk tributary project. I've only been to New York City on day trips when I was at West Point, and I thought this would be a once-in-a-lifetime opportunity to do something really different."

And a chance to test-drive an old relationship in the same time zone with Carl, a classmate from West Point who became a developer and engineered the offer.

"But after yesterday . . ." She felt Garcia watching her and swallowed hard, "My family has no place to live. Daddy's too old to start farming from scratch and too proud to ask for help. What I'm trying to say, sir, is I have to take care of my family. So I will resign my commission and hire on with the Corps as a civilian contractor here in the Delta."

"You'll certainly make more money as a contractor."

The colonel's adjutant knocked on the open door again and handed Garcia two sheets of paper. Garcia read each one and said to Chow, "That's quite a disparity between their bids. Do you know Glenn Mooney and Percy Dickinson?"

"No, sir."

"One looks like a fortune in profit. The other too low to be true."

"I'm not sure what to advise, sir."

Clementine Price said, "Colonel, may I speak?"

"Do you know Glenn Mooney and Percy Dickinson?"

"Cotton and soybean farmers, sir. When their machines are free, they'll contract to the Corps."

"They've submitted competing emergency-basis bids. One is so low it makes me wonder. What can you tell me about them?"

Clementine admired that he would ask her opinion. She wanted to do right by him and couched her answer diplomatically but transparently.

"Well, sir, Glenn Mooney appears to be doing fine. He's mighty busy, bless his heart—just got his hands on another four-hundred acres, old Mrs. Eddison's place. And if Glenn thought he was busy before, now he's got to grade some wicked washouts before he can plant again."

"And Dickinson?"

"Percy Dickinson keeps his ditches clean."

"I gather that's a local expression of admiration?"

"Yes, sir. Although new research suggests that vegetated ditches actually mitigate pesticide runoff."

"Are you connected with either of these men, Lieutenant Price?"

"No, sir. I have no connection of any compromising sort to Mr. Dickinson or Mr. Mooney. Although there is one connection I should mention. I am hoping that Percy Dickinson's Uncle Bob might find room for my father in the repair shop at his John Deere dealership."

Robert Garcia considered that, briefly. "The connection sounds tangential in the extreme and a long stretch from anything resembling corruption." He turned to his adjutant. "Come back in five minutes."

Garcia went to the window and stared out at the *Mary Ann*. "Clementine, what made you think a runaway boat could plug a crevasse?"

"Sir, I had the advantage of seeing the situation from overhead. I saw a boil, and at the same time I saw something that could be used to dam that leak before it ruptured. And since the *Mary Ann* didn't have any passengers aboard, it seemed worth the risk to try. You'd have done the same, sir, faster than I, if you had my aerial perspective."

"Maybe. But I'm new to your river. Though I've had my own adventures with water. And I also remember living 'outside the levee.'"

"Yes, sir?"

Garcia closed the door, sat down in an armchair, and gestured for Clementine to sit in the other. The Boat groaned and lurched, its engines straining below. Finally, he spoke.

"I'm a 'Marielito.' I was thirteen years old when I escaped from Cuba on the Mariel boatlift. A hundred people crammed in an old trawler that stank of shrimp and diesel fuel and sweat. The weather was crazy—so dark, and the ocean was practically black, with waves crashing over the sides slamming us against each other. Everybody was seasick. I saw an old woman lean over the side to throw up. A wave grabbed her like a shark, and she was gone. . . . I'll never forget, when we finally got to Key West, I saw a Coca-Cola machine gleaming at the end of the dock. Welcome to America!"

He cast her a self-mocking smile. "The next time I felt that welcome was when I entered West Point—and I'm sure you remember how 'warmly' we plebes were greeted our first year."

Clementine smiled back. "Yes, sir."

"But I never doubted I was welcome if I gave what was required. And I have no doubt it was the same for you. Can you guess who submitted the lowest bid?"

"Mooney, sir."

"Known for bidding low and making it back with add-ons?"

"I'm not saying he's so crooked you could screw him in the ground. . . ."

"But?"

"Could be he's . . . optimistic."

Garcia stood and opened the door. "Captain Chow! Award the contract to Dickinson."

"The higher bid, sir?"

"Affirmative."

Colonel Garcia sat back down in his armchair and looked her directly in the eyes. "Let me suggest a counter-proposal to resigning your commission."

"Yes, sir?"

"As I said, I'm new to your river. You know it intimately. I'm new to this district. You were born here. You know the people. Let me arrange a transfer to Memphis to be my adjutant."

"But you already have Captain Chow. Sir."

Colonel Garcia gave her a stern look. Clementine wondered whether he had reconsidered offering a plum assignment to an officer who repeatedly seemed to say the wrong thing at the wrong time. But he pressed on.

"General Penn warned me when I was selected for the Memphis District—which covers 25,000 square miles in six states—the *core* of the Corps—that for every friend I made I'd make a dozen enemies. Everybody wants something from the district commander, usually something different and often completely opposite. The farmers want less water and the fisherman want more. The barge companies say the water is too low, and then it rains and it's too high. The cities want riverfront parks that look pretty and don't flood. The environmentalists and hunters want us to flood the wetlands and bayous, and the farmers want us to drain them so they can plant more crops. In other words, Clementine, you are needed here."

A welling of emotion took her by surprise. "Thank you, sir. I would be so glad to be back home."

"Use the rest of your leave to get your family resettled and report in two weeks; I'll take care of the admin on the transfer. And Lieutenant Price, may I suggest?"

"Yes, sir?"

"You've sustained a major loss, the kind of trauma event that can lead to PTSD. The army has people and procedures standing by to help our soldiers work through these problems, completely confidentially. I encourage you to take advantage of them." He handed her a business card with a list of names and phone numbers.

"Thank you for your concern, sir. But I've survived a lot of floods and no one was shooting at us. Save those counselors for the soldiers who earned it."

The colonel gestured at his desk. "I read your record, Clementine. You took care of your people when they came under fire."

"It wasn't as big a deal as it sounded, sir. Any farmer knows when you see a job that needs to be done, do it." She meant that. West Point conditioned officers to observe closely and act decisively. It was her job to look out for the troops for whom she was responsible.

Colonel Garcia offered the earnest young woman an indulgent smile. "Modesty is a fine quality in a soldier, Lieutenant. But so is performing well and thoroughly. It is an officer's duty to keep herself in top shape."

3

The Minister's Daughter

The plaque on the steel door read, "This chapel was built by the Delta Prison Chapel Society—with a generous contribution from Mr. Johnny Cash—which believes that every sinner deserves an opportunity to know God."

Nathan Flowers already knew God. They'd cut a deal. God had pulled him from the river, woke him up handcuffed to a hospital bed, added five years to his sentence for attempted escape, and made room for him in the most crowded, hardest time maximum security prison in the state. What did Nathan Flowers get out of it? They never pinned the drunk watchman on him.

Call it even. Plus, in addition to ducking a murder conviction, he had the opportunity in his new home to double-up such heavy connections with Pure Dominion white brothers that the blacks and Mexicans didn't dare try to hurt him. So he was not interested in knowing God any better. But the good-looking girl at the pulpit was another story. Mid-twenties, he guessed, when she introduced herself in a low, confident voice with just a hint of Delta drawl, none of the banjo-string nasal twang he was used to back in the hills.

"Good morning, gentlemen. My name is Mary Kay Blankenship."

She passed out xeroxed sheets of a hymn, nodded to the colored boy at the piano—who, with his flowery bow tie, Nathan figured for a fairy—and began to lead the men in "When the Roll is Called Up Yonder." Fortunately, the boy played in a thunderous rolling gospel style and she had a good strong voice, for she was pretty much singing a solo.

When His chosen ones shall gather to their home beyond the skies,
And the roll is called up yonder, I'll be there.

She smiled at her stone-faced—and in many cases, stoned—congregation and said, "Y'all know something about roll call, don't you?"

There was the faintest of acknowledgments, a few grunts.

Nathan rewarded her with a rare grin—a jack-o-lantern cave of misshapen yellow and missing teeth he owed to sugar and fistfights. Mary Kay smiled back and pressed on, as if encouraged.

"I'm here to tell y'all about a bigger, more important roll call—not by wardens, not by correctional officers. I'm talking about God's final roll call, the ultimate accounting of what we've all done with our time on earth. And unlike the judges and juries and parole boards and COs y'all deal with here, God knows the real truth about what you did or didn't do; God knows what's in all of our hearts; and God can pardon us—because we're *all of us* sinners—and guide us to a better future no matter how dark and sorrowful our past."

As she spoke, she left the pulpit and began to walk among the men, looking into their faces until they were forced to meet her intense green eyes. The prisoners had self-segregated—as usual—with blacks and whites and Hispanics sitting in separate sections. She prowled confidently among the sullen, hostile groups, displaying neither fear nor pity. Nathan was reminded of a strong, sleek cat, who could vault effortlessly from ground to rooftop with no preparation. He half expected her to explode into a backflip at any moment, she seemed in such total command of her body. She was sure nice to look at, dressed in low-heeled black suede boots and a pleated skirt that was mostly black when she stood still, but when she walked it flared open in swirling panels of bright green, yellow, and red. She could just as well be dancing at a fancy party as pacing around a prison chapel. A slim-fitting black turtleneck sweater, which looked soft enough to pet, was accented by a large gold pendant of a dove in flight. Her shoulder-length hair was on springs, coiling into glossy curls when she got excited, and relaxing into a smooth chestnut dome when her voice got soft and serious.

"'Judge not, lest ye be judged.' That's from the book of Matthew, Chapter 7, Verse 1, in the New Testament. What Jesus means by that is that if a man—or woman—thinks so highly of themselves that they can pass judgment on their fellow man, they too will be judged—and sentenced—just as harshly when their own turn comes to be judged by God Almighty."

Nathan saw in his peripheral vision that Mason, the cruelest of the prison guards who never missed an opportunity to torture any living creature, was growing fidgety. Mary Kay Blankenship seemed to sense this, as she pivoted to speak straight at him.

"In other words, whatever punishment you have doled out as a self-appointed judge and jury will be dealt right back to you, by God—who might see fit to throw in a little extra, just to even the scales. 'Why do you see the splinter in your neighbor's eye, but do not notice the log in your own eye?' Matthew 1:3."

What Nathan could see of Mason's eye, hooded and puffy and shaded by his cap, was looking red and slightly moist, as he fiddled with his key ring.

This was power, he marveled, watching the men watch her. And Mason wasn't the only one listening close. He could learn a lot from Mary Kay Blankenship.

"Let's turn over our song sheet and sing one of my favorites, 'Help Somebody Today.'" She nodded again at the piano player. "Burton, will you play us in?"

Nathan couldn't read music at all, and could only read words at a fifth-grade level, but he forced himself to join in, watching the black dots on the page rise up and down just as the melody went higher and lower, and trying to make his rough voice do likewise:

Many have burdens too heavy to bear. Help somebody today.
Grief is the portion of some ev'rywhere. Help somebody today.
Let sorrow be ended, the friendless befriended. O help somebody today.

Nathan scanned the chapel without lifting his head from the music and saw a couple of others trying to keep up with her song. Was she promising she could somehow get them out of prison? Or was it more like they could fix the messed-up stuff in their heads that got them locked up in the first place? At the close of the service, he hung back as the inmates shuffled out so he could get close enough to speak. "Excuse me, ma'am, I have a question for you."

Mary Kay signaled Mason, who by now looked totally whipped, that it was all right to allow the prisoner to approach. Nathan took a few tentative steps toward her, not wanting to seem threatening; to his surprise, she closed the distance between them, with an open gaze directly into his eyes that acknowledged him not just as a fellow human being, but as a man. She was close enough for him to smell her perfume. He spoke as clearly as he could without revealing his toothless gums.

"Most preacher ladies wear a cross, but you have a bird around your neck. How come?"

"To me, wearing a cross would be like wearing a guillotine or an electric chair," she replied, touching the dove on her chest. "Crucifixion was a barbaric practice that killed criminals as well as innocent people—our Lord Jesus Christ was one of the thousands who were unjustly executed. The reason I minister in prisons is that they are, unfortunately, filled with both the guilty and the innocent—some may only be guilty of having a different skin color—and some will be put to death by a needle on a gurney. I choose to express my faith with the sign of the dove, which is the symbol of peace and hope and the Holy Spirit."

She held out the pendant for Nathan to touch. The dove was suspended from its chain by what appeared to be a rope. No, not a rope. He jerked back his hand.

"Is that *a snake*?"

"A serpent. Jesus told his disciples 'Behold, I send you out as sheep in the midst of wolves. Therefore, be wise as serpents and harmless as doves.' Matthew 10:16."

"What do the preachers in your church say about that?"

"Well, I guess you'd have to ask my father, Reverend Keeler Blankenship of the First Methodist Church of Bliss. I don't believe I caught your name. Mine is Mary Kay."

"I'm Nathan. Nathan Flowers."

"What are you in for, Mr. Flowers?"

"Dragging a nig—a colored man with a truck."

Mary Kay stiffened.

Nathan said, "I guess I have a lot of hate in my heart." He hiked up a sleeve. Tattooed on his rock-hard arm was a swastika formed by lightning bolts.

Mary Kay recovered her composure. "God can help you purge that hate and replace it with love and hope. But He doesn't just wave His magic wand and *poof!* you're reborn. It's a partnership. You'll have to work very hard if you truly want to become a new, better man."

"Could you help? I mean, help show me? How to be a new man?"

"I'd be proud to."

Mary Kay held out her hand. Nathan hesitated, then grasped it firmly. It was both soft and strong. She held on long enough for him to feel its warmth. "I'll see you next week, Nathan."

Book Two

The Secret Place of Thunder

10 Years Later

4

Reverend Nathan Flowers

Day 29
Wednesday

Nathan Flowers stopped his rental car at the chain-link gate to the private plane apron at Missouri's Cape Girardeau Regional Airport, one hundred miles upriver from his Hilltop Fellowship Church. The Embraer Lineage 1000 corporate jet crowding the apron was so long the tail was invisible in the wind-driven rain. Flowers lowered his window to speak into the security phone and got a face full of cold water. *Thank you, Lord.* He'd prayed for rain and been rewarded—teeming rain like the Mississippi Valley hadn't seen in ten years—twenty-nine days in a row, with more on the way.

"I'm expected aboard tail number eight-two-three-three-Romeo-Echo."

"Your name, sir?"

"Schottkohler." It was a believable-sounding alias in the Midwest where German names were common. Manufactured of unrelated phrases that translated to "bulkhead" and "charcoal burner," Schottkohler looked real in print and was pronounced, simply, "shot caller."

The gate slid open and closed behind the car. An attendant sprinted from the private plane terminal and opened the inside gate. Flowers parked beside the Embraer, which lowered its self-contained airstairs for him.

The cabin was spacious. In commercial configuration it would seat one hundred passengers. This one was set up to coddle a dozen, and lavishly decorated with Frederic Remington oil paintings and rosewood paneling in a style that mimicked a men's club, right down to the lingering aroma of Ramon Allones Havana cigars.

"Reverend Schottkohler, I presume?" said the jet's tall, rangy, prematurely white-haired owner, with a condescending wink for their secrets.

Cedric Colson was the richest, by far, of the wealthy men who worshipped in Nathan Flowers's megachurch and the sharpest operator. Colson was also the most full of himself, which was saying a lot. Ceaselessly driven to compete, to win every negotiation, dominate every meeting, Colson pulled a bully's stunt now. He shoved a big hand in Flowers's face.

"What is this hand?"

Colson swiveled it revealing first his pink palm, then the back veined and speckled with spots and bruises and ribbed with a surprising amount of muscle.

Nathan Flowers watched Colson's eyes for the telltale contraction of the irises that would telegraph a sucker punch.

Colson said, "This is the hand that writes the check."

The threat was blunt and deadly. Colson would stop writing checks whenever he felt like it. Its timing couldn't be worse this pouring-wet morning, and Flowers knew he had to nip it in the bud.

"Not today," he answered mildly.

"'Not today?' What do you mean, not today?"

The way to control the very rich was to surprise them.

"You're forgetting that I'm here for cash today, not checks. Your hand is scheduled to hand me an airline roll-on bag stuffed with used fifties and hundreds."

Colson groused as usual about the cash. "Unlike the checks I give your Hilltop Foundation, I can't write-off cash with the tax man."

Nathan Flowers reached past Colson to swing aside a large Remington oil on an invisible hinge. He slid open a hidden panel behind it. Mounted under glass was a flag that depicted—in stark white on a scarlet field—a Mississippi River barge fleet, a cotton boll, and an ear of corn. Lettered, also in white, was the motto—Pure Blood, Pure Faith, Pure Power.

Colson gazed proudly at the flag.

Hoping he had defused Colson for the moment at least, Flowers said with easy humor, "Considering your many up-front contributions of both checks and cash, I promise you that Founding Fathers will pay no taxes in the Republic of Alluvia."

"They better not, or I'll revolt." Colson barked harsh laughter.

But any pretense to good humor died with his suspicion. The distrust twisting his face put Nathan Flowers in mind of a greedy grocer who'd caught him lifting a package of fancy steaks.

"How much longer, Reverend? How many more checks? How many more bags of cash?"

Nathan Flowers had met Cedric Colson five years ago in a room full of rich men—the "Deacons' Lounge" in the back of an abandoned department store in a dying shopping mall where Flowers had preached to Hilltop's original congregation.

Flowers was building a new, permanent Hilltop campus. Colson had already earned fortunes trading commodities and consolidating pipelines and was launching the modern American fertilizer industry on the cheap fracked gas that his pipelines transported. Betting that the fertilizer enterprise would rake in the kind of money that bought access to governors and swung votes in state houses, Flowers persuaded his wealthiest members to invite Colson to a service. Then he invited Colson to tour the construction site where the new church was rising from the old Tomato floodplain.

Colson had canceled twice. When he finally appeared, he was wary. Flowers had done his research and learned that the richer Colson got, the stingier he got, which meant he was leery of being hit up for a big donation. Flowers walked him to the bank of the Mississippi River and into the shadows of a dense and orderly forest of cellar piers so tall they seemed to touch the sky and so slender they had to be temporarily guyed with spider webs of cabling.

"You building a church on stilts?" Colson joked, with an unmistakable warning not to count on him to donate to cover cost overruns. "Hope you can afford enough elevators to lift your congregation forty feet high."

"Hilltop Fellowship is blessed with generous members who can afford elevators. But we don't need elevators. What you call stilts are piers. That hundred-acre field by the levee is our borrow pit. We'll bury these piers with the soil we dig out and anchor our church atop a new tableland four stories above the flood. Folks from Tennessee, Arkansas, and Missouri will see our steeple lighted by a golden dove. Senator Garfield, our honorary archdeacon, bless his soul, says we'll shine day and night like a lighthouse beacon for shipwrecked souls."

Colson took a long second look at the piers, then up and down the river. Finally, he nodded, muttering, "Yessir, Garfield mentioned that. I see what he meant, now."

It was time to open a forthright conversation with a dance of code words. Flowers put some preacher's quaver in his voice.

"You know, I look up in that empty air and the Lord tells me we'll soon be up there hearing our mighty organ and our sixty-voice choir sending shivers down our spines. And I ask myself, what hymn do I want to hear first? What song of praise shall we raise to God? And the Lord's answer comes up the same every time. Can you guess what hymn I mean?"

Everyone knew that the now-celebrated Reverend Flowers had been locked up for a white supremacist's hate crime. But Colson hesitated to take the bait, not sure to trust a man of God with his true feelings. Nathan answered for him.

"'There is Power in the Blood' is my favorite hymn." He quoted a telling line. "'Would you over evil a victory win?'"

Hard eyes softening, Colson quoted back: "'Would you be much whiter than snow?'"

Flowers said, "I'm not surprised to hear that we have in common pure national values."

"Pure" opened the door wider. So did "national."

"Reverend Flowers, it's clear to me that we share a deep Anglo-Saxon heritage." Soon, Colson was boasting that genealogists had traced his family lineage back to Robert I, King of Scots, on his father's side, and William the Conqueror on his mother's. He thrust out his hand. "I'm proud to meet a fellow patriot."

Flowers grew grave. Enough pussyfooting. Time for honest men to speak the truth. Time to stand up in perilous times. Time to act. "Could such rich lineage inspire a patriot to take America back?"

Colson did not have to ask, *Back from whom?*

The gloves were off. They were on the same page now. Proud members of their exclusive tribe. DNA tests, Colson announced, proved that there were no "Africoon intrusions" in his bloodlines.

Nathan Flowers did not raise the obvious objection that after four hundred years inhabiting the same continent, white Americans who claimed no African blood flowed in their veins were either lying or delusional. The fact that Cedric Colson believed in his heart that "pure" white bloodlines made him superior crippled him with a blind spot like a bullseye. But Flowers—helped by Mary Kay to become "a new, better man," and amassing their ever-expanding congregation—had had his eyes opened to a practical observation: hatred could be a tool. And so could love. The key was to tell his followers what they wanted to hear—whether to love their neighbors or hate them. People willing to be led by hatred—or love—were equally blind to reason, logic, and truth, and just as easily misled. And that was the kind of above-it-all power that even Colson's money couldn't buy.

The pilot's voice crackled on the jet's PA system. "Wheels up, Mr. Colson?"

Colson ignored it. "How much longer, Reverend?" he demanded, again.

"Eleven days."

"What?"

Nathan Flowers said, "The Republic of Alluvia goes to war in eleven days."

"War in eleven days? What makes you so sure?"

"The weather is almost ready. So am I."

Cedric Colson stared hard. "You are either the greatest con artist who ever lived. Or the real McCoy."

Nathan Flowers said nothing.

"Eleven days?"

"Eleven days."

"God dammit. You've got so much flim-flam in you it's pouring out of your ears. But there comes a time when the man putting up the money has to trust what he believes. And I believe that in your heart, you are a patriot." Colson touched his phone and ordered, "Wheels up, Tommy."

Jet engines whined.

Colson retrieved the airline roll-on bag from its regular spot behind the bar. "You're my general, Reverend, the general of my army. You dream big, like me."

Bigger, thought Flowers.

Colson, of course, took his silence for agreement and joked, "Okay, we've got eleven more days to declare independence before they catch us." He handed over the roll-on bag. "Here you go, General. Let's shake on it." Nathan Flowers closed his hand over Colson's fingers and bent them sharply backward, forcing the older man to drop to his knees in a futile attempt to relieve the pain tearing his arm.

"Wha—" he gasped.

"No one will catch me. I am beyond their imagination."

Flowers clamped Colson's bony jaw in his other hand and twisted him around so he was facing Alluvia's flag. "Our pure-blood white nation will rule the heartland of the American continent. White men will prosper farming the richest soil in the world and navigating the mightiest river. You are one of the founding fathers of this pure nation, and our Anglo-Saxon race will thank you for centuries. But you are *not* its only founder."

"My hand! You're breaking my—"

"I will lead Alluvia to victory with or without you. With or without your money. Do you want to continue to be part of it?"

"*Yes.*"

Flowers tightened his grip. "Eleven days. For the next eleven days I want you and your money and your jet plane at my command twenty-four hours a day. Will you make that happen?"

"*Yes.*"

Nathan Flowers helped Cedric Colson to his feet and handed him the phone he had dropped. "Tell your pilots, first stop St. Louis."

5

The Acting Commander

Day 30
Thursday

Major Clementine Price urged her Jeep past ninety and hit the wipers to High.

At 5:45 a.m. she didn't have much company on this flat, rural stretch of I-55 north of Memphis, but she had an alibi ready in case she blew past a speed trap. *Officer, I've just been named acting commander of the Army Corps of Engineers Memphis District, to replace my mentor—the long-serving Colonel Robert Garcia, who has been promoted to New Orleans District Commander. Today I have an urgent appointment in Dell, Arkansas—population 251—to address a small group of self-important landowners at their weekly breakfast. Yes, Officer, I realize the entire Mississippi Valley is bracing for the flood of the century, but six months ago I promised my old friend Steve Stevenson I'd come speak and I always keep my promises. Steve was a favorite of my Aunt Martha's and introduced me to Congressman Garfield who nominated me to West Point. How could I say no?*

She would not waste the trip. She'd had her adjutant schedule meetings, site visits, and inspections in the area: a quick tour of Helena's slack water harbor; meet and greet with the St. Francis Levee and Drainage District Board of Directors; inspecting a new relief well at Golden Lake; lunch in Blytheville with the Arkansas Waterways Commission; and an emergency flood planning meeting at Bliss City Hall, which her best friend Libby—who had gotten herself elected mayor of Bliss—had rescheduled so Clementine could attend.

Robert would never have said yes in the first place. The Cuban Sphinx had a knack for keeping his constituents at a friendly arms' length; he'd acknowledge the request, flash his dazzling smile, reply politely, and then do whatever he was planning to do in the first place. But Robert wasn't born and reared here. These were her people. And some of them could be very helpful in her lifelong mission to transform the way the Corps managed the Mississippi River. A mission she could only accomplish if she rose to become the next General Penn (and first female Mississippi Valley Division commander).

The rain accelerated from heavy to torrential, and the Jeep started hydroplaning.

It was rain the likes of which hadn't poured since Tomato was washed away. The river had run low for many summers, parched by droughts. But the rain returned with a vengeance, devastating last fall's harvest, soaking the ground all winter until the soil could drink no more, and falling harder this spring than in the entire past decade.

The exit signs ticked off the geography of her childhood: Joiner, Bassett, Marie, Keiser, Victoria, Luxora, Burdette—tiny farming towns, some of them now unincorporated or entirely depopulated like Tomato. She turned off the interstate early and took the back roads into Dell to get a look at the Little River, a tributary of the Mississippi and part of the Corps' flood control structure in the Delta.

As she feared, the Little River was spilling its banks into fields and ditches. There was no way any farmer would get a crop planted this season; even if the rain stopped tomorrow, it would take months for the ground to dry. People who owned ground would do just fine. The governor would declare a state of emergency and government subsidies would flow. The real victims would be the supporting players in the agricultural economy: tenant farmers, equipment dealers, spray pilots, local stores, and small banks. Exactly the kind of businesses that used to populate Dell's Main Street when she was a child.

Today there were just three downtown destinations: the post office, the Baptist Church, and this morning's destination, the Pecan Grove Inn—all three heavily subsidized and beautified through the largesse of Steve Stevenson.

A text bonged as she stepped into the lobby.

HEY CLEM, YOUR PUBLIC SKED SAYS U R IN DELL. CAN U COME SEE MY SILT XPERIMNT? AND BRING STEVE?

She couldn't say no to her little brother Will either. Maybe swing back through Dell on her way from the Waterways lunch to Libby in Bliss.

WILL TRY. ETA TBA

Will had earned a Bachelor of Science in Agriculture degree at University of Arkansas Fayetteville and was now working on a master's in Agronomy nearby at U. of A. Jonesboro. Clementine had steered

Will toward his topic—comparing crop yields from chemically fertilized ground versus the naturally rich alluvial soil in the floodplain. Lord knows Will had heard her rant and rave on the subject for as long as he could remember. *When the river is running high it dumps three tons of nutritious sediment into the Gulf of Mexico every second! One-hundred-and-eighty tons every minute! It feeds algae blooms that consume oxygen and drives fish and shrimp out of a 'dead zone' bigger than the state of New Jersey. And how do we replace that nutritious sediment? How? Barges heaped to the gunnels with chemical fertilizer, pushed back* <u>*up*</u> *that same river by towboats that burn ten thousand gallons a day of fossil fuel!*

Will joked that he chose his topic to shut her up. But Steve Stevenson, tickled by the prospect of sticking it to Big Ag, had contributed a hundred acres for her brother to experiment on. Steve, a mountain of a fat man with a personality on the same scale, loved secrets, drama, and the power of owning Delta ground. He gave Clementine a conspiratorial wink as she approached the podium.

Six months ago on the "ambassador circuit," she would have delivered a cozy talk "Behind the Scenes at USACE," or "Welcome Aboard *Mississippi V*, the Hardest Working Showboat on the River." Today however, with the strong possibility of flood on everyone's mind, she preached the Corps' Gospel: the levees were stronger than they'd ever been.

"Good thing, little lady," shouted a crusty old farmer, "because so's the rain. Thirty days in a row with more on the way."

"Mr. Cook," she grinned back at him, "you could write your Congressman to stop the rain. But instead, why not ask him to increase the Corps' levee-building appropriation?"

The old man responded with barely enough of a laugh to be civil—a deliberate reminder that people who owned ground in the Delta stood atop the social heap and that even before the Prices lost theirs, they had come from the wrong side of the levee.

But others demanded warmly that she sit with them for a fresh round of coffee. Lester Gill, the Great White Hunter—who appeared to be eating more ducks than he was bagging—asked how was her daddy doing? Getting along just fine at John Deere. And mother? Happy as a jaybird in a cherry tree. Ten years off the farm, she still doesn't miss mud on her rugs.

They had the kindness not to ask about her brother Jackson, lost to OxyContin, rescued by a Louisiana Cajun woman, and lost again when she took him home to the swamps of Atchafalaya. They did remark on Kevin, who had parlayed his small share of the sale of their ground into some soybean acreage inside the levee. Whatever happened to Abram? Seed salesman for Monsanto, based up in St. Louis. Her little brother Will?

"Will's fixing to turn his senior project into a master's thesis."

"What's it about?"

"Something way over my head," Clementine smiled and whispered Will's invitation into Steve Stevenson's ear, adding, "I'll text a heads up when I leave Blytheville."

Steve raised his eyebrows and nodded.

Lester Gill asked how was Uncle Chance.

That was complicated. She had not seen Chance Price since the flood. He had turned his back on the family, which hurt and confused her. Which was none of their business. She said only, "Working for Hilltop."

"Hilltop," snickered Mr. Cook. "They call themselves a megachurch. I call 'em a mega-country club."

"Clem, you still got Chance's Air Tractor?"

"I swapped out the old radial motor for a turbo-prop."

That met approving rumbles from men who could rebuild any machine they owned. Then Mr. Cook said, "Well, Clementine, we hope we'll see you again."

"Why wouldn't you?" Here comes the knife, she thought, with a swift eye-to-eye exchange with Steve.

The old farmer didn't disappoint. "You said you was '*acting* commander.' Don't have a permanent ring, do it?"

With that, Mr. Cook stood to signal breakfast was adjourned and the room emptied, except for Clementine and Steve Stevenson, who helped himself to a third pecan roll and another cup of coffee.

"Don't let that old viper sink his fangs in you, Clementine. You just shake him off, like a skinny little garden snake."

"He's got a gift for hitting where it hurts."

"I know how he would treat this roly-poly fairy if I didn't have six thousand acres. It must shrivel his soul knowing that if he hadn't married Bernice with her daddy's ground and half-share of the Burdette cotton gin, he'd still be bagging groceries at the Piggly Wiggly."

Clementine had to laugh. "And how venomous he'd be if he knew I wanted to take away his fertilizer and flood his fields with river sediment every spring. I'd just as soon be bit by a cottonmouth."

"Mr. Cook wouldn't mind not spending a hundred dollars an acre on fertilizer. That's how you'll get what you want for your river, Clementine; if you can sell the farmers, they'll vote their pocketbooks and the government will get the message."

Clementine sighed. "You're reminding me that whenever I'd go off on a tear about working *with* Nature, like Eads did, instead of battling it like the Corps does, Robert would remind me that monumental change takes long-term planning. And time." She checked her watch: 7:30. She was falling behind. She stood up and said, "Speaking of time. Shall we go?"

Steve wiped his mouth daintily, flicked crumbs off his shelf of a stomach, and pushed the dwindling plate of rolls toward Clementine, who shook her head no and inched toward the door. "You'll be sorry when your stomach starts rumbling after your fifth meeting today with no lunch," he warned, reaching for the napkin dispenser. "Here, I'll make you a doggie bag." He wrapped her snack, helped himself to a fourth roll, plucked a single pecan off the sticky white icing, and held it up for examination.

"When I was growing up in the 1960s, all the large farms had a pecan grove. I remember in the fall the trees would be covered with Monarch butterflies. I thought it was one of the wonders of the world. A tree—with brown leaves because there had already been a frost—and the pecans were opening on the top, and it was just hung with thousands and thousands of these butterflies attached, one to another, in living chains."

He put the pecan back on the roll and took a bite. "You never see butterflies around here now—or bees—and there are hardly any birds because the pesticides have killed all the insects they feed on. Hell, there are hardly any shade trees now. We've cut 'em down to make bigger and bigger turnrows for bigger and bigger machines. We don't even grow real cotton anymore—it's all GMO, Bollgard—Hon, I know your brother Abram works for Monsanto and everybody has got to make a living somehow—"

Clementine interrupted. "Steve, I've got wall-to-wall appointments all day, and I'm the star attraction at Libby's flood prep meeting, for which I cannot be late. And I want to make time to show you Will's silt project."

Steve waved to the busboy who had valet-parked his pickup truck. "Farming has completely lost touch with the natural world. It's just an open-air factory now. Self-driving tractors, chemicals to kill weeds and insects, and then to kill the plants themselves for harvesting. Six-hundred-thousand-dollar, eight-row cotton pickers driven by minimum-wage high school dropouts who've managed to pass a drug test. Then the cotton's hauled to the gin—another factory—a million-dollar machine operated by three Mexicans with fake Social Security cards."

"I gotta go, Steve. I'll text you from Blytheville."

Steve said, "I'll walk you out." Clementine helped him stand and propelled him toward the door.

"And if it's a short crop, the government will step in and make up the difference. One year, I didn't grow a stalk of cotton. I got my entire cotton crop out of the post office, in a check from the USDA. A lot of people call that farmer welfare; and I won't argue with them."

They had reached the porte cochere, where a fire-engine red Chevy Silverado was idling with the driver's door open. Steve dug a five-dollar bill out of his back pocket for the busboy. "To me, modern farmers are no different than little boys playing in the dirt with their toy bulldozers, except their toys are a hundred times bigger and a thousand times more expensive."

"Sounds just like the army," said Clementine. "See you later."

6

The Parsonage

Day 30
Thursday

Thirty straight days of rain were making Mary Kay Flowers—and everyone at Hilltop Fellowship Church—work a little harder to live up to the megachurch's motto: "Have you helped your neighbor today?"

The front hall of the parsonage looked like a camping store with a sale on slickers and rubber boots. Mary Kay's Karastan rugs were covered with plastic runners, and she had replaced their antique oak hall tree with a metal coatrack to save it from drip stains. Every room in the house smelled of mildew, even with the dehumidifiers running full blast day and night. She had given up on her hair entirely.

This morning there was standing water on the front walk. Mary Kay tugged on cobalt-blue boots, slid a yellow poncho over her head, and ran out under a big red umbrella to rescue the morning papers from their jumbo-size newspaper tube. She shivered at the sight of the rain-pocked Mississippi. Though far below the Hilltop campus, it grabbed the eye, shouldering a wide, gray-brown swath between the sodden shores of Arkansas and Tennessee. The brackish color, and the breadth where it had begun to submerge swamps and sandbars and penetrate the backwaters on the far shore, left no doubt the Mississippi was rising.

She retreated indoors and spread the moist newspapers on the kitchen floor to dry. They subscribed to all the Mid-South and Delta local papers—on newsprint—as well as the *Washington Post*, the *Wall Street Journal*, and the *New York Times*. Nathan always wanted the big picture, even while laser-focused on building the Delta's largest, fastest-growing megachurch. Wait 'til she read him the Memphis *Commercial Appeal*.

She filled her coffee mug and sat beside Cora, their three-year-old, who was absorbed in her picture book, *The Mixed-Up Chameleon*. Four-year-old Gabriel was puzzling over a chessboard as Nathan coached him through a game.

"Black Knight to D4, son."

Nathan paced the kitchen, concentrating on three separate, simultaneous matches: one on his laptop against a player online; one on his iPad against an app; and one with actual chessmen with Gabriel physically moving the pieces according to his father's instructions. Life on Earth, Nathan believed, never offered the luxury of battling a single opponent at one time, in one place.

Mary Kay cleared her throat dramatically.

"Front page Memphis *Commercial Appeal*—above the fold!"

NEW BARGE WHARF FOR HILLTOP
By Francine Rizzo, Senior Correspondent

HILLTOP VILLAGE, Ark. — The Hilltop Fellowship megachurch broke ground Tuesday for a liquid natural gas (LNG) barge wharf, the final stage of a state-of-the-art, all-renewable energy power plant on the riverside section of the church's ever-expanding campus. Addressing a crowd of members, contractors, workers and political and business leaders huddled under a tent in a steady downpour, Rev. Nathan Flowers stated that the power plant was more urgently needed than ever, due to the protracted power outages caused by heavy rains and flash flooding.

Hilltop already supplies most of its own energy through solar panels installed on every roof in the 30-acre campus. However, incessant rain and heavy cloud cover have demonstrated the limitations of solar power alone, noted Rev. Flowers.

Since its founding five years ago, Hilltop has erected dozens of new structures, the most remarkable of which is the site itself: a manmade plateau, elevated 40 feet above the surrounding terrain and connected by a four-lane causeway to the county highway.

Nathan grinned. "Why does the media love that word 'plateau?' It's a 'tableland,' like in the Bible and all our hymnals." His winning smile was the handiwork of Memphis's top cosmetic dentist Dr. Rudolf Stern, a Vanderbilt classmate of Mary Kay's father, who had replaced his rotted molars with implants, ground his smashed front teeth down to stumps, and capped them all. The expensive and painful procedure had been well worth it, as Nathan learned to use his smile to project warmth, confidence, sympathy, and delight.

> Hilltop's 22,000 members fill the 6,000-seat sanctuary at services from dawn to dusk on Sundays, with additional activities and worship throughout the week. On a clear day the church boasts views of Tennessee, Arkansas and the Missouri Bootheel. Residents of those states can look up and see the golden dove that crowns the sanctuary's tower, "glowing day and night like a lighthouse beacon for shipwrecked souls," in the words of Arkansas Senator Eustace Garfield, one of the non-denominational church's early supporters.
>
> Libby Whitcomb Winters, the mayor of Bliss, Arkansas, six miles south of Hilltop, said, "That church is a blessing for our city and all the surrounding small towns who are struggling to provide services to their citizens without over-taxing them."

A horn honked outside. A sunshine yellow shuttle bus was arriving to take the Flowers children to Hilltop's preschool. Ordinarily Mary Kay would walk them across the campus herself, but the once-manicured lawns, paths, and gardens had melted into a mire too deep for little legs to navigate. She inserted Gabe and Cora into their boots and slickers and ran them down the front walk under the big umbrella to the patient, smiling driver.

Chance Price—a retired crop duster pilot whose people were flooded out of the old town of Tomato ten years ago—had gratefully sold his share of their abandoned farm to Hilltop, in exchange for lifetime housing and steady work. With his buzz cut, protruding ears, and horsey features, he was frequently underestimated as a country rube—an impression, Mary Kay had noticed, that he delighted in quietly skewering with his sophisticated grasp of history, biochemistry, and aviation. There was always a plastic tub full of library books on the floor beside him.

"What are you reading this week, Chance?"

"Gaddis's new one. Leadership and grand strategy. I think the Reverend would like it." He rotated the yellow crop duster model he kept on the dashboard so the little plane's long nose pointed at Gabe as he climbed into the bus.

"Gabriel! Your plane's fixed good as new."

"Can I spray crops again?"

"Soon as it stops raining."

Mary Kay hurried back inside, then stopped in the kitchen doorway to regard her husband, the former wild animal who had voluntarily tamed himself. Nathan felt her eyes on him and looked up. With his new smile had come a new voice, through grueling sessions with a speech therapist who recalibrated his whiny twang into a silken baritone.

"Mary Kay, you've got that reporter eating out of your hand—listen." Nathan picked up reading where Mary Kay had left off.

> Nathan Flowers' by-now-well-known personal story of redemption has landed him on the covers of national magazines, on network television and on the front pages of major newspapers.
>
> Jailed for participating in a violent hate crime, he met his future wife Mary Kay Blankenship when she was ministering in Flowers' prison.
>
> "You know what Willy Sutton the bank robber said when asked why he robbed banks?" asked Mrs. Flowers. "'Because that's where the money is.' That's why I went to minister in jails: that's where the sinners are. And I have to admit, Nathan was one of the worst sinners I ever encountered."

They laughed, and Nathan stood to pull out the chair for his wife, kissing the top of her head. She squeezed his hand and resumed reading.

> That encounter changed the course of both their lives, with Flowers renouncing his extremist beliefs and educating himself in the prison library in history and civil engineering, eventually becoming an ordained minister with a

Bachelor of Science degree in water management and land use.

"Nathan was my biggest challenge," said Mrs. Flowers, who, with her father the Reverend Keeler T. Blankenship of Bliss's First Methodist Church, successfully lobbied the governor to commute Flowers' sentence, promising that they would be responsible for him.

They were wed the day after his release and established their first church in the empty Goldsmiths Annex department store in a failing shopping mall. The following year, they broke ground for Hilltop Fellowship.

She looked up and saw he had begun clearing the breakfast table.

In truth, of course, Nathan's transformation had not come instantly, like Paul's on the road to Damascus. Mary Kay thought of it more as an excavation, scraping away the hard crust of ignorance and resentment to reveal a will of iron and a keen intellect that could both absorb and synthesize information rapidly. Most gratifying was his deep hunger for human connection; he was an ardent and tender lover and a generous partner—proof that God's goodness was in him all along.

The incorporated Hilltop Village encompasses 600 acres of what was once the small farming town of Tomato, which was destroyed by the flood of 2008. To protect the church campus from the regular flooding that plagued Tomato, its levee was engineered to exceed United States Army Corps of Engineers (USACE) floodplain standards, with an innovative design by Rev. Flowers himself.

Hilltop recently expanded its dock for the fleet of ferryboats it operates to transport members living across and up the river in Tennessee and Missouri. It has also filed applications to construct an airplane runway and helicopter pad, but Rev. Flowers dismissed those plans as "only speculative."

The phone rang. Caller ID said First Methodist Bliss. Mary Kay's father read the *Commercial Appeal*, too. She pictured him hunched over it with steam coming out of his ears.

"Good morning, Daddy."

"Aren't you and your Reverend biting off more than you can chew?"

"What makes you say that?" she asked brightly.

"Y'all are acting like a city-state, not a house of worship. A power plant? And a *runway*?"

"We haven't even applied for the runway yet. But we do need it. Nathan has to drive ninety miles to Memphis every time he flies anywhere because there's no place to land a jet around here." Then, worried she might sound selfish, she added, "It would be helpful to local businessmen and farmers too, to have access to a bigger airport than Bliss's little old municipal landing strip."

"An *airport*? Not just a runway but an actual airport? Mary Kay, don't you forget what God did to King Nebuchadnezzar and his empire of Babylon."

"I know that story, Daddy. God made Nebuchadnezzar insane, and he spent seven years in a field thinking he was a wild animal. That has nothing to do with what we're doing at Hilltop. Our mission is to help our community, and since we live in a world where no one wants to pay taxes for things like schools and libraries and hospitals and public transportation, we're filling the void. How's Mother?"

"Hasn't gotten out of bed yet today. She's supposed to exercise her new hip, but she says it's too rainy to go outside and too depressing indoors. I'm at my wits' end with that woman."

"I'll run over after lunch and bring her to the water exercise class at our pool and then we can pick up the children together. Gabe and Cora always cheer her up. Good-bye, Daddy."

Nathan reached over and gave her hand an affectionate pat. "Your daddy means well, darling. He's just stuck in his ways." Then, suddenly serious, he asked, "Any regrets, Mary Kay?"

"Yes. You should have woken me when you got back last night."

"At three in the morning, only a monster would wake a sleeping angel. Any more regrets?"

"Not one!" Daughter, niece, and grandchild of ministers, she had seen plenty of disappointed brides and empty-shell marriages—in the parsonage as well as the congregation—to know how lucky they were that daily burdens had not ground the edge off their love. She gave Nathan full credit for that. She had never known anyone who could focus so finely on so many things at once.

Nathan's cell phone shrieked—the "emergency" ring tone. He held it to his ear, listened for a full minute in silence, then said "I'm on my way."

He asked Mary Kay, "Would you call Randy, please, and tell him he'll have to preach tonight? And probably tomorrow."

"Oh, I was hoping to have you home for a while."

"I'm sorry, darling. Some poor fools in Potosi are fixing to take one of our preachers hostage. It could be a long night, or two. And, yes, dear, I will be careful. But don't you worry. Sinners know that there were no sinners more dangerous than Reverend Flowers before he was saved."

"Don't joke! I'm asking you, please don't take chances."

"Darling, if you hadn't taken chances, who would have saved me?"

"You're not a twenty-year-old anymore. You're a minister and a husband and a father. Thousands in our church depend on you, and three of us here in your home. The kids in jail are tougher than ever. Please be careful."

Nathan Flowers said, "I give you my word in the name of God and our love, I am always careful."

7

The Mayor

Day 30
Thursday

It was still only mid-morning when Mayor Libby Whitcomb Winters spotted a dead man floating down the river, but it felt like a long day already. She had started at dawn, telephoning her agency heads at home to stockpile sand, clay, bags, and poly sheeting, to line up trucks and manpower, and to rent and borrow every pump they could get their hands on. The Bliss highwater gauge that the Corps maintained just above the city at Mile 801 had recorded forty feet.

Up a full foot, with more rain on the way, the pressure from all that water was driving seepage through the three-story levee that protected Bliss's Old District. Main Street banks and shops, the hospital, the many churches that lifted great steeples to the sky, and mansions built back when fortunes were made shipping on the river, all had water in their cellars. Even in the old cotton warehouses that had been converted to loft apartments, upscale millennials were experiencing their first taste of what the developers sold as "historic riverfront lifestyle."

Libby sympathized. She too lived in the Old District with Rolly, their two children, and her mother—finally retired and working harder than ever looking after the boys—in a large Victorian that had been a halfway house before they became pioneers in Bliss's first gentrification experiment. Nothing like rain and a rising river to make a grand old house show its age. Rolly was patching the roof, buckets were catching new leaks, and she'd scraped the heck out of her leg falling through a rotted step on the front porch.

Things could be much worse—much worse—she discovered when she telephoned her Mississippi Valley Mayors' Initiative counterpart in St. Louis, three hundred miles upriver where the Missouri joined the Mississippi and doubled it with the waters of the Great Plains. Mayor Francis Killing was leading an early morning media inspection of St. Louis's new floodwall. He answered his cell with a cheerful, "Morning, Mayor Winters." Next second, he let loose a frightened, "*Whoa!*"

Libby heard cries of alarm and whooping sirens. When Mayor Killing finally got back on the phone, he was no longer cheerful. Water penetrating their brand-new floodwall had lifted the street they were standing on.

"*The asphalt! Right under our feet!*"

Public Works crews were frantically pouring concrete to stabilize it. If that wall collapsed, St. Louis's famous Gateway Arch would be standing in a lake.

Libby's city could not survive such a flood. Bliss's grip on the future was frail in spite of her initial successes at stemming decay and firing the deadwood at a corrupt and bungling city hall. In the years since her childhood, Bliss had become two cities, the "Old District," and a new town of Walmart and Home Depot, motels and franchise restaurants, and subdivisions of fancy houses clustered around the interstate cloverleaf, where most of the money had gone. She could brag about their new industrial park and getting a gas-fired plant built at the former air force base. If she could somehow knit the old and new parts together, Bliss could be the new capital of the Mid-South. Never one to wait patiently, Mayor Winters's "Welcome to Bliss" billboards already proclaimed on every road into the city, "Move Over Memphis!"

And the river that threatened Bliss was so much bigger than St. Louis's. By the time it got here, the combined forces of the Mississippi and the Missouri were doubled again by the mighty Ohio, which was fed by mountain streams and huge rivers in fifteen states.

When she finally got off the phone, Rolly was laying out breakfast for the boys.

"Where's the Black Panther?" asked Rolly Jr., eleven.

"Uncle Duvall is covering for me so I can eat breakfast with you guys. He says, 'Yo!' to you all."

Duvall McCoy—ex-Air Force special tactics, like Rolly—was one of the African American stars Rolly was shepherding up the ranks of Bliss's Metropolitan Police. The kids had thrilled to the sight of him leaping through the trees like the Black Panther when he came over Saturday to help saw a dead limb threatening more holes in their roof.

"When does Uncle Duvall eat breakfast?" Kevin was nine.

"Uncle Duvall is so tough he doesn't need breakfast. Just gnaws on a bullet if he gets hungry."

"Rol?"

"Yes, dear?"

"If you say something like that, they'll be eating bullets themselves."

Rolly Winters turned to his sons. "You guys never touch guns and you never touch bullets. Right?"

"Yes, sir."

"I shouldn't be jiving like that. Your Momma's right."

Libby slung her arm over his broad shoulder. "I should get going."

"Careful out there, Libby. More cloudbursts last night. News showed some fool drowned where the road washed out. Thought his all-wheel drive made him a steamboat. Floated a half mile into the fields. No one there to pull him out when he flipped over and busted the windows."

"I promise not to be a steamboat. Are you OK here?"

"We're doing fine," said Rolly. "Here's Mother June now."

"Grandma!" the boys chorused.

Libby's mother rushed in from her apartment in the back of the house, apologizing for sleeping late, but she'd been up half the night sitting with Mrs. Dilbert who had bronchitis.

"Mama! Mrs. Dilbert can afford to hire a nurse."

"No friend of mine needs hired help." She took the homework Rolly Jr. waved at her and handed Kevin a new drowned beetle for his collection.

Libby kissed Rolly and was out the door to see with her own eyes what the river was fixing to do to Bliss. She stopped by her office to straighten out a few people, then put on a cherry-red raincoat with an oversize hood big enough to accommodate a Sunday church hat, climbed into the ten-year-old mayoral Chevy Suburban, and drove herself to the levee that was supposed to defend their city from oblivion.

She parked on top, on Levee Street itself, to look directly at the enemy.

Normally she would look down twenty feet or more. This morning they were eye to eye. The river was thick with debris. Branches, tree trunks and pieces of plastic floated swiftly on the current, stark evidence of damage suffered farther up. A gas-bloated razorback hog floated on its back, rigor-mortis-stiffened legs pointing at the clouds. A thick cottonmouth snake swam after it, slithered onto the carcass, and coiled into a ball between its legs. Libby shuddered. No wonder few Bliss citizens had a clear concept of the threat. The levees that contained the river hid its savagery.

She turned her face downriver, where the old steel mill loomed like a gray city without windows. She'd helped get it up and running again, partially at least. She was proud of the conveyor belts lifting Minnesota iron ore from hopper barges to the blast furnace, proud of the electromagnets whisking scrap metal to the arc furnace, and proud of the return of high-paying jobs, now that Bliss was again a regular stop for the barge fleets that floated special alloy steel down to south Louisiana for export.

A clump of flotsam caught her attention. It was round as a person's head. The water sucked it under. Libby stared at the empty, liquid coil, unsure, half expecting to see an arm thrashing to the surface. . . . Probably a lost basketball from pickup b-ball at one of the rundown levee parks where a bad bounce meant the end of the game. Except it was raining too hard for b-ball.

What looked like an arm rose lazily from the water near where the basketball had disappeared. Probably a tree branch rotating in an eddy. But she jumped from the SUV and followed after it, running as fast as she could in her high heels, trying to keep up with the current.

A trick of the flow whipped it closer.

"Mercy!"

It was a man. His arm rose again, a muscular, pale white arm blackened by tattoos. She ran to where the water scoured the slippery edge. She was a strong swimmer, thanks to luring the YMCA back to Bliss and doing daily laps (dropping thirty pounds in the process), but no one could swim in that. The Mississippi flowed like a solid thing, dense and unyielding. It would sweep her along as effortlessly and relentlessly as it was sweeping the man.

She was dialing 911 when his body rotated on the current and she saw his face. Or what was left where his face had been. She told the 911 dispatcher to send the marine patrol, then speed-dialed her husband.

"Homicide," Rolly answered in that rich, chocolate voice that promised, everything is going to be fine soon as you tell me your troubles. "Chief Winters."

"I just told Marine there's a floater off South End. Looks like someone took a shotgun to his face." Even as she spoke, the body took another lazy twirl, and disappeared inside a wave. "He just sank."

"They warned me not to sleep with the mayor," Rolly groaned, nudging her toward the gallows humor that had gotten her through her days as a street cop. "How long in the water?"

"Looked fresh."

"River View Houses," Rolly grunted. As a source of bodies in the river, shootouts at the public housing projects—River View Houses upstream and South End Houses down—were running neck and neck with gambling casino suicides.

"Except I saw a Pure Dominion tattoo on his arm."

"You sure? PD usually wins gunfights."

The Arkansas prison gang had expanded up and down the Mississippi Valley, west onto the Plains, and east into Appalachia. Pure Dominion owed much of its success to the Corrections Department's effort to break the gang by dispersing its leaders. Transferred out of state to Tennessee, Mississippi, Louisiana, Kansas, and Kentucky prisons, the PD bosses who ruled inside the prisons—and their shot callers who served as their agents and enforcers both inside and out—were as enterprising as Silicon Valley venture capitalists.

"I'm sure. Double lightning bolts around a '16' and a '4.'"

When Rolly made chief of Bliss Metro Homicide, he had landed a Black Lives Matter grant to pay for a part-time hate crime squad, and Libby had snagged some money from the Justice Department. Rolly and Duvall McCoy had been tracing the command structure of Pure Dominion through databases maintained by the Southern Poverty Law Center and the Anti-Defamation League. He and Libby both knew prison-gang tattoos, especially those inked by white supremacists.

"Has he popped up again?"

"Gone."

"Will I see you for supper?"

"Depends how long the flood meeting goes. I'll call you."

"Take care of yourself, Libby."

The mayor got back in her SUV and drove north, out of the city. Upriver was a floating eyesore that made her blood boil every time she saw it. Scarlet letters twenty feet high glared like the Devil, night and day: Noah's Lucky Ark Casino.

Gambling was legal in Arkansas only on riverboats, which the state's legislature interpreted as "offshore," not on state land. Noah's "riverboat"—permanently moored on barges—was a gigantic, grotesque, fake-wood "ark" three stories high, with cartoonish pairs of animal heads sticking out of false windows rimmed with neon. Like any casino, the Lucky Ark drew a loose, criminal element, encouraged drugs and drinking, and caused endless pain and suffering to the families of addicted gamblers—leaving Bliss's first responders, hospitals, and social services to sweep up the mess.

And speaking of Noah, some marketing fool in a warm, dry TV studio had come up with a rain joke: a biblical-looking Noah animation with a white beard and a Flintstones umbrella who ticked off the consecutive days of rain. Amid the daily reports of people driven from their homes by local flooding, and drownings like the one that had Rolly in a lather this morning, the cartoon Noah did his rain dance on his ark calendar, which measured to forty days. Today made it thirty in a row: drenching rain in Kansas, Illinois, Nebraska, Iowa, St. Paul, Chicago, Pittsburgh, and Cincinnati. Rain over every river that fed the Mississippi.

She drove farther upstream under the interstate connector bridge that spanned the channel with an airy arch of girders. Four miles north, the levee curved inland where Tomato used to be.

Libby still could not believe Clementine's farm was gone. She had practically lived with the Prices during the summers. While her mother worked the night shift at the hospital, she and Clem would share a bed on the sleeping porch, tell ghost stories, and confide their deepest secret dreams. She learned to drive a tractor like a real farmer's daughter, how to gut a catfish, and how to put up their abundant garden's fresh fruit and vegetables into boiling hot jars. She even got to ride on Uncle Chase's towboat and still remembered with a pounding heart when Clementine fell off and nearly drowned.

The Price home place was now occupied by an enormous lake and a vast hill of earth with a flat top. On that tableland spread the Hilltop Fellowship campus. The sanctuary itself loomed hard beside the river, the golden dove on its steeple glimmering through the rain and fog.

Libby was eying that higher ground as a primary shelter for flood refugees if the worst happened to Bliss. Reverend Flowers and his wife Mary Kay had already offered any resources the church could provide, and Hilltop's operations manager would be at this afternoon's flood preparedness meeting. Libby hoped to use the church's fleet of yellow vans to augment the decrepit city buses. The new causeway that Hilltop had built to welcome parishioners driving from the interstate highway also connected to the county road on top of the mainline levee; that meant people in Bliss had two routes to safety. Three counting the ferry dock, if the river wasn't too wild for boats.

Driving back to the city, she passed under the interstate connector bridge again. An awful picture grabbed hold of her brain—thousands of people climbing the bridge to get above the roiling high water, huddled all night in the rain, cold, wet, and hungry.

***

Clementine Price raced from her lunch meeting in Blytheville to Steve Stevenson's home place—ten-square miles of Delta ground that stretched as flat and endless as an ocean. Steve, thank God, was waiting in his Silverado and she followed him on a cratered gravel road across bare, sodden fields and onto a turn-row so muddy it spattered her windows to the roof line. Through the rain, she saw Will in a yellow windbreaker, perched on the tailgate of his rusty Ford F-150 parked beside an orange fiberglass tank the size of a stretch limo. The tank, stenciled AG-SCI DEPT, sat on a lowboy flatbed trailer next to a drainage ditch which was running like a raging river. Will had a portable pump sucking water out of the ditch and into the tank.

Clementine parked alongside Steve and helped him disgorge his mass from the truck. The fat man was draped in a fern-colored poncho that Clementine swore had been fashioned from a pup tent—indeed, as she grabbed his plump hand to steady him onto the truck's reinforced running board, she glimpsed an *LL Bean Mountain Light Two-Person Tent* label.

Steve adjusted his oilcloth fedora to a jaunty angle.

"Let's see what the mad scientist is up to."

Clementine hugged her brother as hard as she could through her slippery raincoat. He'd put on muscle since she had last seen him and grown a beard—like every millennial she knew who wasn't in the service. With his crown of curly sandy-blonde hair peeking out from his hood, he looked like a Christian disciple in a Renaissance painting.

Steve shouted to be heard over the rush of water and the growl of the pump. "Is that a septic tank?"

"Yes, sir. We're separating the silt and sediment from the chemical run-off in river water. Just like in a septic system, the solids—silt and sediment in this case—sink to the bottom, while the liquids rise and flow out. The silt contains the nutrients that make 'alluvial' soil so rich."

Will jumped off the platform and ran to the other end of the tank where a white plastic pipe emerged near the top and angled down to a patch of tall grass. "The water flows into this enclosed wetland we created—basically, a leach field—which we're testing for pesticide residue to see if we can clean it enough to recycle."

Steve looked skeptically at Will's homemade contraption. "Your wetland is occupying acreage that's not producing any crops."

"Yes, sir. Ideally the leach field can be siphoned underground with French drains, below your crop roots, and any contaminants would be absorbed by transpiration."

Steve said, "Can we continue this technical discussion in the dry comfort of my capacious club cab?"

They slogged through the ankle-high mud to the Silverado. Will climbed in first, revealing a taut band of bare skin above his tight Levis as he maneuvered himself into the small back seat. Clementine watched Steve gape in open appreciation of this fine specimen of young manhood.

With the AC and defogger running at full blast, and the rain battering the roof, they had to yell at each other.

"The septic tank is just a model, to test the concept," Will explained. "If it works, the next step is to construct—with Steve's permission—an underground version, based on an Imhoff tank."

"Layman's terms," pleaded Steve.

"That is way down the road," Clementine interjected, noticing that Steve's patience was wearing thin. "The main thing is that Steve has given you the opportunity to experiment." She smiled warmly at her old friend. "Thank you for being Will's guinea pig, Steve. I think he's working on something very important for our planet. That could also be very remunerative."

"I like remunerative," said Steve, revving the motor in a clear signal that the site visit was concluded. "But this little guinea pig is going home to a warm bath and a hot rum toddy." He laughed his big laugh and patted Clementine's cheek. "Let me know when you're ready to top-dress my cotton with Mississippi River fairy dust."

Clementine and Will sheltered inside her Jeep while the rain pelted down. She spoke first. "Tell me something honestly: I caught Steve ogling your butt, and it's a very nice butt, for sure. Has he ever made a pass at you?"

Will stared at her, then rolled his eyes and laughed. "Do you think Steve is the first gay man who's ever 'ogled' me? I've seen him eyeing me, and I take it as a compliment. And for the record, I've seen lots of men—and women—ogle you, too. You're a good-looking woman, Clem, you should appreciate being stared at."

"Has he ever made a pass at you?" she repeated.

"No ma'am—Major—he has not. And for the record, to prove your little brother is capable of defending himself against molestation, the second time I caught him rubbernecking my ass, I called him on it."

"What did he do?"

"He said 'Just because I've ordered my dinner doesn't mean I can't look at the menu.'"

Clementine burst into laughter. "I'll steal that line next time I ogle someone."

Both their phones chirped with incoming texts.

"The WhetherChannel," Will grinned. "You're copied."

"Your geek friends at U of A are doing some impressive meteorology, I have to say," said Clementine, scrolling through the text.

"Hey, look at this." Will tapped his phone and a weather simulation appeared. "This is lots worse than what NOAA and the other Weather Channel are predicting: flash flooding on all the tributaries—St. Francis, the White, the Red, the Arkansas, the Black, and the Yazoo."

Clem said, "I haven't seen any forecasts like that."

"My bros hacked into remote sensors the National Weather Service is beta testing."

"Are you serious?"

"Our WhetherChannel might know something the grown-ups don't."

The rain had eased but she drove Will directly to his truck anyway. "Be safe, Will. I love you."

She turned the vehicle around and was struck again by how flat this natural extension of the Bliss Basin was. For twenty miles, nothing but a few old Native burial mounds stood between her brother's experiment and the Mississippi River. She lowered her window.

"Will—worst case, do you have a plan to get to higher ground?"

Will's grin tightened, and he suddenly looked less the carefree boy. "Always."

8

The Weatherman

Day 30
Thursday

Half the nuclear missile silos hidden under the Great Plains had been decommissioned in the 1990s. Hundred-foot-tall weapons aimed at the former Soviet Union were hoisted to the surface and trucked away in pieces. Some empty silos were filled. Some of the deep shafts were sealed. Others were put to new purpose, bought from the government for eccentric vacation homes or impenetrable survivalist retreats. It was quiet fifteen stories under the prairie—silent if your generator was housed in a separate shaft—and people spoke softly.

"The weather is still on your side, Shot Caller. My models project thunderstorms over the entire Mississippi watershed. On the Plains, the Upper Mississippi Valley, the Ohio Valley. The Missouri River is nearing flood stage. The Ohio River is nearing flood stage. The St. Francis River, the White, the Arkansas, and the Red are nearing flood stage."

The Shot Caller's gaze roved over the silent monitors that bathed the Weatherman's studio in cold blue light. He studied each knowledgeably: the graphic displays of radar-detected precipitation, rain cores, storm cells, and automated real-time rainfall reports; and Network Control's map of cloud-to-ground and intra-cloud lightning flashes, which indicated the time, location, and power of every strike. The Weather Channel, muted on a flat screen TV, had their Noah cartoon ticking off day thirty.

"When?"

He visited regularly, dressed like a Midwestern insurance agent in a sport coat and tie, his face hidden by a black mask that covered his eyes, his forehead, and his nose. The Weatherman liked these visits. The Shot Caller was focused but serene, demanding yet always respectful. There was no question who was boss, but he never rubbed your face in it.

"Flash floods start next week."

"Where?"

"Water, water, everywhere."

"How much for Arkansas and Tennessee?"

The Weatherman brought up the highwater gauge readings at Caruthersville, Missouri; Bliss, Arkansas; and Memphis, Tennessee. "I can't guarantee Memphis, yet, though it's looking good, but I promise oceans for Bliss."

"Louisiana?"

"Like I said, the weather is on your side. Rain is filling the tributaries—the Arkansas, the Black, St. Francis, and the Yazoo—and the tributaries have nowhere else to go. The Mississippi River will storm into Louisiana brimful. Look out New Orleans. Baton Rouge. Port of South Louisiana."

The Shot Caller faced the Weatherman. "Where is your bitch?"

"I gave him a few days off."

"Why?"

"I love it down here. I could stay forever. But the bitch gets claustrophobic. He says it reminds him of jail." The mask could not hide from a sharp observer what the Shot Caller was thinking. His body revealed it for him, a trifle stiffer, hardening a little. The Weatherman tried to soothe him with a smile, "I tell him it reminds me of jail, too, but only the good parts."

"Do you trust him to come back?" The Shot Caller's voice was no louder, but no longer soft.

The Weatherman decided that it was time to demonstrate that he was not the kind of "jail-brains" that the Shot Caller despised, but a fucking genius who deserved the best weather station money could buy. He tapped his touch screen. On the wall of monitors, the lightning strike graphic was replaced by a map of the United States. A single red dot pulsed near the middle. Another tap zoomed-in the map on the city of Bliss, Arkansas.

"I trust him to come back because the bitch knows that *I* know where he is. Every second, every hour, every day."

"How?"

"GPS ankle monitor."

"You're not a parole officer. What's to stop him from chiseling it off?"

The Weatherman knew that the Shot Caller was not happy. Still, he could not resist strutting his stuff, so he answered with a smug smile, "The bitch is not suicidal."

"What does that mean?"

"He knows that the monitor is, shall we say, tamper-resistant."

"How resistant?"

"Any attempt to remove it will blow his foot off."

"With what?"

"C4," said the Weatherman, expecting an awed, "Cool!" or at least an approving nod. What he got was silence that went on and on and on, darker and colder with every second ticking mutely on the monitor clocks.

Nathan Flowers was reminded that the more "big brains" he recruited, the more craziness got in his way. He should whale on this dumb son of a bitch right now. Shower him in blood and pain. Yet at this crucial point, he needed them pulling together. So, he said what the self-satisfied "big brain" wanted to hear: "Ingenious."

He stepped into the wooden cage that Weatherman had rigged for an elevator. It was the lowest-tech thing in the silo, a work of engineering centuries simpler than the ankle monitor. With the cage suspended from a pulley topside with a counterweight, you ascended by pulling on a stationary rope.

"Problem is, like you just told me, the weather is moving our way." He raised his voice. "Get your bitch back down here. Now! Before something pops his trigger and he does some stupid thing bitches do."

"You got it, Shot Caller. I'll get him back right away."

The Weatherman listened to the soft creak of the elevator ascending. He *did* like it down here, liked it better than anyplace he had ever lived, which meant he owed the Shot Caller big time. No way he would ever disappoint him. Problem was, the bitch was not answering his phone.

9

Preparing for the Worst

Day 30
Thursday

Clementine Price knew the entrance codes to Bliss City Hall and let herself in the side door ten minutes before the emergency flood planning meeting was set to begin.

Built in 1939 as a WPA project, the municipal headquarters had everything a small southern city could have wanted eighty years ago—including an acoustically perfect four-hundred-seat auditorium where Libby's mother had taken the girls to hear Clementine's first chamber music concert. Schubert's "Trout" Quintet had become study music that carried her from high school through West Point and every graduate course she had taken since. But the building was cramped and antiquated by current standards, cold in the winter and beastly hot in spring, summer, and fall. The air conditioning had broken. Custodians circled chairs and tables on the auditorium stage, where the hot air could rise into the fly space, and positioned portable fans on the floor in hopes of creating the semblance of cool air. The roof had started to leak, so plastic tubs were being requisitioned. Someone had the foresight to bring in a trash can for umbrellas, where Clementine deposited hers.

Libby was there already, in the wings, illuminated by a fly-specked window, her papers spread out on the padded leather cover of the old Chickering grand piano that had remained even though chamber music concerts had ceased decades ago. The mayor frequently blew off steam by pounding out Stevie Wonder, gospel, or Beethoven on the old war horse, which was serviced regularly by a blind piano tuner who Libby paid out of her own pocket.

"Your Honor!" Clementine greeted her with a hug and gave a firm handshake to her chief of staff, Sharon, a polished young African American woman Libby was grooming to run for the General Assembly.

"Wow, that's a long list of presentations," she said, reading warily over Libby's shoulder.

"Every dog has to protect his territory," said Libby, "but Sharon is keeper of the stopwatch. After five minutes they get the gong." Sharon demonstrated the "gong" on her phone—a recording of thunderous applause.

"I know at least one chief of police who will think that's the real thing," laughed Clementine.

Libby rolled her eyes. "Seventeen months until he retires. I've set up my own Billy Bob Owen Advent calendar to count the days." She walked Clementine into the corridor to make sure they weren't overheard badmouthing one of her key players. "Seriously though, all he can talk about is his anti-looting plan and how he's going to maintain law and order during a flood. If what they're predicting comes true, those looters will be swimming for their lives. I need him to wrap his head around the concept of evacuation—right?"

"Right." Clementine took her by the shoulders and looked directly into her eyes. "I am not going to sugarcoat this. The weather models indicate that multiple flood crests could head our way. The river is already full, which will slow down the flood crests, and slow-moving crests are the most dangerous. They can crevasse levees—suddenly break through with a force that can turn Bliss into an instant lake."

"Worse than 1927?"

Clementine hugged her friend hard and tried to lighten up. "*Could* be, not will be. Many variables can work in our favor. And the levees are stronger than ever."

They walked back onto the auditorium stage, which was filling with department heads, civic leaders from local businesses and not-for-profit agencies, and clergymen and women—many of whom Clementine had known most of her life, but plenty of new faces as well. One of them came up and introduced himself.

"Major Price, I'm Andrew Wells, the facilities manager from Hilltop Fellowship Church." Wells had a buzz cut, a no-nonsense manner, and a neutral accent—marking him as a newcomer to the Delta. "Your predecessor Colonel Garcia spoke so highly of you all these years. He was so easy to work with, helping Hilltop get all the variances and construction permits we needed. I'm grateful he left the district in such capable hands."

Clementine took flattery like this with a grain of salt—remembering Robert's warning that everyone wanted something from the Corps—and gave Wells an enigmatic smile that would have done the Cuban Sphinx proud. Wells continued, "I've already told Mayor Winters that Hilltop is standing by to offer temporary shelter, transportation on church vans and ferries, meals from the church's food pantry, and on-site counseling for flood victims. And volunteers from our congregation have started collecting emergency supplies—flashlights, bottled water, canned food, you know—that people can use to assemble their own disaster kits. We've also set up an animal rescue and boarding facility at Hilltop, for pets and small domestic animals. It's open now, free of charge of course, to anyone who wants to deliver their pet to us in advance for safekeeping."

"That's very farsighted, Mr. Wells."

"The pet shelter was Mrs. Flowers's idea. She doesn't want anyone to drown because it took an extra five minutes to get Fluffy into the carrier."

Clementine flashed on her last sight of their farm, with the chickens on the roof and the pigs and cattle trying to swim. She wanted to end this conversation and saw a familiar white head hovering behind Wells.

"That's so true, Mr. Wells. Do you know Dr. Sudbury, the CEO of Stevenson Memorial Hospital?" She suspected he did but didn't want to hear about it. "I've known Dr. Sudbury since I was a little girl—my great Aunt Martha was on the hospital board when Dr. Sudbury was still in his internship. He brought that institution into the twenty-first century, against some mighty stiff headwinds." Clementine knew how susceptible the good doctor was to shameless flattery, and she laid it on thick, realizing what an asset Stevenson Memorial could be. She took his arm and steered him toward Libby. "Your hospital is the tallest building in Bliss, isn't it? And you just last year moved all your generators to the roof—so wisely!" Libby was now within earshot and Clementine addressed her directly. "I wonder, Dr. Sudbury, if your hospital might be able to set up a space for Bliss's first responders to go between shifts?"

Libby caught Clementine's pass and ran with it. Daughter of a nurse, wife of a cop, and a former cop herself, Libby knew firsthand the toll that prolonged emergencies took on frontline workers. "On the top floor, maybe, Dr. Sudbury? Chance to close their eyes for a few hours, take a shower, and get a bite to eat?"

"Stevenson Hospital is the perfect place for that, with emergency medical care on site," added Clementine. "It could also be the designated meeting place for first responders to go if they've gotten separated from their families—their children would know to come there."

Dr. Sudbury nodded obediently. His assistant took notes.

Libby pointed to her watch. "Five minutes," she mouthed. Clementine checked her phone for messages one more time before the meeting got underway. It suddenly vibrated and shrilled "Reveille"—the custom alert sound that senior Mississippi Valley Division officers programmed for a "Penn-to-gram."

Heads whipped around at the bugle sound. Clementine pocketed her phone, caught Libby's eye, held up her index finger—wait one minute—and stepped into the wings to read the urgent text from Lieutenant-General Clinton Penn that none dared let go unanswered for more than sixty seconds.

> DISTRICT COMMANDERS MISSISSIPPI VALLEY, EXCEPT ST. PAUL AND ROCK ISLAND, REPORT 0800 TOMORROW MV MISSISSIPPI, NEW ORLEANS. LODGING ABOARD.

Libby came over to see what was holding things up.

"New orders. New Orleans early tomorrow morning. General Penn. Attendance not optional."

"Sounds big," said Libby, sensing she was about to lose her star speaker.

"Libby, I hate to do this but you're going to have to cover for me here. I know the meeting was moved on my account. But tomorrow has just been totally blown up, and probably the day after, too. I've got to get back to Memphis and see what I can salvage of the rest of my week."

Libby did not hide her irritation. "OK, Major, give me your talking points. I'll deliver them."

"The main thing is you have to have a solid evacuation plan with multiple fallback positions."

"I've identified three evacuation routes."

"That's not enough. They could all be impassable. You should have six, at least. And every citizen needs to know *all* the routes to safety, not just one or two."

"What if your flood doesn't come?"

"Pray it doesn't."

"At what point in time can you guarantee the river will flood?"

"Weather is not yet an exact science. Thunderstorms and flash floods alter models overnight."

"I'm not talking about science. I am talking about people. Dammit, Clem. People aren't an exact science, either."

"What are driving at, Libby?"

"I'll only get one shot. If your flood doesn't come this time, they won't run *next time* they're told a flood is coming. They won't leave their homes before they're under your 'instant lake.'"

"Libby, it's my job to warn everyone of worst case—Oh, for pity's sake, don't cry." Clementine edged Libby further into the wings and got her behind the curtain.

Libby shook her head, angry at her tears. "It's not you. It's just that I saw . . . I saw a body in the river. And I just don't want to see a whole bunch of them."

"Drowned?"

"Shotgunned—a gang thing." She shook her head again. "I don't know what's gotten into me. I've seen tons of bodies. I'll bet I saw more bodies when I was a cop than you saw in Afghanistan. At first I was yukking around with Rolly like we used to on the force—stupid stuff you say to close your eyes. Twenty minutes later I was driving under the interstate bridge and for a second I swore I could see a thousand people climbing it trying to escape the flood. They looked so scared—It's OK. You have to go to New Orleans. I'm fine. Go."

"Soon as I get back, we'll have a glass of wine?"

"A bottle."

"Your place. I'll bring the bottle."

"Who's going to be in New Orleans?"

"Division brass, minus the upper river districts where flooding's already started."

"Colonel Garcia?"

"Sure. Robert's the new District Commander of New Orleans—you know that. Why do you ask?"

"Say hi for Rolly and me. Tell him we all miss him. I'll bet you're looking forward to seeing him."

"Of course," said Clementine. "I miss him, too."

10

The General

Day 31
Friday

"Colonel Garcia!" roared Lieutenant-General Clinton Penn—Commander of the Mississippi Valley Division and President of the Mississippi River Commission—"How in blue blazes did you get your paws on a blimp?"

Robert Garcia left it to a more reckless officer than he to inform Clinton Penn that the 250-foot-long *Wingfoot Four,* Goodyear's newest addition to its aerial television camera fleet, was not a blimp, but a semi-rigid dirigible airship. It was more maneuverable than a blimp, faster, quieter—ideal for the confabulation Penn had ordered—and carried a bigger payload. Sixteen Army Corps of Engineers officers were seated in comfortable armchairs, transfixed by the view three thousand feet below *Wingfoot*'s glass-bottomed gondola.

"You made it clear the mission required a bird's-eye view, sir," Garcia answered with an easy smile. A roaring, "country-boy" General Penn was an amiable General Penn. A soft-spoken General Penn sprang surprises, none of them pleasant. *Roar on, sir.* "Otherwise, all credit to the kindness of our friends at Goodyear." (And to the weather gods. If the rain hadn't thinned, he would be host to a bored three-star general staring at clouds.)

General Penn—a tall, well-built soldier in combat camouflage who appeared ageless thanks to a face smooth as limestone and an arresting mane of iron-gray hair—marched up and down the center aisle narrating the scene beneath the shifting checkerboard of rain and clouds. "Can you believe that this hive of industry was once only sugar plantations? Louisiana's fabled Gold Coast, the River Road. Look at it now!"

A vast inland port lined the Mississippi River from New Orleans to Baton Rouge.

"Fifty-four *miles* of deepwater docks and oil refineries. Ships and barge fleets as far as you can see. The busiest tonnage port in the United States.

Busiest in the western hemisphere. Second busiest in the whole world. The Port of South Louisiana."

Penn had summoned his long-serving deputy division commander, his district commanders, and some old comrades from the neighboring Northwestern, Southwestern, and Great Lakes and Ohio Divisions, and his favorite personal adjutant, the adoring Captain Margaret Standfast.

Standfast's ruddy, round cheeks and enormous brown eyes made her look like innocence personified. There was gossip, of course—typical speculation when a pretty young adjutant served a much older, charismatic senior rater—but Garcia did not believe a word of it. For one thing, he knew Mrs. Penn. She could play the general's gracious wife, but she was at heart a tough old farm girl who would not abide being humiliated by a philandering husband. Nor did he see Penn chasing women thirty years his junior. He was a man of outsize passions, but these passions embraced the United States Corps of Army Engineers and his relentless adversary, the Mississippi River. It was Garcia's opinion that Margaret's wide-eyed admiration was a clever smokescreen for her own ambition. As Penn's gatekeeper, she had accumulated immense power for a mere captain, but kept it well hidden under a veneer of wholesome innocence.

Garcia glanced at Clementine. Speaking of hiding it well. Only if you had worked with Clementine Price for ten years would you realize she was on high alert, sensing something was up while smoothly concealing her concern and her determination to scope it out.

A natural showman, Penn wove dramatic descriptions with flourishes of detail and interrupted himself with silent pauses that allowed them to drink in the inland port's astonishing immensity.

"Talk about a 'target rich environment,' gentlemen. And ladies." Brisk nods for Major Price and Captain Standfast. "Docks, cranes, warehouses, tank farms, chemical plants, and gasoline refineries. If an enemy air force was attacking—instead of a flood—they wouldn't need smart bombs. Just drop dynamite."

The levees were tall, the channel deep, welcoming gigantic tankers and freighters from the oceans of the world. Industry and commerce crowded up against housing tracts, antebellum mansions, and sugarcane fields rutted from the wet spring harvest.

Garcia was struck by one particularly haphazard juxtaposition of the silver prilling towers of a fertilizer plant, a red-roofed suburban subdivision, and a plantation house with a dark green polo field. The polo field shimmered like an emerald set in a ring of rubies. A towboat was backing a fleet of covered hopper barges alongside the fertilizer wharf.

General Penn steered their attention to the densely woven net of railroads, highways, bridges, and canals that converged below. "It's a tighter choke point than the Strait of Malacca. There's Interstate 10, the southern Atlantic-Pacific artery. I-55 to St. Louis and Chicago and Detroit. I-59 to the Northeast. The Illinois Central Railroad. Canadian Pacific Railroad. Kansas City Southern. The Union Pacific. Mississippi and Ohio river barges. Pipelines to the Gulf of Mexico.

"A flood that ties this port in knots strangles our nation. A flood that destroys it slashes the country in half and sets the economy back sixty years. How can we move energy into the Heartland and cotton, grain, gas, and steel out if the Port of South Louisiana is underwater?"

Garcia sensed Clementine's eyes on him and exchanged a swift private glance with her. She looked certain that General Penn was leading up to something big but couldn't yet reckon what. Garcia had an inkling, but he wasn't going to jump the gun by guessing the worst.

Baton Rouge slid astern of the airship. Cropland edged the levees. General Penn stopped talking, leaving his people to digest the details of his presentation and speculate on their meaning.

Wingfoot continued northwesterly up the river. On Colonel Garcia's orders, however, her pilots no longer traced its twists and turns, but flew a straight course, crossing the many bends like a dollar sign's vertical stroke. A new presence took shape in the west—another river edging close, converging with the Mississippi.

Garcia stepped into the cockpit for a word with the pilots. The big airship altered course a few degrees and descended a thousand feet. Garcia returned to his seat and minutes later was rewarded with murmurs of satisfaction from every officer in the gondola. Three prongs of water could be seen connecting the now-parallel rivers like a lopsided trident. The rivers raged, murky water near flood stage, but the connections imposed order, thanks to feats of engineering that were astonishingly immense and incredibly bold.

"Gentlemen and ladies," General Penn resumed his narration proudly. "Gaze upon six structures that represent everything the Army Corps of Engineers stands for. Writ large! Along this treacherous stretch, the Mississippi flows so close to his neighbors the Red River and the Atchafalaya River that levees alone can't keep them apart. Were they to unite, unbridled, our nation would suffer a catastrophe.

"The Atchafalaya is a thirsty river. Originally she was a tributary, giving her water and the Red River's water to the Mississippi. But the Atchafalaya has grown herself into a *dis*tributary. A greedy one and, as I said, a thirsty one—a *seductress* with a ravening maw that grows bigger, deeper, and wider every year. Every advantage is hers—her bed is low, her route short. If we let her, she would suck every drop of Mr. Mississippi straight to the Gulf of Mexico—stranding the city of New Orleans and the entire Port of South Louisiana."

Penn glowered down at the treacherous Atchafalaya like a preacher castigating Jezebel. "To ensure that never happens, we built ourselves the Old River Control Structure—a big valve to control how much water we will allow her to steal.

"It's the biggest valve mankind has ever built in the history of the world. It's got six parts—a lock, a dam, three flow-control structures, and a hydro-power plant—and one purpose: prevent Mr. Mississippi from co-mingling with Miss Atchafalaya."

In the water-bound land of curves seen from above—the meandering rivers, the twisting streams, the sinuous swamps—the Corps' work was distinguished by hard, straight lines.

"First thing you see coming up is the navigation lock. Having prevented the rivers from co-mingling, we've built a back door to allow barge fleets to move between them."

The lock connecting the Mississippi and the Atchafalaya ran like a laser beam for a full mile.

"Here comes an earth dam. A humongous earth dam. Taller than a ten-story building and weighing five hundred million tons. Who can tell me why we built a dam weighing five hundred million tons?" He raked the gondola with a stony gaze. Career officers who had cycled recently into the division looked like they wished they were back in the bone-dry deserts where they'd last served.

It struck Garcia, not for the first time, that an officer could learn a lot from General Penn about letting his people figure out for themselves what was going on. Few if any of these West Point stars knew the Mississippi like Penn did. The idea behind the "blimp trip" was to let them absorb reality for themselves. Penn cast Garcia a thin smile. "Obviously, you know why we built that dam, Colonel Garcia, as our blimp is floating over your new district—Major Price! You appear eager to elucidate."

Garcia hid a smile when Clementine let her soft Delta accent grow a little thicker to drawl, "Well, sir, the Mississippi used to meander down to the Atchafalaya—you can see just a trace of that old meander behind the earthworks. Until the Corps dammed it and chased him back into his own bed."

"Well put, Major Price. Incidentally, officers new to the division would do well to read Major Price's report on last winter's barge pile-up that came within a cat's whisker of taking out the Harahan Bridge. All right, now we're floating over the heart of the system, the flow-control structures."

They looked, Garcia thought, like giant zippers stretched across the channels. The individual gates within them stood as neat and orderly as zipper teeth.

"Think of them as a series of mini-valves within the big valve," said General Penn, adding with a sly smile, "If you can call a football-field-and-a-half-long concrete-and-steel Auxiliary Structure flow-control gate a 'mini' valve. Or that double-football-field-long Low Sill Structure flow-control gate 'mini.' Not to mention that 'mini' half-mile-wide Overbank Control Structure standing by to open its gates for extreme highwater."

Garcia spoke up, asking, "General, is it true that during the flood of 1973 they sent a television camera down to make sure floodwaters hadn't scoured under the Old River Structure?"

"Damn straight. I was there."

Colonel Hardy of the St. Louis district piped up, with an ingratiating, "Surely you weren't serving all those years back, sir."

"I was still a cadet—just a country boy who got hisself to West Point—but I wangled an internship down here. We sank a bore hole to inspect the state of our concrete, and I helped waterproof the camera. Do you know what we saw on the TV? Concrete? Heck no. Fish! Catfish swimming *under* our two-hundred-thousand-ton control-gate structure." He laughed. "Let me tell you, boys, that was touch-and-go for a while."

The general sobered abruptly. "You all have heard the complaints now and then that the Corps tries to assume the role of Almighty God. Well, I'll leave that judgment to the preachers. But I will say this. If the Atchafalaya ever gets her hooks into our Mississippi, she'll make hurricanes and oil spills and floods a gentle memory by comparison. That's why the Corps builds 'em strong. Take us home, Colonel Garcia! We see the big picture."

As the stately airship sailed through her turn, Robert Garcia traced the thin line of the main levee from where it continued north of the Old River Structure and disappeared in the rain a few miles up the river. He was thinking about famous screw-ups in military history. The French army built impregnable fortresses on the Maginot line. But Nazi tanks hung a right and detoured around them. Or, as his grandfather, his heartbroken *Abuelito,* always mourned: "We had the gardener string barbed wire around the front gate; Fidel Castro's Communists smashed our kitchen door."

***

"Will you men join me in prayer?" asked Nathan Flowers. They had settled into his host's private office, a glassed-in belvedere atop the roof of his Greek Revival plantation house that offered views up the Mississippi River almost to Baton Rouge.

Peter Fleming, a lavish contributor to the Hilltop Fellowship Church, bowed his head and closed his eyes. Cedric Colson, who had stationed himself in a window that overlooked Fleming's barge wharf bowed his head too, but kept his eyes wide open.

Flowers fixed his own eyes on Fleming's polo field. It had been planted in dark-green Bermuda grass, Fleming boasted, by the same turf expert who managed the Guards Polo Club in Windsor, England. A faint odor of ammonia wafting from the fertilizer plant penetrated his office although the windows were closed and the AC system kept it cool and dry.

"Thank you, Lord, for blessing your Hilltop Fellowship Church with visionary men. Thank you for your servant Peter who supports your work with ceaseless generosity. Thank you for your servant Cedric who slings his strong arm around the shoulders of your churchmen. And may we ask, Lord, if it pleases you, that you provide guidance to these men that they may conduct their business righteously, that each might enjoy the satisfaction of serving You by helping his neighbor."

Cedric Colson could not resist a self-satisfied smirk—lording it over Peter Fleming because innocent Peter was only part of the church and not in on the secret of Alluvia. Flowers shot Colson a warning look. The smirk flared out abruptly and the self-satisfied fool shut his eyes.

"Amen."

Fleming and Colson repeated, "Amen," and Flowers said with a smile, "I hope you forgive the direct pitch, but I'm sure that the business you are hoping to conclude deserves support from the highest level."

Peter Fleming laughed. But Cedric Colson spoke gravely. "We're not quite shaking hands, Reverend. Thank the Lord you needed a lift to minister to the Baton Rouge jailhouse just when I was flying down here. I'm praying you'll see a way to straighten us out."

Nathan Flowers asked, innocently, "What is the point of contention?" It was, in fact, about the barge wharf, a fleet of jumbos that Fleming's factory was loading with fertilizer.

"Loyalty," said Peter Fleming.

Colson reddened. "Pete, I've bought a lot of companies in my day and I intend to buy more. So I know there comes a time when the man putting up the money has a right to be accommodated on a small matter."

"I couldn't agree more," said Fleming, "which is why I tried so hard to help you understand that this is no small matter."

Nathan Flowers spoke softly. "Mr. Fleming, Peter, may I ask the nature of the matter?"

"Of course, Reverend. Back in the day—long before Mr. Colson entered the fertilizer industry—when natural gas got so expensive it almost drove us out of business, and the Chinese undercut us at every turn by subsidizing their ammonia industry—I weathered those times thanks to a Midwestern distributor who gave me every break to sell my fertilizer to his customers. Hank Morrison, of Morrison Grain and Fertilizer in Missouri. He's not quite so ready as me to sell out and retire. Young wife, kids in school. He's trying to keep afloat 'til they're all cared for, but it's getting harder to float with the big boys consolidating the business."

Fleming sprang to his feet, bounded across the belvedere, and pointed at his wharf. "Hank can't get product. I promised him those barges. Thirty jumbo hoppers of prime urea ammonium nitrate and granular urea with 46 percent nitrogen content."

"You would let this huge deal collapse over a few barges?" asked Colson, sounding scornful, incredulous, and superior.

"They are not a 'few' to Hank Morrison," Fleming shot back. "At this moment, they're everything. Hank was there for me; I'll be there for him. Reverend, do you understand?"

Nathan Flowers needed Peter Fleming's barges a thousand times more than the dueling businessmen, which was why he found himself in Louisiana trying to maneuver their cargo into Cedric Colson's possession. Fertilizer was the prime ingredient of the blasting agent ANFO—an explosive mix of ammonium-nitrate and fuel-oil—and there was enough in those barges to level mountains.

"It's not always easy being a Christian, is it?" he asked. "Which is why, at moments like these, I turn to the Bible. . . ."

Two hours later, Colson's big jet was rising from Baton Rouge and circling north over the Atchafalaya Floodway.

"King Solomon!" Colson crowed. "Pete actually fell for King Solomon."

"He didn't fall for it," said Nathan Flowers. "He focused on the prospect of nothing."

Flowers pressed his face to the window, peered down through a hole in the clouds, and oriented himself by tracing the Atchafalaya River up to its beginning at the confluence of the Red and the Mississippi. Seen from several thousand feet above, the Army Corps of Engineers' Old River Control Structure looked like a crooked fork. Rivers that flowed from distant Texas, Wyoming, and the Appalachian Mountains were suddenly side by side, close enough to touch each other. *Like me and Mary Kay in the prison chapel.* Maybe. But one thing was for sure: The Control Structure looked like the Corps was stabbing the Mississippi in the back with that fork.

11

The Floodway

Day 31
Friday

"Home" for the Corps that night was *Mississippi V,* dockside in New Orleans, where General Penn's officers would sleep onboard in The Boat's staterooms. The Boat was cost-effective, logistically efficient, and private.

Clementine Price noticed there were no civilians among the support people; every deckhand, A-V tech, and steward was U. S. Army. The same had prevailed on Garcia's dirigible—career soldiers, lifers who could be trusted to keep their mouths shut; not even the senior civilian engineers were allowed to attend. She watched Robert for a clue. If the Cuban Sphinx knew what General Penn had up his sleeve, he was not offering to share it.

Penn seated them around a big table set with water glasses, pens, notepads, and laptop power ports. He cut his usual imposing figure, but he looked anxious, Clementine thought, his normally rosy cheeks pale, his eyes bleak. He hadn't loosed a single belly laugh since they got off the dirigible. It seemed to her that he was suffering a grim desolation that mirrored the weather projected on the flat screens.

"By now it should be clear to all that the Port of South Louisiana is our top priority. It should also be clear that we are very possibly looking at worst-case weather. And, it should be especially clear that it is up to the Mississippi Valley Division to ensure that the Port of South Louisiana does not flood—Major Price!"

"Yes, sir."

"We will work our way downriver from Cairo, Illinois. What options can the Memphis District offer to protect the Port of South Louisiana?"

"Birds Point-New Madrid Floodway, sir—immediately below Cairo—can divert 550,000 cubic feet per second of a 'project flood,'" she answered, using the Corps term for a giant flood that challenged every element of the entire system they had engineered to keep the Mississippi inside the levees.

Penn growled, "That would be just fine, except the environmentalists stopped us from sealing the exit so the water just rushes back into the river at New Madrid." He enunciated "environmentalists" in nine syllables, that clearly translated into "lunatics with their insane idea to so-call restore a so-called natural river."

That sent the general on a tear every officer in the room had heard before.

"We cannot afford the luxury of a 'natural river' any more than physicians can accept 'natural cancer.' We are responsible for protecting railroads, highways, airfields, industry vital to defense and the economy, dozens of slack water harbors, and *five hundred million acres* of the most productive agricultural ground in the world. Not to mention the Port of South Louisiana, which is what we're here to settle. What else can the Memphis District do to save our nation's paramount inland port, Major Price?"

Clementine hesitated. Her scrupulously maintained levees would not help Louisiana. What was he driving at?

"What about the Bliss Bends?"

"Sir?" asked Clementine, baffled.

"*The Bliss Bends!* A twisty corkscrew in the river above Bliss, Arkansas! We dug a chute down the middle, straightened the channel sixty years ago. Before your time, Major Price. The best way to prevent flooding is to speed up the river, make it carry more water by making it flow faster and smoother. The Bliss Bends used to slow down the water. Used to trap it above the city—gathered it like the cone of a funnel. The city levee was the spout. A terrific amount of water would be bottled up and come shooting through, undermining Levee Street, jumping the banks, wiping out all the little villages that used to be along there. It was just awful."

Penn stared at her. She said, "Yes, sir. I—"

"The Corps erased those sharp curves with cut-offs—lengthening the spout and eliminating the cone. The river shoots through faster and doesn't build up such pressure behind it. Since then, instead of backing up at the bends and flooding the basin, the water runs in a straight line."

"I'm afraid I don't understand, sir." She glanced toward Captain Standfast. No help there. Round cheeks flattening, eyes blank as an executioner's, Penn's adjutant looked ready to impale Clementine on the general's orders.

He said, "Major Price, you've got a natural, built-in floodway right there. The Bliss Bends Basin has darn near the capacity of the Birds Point spillway."

"What about Bliss?"

"What about it, Major Price?"

"It's a city, sir."

"Folks in Bliss'll be fine. I built their levees, Major Price. You forget that for many years before I took command of the Mississippi Valley Division, I held the Memphis District. I oversaw every project. Their levees are strong."

"The mainline levee is superb, General," Clementine replied smoothly. "Seepage into old cellars is minimal, far less than it used to be. What concerns me, sir, worst case, are the back levees, behind the city on the inland side. They're just old county levees. Can they be relied on to prevent the floodwater racing out of the Bliss Bends from sneaking in the city's back door?"

He stared at her hard. Was he willing to risk a breach at Bliss to provide relief downriver? Whatever he meant, General Penn ignored the gist of her answer, saying, "Exactly, Major Price. If the Bliss Basin doesn't provide enough relief, water will divert west toward the Little River, and on into the St. Francis Basin. A natural floodway with a hundred times the capacity of Birds Point."

But surely he knew that the cotton, rice, and soybean farms in the Delta west of Bliss were not a designated floodway like those where the Corps paid landholders for easements. From the corner of her eye, she saw Garcia lift his chin, his old signal of "chin up, don't let the bastards goad you into a mistake."

General Penn seemed to anticipate her objection. "Major Price, we prepare for 'worst case,' to use your phrase, by considering all options. I am sure you will set your engineers' minds to linger upon various worst case means of offering relief downriver."

Welcome to the army, as Robert taught her. Every army in the history of warfare. She said, "Yes, sir." Not to would be to get kicked out of the loop and lose all hope of making a difference.

General Penn moved on to Colonel Bradley, commander of the Vicksburg District, who surprised no one by bragging about his levees and reminding them that during the 2011 flood, which he called a "flood event," 2,300,000 cubic feet of water flowed past Vicksburg per second.

General Penn interrupted, "What will the Vicksburg District do to spare the Port of South Louisiana from some of the water you've contained?"

"Well, sir, as the general is surely aware, sir, we have no floodways and no reservoirs in the Vicksburg District."

"Provided we survive this flood, I suggest you and your engineers work up proposals to change that situation so the Vicksburg District might contribute to the effort to protect the Port of South Louisiana, Baton Rouge, and New Orleans. As it stands now, the Vicksburg policy appears to be to pass the water on."

Clementine Price and Robert Garcia shared another lightning look, and she could hear him asking, "You think you have troubles with Penn? How would you like to be Colonel Bradley from Vicksburg?" At least Penn hadn't suggested that she work up an actual plan to breach the Bliss Basin levee. Or would that come in the form of a directive from headquarters?

Bradley said, "Yes, General, but may I ask the general to please remember that the 2011 flood broke records, but our levees stood strong? We saved over four million people, ten million acres, and $100 billion in damage—"

"Colonel Garcia, you're up."

Robert Garcia was ready with assurances. "If the Old River Control Structure is unable to disperse all the floodwater, the Morganza spillway stands ready to discharge an additional 600,000 cubic feet per second. But all at the price of the inundation of southwestern Louisiana by the Atchafalaya River."

"I know the physical geography," Penn said in a quiet voice dripping with menace. The room grew still as all remembered how even the general's favorites could suffer his changes of heart. "I want you to consider this, Colonel Garcia: it's clear to me that the Old River Control Structure makes you anxious; I sympathize, to a degree. As I mentioned earlier aboard your blimp, a scour hole in '73 almost undermined the Control Structure. It would have been catastrophic, leaving our greatest inland port high and dry and permitting the Gulf of Mexico to drown the city of New Orleans. We repaired it best we could and relieved some potential pressure by erecting a brand-new auxiliary structure. But remember that fear and doubt can undermine the Corps as severely as Mother Nature."

"Yes, sir. And may I add, sir, that the newly improved Bonnet Carré Spillway can divert up to 300,000 cubic feet a second into Lake Pontchartrain. Some low-lying neighborhoods of New Orleans might flood a bit if Lake Pontchartrain is raised too high by spillway influx, which raises a difficult question. Given the city's repeated battering by

Mother Nature since Hurricane Katrina, I am duty-bound to ask you how much flooding would be politically acceptable?"

If anyone in the meeting doubted that Garcia still enjoyed some degree of fair-haired status, they didn't after General Penn responded to Garcia's carefully measured statement by saying, "You boys keep my options open. I'll deal with the politicians—Major Price!"

"Yes, sir."

"What is the condition of your Birds Point fuse plug levee?"

"The fuse plug levee is standing by to erode, sir, if water tops it."

Like a home circuit breaker programmed to fail before an electrical fault sets the whole house on fire, the Birds Point fuse plug levee was designed to divert extreme high water before it breached the main levee. It was slightly lower than the main levee, and the river rushing over it would erode an opening to shunt excess water into the Birds Point-New Madrid floodway—a two hundred square-mile stretch of low-lying farms and wetlands as big as Chicago.

"Have the sapper pipes been charged with blasting liquids?"

"No, sir. On your orders, no explosives have been pumped into the fuse plug sapper pipes."

"Keep it that way. Last darned thing I ever want to see again on TV is the Corps dynamiting levees. We saved Cairo in 2011 and what did the TV show? Cairo not flooded and no citizens drowned? *No!* The TV showed exploding levees and drowned cows—which I still believe was stock footage of cattle from some other flood. That fuse levee had not been called to serve since 1937. Folks commenced to thinking it was permanent and the floodway was permanently not underwater. 'Til they woke up to swamps and fields flooded on CNN. It's a *floodway*. It's supposed to flood. Just like Colonel Garcia's Atchafalaya Floodway is supposed to flood. We pay property owners good money for flowage easements. But one dead animal floating by—or some fool who refused to evacuate sitting on his roof in the middle of a lake—and the Corps is in the doghouse. That's why we've gone back to old-fashioned fuse levees."

"Yes, sir."

"Trouble with a fuse levee is we have to wait for the river to overtop it. But on the other hand," Penn smiled, "the environmentalists cotton to the idea it's 'natural.'"

Amen to that! thought Clementine, wondering if General Penn remembered or had ever noticed that she had overseen the restoration of the 'natural' fuse levee at Birds Point. Probably not. Generals tended not to notice majors. (Though he had remembered her report on the Harahan bridge pile-up, bless his heart.)

"No explosives unless you hear different directly from me, Major Price."

"Yes, sir." She debated whether she should point out that if he changed his mind it would take at least a full day and half to barge the blasting explosives against flood currents from Memphis up to Cairo. Should she suggest moving them closer, now? Or let that sleeping dog snooze, at least for a while? Did she have the nerve to arrange a nice surprise for him?

"And Major Price?"

"Yes, General?"

"Can I assume that stretch of fuse plug levee is properly maintained?"

"Yes, sir. The crown is kept clear of vegetation by contract with J. B. Hanley. If the river tops it, it will melt as it was designed to."

"You assumed temporary command three weeks ago, Major Price. When is the last time you actually clapped eyes on the Birds Point levee?"

"Tuesday, sir."

Penn looked surprised. "Good job, Major Price."

Thank God for Snoopy! Uncle Chance's old Air Tractor allowed her to inspect her far-flung 25,000-square-mile district a lot faster and more often than driving or flying commercial.

"All right, we're all in agreement. This meeting is adjourned. I'll see you in the officers' mess at 1800."

Clementine was not in agreement at all. She went straight to her stateroom, telephoned her headquarters, and directed her officers and engineers to re-inspect every levee and flood protection system above and below the Bliss Bends. Jesse Corliss, the civilian chief engineer she asked to take charge of the re-inspection, was an old friend who had been a generous show-er-of-the-ropes when she first arrived in the Memphis District as a newly minted captain.

"And have another look at Bliss's back levee," she told him.

"I toured the back levee with the county engineer two weeks ago. Tip-top."

"Can't hurt to look again, Jesse," said Clementine. "Do you have the time, or shall I tap someone else?"

"I'll do it," said Corliss.

"We'll want to deploy bags and sand along the back levee. And—just to be on the safe side—let's have a half mile of Tiger Dams ready to be filled. Lay them out now on their straps; corkscrews standing by to stake 'em down."

Tiger Dams were fifty-foot-long vinyl tubes they could fill with water from city fire hydrants. Laid end to end atop a levee, they made a three-foot-high flood barrier. Two Tiger Dams stacked side by side, supporting a third dam on top, created six feet of protection.

"You got it, Major. So what's the situation in New Orleans?"

"Challenging."

It was clear, now, why General Penn held the meeting in the privacy of The Boat. He'd received orders from on high that New Orleans and the Port of South Louisiana were top priority. If the worst of the current forecast models held true—if the weather generated a project flood—somewhere else had to be sacrificed. And that somewhere was Bliss.

***

She forced herself to maintain an even keel at the large oval dining table where General Penn was playing gracious host even while underscoring the seriousness of the situation by not ordering wine. As stewards stood by to top up water glasses after every sip, she listened for an opportunity to reopen the discussion in some way that might establish a line of communication with Penn that she could take up tomorrow.

Finally, she got an assist from Robert.

"When I was at West Point," Colonel Hardy from the St. Louis district bloviated, "the only gut courses were environmental science and—"

Garcia—who had already made an enemy of Hardy by beating him out of the New Orleans promotion—cut him off and called down the table. "Major Price, didn't you win the Environmental Engineering Prize at West Point?"

"Yes, sir. For a modern-day application of James Eads's jetty system."

And she was off and running with her by now well-practiced tale of re-enacting Eads's diving bell experiment, which she introduced by saying, simply, "I had to get into West Point. The Academy was the only way I could afford a first-class engineering education." Hearing that, General Penn actually put down his knife and fork to listen and occasionally emitted a chuckle as she spun her yarn.

"Do I recall correctly, Major Price," he asked, "that Eads used a whiskey barrel?"

"You are correct, sir. A forty-gallon whiskey barrel, three feet high, two feet wide at its widest. There was barely room for his shoulders."

"But you employed an actual farm bell?"

"I didn't have a barrel."

"Well, I'll be."

Having finally nailed Penn's attention, she talked as fast as she could to hold it. "Why do Eads's jetties still work today? Elegant engineering—underpinned by Eads's intimate understanding of the Mississippi River. Eads walked its floor, held its silt in his hands, tasted its mud, felt its currents and whirlpools shove and tear at his body. It was personal. That's what gave him the courage to put his money where his mouth—"

"What money?" Colonel Hardy interrupted.

"Eads offered to build the project *with his own money* and not charge the government a penny if he failed. Can you imagine such confidence, Colonel Hardy?" Hardy looked nonplussed and a smile puffed Margaret Standfast's cheeks as if she thought, Score one for the women!

"All in the face of powerful resistance from our predecessors at the Corps of Engineers and politicians who were fixated on building ever higher levees and ever stronger flood walls, as if they could confine the river into submission. Enfilade it like a human enemy. Eads knew not to pit man against nature, because nature is patient. Nature will always win."

She pushed her empty plate away and leaned in, lowering her voice so her audience had to listen closely. Garcia had seen her deploy this instinctive tactic so successfully over the years that he had adopted it himself.

"Eads didn't try to conquer the river by brute force. By building those jetties below the port of New Orleans, where the Mississippi empties into the Gulf of Mexico, he narrowed the outlet so the water would flow faster and carve a deeper channel. It dredged itself—with its own current. Ships no longer ran aground on pileups of silt and sand. Basically, Eads got the Mississippi to power-wash itself!"

Clementine got what she was hoping for from General Penn, the genial belly laugh that famously persuaded farmers, environmentalists, and local governments not to think of the Corps as occupying the Mississippi Valley like an invading army, just because it had been constructing dams, locks, jetties, levees, cutoffs, weirs, and floodways wherever it pleased for a hundred years.

"To this day," she added soberly, "Eads's jetties are vital to the Memphis District. The Bliss Bends Cutoff would silt up without them. But I wish I knew what Eads would have done with flash flooding. They didn't have so much of that back in the 1800s."

"All mighty interesting," General Penn said softly, rising from his chair, prompting the rest to leap to their feet. "But I'm turning in for a good night's sleep, which I recommend to all of you. We've got big days coming up and hard work. We'll need our strength. Good night, everyone. Godspeed home to your districts in the morning,"

Halfway to the door, he turned back and said, "Clementine, you are quite the storyteller."

"Thank you, sir."

"Have you ever considered entertaining on the stage?"

"No, sir, I'm just a country girl who got herself to West Point."

12

At Last

Day 31–32
Friday and Saturday

The rest of the district commanders gradually drifted away, leaving Clementine Price and Robert Garcia alone in the mess while the stewards cleared and reset for breakfast. They hadn't seen each other since his farewell party in Memphis three weeks ago, and Clementine was shaken to realize how much she had missed his daily presence in her life.

"Well-played with the Eads story. General Penn knows who you are, now. And where you come from."

"I'm just praying I can talk him out of this Bliss Bends thing."

"The general has to look at options. God willing it won't come to it. If the weather saves us."

"I hope I earned enough goodwill at supper to talk to him again. Otherwise, Bliss is on its own."

"Not so. Bliss has you looking out for it."

The rain outside got louder. The last waiter on duty walked by with a sly grin. Without breaking stride, he passed Garcia a wine bottle wrapped in a napkin. "Good to see you, again, sir."

Clementine watched with satisfaction as Garcia unfolded a fine Laguiole penknife to cut the foil from the bottle and pull the cork. It had been her farewell gift to him. "An elegant tool for an elegant officer. Bon Voyage," said her card.

They clinked the empty water glasses he filled and sipped the wine, a rich white Picpoul. "I wonder," she said, "how your friend the waiter just happened to know your latest favorite wine."

"Plan ahead," said Garcia. "The Corps' marching song."

"Is that how you got the blimp?"

"Dirigible, and you're asking the wrong question. The question isn't how did I get the dirigible, but why did I get the dirigible."

"Because General Penn wanted it," Clementine answered, falling easily into their old mentor-protégé relationship.

"General Penn is too busy running the Corps' most important division to waste time and effort wondering if he wants a dirigible. He had already solved the problem by asking me to give his people a "show," as he put it. When I figured out he wanted a dramatic overview that would stick in everyone's head, all I had to do was remember the name of a guy at Goodyear I did a favor for. I will be rewarded with six months or a year of Penn not second-guessing me in my new command."

"Did you know what he had in mind for Bliss?"

"No. I only knew that he had something big up his sleeve and was determined to get his entire division on board."

"Colonel?"

They had been on a first-name basis, in private, since he made her deputy commander years ago, and Clementine only addressed him as "Colonel" when she was joking or they were in public. Or when she was dead serious.

"What is it?"

"Why is Penn so obsessed with saving Cairo? It's a dying city. The population's down to just a couple of thousand people. It's smaller than most towns."

"Cairo sticks in people's minds. The Corps has been defending it from the river for a hundred years, since back when it was an important city, and the media all know its name. So General Penn knows that if something happens to Cairo, he'll end up grilled on a congressional hot seat."

"Robert, what can I do about this?"

"Again, wrong question. Ask yourself how you can reward him for accepting my recommendation to make you acting commander."

"There isn't time to 'get a blimp.' I have to change his mind now."

"Clementine. The Mississippi Valley Division is the most important in the Corps. If every other division turned traitor and sold out to China, who would ever notice? The Mississippi Valley Division *is* the Corps. And General Penn is its commander, has been for a long, long time, and having made fast friends everywhere, he will command it until he retires. If the Secretary of Defense offered a fourth star and chair of the Joint Chiefs of Staff, Penn would decline the promotion. He likes commanding a by-and-large benign occupying army. And he takes his job very seriously. Two jobs: keep river traffic in the channel, and river water off the farms.

"Now he's been directed to perform two additional, extremely specific jobs: keep the Port of South Louisiana functioning, and New Orleans no wetter than usual. With emphasis on the port. Does he realize what can happen to Bliss? He realizes what *might* happen. He hopes it doesn't. But he will save the Port of South Louisiana and the city of New Orleans at all costs."

"I don't know what to do." At least she had put her people on alert.

"Clementine, you have more reason than most to fear the flood," he said gently. "But trust me. Just do your job and stay out of his."

"Those are direct contradictions."

"Welcome to the army."

Clementine did not know what to say to that. But Garcia was not done. He said, "Everybody knows that I ended up in the Corps at General Penn's invitation."

"Because his son served under you in Iraq. And you saved his life."

"I did my job. What people don't know is why I accepted his offer."

"It was a heck of a career move."

"Not one I wanted."

"Then why'd you take it?"

"I told myself that I owed my children a father they'd see alive while they grew up."

"Told yourself? Meaning . . . ?"

"Truth was, I enjoyed it too much."

"Enjoyed what too much?"

"Battle. Combat. Maybe even killing. The general offered me an honorable way out. Saved my soul—at the expense of giving up some excitement. I am grateful to him."

"All these years," Clementine marveled, "I've thought of you as the classic engineer: driven to make order out chaos. I never understood that other part."

"No way you could. I'm as private as you are, Clementine."

The dining room grew so quiet she could hear the rain outside the steel walls. She finally broke the silence by asking, with forced lightness, "So, what's it like in New Orleans?"

"I'm a little at sea," Garcia answered seriously. "New Orleans is very baroque—so many local customs and power brokers and tribes. It reminds me of Cuba. Those who stayed under Castro had to be willfully blind to danger all around them. But in Cuba the evils were manmade. In New Orleans, it's geography. They live fifteen feet below sea level. They can drown in their sleep. Needless to say, they deeply distrust outsiders. Just like your Delta people did," he smiled. "At least when I first got there."

"The New Orleans district must have at least one ambitious young 'Lieutenant Price' to show you the ropes."

Garcia's smile widened. "I haven't found anyone like you, Clementine." He looked around the empty mess. "Why don't we let them shut down? Feel like a walk?"

"Why don't we go up to the chart room?"

"What for?"

"Have a look at the weather."

"Of course." He tucked the wine bottle into a capacious pocket and took both their empty glasses in one big hand.

They climbed to the wheelhouse, occasionally bumping shoulders as they navigated the narrow corridors and stairs. Clementine inhaled the smell of him, soap and mint and Brylcreem, and allowed the wine to go to her head. They reached the top of the stairs that led to the Texas deck and stepped through the curtain that shielded the wheelhouse from the lights. With The Boat moored dockside, there was only one officer on watch, a very junior lieutenant who saluted them and froze at attention. His combat uniform name tape read, "Pickett."

"Chartroom computers online, Lieutenant Pickett?"

"Yes, sir, Colonel."

They stepped into the dimly lit bay directly behind the wheelhouse and Robert drew the curtain. Clementine briefly studied the monitors streaming the latest data from the National Weather Service and National Severe Storms Laboratory. "The same, only more."

They sat, side by side, on a narrow navigator's bench in the corner, their faces illuminated by the screens in chiaroscuro.

"Robert? . . . Was it hard to persuade General Penn to make me acting commander?"

"Not really. He knew I had every reason to leave my district in the most capable hands."

"You're a close old file. I had no idea you were campaigning to take over New Orleans."

Garcia took out the wine bottle and poured them each a second glass. "You were the reason I wanted the New Orleans appointment."

"To make room for your protégé to advance? That's chivalrous of you."

"I was willing to step sideways as long as I could get away from the Memphis district."

Clementine looked down into her glass. "To get away from me?"

"To get away from us. From an impossible situation. I had fallen in love with you. And I believe you had fallen in love with me."

She turned to look him in the face. His usually perfectly composed features wore an expression she had never seen before, of unspeakable sadness and longing.

"Yes, I had fallen in love with you," she whispered. "I am in love with you."

They sat silently for several minutes listening to the hum of the computers. She hoped it would drown out the sound of her pounding heart. Eyes forward, they leaned into each other, shoulders pressing together, then arms, knees and feet, all trying to become one. She had fantasized about this moment for years. Now that it was actually happening, she was paralyzed.

Garcia stood. "I'm going down to my stateroom. If you would like to join me, tap on 806. Please don't if you don't want to."

Clementine loitered outside her own stateroom until there was a witness to see her entering it alone. It turned out to be Captain Standfast. Clementine started to let herself in, waving good night.

"Major Price?"

"Yes, Margaret?" said Clementine, thinking, Oh my God, did she spot us going up to the wheelhouse?

"I loved your story at dinner, ma'am."

Clementine opened her door. "Thank you, Margaret. I appreciate that. Good night."

Clementine closed the door and waited five minutes, double checked that there were no security cameras in the hallway, then made her way quickly to Robert's door, hoping he hadn't given up on her. He answered after a single tap and she slipped in, unseen.

They stood and stared at each other. Robert had already removed his bulky jacket and combat boots, and was barefoot, wearing only trousers and a snug tee shirt. The skin that never saw the sun was as pale as hers;

his arms ropy with muscle, his torso lean as a knife. He opened his arms, inviting her to step closer.

Clementine sat on the nearest chair, hurriedly unlaced her boots, tugged open the top button of her camouflage uniform, and started to pull it over her head.

Robert gently put it back on and knelt beside her. "Don't rush things, Clementine. I've waited ten years for this, and I want to enjoy every moment."

He pressed soft fingers on her forehead, on the tip of her nose, each earlobe, each cheek, then her lips. "I wish to become better acquainted with all the parts of you that I've only been able to look at and couldn't touch. Do I have your permission, Major?"

Clementine nodded. She didn't trust herself to speak. Robert then retraced his journey, this time with his lips. When his mouth reached hers, she seized it hungrily, wrapped her arms around him and pulled him closer.

When they finally caught their breath, Clementine said "Sorry. Pent-up demand."

Robert burst into joyful laughter, and she did too, grasping both his hands and slowly, teasingly, kissing each individual finger. "Sauce for the goose is sauce for the gander, Colonel," she said between kisses. "I've been lusting after you for ten years, too."

She paused when she reached his wedding ring.

"Would you feel better if I took that off?" asked Robert, as he began to tug at it. The untanned flesh hidden by the gold band glared at Clementine like a rebuke.

She put her hand over his. *I want him no matter what. And we may never have this chance again. Time to change the subject.* She turned his hand over and softly traced the lines in his palm with her forefinger.

"I can tell that somewhere in the middle of your life your own desires have been—or will be—set aside in order to serve the needs of others."

"What?"

"Libby taught me to read palms when we were in sixth grade, so I can see right through you, Robert." She kissed the center of his palm. "Here's your heart line. It shows that you are picky when it comes to love."

"Well, judging by present company, it's true. I am picky. Very. However, I haven't yet concluded my inspection. Do I still have your permission?"

Methodically, tauntingly, and exceedingly pleasurably, he investigated her wrists, palms, fingers, and throat. When he made his way around to the nape of Clementine's neck and started in on the downy blond peach fuzz nestled beneath her smooth, thick roll of strawberry blond hair, she slid her jacket off, stood, and walked to the bed.

She removed a bobby pin and a Victory Roll cascaded.

She handed Robert the pin.

"Keep track of these, please. I didn't think I'd need extras."

13

The Hate Crime Unit

Day 32
Saturday

"Incredible," marveled Bliss Metro Chief of Homicide Rolly Winters. "I figured he'd be in Memphis by now."

"You *know* him?" asked Duvall McCoy. It was after midnight. Duvall had just gotten back from retrieving a fugitive in West Memphis.

"Libby saw him floating by yesterday."

The body had turned up in a patch of still water shielded by an abandoned wharf, well within Bliss city limits. It had been pinned there when its left leg jammed between creosoted pilings.

Rolly illuminated it with a little LED flashlight.

Duvall McCoy snapped photos with his phone while they waited for the medical examiner to pronounce it dead.

"How do you know it's the same guy? He's got no face."

"He had no face yesterday, either. Libby spotted his PD ink."

Duvall leaned over the water to focus tightly on the Pure Dominion lightning bolts that blackened the dead man's arm. Rolly held him by his belt.

"Good job," he told the young street cops, one white, one black, who had found the corpse. Posting the mantra, *Call It In, Don't Touch,* on roll call bulletin boards had had the desired effect. Bliss Metro's patrol officers were becoming an asset instead of the pain in the butt they'd been when he first joined the force.

The quiet Duvall, as tall as Rolly but nowhere near as wide, got grins out of them by adding over his shoulder with mock solemnity, "Your Homicide Department appreciates the opportunity to examine a murder victim for clues before he is separated from them."

Equally satisfying was that the fact that the black and white team seemed to get along like good street cops had to. Rolly and Duvall took that as a modest victory for their initiative to diversify Bliss Metro's all-white ranks, in hopes that partnering rookies from the suburbs with rookies from the housing projects might yield the kind of policing that could keep the peace without routinely breaking heads.

An assistant medical examiner arrived under an umbrella, looked, pronounced, and left. Rolly and Duvall went to work, helped by the cops, and managed to pry the body loose from the piling and out of the water without anyone falling in.

"What's he got on his leg?"

Rolly focused his LED glare on the leg that had stuck in the pilings. "I'll be. That's what got caught."

"Is that an ankle bracelet?" asked the black cop.

"ID'ing him ought to be a cinch. Wait for his parole officer to slap the cuffs on him."

The white cop knelt down and leaned in close.

"Don't touch that!" Rolly and Duvall shouted in unison.

Both detectives had been to war—veterans of an air force outfit specializing in low-visibility, high-impact intrusions. Rolly had continued with the reserves, teaching what he used to lead until they posted him back to the Middle East for a year, which was where the comrades had hooked up again, Duvall having re-upped following a rocky re-entry to civilian existence.

They shared survivors' respect for improvised explosive devices.

Neither had ever seen an ankle monitor rigged as an IED, but there was something about this one they didn't like. (The cuff was the giveaway, Duvall later reckoned during their "after action review" over a couple of beers. It looked a hair thicker than usual. The dense C4 putty the bomb maker had worked around the steel had bulked up the fabric sleeve.)

"That is one mean parole officer," said Rolly.

The street cops cracked up.

Duvall said, "I'll get a closer look."

Rolly held him back with a big hand. "Settle down. We'll bring in the pros before somebody gets killed."

Duvall did not like that. He looked pumped to charge and tear the thing apart with his bare hands.

Rolly said, "String yellow tape before some damned fool blows it up."

Duvall McCoy backed off and recruited the street coops to string Police Line tape at a distance. Rolly Winters called for the bomb squad.

***

The road to perdition with a pit stop in paradise? Robert wondered. They lay like perfectly matched spoons in the narrow berth. The lights were off but the drapes were open, with The Boat's deck lights illuminating the stateroom just enough for him to see the deep curve of her waist and the swell of her hip, where he rested one hand. He wouldn't be the only man in his New Orleans parish this Sunday to enter the confessional and perfunctorily recite that he had had carnal relations with a woman not his wife. But this didn't feel like adultery, although of course technically it was. Clementine was his true love, his only love. She must know that.

He stroked the cascade of strawberry blond hair that covered the pillow and most of her torso. It was so long, and there was so much of it. He never suspected. How many more delicious secrets were there to discover in this miraculous woman?

Clementine stirred and turned her head so her face was in profile. A woman with a jawline like that should not be trifled with, Robert realized.

"Clementine? Are you awake?"

She kept her eyes closed and smiled. "What did you have in mind?"

"Lots. But first I want to make sure you know that you are the only woman in my life. From practically the moment we met."

She turned to face him, with an arched eyebrow. "Robert, I appreciate your romantic spirit, but how can I be the only woman in your life when you have a wife *and* this is the first time we've gone to bed together?"

"I do have a wife. Rita gave up her own career to support mine, and she's a wonderful mother. Her life totally revolves around the children. We've become co-administrators of a family."

"What do you mean by 'co-administrators?'"

"I mean we haven't slept together since Candace was conceived, nearly twelve years ago."

"Seriously?"

"Rita's a strict Catholic. She doesn't believe in birth control or abortion, which pretty much eliminates the possibility of having sex, if you've decided that four children are enough. . . . It's not like we hate each other. We never fight, we're considerate of one another, but we barely talk unless it's about the kids."

"So, you maintain this charade for your children?"

"It's not entirely a charade. Our children are growing up in a warm home. At least it's warm for them."

"You've been celibate for twelve years? How?"

"It wasn't the first time for me. Before I entered the Academy, I considered the priesthood. To see if I could handle it, I practiced being celibate for six months. I couldn't hack it, but I was only seventeen. It was easier as an adult, like you just turn off a switch inside yourself. Except now that it's back on, I can't extinguish it."

Clementine slung a long leg over his thigh and pressed her belly into the bulge that suddenly announced itself in the "on" position. "Nor do I want you to extinguish it," she teased. "But you must know that I have not been celibate for the last decade. And why should I have been? You were not available, and," she gently touched his face, "you are still not available, legally."

"I'm not pretending to be rational. Of course you were dating. You're a beautiful, accomplished single woman, why wouldn't you have boatloads of suitors?"

"I don't recall having boatloads, Robert."

"Well, I've seen some of your boyfriends over the years. I know I had no right to be, but I was insanely jealous of every one. Especially that tall redhead—your classmate from West Point, the one from New York City?"

"Carl?"

"Yes, Carl. I saw him pick you up from headquarters one afternoon, after work. He put his arm around you, you kissed him, and the two of you headed out for the night, smiling and laughing. I wanted to run after you, slap him with a glove, and challenge him to a duel. Right there on Main Street!"

Clementine burst out laughing. Robert had to laugh too, realizing he sounded like a caricature of a hot-blooded Cuban.

"Robert, you must have noticed that I never married any of those guys I dated—even Carl, who asked repeatedly. Actually, I think you should be grateful that I've had some experience with men and love and sex. I was looking for a soulmate, but my soulmate was right there in front of my eyes every day. And he was my commander to boot—my boss!"

"Not anymore. You are no longer in my chain of command."

"Does that mean that I can give you a direct order, then? I think it's one we'll both enjoy."

***

Bliss Metro's bomb squad arrived with lights and sirens, which drew an audience despite the hour—a reporter with a video camera from Bliss's NBC affiliate, a couple of homeless men, and a working girl who was having a terrible night in the rain. Rolly explained, firmly, that even though the TV reporter's press pass permitted him to cross police lines, he was not ducking under this particular yellow tape until the IED was safely defused. All watched from a distance as a secondhand robot recently purchased with a Homeland Security grant labored for an hour before the booby-trapped ankle monitor blew up with a flash.

"Great," said Rolly, his ears ringing. "Now the supremacist bigot minus a face is short a leg."

"And his bracelet's in the river."

"So's the robot."

"Who gets to tell the mayor the bomb squad has to buy a new one?" asked Duvall. "Senior officer at the crime scene, Chief?"

Rolly Winters gazed upon the body with fresh interest: secondhand or not, the robot had been first-class and the officer operating it had learned his trade in Baghdad; so the bomb maker was no amateur.

"The PD tattoo says the bigot was a convict. Maybe CODIS has him."

The FBI's Combined DNA Index System kept local, state, and national databases. When it came to DNA, the Supreme Court had ruled mostly in law enforcement's favor on Fourth Amendment search and seizure issues. If the sample that Bliss Metro's Hate Crimes Unit uploaded got a hit, the city lawyers could get started on nailing a name. It should not take long. Not with everyone intensely curious about who fitted a white supremacist with an exploding ankle monitor.

***

When the Weatherman checked his map screen for his bitch's monitor for the tenth time that night, his body went rigid and his breath came short. The pulsing red GPS dot had disappeared. He hit "Search" and scanned back for its last appearance. It had stopped pulsing twelve minutes earlier, while still in Bliss, Arkansas. The Weatherman stared at the record of what no longer existed. The thing with bitches was they were usually kept in line by the threat of violence. But looking back, he wondered if this one had just hung out with him by choice. Seemed to. Funny thing was, after he gave him the time off, the Weatherman had missed him.

But no good deed goes unpunished. How did the bitch thank him for the time off? Blew himself up. Which put the Weatherman in scalding hot water. He had to find out what happened, and if it threatened the Shot Caller. But the answer wasn't something he could find in the data. Media reports wouldn't have deep truth. He needed people on the ground to tell him what had happened. But he was too isolated down here. He had no one on the ground. Only himself, underground. Trapped and helpless, he did the bravest thing he had ever done in his life, keyed his telephone with a trembling finger, and left a message that said, "Shot Caller, I am really, really sorry, but there is a problem that might cause you a problem."

***

False dawn was seeping through the window. Clementine Price checked the clock on the nightstand. Just past 4 a.m.

"Robert, was it really love at first sight for you when we met? I mean, you were only three weeks into your new post, besieged by reporters, contractors, duck hunters, and God Almighty General Penn himself. Did you really see me that way on such a crazy day?"

"It wasn't that crazy a day until you walked in."

Clementine kissed him on the forehead and started to slip out of the berth. "I better get back to my own bed before General Penn bugles 'Reveille.'"

Robert sat up and pulled her back. He held her face in his hands and looked directly into her eyes. "Clementine, if we continue to see each other—and I intend to if you'll have me—we are risking our careers if we get caught."

"I know that, Robert."

"And as a woman, the ax would fall harder on you than me. You'd be painted as a scheming Jezebel. I'd get a rap on the knuckles publicly, and a private slap on the back telling me how lucky I was to get such a fine piece of ass."

"I know that too."

"And one more thing, just so we are crystal clear and there are no delusions between us. You know that I am extremely ambitious, but my ambition is to rise up the ranks. Period. At some point I'll accumulate enough stars to retire at the top of the heap. But your ambition is to rise up the ranks as a means to an end. Your ambition is to change the Corps' mission. To change how we treat the river, like you told me your first day as my adjutant. You are rising up the ranks with a greater purpose than I am. You must think very clearly about what is most valuable to you, and how much you are willing to risk by being lovers."

"I understand the risk."

"Think on it. Think on it hard."

"I think you are worth it."

He held her close for a long moment. "Then good night, my darling Clementine. Thank you for the happiest night of my life."

"I've always dreamed of you saying that to me, 'my darling Clementine.' When I was a kid, they teased me about my name—in that song Clementine is a clumsy oaf with big feet. But when you say it, I feel beautiful."

"I adore you."

Robert had already disembarked by the time Clementine left The Boat for New Orleans's Lakefront Airport, where Snoopy was parked.

Just as she was completing her preflight, an attendant came running out on the apron and handed her a manila envelope.

"An officer left this for you, ma'am. Asked to be sure I give it to you personally."

Clementine thanked him and settled into the cockpit. She turned over the envelope, and recognized Robert's handwriting.

Inside was a fifty-count card of bobby pins—blonde and written on the back of the card in his elegant cursive:

For next time, my darling Clementine.

"So I wait for you like a lonely house
until you will see me again and live in me.
'Til then my windows ache."
—Pablo Neruda

14

The Coach

Day 32
Saturday

"Chief Owen, it's Reverend Flowers. I hope I'm not interrupting anything."

"Just catching up with paperwork, Reverend. What can I do for you?"

"On Saturday afternoon? I'd say the taxpayers get their policing dollars-worth out of you, Chief." Flowers had checked before he telephoned. Mrs. Owen was visiting their grandchildren in Memphis, which meant that Chief Billy Bob was sneaking an unmarked police car into the back parking lot of the Motel 6. Flowers already had photos of a recent tryst on his laptop, which established the girl's youth and skin shade in case the chief ever became a problem. His potbelly, thick jowls, and please-me sneer embodied the nightmare of a crooked cracker cop. But for now, Billy Bob Owen was an upstanding member of the Hilltop Fellowship.

"So what can I do for you, Reverend?"

"You sound rushed," said Flowers. "I won't take much of your time. I was just wondering if you can satisfy some personal curiosity—without violating police protocol, of course. I saw on the news about that fellow they pulled out of the river. He wouldn't be one of our parishioners, would he?"

"Doubt it, Reverend."

"Well between you, me, and the lamp post, I'm aware of at least one husband who's not been home in a few nights. What happened? Shotguns? Explosions?"

"Pretty complicated, is all I can say. But seeing as how he probably met his demise in the River View project, I'd feel safe in guessing he's not one of Hilltop's."

"Was he a resident of River View Houses?"

"I'm more inclined to conclude he was calling on an acquaintance."

Nathan Flowers said, "Now, Chief, we both know it's been a long while since I was, shall we say, 'street smart,' so I'm a little confused by your meaning. Are you suggesting the victim was visiting a girlfriend or paying for service at a brothel?"

The chief laughed. "Bless your soul, Reverend Flowers, let's say not all the dark-skinned ladies *sell* their favors in River View. Most just give them away."

"Are you saying the woman shot him?"

"My best guess is that her boyfriend shot him."

"Did you catch him?"

"Not yet. We don't have his name, at this time. But it was clearly a boyfriend thing. Keep in mind, your average River View male tends to shoot first and plan ahead later. Meantime, Reverend, as much as I'm enjoying our conversation, I gotta get back to work."

"Thank you for putting my mind at ease, Chief. I will see you in church tomorrow morning."

"Amen to that, Reverend."

Flowers hung up and stared inquiringly at Billy Bob's photograph. The chief had offered not a word about the explosion. Were the cops working that angle? Had to be. It was too strange not to. Billy Bob had made it clear that he couldn't care less, but some sharper cop on the homicide squad would get onto it, or at least try. Flowers figured that in theory, at least, time was on his side. Homicide's first job would be solving the murder, not an explosion on a dead body. But he had to get to the bottom of this to make sure it didn't sneak up behind him at the worst possible moment.

***

Clementine Price left her raincoat and boots to dry in her foyer, where all-weather vinyl mats protected the vintage parquet. Although she rented her sixteenth-floor apartment in the historic Number 10 Main Street building in downtown Memphis, she treated it as her own property. Just a five-minute walk from district headquarters, it offered 180-degree views of her Mississippi River to the west and a fitness center, which she'd reluctantly embraced as an alternative to a daily five-mile run in pouring rain. Not lost on anyone was its altitude. As Libby pointed out when she first saw it, "Girl, you got yourself the highest ground in town."

She had furnished it with antiques inherited from Aunt Martha—including a massive mahogany dining table with extra leaves and chairs to seat twelve guests, and place settings of gold-rimmed Haviland china and monogrammed Della Robbia silver, which Clementine used every Thanksgiving, Christmas, and Easter for the "orphans" dinners she hosted for friends and soldier colleagues who otherwise had no place to go. Her elegant home was a surprise to those who expected hard-driving Major Price to live in an efficiency apartment with a hotplate and an air mattress.

It was a surprise to her as well, after a childhood of often-drenched decor broken up for kindling, then living out of a deployment bag her first ten years in the army, to discover that she actually enjoyed beautiful surroundings. Her living room was unabashedly opulent: she'd sewn silk shantung drapes to frame her views of the river and re-upholstered Aunt Martha's Edwardian parlor suite with extravagant swaths of damask and brocade.

Framed in white oak and hung gallery-style from the picture molding along the high ceilings were fifteen full-scale reproductions of the phantasmagoric *Ancient Courses: Mississippi River Meander Belt.* She had discovered the maps her first year at West Point, and they had blown her mind. In a 1944 Army Corps study titled *Geological Investigation of the Alluvial Valley of the Lower Mississippi River*, the young geologist Harold Fisk had illustrated the shape-shifting flow of the river by drawing swirls and curlicues in vibrant shades of red, yellow, blue, and green that represented the Mississippi's changing course in the eighteenth, nineteenth, and twentieth centuries. To her scientist's eye, what looked like an LSD trip was a gobsmacking visualization of just how uncontainably far and wide the river had traveled those three centuries, restlessly carving new paths for itself and spreading floodplains and bayous in its wake. The framed set had been a housewarming gift from Steve Stevenson, and she never tired of studying them.

The guest bedroom, which doubled as her office and sewing room, had an entire wall arrayed top to bottom with thirty-five historic photographs of Tomato, a gift from Robert for her thirty-fifth birthday. Most of the rare images had been new to her. They ranged from the town's heyday in the early 1900s when it boasted three stores, three churches, and a schoolhouse; through the Depression and the devastating flood of 1937 that prompted the town to relocate a mile and a half inland (she loved the picture of mules pulling the general store to its new destination on log rollers); up through 1968, when the last store, which had already been moved three times, disappeared into the Mississippi River. She suspected Robert had pulled strings with his contacts at the local newspapers and historical societies and had planned the gift years in advance.

She wondered if he had also planned last night years in advance. She had so often fantasized about going to bed with him but could never come up with a scenario that didn't result in a scandal with one or both of them resigning in disgrace. Was it possible now to be secret long-distance lovers?

She dropped her deployment bag on her bedroom floor and tried to picture the two of them in there, making love in the big Victorian four-poster. Five minutes from her office—his former office. In a doorman building. Bumping into colleagues on the street. Impossible. They'd have to conduct their affair far afield, where neither was known.

She checked the rain gauge outside her window—three more inches just since she'd gone to Bliss and New Orleans—and surveyed the river below as it surged ever higher against the natural bluff that protected downtown Memphis. She brewed coffee and read Robert's bobby pin card again—she'd already read it a dozen times this morning. She Googled Pablo Neruda, discovered the excerpt of the poem was in a collection called *100 Love Sonnets* and ordered the book. She sent her daily "good morning" texts to her mother, father, and Aunt Rhonda—later than usual today as she hadn't gotten back from New Orleans until noon—and set up her laptop for her weekly life-coaching session via Skype.

Before West Point, Clementine had never met anyone who went to a shrink—or at least admitted to it. But every ambitious officer had a personal life coach. Field Manual 6-22 (Leadership Development) left no doubt: "The gravity of the army mission and the dynamic nature of the world make continuous learning and self-development crucial to personal success and national security."

"Life coach" carried none of the stigma of "therapist." The sessions with her coach were driven entirely by goals she set for herself, not what a psychiatrist might identify as a neurosis. They went part and parcel with acquiring graduate degrees and certifications in new skills like Clementine's two master's (MS in environmental planning and MPA in public administration); her graduate certificate in sustainable agriculture; the Excellence in Competition points she was slowly earning toward the Distinguished Pistol Shot Badge; and her better-late-than-never ASEL (airplane single-engine land) certificate and Instrument Flight Rules rating for her private pilot license. If the exchanges with her coach occasionally lapsed from the professional to the personal, that was nobody's business. Even though the armed forces paid the officer's coach, every word between them was strictly confidential.

Five minutes before the session was scheduled to begin, she set the laptop on the marble library table next to the settee with the camera at eye level and typed in her Skype handle and password.

Her landline rang. "Unavailable" read the caller ID. Probably a robo-call, but on a hunch she picked up.

"My darling Clementine."

Her heart leapt. "Robert!"

"I'm calling you like a drug dealer! I paid cash for a 'burner' phone. Here, write down the number—but only call from your personal landline."

Clementine quickly typed it into her laptop and named the file Burner. "Robert, you have quite a knack for covert operations. Is there something in your past you haven't told me about?"

"Plenty, my darling, but no, I was never a spy. And actually, what we're doing really falls under the category of *clandestine* ops—secrecy as opposed to plausible deniability. Listen, I've got to go. I mailed you some travel brochures, so we can start planning our next rendezvous."

"Thank you for the bobby pins. And the poem. I've read it so many times I've memorized it. And I've just ordered the entire volume."

"Good. We can read them to each other. Until then, my darling:

'And one by one
the nights between our separated cities
are joined to the night that unites us.'

I adore you."

Clementine put down the phone and felt her heart. It was pounding again, literally. She closed her eyes and started to replay their night together, step by step.

"Clementine? Are you awake?"

Robert had said that last night, but this wasn't Robert's voice—this was her coach's voice! He was on-screen, trying to get her attention.

"Sorry, Tom. I just flew back from New Orleans and didn't get much sleep last night." All true, if incomplete. We'll see where the session goes, she thought, and started the stopwatch on her phone to count down forty-five minutes.

Tom O'Donnell coached from his home office in the Hay Adams neighborhood of Washington, DC, where he lived with his husband who he never talked about, but Clementine had wormed out of him that his name was Patrick and he was a musician.

"No problem, Clementine. I won't ask about the weather because I just checked it for Memphis. Anything you'd like to celebrate this week?"

She reran in her mind the meetings in Arkansas, Robert's dirigible ride over the New Orleans District, General Penn's orders to save the Port of South Louisiana at all costs, and her ecstatic night with Robert.

"I think I am doing a better job of controlling my time," she began. "That idea we came up with to send a 'good morning' text every day to Momma, Daddy, and Aunt Rhonda has really cut down on the number of frantic phone calls I get—at the worst possible time—asking me to solve a nonexistent problem for them. It's ironic that the one relative I wish I had *more* contact with has disappeared."

"And which relative is that?" Tom asked, with practiced neutrality.

"My Uncle Chance. I've told you I was closer to him than to my own father, but Chance has completely separated himself from our entire family since the flood. In any case, I would like to celebrate being in more control of my private schedule, especially since the public one seems to be growing fast."

"How so?"

"I'm learning that an 'acting commander' has to make herself twice as visible to be effective."

"How long will you be 'acting'?"

"I serve purely at the pleasure of General Penn. I could be out on my ear tomorrow. Or temporary until retirement. At least until the selection board chooses the next permanent commander."

"Does that bother you?"

"Honestly? Yes. . . . But I don't have a right to be bothered. District commanding officer is almost always a full colonel. And I am way too young to be a full colonel. On the other hand, I know the Memphis District better than anyone, and I know what it needs. Robert was a brilliant CO. I learned so much from him."

"Robert being Colonel Garcia?"

"Yes. Of course."

"Any other reasons to be bothered?"

His question stopped her cold for a moment. She took a breath. "I'm afraid of letting Libby down."

"Letting Libby down how?"

She told him half the truth. "I have to help her rally the public behind a worst-case evacuation plan—in case Bliss is flooded." No way was she going to tell Tom, or anyone outside the division, Penn's plan for protecting the Port of South Louisiana.

"Do you have a plan to help rally the public?"

"I'm going directly to the people. Starting tomorrow, actually—visiting churches and speaking to their congregations."

"Are you comfortable doing that?"

"Oh, gosh, yes. Churches down here are very welcoming. Though, I must admit . . ."

Tom waited. He wasn't about to prompt her, she knew.

"I have to admit that I am not looking forward to . . . one of them—dreading, actually."

Tom waited.

Clementine said, "Hilltop. The megachurch I might have mentioned. . . . The church where our farm was. Where my Uncle Chance works now."

"I gather you've gone there rarely."

"Never."

"Not even in the course of your work?"

"No. When the church applied for permits to build, Colonel Garcia ordered me to recuse myself. The Corps has such power we have to be scrupulous about even a hint of self-interest or prejudice. Colonel Garcia and his then-deputy commander managed all the Hilltop applications. When I advanced to deputy, he made me manager of other projects, like the Birds Point fuse levee. It might sound like an abundance of caution, but actually, I think Robert—Colonel Garcia—shielded me from having to watch the church make our ground disappear."

"What's it's like to look down when you fly over in your airplane?"

"I've never flown over it."

"But you've told me you fly up and down the river often."

"When I get to Hilltop, I sort of hang a left—loop west around it, like . . . make a detour." She looked at the stopwatch. The time had flown. Now suddenly it seemed to have stopped dead.

Tom waited.

Clementine stared at the stopwatch. The seconds crept. Two minutes to go.

"By the way," she said.

"Yes."

"Robert?"

"Colonel Garcia?"

"We finally got together. In bed. After all these years. He admitted he was in love with me. And I admitted I was in love with him. It was—he was—everything I'd dreamed of."

"If we were friends over coffee, I would say, 'Congratulations.' However, as your coach, I have to ask about fraternization."

"Army Regulation 600-20 prohibits relationships that degrade unit morale due to a perception of impartiality or favoritism. But he's no longer my CO. Adultery is another problem. Technically, we could be prosecuted for violating the Uniform Code of Military Justice. Hopefully, no one would make a big deal of it if we're discreet."

"You mean if you don't get caught. What if you were?"

"We'd probably get off with letters of reprimand. But letters of reprimand can wreck your career. I understand I am taking a big risk."

"What's next?" Tom asked.

"I have no idea. Like most colonel's wives, his has sacrificed any career she might have had to follow Robert wherever he's assigned. And she's a great mother to their children. All four of them. Including a little girl who looks up to me. Candace. She wants to be a pilot."

"Are you close with his wife?"

"No."

The Skype connection was sharp enough to show Tom's eyebrow rise skeptically. He said, "I asked because you and Robert served together ten years. You were his deputy for three."

"I guess I didn't want to be close to her. I doubt she'd give him a divorce and to be honest, I can't imagine he would ask for one. At least not before the children are grown. And that's a long way off." She paused. "It's like I borrowed him."

"Do you think that's a wise way to view what happened?"

"It would be. If I didn't want to borrow him again."

15

Salt of the Earth

Day 33
Sunday

Early Sunday morning, the five-deck towboat *Delta Lady* sat rock-steady in the middle of the river, taking fuel from Bliss Marine. Her engines thundered, holding the fleet of barges she was pushing stationary against the current. A wholesale butcher's skiff bounced across the water with a delivery. Deckhands humped the fresh meat into the galley. The butcher went forward to the doghouse—a rigging locker and workshop on the weather deck.

Joey, *Delta Lady's* chief mate, was waiting for him. He was a short, powerful man with some yellow teeth, a shaved head, and a blue tattoo on his ham hock arm that read, "White Pride World Wide." At his feet was a ninety-six-gallon, heavy-duty trash can liner. It looked full. Its mouth was loosely tied.

"His name is Richie. He shotgunned the Weatherman's bitch."

"For sure?"

"I'm sure. But the Shot Caller wants to confirm it." He handed the skiff driver a garage door opener. "He's gagged with a whiffle ball so he don't suffocate. Gives you any trouble, here you go."

"What's this?"

"Zapper. I put shock cuffs on his arms and legs."

"They work?"

Joey touched the opener's switch. The trash bag twisted as if the plastic were alive. An explosive breath whistled through the whiffle-ball gag, which muffled Richie's scream.

"Cool."

"Don't overdo it. Give him a heart attack and Shot Caller will put the bracelets on *you*."

***

Clementine Price parked her Jeep in front of Libby's Old District Victorian at 7:30 Sunday morning and texted "I'm here." Libby was doing her the kindness of accompanying her to not one but two church services, and the second visit was to Hilltop Fellowship. She needed her old friend at her side for that.

Libby hoisted herself into the passenger seat, ducking her head like a perp in a squad car to protect the church hat straining the seams of her red raincoat's enormous hood.

"Have I seen that one before?" Clementine asked.

"Probably," Libby replied, checking her makeup in the visor mirror. "I never wear a new hat when it's raining."

Libby was a connoisseur of church hats, and Rolly had built her a facsimile millinery store—complete with plastic model heads—in one of their home's many bedrooms so she could properly store and inventory them, with a spreadsheet of which hat she'd worn to which church and when. Even in Afghanistan, Clementine would get a picture every week of Libby's Sunday morning headgear along with the title of the sermon that had been preached. Her all-time favorite was about Lot's wife: "She Was Exalted. She Halted. She Was Salted."

"New Salvation Baptist Church is in the old Goldsmiths department store, right?"

"Which became a Barnes & Noble when all the department stores went out of business and then Barnes & Noble closed it. Reverend Eddie Parker has tripled his congregation since then, which is why they now have the extra early morning service, and they just broke through to the next boarded-up section to get more space. Even though they don't pay taxes I'd rather have a busy church than abandoned buildings any day. Rolly and I actually considered joining New Salvation. But that would paint a big target on my back—can you imagine, the *mayor* has abandoned the church of her *childhood*! Who does she think she is?— So it's simpler just to stick to our old AME and go visiting in my official capacity. Which is also a fine way to find out what folks are thinking and worrying about."

"I know. I visited every church, mosque, and synagogue in Memphis at least once in *my* official capacity as Robert's deputy commander." Clementine turned into the pot-holed parking lot, which was already half full.

"Where do you rate Reverend Parker on your Sanctified Spectrum?" Clementine asked. ("One" being White-Bread-Presbyterian and "ten" being Holy-Roller-Speaking-in-Tongues.)

"Six, maybe seven, depending on his audience. He knows how to play the room. So how was New Orleans? And Robert?"

Clementine snapped open her golf umbrella and pulled Libby under it. Even in high heels and an enormous hat, she only came up to Clementine's earlobe. "I'll tell you about it after church."

They picked their way through the puddles toward the lighted church sign and message board that read:

WELCOME TO BLISS NEW SALVATION BAPTIST CHURCH
TODAY'S SERMON
DOES GOD HAVE A PLAN B FOR US?

The entryway had boot trays and benches for changing into church shoes. Clementine got a closer look at Libby's *chapeau*. Bright fuchsia silk, trimmed with iridescent aquamarine and emerald peacock feathers, it was shaped like a man's bowler on steroids. Libby always calibrated her wardrobe to stand out, but not outshine the most lavishly dressed women in the room; so, Clementine figured, this was a church where the ladies really put on the dog. She was glad she'd chosen to wear her dress uniform skirt and heels instead of trousers, and all the chest candy she'd earned.

"Come meet Reverend Eddie." Libby steered Clementine into the sanctuary where church mothers were distributing bulletins, paper fans on wooden sticks, and envelopes for the offering. Fluorescent tubes buzzed overhead. The walls were covered with fake wood rec-room paneling, and the pews were varying shades of varnished wood—hand-me-downs scavenged from other churches. Ushers and deacons wearing well-pressed dark suits with identical red ties and gold cross lapel pins were placing buckets under rain drips.

Church nurses dressed in white—Libby's mother was still a church nurse at the First AME and proudly wore her real RN hat—prepared their supplies of aspirin, Kleenex, smelling salts, and Dixie cups of water covered with paper napkins. The organist removing the cover from the Hammond B3 was one of the area's top jazz players, Clementine knew, looking a little worse for wear, as if he'd come straight from a Saturday night gig that actually paid money to play early this morning for the Glory of God.

The large floral display on the altar had to be a gift from Steve Stevenson, who paid Bliss's top florist to provide arrangements for any church in town as long as they were made with native plants. Since nothing had bloomed yet this soggy spring, it was artfully composed of last fall's cotton bolls, dried stalks of golden milo, bittersweet vines, and firethorn berries.

Reverend Eddie Parker, resplendent in a black robe accented with crimson, was up front helping a teenager—his son Morris, it turned out—hook up a sound system and speakers that looked far more powerful than necessary for the room. Clementine braced her ears for a high-decibel experience. In the choir loft, the electric guitar and electric bass player were warming up, the drummer was testing his traps and bass drum, and another teenage boy was positioning additional speakers on the side of the choir area.

Libby noticed her staring at the stack of speakers and whispered, "Reverend Eddie's a whooper, but he doesn't bust your eardrums. Something special must be going on today."

Like an actor hearing his entrance cue, Reverend Eddie strode over and flashed a blinding smile. Clementine was reminded of the sermon title Libby had sent on the power of the tongue: "The Little Red Devil Behind the Pearly White Gates."

"Mayor Winters, it's a blessing to see you! And is this Major Price, who we've heard so much about?" He gripped Clementine's hand in a sandwich between both of his powerful, soft hands. "I hope you'll both say a few words to our congregation this morning—Look! Here comes another lady to bless us with a few words. The outreach minister of Hilltop—and her fine-looking youngsters. Good morning, Mrs. Flowers."

"Good morning, Reverend Parker. Good morning, Libby! Gabe and Cora, can you say hello to Reverend Parker and Mayor Winters?"

Little Gabe, dressed in a plaid jacket and a yellow bow tie, dutifully stepped forward and held out a tiny hand, then ran to Libby and tugged on the fringe of her shimmering peacock-patterned scarf. "You're the mayor," he said, face upturned in wonder. "I see you on TV!"

Libby crouched down, beaming, to shake his hand. Cora rushed forward to hug her. "I'm Cora. Can I touch your hat?"

Clementine watched Libby melt. As much as she loved her rambunctious boys, she had longed for a daughter. May Kay corralled her starstruck children and the two women hugged warmly.

"Mary Kay," said Libby, adjusting her now lopsided chapeau, "Meet my friend Major Clementine Price."

Mary Kay Flowers took Clementine's hand and raised her gaze to look the tall army officer in her eye. "I'm so glad you'll be visiting Hilltop today. I imagine it might hurt to return to your old home place. Is there is anything I can do to make it easier?"

"You just did," said Clementine, deeply touched. "Thank you for thinking of me."

Mary Kay gave her hand another squeeze and said to Reverend Eddie, "Forgive me, Reverend, I over-scheduled this morning. Could I ask you to deliver Hilltop's message for me?"

"Mrs. Flowers's 'outreach,'" Reverend Eddie said to Libby and Clementine, "is longer than Sonny Liston's. What shall I say, Mrs. Flowers?"

"If there is a flood, Hilltop will coordinate our buses with the Bliss city buses. But in case there aren't enough buses, or the roads aren't passable, Reverend Flowers has chartered a riverboat, which is standing by to carry thousands to Hilltop."

Clementine Price made an instant decision not to object that the Coast Guard would probably shut the river to navigation, or that boarding thousands of people in flood conditions would be a nightmare. Better to let the "ark" idea encourage them to evacuate. And, indeed, Reverend Eddie said, "I'll read from Genesis. 'The Lord said unto Noah, Come thou and all thy house into the ark."

"Hilltop's ark for Bliss," said Mary Kay, and swept away with warm smiles for all.

Libby said, "Reverend, you just heard we have another congregation to visit this morning, so if you could introduce us *before* your sermon . . ."

Reverend Parker let out a raucous laugh. "Yes, I know my reputation for long services. I just can't stop preaching when the preaching come. I've got to run, 'til God says well done. Don't worry, Sister Winters, I'll introduce you right after the offering."

He escorted them to a middle row near the side aisle where they could quietly slip out and bustled off. Libby and Clementine remained standing as a spontaneous receiving line formed, led by Reverend Parker's wife Anita, principal of the Southside Elementary School and the church's choir director. Libby gave every one of them a hug and then introduced them to "Major Price, head of the Memphis District Army Corps of Engineers and my best friend since first grade."

By the time the service began, Clementine had committed to speaking at a Vacation Bible Camp, interviewing an applicant to ASU Mid-South's Department of Military Science program, and hosting field trips to Corps construction sites for the science and technology magnet school and for Bliss's Never-Too-Late "tough-love" boys summer camp.

At last, Reverend Eddie bounded to the pulpit.

"Come on, come on," he sang. "Don't you want to go?"

The congregation sang back, "Yes, I want to go." The guitar, bass, drums, and the Hammond B3 joined in, exactly on key, and the service flowed seamlessly from song to song—no hymnals—to prayers led by deacons, church mothers, and ordinary members of the congregation. Some knelt on the floor, facing the pew, their hands tightly folded in prayer; others moaned, wept, shouted with joy, waved praise hands, shook tambourines, clapped, stood up and stomped and twirled. A tall lady in a leopard-print dress near Clementine spun so fast her glasses flew. Before Clementine could reach into the aisle, a church nurse appeared to rescue them and gently steered the whirling dervish to safety.

The action was punctuated with cries of "Thank you, Jesus," "Have Mercy, Lord," "Hallelujah," "Yes, Lord Jesus." Little children rocked in the arms of mothers, fathers, grandmothers, and grandfathers. All were having private, direct contact with the Lord, Clementine thought, including Libby, who was singing softly, chanting, and occasionally waving praise hands.

Clementine allowed herself to drift on the waves of sound. She was no stranger to black churches. But for some reason that she didn't understand at first, she felt compelled to imprint each face on her memory: three sisters in pink with fountains of braids and pink butterfly barrettes spouting from their heads; a white haired couple, stooped and immaculately dressed, fanning themselves, lips moving silently; a young man cradling a baby who wouldn't stop crying; a round young woman with sparkly makeup, a grill, a cross tattoo on both her bare arms, and a spangled top hat; an emaciated old lady in black, hugging her dog-eared Bible; a teenager with cerebral palsy in a wheelchair, tended by a kind-faced woman Clementine recognized from high school, looking gray and worn. These were working folks—especially at the early Sunday service, many probably had afternoon shifts or second jobs to get to today. Others likely had family members to look after.

Suddenly she knew with cold certainty that they were the innocents in the line of General Penn's fire. She envisioned water smashing through the ceiling, drowning the congregation in a tsunami of mud. Then dead silence. She began to weep. Libby wrapped her arm around Clementine's shoulder and hugged her tightly. She thinks I'm feeling the spirit, Clementine thought. I can't tell her the truth. I can't save them.

"Before we offer up our financial gifts to the Lord," announced Reverend Eddie from the pulpit, "and introduce our guests, I'd like us to turn our attention to a group of young members who have prepared a special presentation for us. Now, I saw some of you giving the hairy eyeball to this fancy sound system we've installed today, and don't worry, we're not fixing to be one of those jack-hammer churches where you have to wear ear plugs or go deaf. But these young folks have put together a Bible story in the language of their generation—and yes, I'm talking about rap—and before you get all high and mighty, just think how your folks or grand-folks thought about James Brown, or BB King, or Chuck Berry, or even Miss Aretha Franklin—the daughter of a minister—doing R & B, the so-called devil's music. Every generation has its own way of expressing itself, and if we want these young folks, especially our young men, to stay in our church and in the path of righteousness, we got to understand their language. So please put your hands together and welcome the Saline Solution—also known as the salt of the earth."

The plump girl with the spangled top hat and grill and the teenage boys who'd helped set up the sound system stepped up, giggling. Reverend Eddie's son Morris passed them handheld mics and two more spangled hats and fired up the background track, and Saline Solution started their moves.

He was from the city but his story wasn't pretty,
His stink would fill your nose, didn't wear no clothes,
Didn't have a room, he was livin' in the tombs.
The man was full of demons, and day and night was screamin'
Shouting curses, the man he needed nurses,
The rude, crude, dude in the nude.

Jesus came to visit and he said, My Man, what is it?
Demons, leave him be, get you gone is my demand.
Those demons went a running, but demons they be cunning

They be sitting there and waiting for more trouble to be making
Another soul to torture, another poor unfortunate
Rude, crude, dude in the nude.

But Jesus thinking big, he looks out and sees some pigs
Chomping on the hillside, and sends those demons for a ride
Into that herd of porkers, upon the Savior's orders
They go running round and down to the lake and drown,
Forever cleaning demons outta that
Rude, crude, dude in the nude.

The congregation roared its approval. Libby turned a wicked smile on Clementine. "Are we up to following that act, Sister Price?"

Libby and Clementine made their way to the altar as the Saline Solution reluctantly returned to their pews. Clementine saluted each one smartly while Libby offered fist bumps to the two boys and a warm hug to the girl with the grill—Daneesha, Libby told her later, a city hall summer intern. Libby stepped up to the pulpit to speak first. Before she finished the boilerplate flood evacuation summary, Clementine leaned in and interrupted.

"All we are asking is please be ready just in case the worst happens. Be ready to heed the call of your mayor, if the alarm sounds. Just like Lot and his family heeded the call of the angels to flee Sodom and Gomorrah before it was destroyed by a mighty hail of fire and brimstone." She glanced at Libby with a wink only her friend could see and embraced the pulpit, wrapping both arms around it as Reverend Eddie had.

"Be ready! Be ready to leave, and don't look back until you're safe. Remember what happened to Lot's wife when she looked back. . . . She was exalted. She halted. And she was salted!"

"*Amen, Sister!*"

16

The Dungeon

Day 33
Sunday

Nathan Flowers had seen enough prisons to understand that total hopelessness was the worst punishment. He made the dungeon under the Hilltop sanctuary look as escape-proof as the ADX—the "supermax" penitentiary in the Rocky Mountains. No one was getting out of this cell. Ever.

Only Pure Dominion's inner circle ever saw it: Flowers's trusted Alluvia disciples, like Robby Bracken, his shaved-skull, red-bearded behemoth of a security chief; Joey, whom he'd put in charge of *Delta Lady;* and Sammy Burke, the warped Chicago business genius who organized his shell companies. Mere "founders" like Cedric Colson had never seen the dungeon, neither had the Weatherman, nor Flowers's inside men who thought they were boss because they ruled the prisons. The exceptions were kidnapped enemies and dangerous fools like jail-brains Richie, who both Joey and Robby Bracken suspected had shotgunned the Weatherman's bitch.

First, Bracken gave Richie a long look around. Lacking even the four-inch slit window of a supermax unit, it was designed to get closer to Hell than a captive could imagine. When Richie's expression said he got it, the red-bearded giant spreadeagled him face up on the cot, wrist and ankle shock cuffs secured to the strap-down rings. Bracken pulled a sensory-deprivation-helmet over his head, covering his eyes and muffling his ears.

Richie heard nothing but his heart beating. He could feel his nose and mouth still exposed to the air. Suddenly, a voice spoke like it was inside his skull.

"Richie?"

Headphones, he realized. The ear mufflers were headphones.

"*Richie!*"

"Yeah?"

"Did you shotgun the bitch?"

"Damn straight."

Nathan Flowers shook his head. Never, ever underestimate the sheer stupidity of jail-brains, he reminded himself. Just when you think you've heard it all along comes a bigger fool. "Care to tell me why?" he asked.

"I heard what he done to that little boy."

Nathan said, "Fact is, that was a rumor that wasn't true. There was no little boy. He never hurt a little boy."

"That's what he said when I shot him."

"But you shot him anyway?"

"You know how in jail you replay and replay what's in your head? I couldn't get it out. It was torture, like when they tase your balls, except you can't pass out. It just kept replaying."

"So you truly believed the bitch was in jail because he had hurt a little boy?"

"Right. It wasn't my fault."

"So you went after him to avenge the little boy."

"Right. But I was misled."

Nathan Flowers asked the main question, the only one that mattered. "You didn't just bump into the bitch and blow him away?"

"No."

"Didn't just run into him by accident?"

"No, I heard he was coming to Bliss. I figured this was my chance."

"How did you hear?"

"A girl told me."

"What girl?"

"Girl in the projects."

"What were you doing with this girl?"

Richie smirked. "What do you think?"

Nathan Flowers raked his knuckles across Richie's face. Blood trickled from his nose. "Which projects? River View or South End?"

"River View."

"Where blacks live free."

"There's niggers in South End, too."

Nathan Flowers said, "Premeditated."

"What?"

"You thought about it ahead of time."

"Right."

"Premeditated murder."

"Premeditated murder? What are you, a fucking judge?" Jail-brains flinched a second after he said it. This time Nathan did not hit him, but said, quietly, "In other words, you had time to consider what your action would do to Alluvia."

"Yeah, but, like I told you, the little boy, I thought he—"

Flowers spoke now to the others who were watching, reminding them of the danger Richie had put them all in. Reminding them of the rule—the law—that decreed that Alluvia crew outside of prisons never did anything to draw the cops. And especially never fought among themselves. "You betrayed Alluvia. You betrayed your comrades in arms. You betrayed your race."

"Come on, man. I didn't rat anybody. I ain't saying I didn't screw up, but I didn't mean to."

Nathan Flowers had heard enough. Richie had confirmed the bad, bad feeling he had about the Weatherman and his bitch—a premonition that he would pay the price for their stupidity. He was enraged by his powerlessness, livid that he could not undo what the morons had done. But he got a hold of himself and spoke calmly in the language his followers wanted to hear. "Kill the nigger-loving son of a bitch."

"Fast or slow?" asked Robby Bracken.

Nathan Flowers looked at his watch. Christ! Almost ten. He had six thousand people waiting upstairs.

"Fast. You've got bell ringers in the tower, and I gotta preach."

Robby Bracken closed both hands around Richie's throat. He made him wait for it just long enough to realize what was coming, and then ruptured his carotid arteries.

17

Hilltop

Day 33
Sunday

"What happened in New Orleans?" Libby asked before Clementine had even turned the ignition key.

Grim stuff at General Penn's meeting I can't tell you about, Clementine thought. A least not yet. Aloud she said, "Seatbelt, please. We're running late." Libby strapped in with a sigh and Clementine peeled out of the parking lot, cutting off a slowpoke sedan she didn't want to get stuck behind.

Libby dug around in her purse for a pack of Kleenex, took off her shoes, and began methodically wiping the mud off her high heels. "I'm listening," she said, with the infinite patience of a mother of two boys.

"Well, after the meeting, Robert and I somehow found ourselves alone, and he told me he left the Memphis District because of me. Because he was in love with me . . . *is* in love with me."

"Honey, I've known that for years. And tell the truth— so have you."

"Part of me hoped it was true, but the other part was terrified—I mean, what could we do about it?"

"Did you figure that out in New Orleans?"

"Yes. And it was . . . it was everything I'd dreamed of. And more. The sex anyway. I don't think I ever really understood what you have with Rolly. Now I do. But . . ."

"But?"

"You know. He has four children. I can't imagine he would leave Rita, not while the kids are around."

On the interstate, Clementine bumped up her wipers and set about her lifelong mission of encouraging slow drivers to stay out of the passing lane.

Libby tightened her seatbelt. "How old is little Candace? Twelve?"

"Eleven."

"Oh, Lord. Well, lots of folks live double, even triple lives. My daddy had a whole second family across town in Hattiesburg, until Mama found out and packed me and everything in the house into the truck she'd just paid off and drove all night to her brother's house in Bliss. I was two and don't even remember my daddy, but obviously he had no problem with the arrangement."

Clementine flashed her high beams and downshifted to pass an RV wallowing in and out of its lane. "Robert is not a bigamist and he's not a womanizer."

"Chill, girl. All I'm saying is that we all compartmentalize—we put on a mask and play the role that's called for at the moment. Rolly uses the same hands to throw down a suspect that he uses to cuddle the boys and make love to me. Remember senior year English lit? Walt Whitman: 'Very well then, I contradict myself; I am large, I contain multitudes.'"

Libby pulled a Dryel pen from her bag and started rubbing at a grease stain on her raincoat. Clementine glanced at her with affection. "That purse of yours sure contains multitudes. What else is in there? A hair dryer? A Shop-Vac? My floor mats could use some attention."

Libby arched an eyebrow, fished out a lint roller and shook it threateningly. "I'm serious, Clementine. You and Robert found a way to . . . let's say, 'accommodate' the situation."

"What do you mean?"

"Have you ever seen an ambitious Army Corps of Engineers officer stay at one post for ten full years?"

"General Penn."

"General Penn is king of the Mississippi Valley. Why would he leave? You know what I'm saying. You two could never bear to part. You were in love—even though you didn't act on it. I'm sure Rita knew and just chose not to think about it. But now that the dam has burst, I am worried you're fixing to have your heart broken. Will you really be satisfied with a part-time man?"

Clementine slammed on the brakes as an instant traffic jam materialized at an exit ramp. "Where in blazes did this come from? It's like Friday afternoon rush hour."

"It's Sunday morning. Hilltop has 22,000 members, remember? This *is* rush hour in these parts." Libby had donned her reading glasses and was now sewing a loose button on her raincoat. "What's happening with your New York City real estate developer?"

"Carl? He's not 'my' developer."

"He's been courting you ever since West Point."

"Actually, I saw Carl just last month; he concocted some kind of business trip to Memphis and we spent a couple of days together—and nights, if you're wondering. Carl is a perfectly dear man; he's smart, he's decent, and he says he loves me. But I don't ache to touch him and smell him and hear his voice. Carl doesn't thrill me. Robert does. Just talking about him now . . . let me put it this way: if I were a guy, I'd have a hard-on."

Libby shrieked with laughter and Clementine cracked up with her. It felt better to laugh than cry. She exited the interstate onto the county road, into another traffic jam. Since Hilltop's founding, Route 118 had swollen into a four-lane divided highway lined with motels, strip malls, and fast food restaurants advertising "Sunday All Day Breakfast Special–15% off for Hilltop Members."

At just the point where the lighted dove on Hilltop's steeple pierced the fog and rain, the road soared on a causeway that traversed low ground and climbed toward the church. "See what I was talking about?" said Libby. "Even in a flood, our buses could drive to high ground."

"True. But they have to get out of Bliss first."

Clementine had been braced all morning to be rocked by memories of her home. But nothing she saw was familiar. She tried to orient herself by the bend of the river. She couldn't find the familiar sight lines or even the trace of a landmark. The natural bank had disappeared under a hulking new mainline levee. Inside the levee was a whole new manmade world—a lake and a mounded plateau that raised the church's campus forty feet above the water. The church itself rose from the far edge of the plateau, towering above the river like a spear driven into the bank.

They inched along the causeway and through the "pearly gates" (Libby's description of the elaborately filigreed, white-painted ironwork). The last time Clementine saw Tomato, it had been submerged under thirty feet of water. Now, it was erased.

A flashing overhead LED sign offered guidance for the faithful.

10 A.M. SERVICE: PARKING LOTS A C FULL
USE D–G, OVERSIZED VEHICLES USE LOT G ONLY
VALET PARKING AVAILABLE LOT E

"Is this a church or a theme park?" Clementine muttered, yanking the emergency brake while she shifted into first gear and danced on the clutch and gas pedal. "Mr. Cook called it a country club. But it's too crowded for that."

"These crowds tell me this church must be doing something right," said Libby. She pulled down the visor mirror and carefully removed her feather-trimmed hat. Beneath it, tightly pinned to her braided updo, was a modest green cloche.

Clementine did a double take. "My hat is large, it contains multitudes?"

"I like to think of it as 'millinery intelligence.'"

Libby raised her hand for a high-five. Clementine let go the gear shift to deliver it. They lurched upward a few more feet. The Jeep's interior was fogging up and Clementine cranked her window open, got a face full of rain, and looked down the hillside to see how far they'd progressed.

"Revetment!" she exclaimed. "What's that doing there?"

"Where?"

"They've laid articulated concrete revetment mats on the hillside."

"Well, why not? Hilltop's right next to the river, in a floodplain."

"The Corps *sinks* revetment to stabilize bends in the riverbank. *Underwater*. It's flexible, so it contours to the channel bottom like fish scales and still deflects the current. It protects the foundation of the levee, the submerged part, from fast-water scouring."

Libby leaned across her to see the linked slabs. "Like big chain mail."

"Exactly! Chain mail. But there's no danger of a flood at this elevation—no current scouring forty feet above the levee. That's what's strange. Flowers is a trained engineer. So he's either building for eternity, or he knows something I don't."

They finally reached the flat plateau. Crawling along behind one of the yellow Hilltop shuttle buses, Clementine wondered if she might run into Uncle Chance this morning. "Look at all this. Library, fitness center—with pool—preschool, day care, community kitchen, addiction treatment, urgent care, broadcast center. It's not a theme park, it's a self-sufficient nation-state! OK, I'll admit it's well-designed. And super green, with the solar tile roofs and vertical gardens. Looks like they have roof gardens too. Hydroponic farming?"

Libby nodded. Clementine parked the Jeep on a porous pavement lot tastefully screened by shade trees and continued to vent. "Look at the size of these trees! Do you know what it costs to buy and plant a mature tree? By the hundreds? I know they have some big donors, but come on, where do they get the *money* for all this?"

The two women shouldered through the crowds toward the main entrance, Clementine holding the golf umbrella as high as she could to avoid pedestrian casualties. Church bells pealed in a descending scale from the twelve-story bell tower.

"Sounds just like the Cadet Chapel carillon."

"Except at West Point," said Libby, "it's one guy on keyboard. Hilltop has human bell ringers, twelve of them, one on each bell." She tilted the umbrella to show Clementine the soaring tower with huge bronze bells rotating in graceful arcs on sturdy wooden axles. "It was one of Mary Kay's wild ideas that turned out, as usual, to be really smart."

Andrew Wells, the buzz-cutted Hilltop facilities manager who'd come to the Bliss emergency planning meeting, was waiting in the cavernous vestibule, where twelve double doors rimmed with metal detectors and "No Firearms" signs funneled the crowds into the sanctuary.

"Welcome Mayor Winters and Major Price. I hope you ladies don't mind speaking *after* Reverend Flowers's sermon; we think the congregation will be most receptive to your message after Reverend Flowers has opened their hearts a little wider."

The facilities manager smoothly cleared a path toward the least-congested doorway, leading the women past a massive carved marble wall listing the HILLTOP FOUNDING FATHERS & MOTHERS. Clementine recognized many of the names: Senator Garfield and all of the congressional representatives from northeastern Arkansas, southeastern Missouri, and southwestern Tennessee; three of the Delta's richest landowners; CEOs of Big Ag, railroad, and shipping companies; and some internationally known foundations.

"Should I walk you around the metal detector, Major?" asked Wells.

"I don't carry a weapon in dress uniform, Mr. Wells."

"Of course, Major."

The congregation was mostly white, but Clementine noticed more than a few black faces, and recognized a number of Hispanic workers from Steve Stevenson's farm, cotton gin, and sand and gravel quarry. She exchanged smiles with several and paused to shake hands with Hector Lopez—Steve's dairy herd manager—and Hector's daughter Paloma, a horticultural-science major at University of Missouri, who Steve was hoping would come back after graduation to work for him. She was pleasantly surprised to see diverse worshippers spread throughout, not sitting in segregated sections. Martin Luther King's famous observation that "the most segregated hour of Christian America is 11 o'clock on Sunday morning" remained true today in the vast majority of the churches she had visited, but not here. She remarked as such to Libby.

Libby said, "Mary Kay's vision. Celebrate in peace with all your neighbors."

Wells led them to their aisle seats—plush, individual, upholstered theater seats, not pews—where Libby deposited her handbag and headed back up the wide aisle to mingle with constituents. Clementine settled in with her program and scanned the growing multitude. She never made a public address without knowing who was in the room.

She estimated the six-thousand-seat auditorium—arena? she couldn't really call it a sanctuary—would be packed by the time the service started, with the adjacent overflow "chapel" filled with another two thousand watching on a Cineplex-size screen. Plus all the people watching live on Hilltop's cable TV channel or later on the church's YouTube channel. This was the largest audience she had ever addressed.

She tried to zero in on individual faces among the throng. People were casually dressed, very casually, as if going shopping at Walmart. Clementine could hear Aunt Martha: "Don't come as you *are*. Come as you *wish to be!*" Still, maybe this church was such an ordinary part of their daily lives they didn't bother to get dressed up. Or couldn't afford to. She scanned the upper tiers for displays of old or new wealth. She waved to contractors she recognized and several Corps engineers and their families. Comfortable, but certainly not rich. This was an Everyman's church. And there was General Penn's Margaret Standfast, sweet and round in her dress blues, giving her a shy little salute when their eyes met. Clementine tossed a friendly wave back at her, wondering how often she drove the four-and-a-half hours from Vicksburg to attend services. Probably had family in the area.

A bank of three screens dominated the second- and third-story space above the stage. (It was definitely a stage, not an altar.) The left screen displayed a vertical scroll of Hilltop's weekly schedule of activities and programs (shop class, computer coding, organic gardening, adult day care), and the center screen showed some kind of real-time, Facebook-style app called Help Your Neighbor Today. Clementine watched in amazement as multiple typed conversations occurred:

-DOWNSIZED FROM TRUCK DRIVING JOB. LICENSED, NO VIOLATIONS. CAN U HELP W/ PART-TIME WORK?

-WHERE LOCATED?

-MO BOOTHEEL.

-MOM W/ ALZHEIMERS, I AM ONLY CAREGIVER, NEED PLUMBER, CARPENTER, ELECTRICIAN

-CALL HILLTOP'S VOLUNTEER BANK, WE CAN SET YOU UP.

-BUSCAN ROPA USADA DE LOS NIÑOS. TAMAÑO 6-8. TAMBIÉN ZAPATOS, TAMAÑO 10-12. DONACIONES POR FAVOR.

-TENGO, ADEMÁS DE ABRIGOS DE INVIERNO Y BOTAS. LOS TRAERÉ A HILLTOP DAY CARE CENTER.

-GRACIAS. DEJA A LA FAMILIA LÓPEZ, POR FAVOR.

On the right screen, she could watch the bell ringers in action, facing each other in a circle. They encompassed such a range of ages and types that they would probably have never encountered one another in daily life; yet here they were, looking into one another's faces as each serenely but energetically grasped a two-foot-long fuzzy striped section of rope with both hands, tugged it toward the floor, let go completely, then swiftly caught and pulled the rope's tail end that was looped like a hangman's noose, let it go, and then grasped and pulled the fuzzy part again.

The screen image was split horizontally, displaying the ringers on the bottom half and the belfry itself on the top, so the audience could see each bell swinging in direct response to a ringer's pull, as the ropes wound and unwound around the rim of the big wooden wheels. Seeing the process made the bells seem even louder, the vibrations palpable. Clementine was reminded of the hypnotic, rhythmic strokes she learned rowing on West

Point's crew team, before she concluded that the Hudson River was too tame for her. In her program were listed the names of each member of Hilltop's "Change Ringers," and "Tower Captains," alongside an invitation to join in: "Change Ringing is a team sport, a musical performance, an ancient art form, and invigorating exercise for all ages. 'Let the Bells of Praise Ring Loud!'" A special guest helper was listed for each of the day's five services.

Below the screens, in the choir loft, Clementine counted sixty-two choristers in emerald-green robes listening intently to a willowy African American man in a state of high animation drilling harmonies and chord changes on a nine-foot concert grand piano. Identified in the program as Reverend Burton Furman, Minister of Music, he also had at his command an orchestra of percussion, brass, woodwind, and string players warming up. Every single name was listed in the program, which noted that all were students or graduates of Hilltop's music academy: "Founded to counteract the decline of music and arts education in our schools, Hilltop Conservatory welcomes all ages and abilities, tuition-free. Now enrolling for summer session. More information at hilltop.org."

Overhead floated a matrix of lighting instruments and speakers, and Clementine counted seven discreetly placed television cameras. Like most non-denominational churches Clementine had visited, ecclesiastical imagery was minimal. The stained-glass windows on the side walls depicted only scenes from nature, no religious figures or symbols, no crosses anywhere. A Jeep-sized golden dove in flight was suspended directly over the pulpit.

The descending bell pattern blossomed into a melody, and all three screens switched over to the ringing room. Clementine noticed that the shortest ringers were standing on apple boxes. The Tower Captain—a smiling giant with a shaved head and a bushy red beard—signaled for silence.

Mary Kay Flowers walked into the frame, dressed in a sky-blue sleeveless sheath and Kelly-green pumps. She was holding the hand of a small dark-haired girl in clean pressed denim overalls. With a smile for the camera, she addressed the congregation.

"Good morning! This is Sally Sanchez, our Helper of the Week, who's going to ring the Call to Worship. Sally is only six, but she noticed during a power outage this past week that they hadn't seen their neighbor Miss Alma for two whole days, and she insisted her mama check on her. When Miss Alma didn't come to her door, Sally's mama called the police, even though she's afraid of police because they might be ICE agents and take her away from her children." Mary Kay paused a moment to let that sink in, and then picked up the irrefutably adorable child and held her so that their faces were side by side. "Turns out Miss Alma had taken a spill and hit her head. She was rushed to Stevenson Memorial Hospital and she's going to be all right, thanks to Sally here."

She said to the child, "Now, Sally, this nice man is Robby Bracken, the Tower Captain, and Robby's going to help you ring a bell." She passed the child to Bracken. The bearded giant nestled Sally in the crook of an arm thick as an Easter ham and placed her little hands around the fuzzy section of his bell rope. "Did you know, Sally," Mary Kay said, "That this woolly part of the rope is called 'the sally'? I think you're destined to be a bell ringer."

"Look to!" Tower Captain Bracken commanded the ringers.

Sally's eyes widened with delight when—with assistance from her bearer—her bell sounded. She clapped her hands and let go of the sally just as Bracken—now with only one free hand—reached for the rising looped tail. No one noticed until it was too late that the loop caught on the buckle of the child's overalls.

Little Sally swatted frantically at the swirling loop and got both her arms entangled. The noose tightened around her shoulders and yanked her up and out of the camera's view. The bell ringers' panicked shouts and Sally's piercing screams were met with gasps and cries as the congregation watched in helpless horror.

"*Catch hold and coil!*" shouted Mary Kay. As the ringers tried to capture their thrashing bell ropes, she kicked off her shoes, grabbed the nearest rope and climbed rapidly—pulling herself up with her arms, using her feet to wrap the rope against itself to make a step on which she stood to reach up for the next stretch of rope. In seconds she climbed out of the frame and vanished.

One by one, all but a single bell fell silent. A single noose, now empty, descended into the ringing room. Bracken grabbed it and silenced the last bell. The child's crying stopped. The congregation watched in breathless suspense. Mary Kay's bare feet appeared at the top of the screen gripping the rope, then her legs, then her torso with the weeping child clinging to her neck and waist. "We're fine," she called and descended hand under hand to the floor.

"'Ring the Bells of Heaven!'" she ordered Bracken and strode out of the frame with Sally still wrapped around her. Bracken signaled his ringers. The screens cut away to the belfry. The pipe organ thundered, and Reverend Furman's musical army lifted their voices:

Ring the bells of heaven! There is joy today,
For a soul, returning from the wild!

Libby slipped in next to Clementine and squeezed her arm. "*Did you see that?*"

Clementine shook her head in disbelief. "That woman is amazing."

Suddenly the lights dimmed, and all three screens flashed white letters on a black background.

TODAY'S SERMON
"THE BORROW PIT"
REV. NATHAN FLOWERS

Reverend Nathan Flowers himself appeared—four of him, actually: three larger than life on the giant screens, and one in person. "Fasten your seatbelt, Clementine," whispered Libby. "That was just a warm-up act. Here comes the main attraction."

18

The Porch Sermon

Day 33
Sunday

Reverend Flowers gripped the sides of the pulpit and smiled. Dressed in pressed khaki pants and a blue denim button-down shirt—no jacket or tie—he spoke in the intimate tones of an avuncular radio host. "Little Sally Sanchez almost flew away from us today, like the angel she is. But my wife Mary Kay must have had a word with the Lord and persuaded Him to let us keep Sally a little longer, on account of all the good she can still do here."

Laughter rippled through the room and the tension was broken. Seeing he had successfully changed the subject, Flowers spread open a large embossed-leather Bible and, like a seasoned showman, let the silence gather before he spoke.

"Luke tells us Jesus's parable in Chapter 7, Verse 39: 'Can the blind lead the blind? Will they not both fall into a pit?'"

He closed his Bible, emerged from behind the pulpit, and prowled the stage. Hilltop's state-of-the-art sound system rendered every word crystal clear, captured by a wireless microphone the color of his brown hair, taped to his forehead at the hairline so invisibly that even the high-definition camera didn't pick it up. Clementine finally figured out the trick when she saw the flat bulge of the power pack and the antennae wire in his back pocket.

"What is a pit? Well, many of us know the 'borrowing pit' where we fall into debt and have to work extra hard and scrimp until we pay it off. Then there's the engineers' term—the borrow pit. Remember? Remember how Hilltop was built, on a great mound of earth dug from the floodplain outside the government levee?"

He pointed at the screens, which were suddenly alive with video of dozens of enormous farm tractors and earthmovers bulldozing a pit out of the Tomato floodplain, pushing the earth up into the hill that would hold the church.

Clementine's stomach turned over. She felt violated, attacked, as if those machines were fire ants crawling all over her naked body. She tried to look away. But an odd straight line riveted her eye—hard edges angling from the swirling mud. A tree trunk, long buried? Or a telephone pole? But it was square, not round.

She half-rose in her seat and she heard her own voice whisper, "No. Please, no." It was not a tree. It was not a pole. It was their chimney, a square shaft of brick and masonry fallen intact when the river smashed the house, all that remained of the ruins. An earthmover snatched it crossways in its bucket and trundled it onto the hill like a fat dog with a prize bone in its jaws. Before Clementine Price could look away, the chimney broke of its own weight and was ground under by machines rushing down the slope for another load.

Libby grabbed her arm. "Clem? Clem, what's wrong?" she whispered.

"Our chimney."

Libby gently pulled her down into her seat. "Are you okay?"

"No." Clementine shut her eyes.

"Remember our 'barn-raising'?" Reverend Flowers continued. "Remember, after the crop was in that year, every member of the congregation who owned a machine brought it here to raise the hill for Hilltop? The borrow pit is the hole the machines left behind that became Hilltop's lake. It was just a big ugly hole in the ground when we got done digging it. But we filled it with water and now it's a beautiful lake where the faithful are baptized, and dads take their boys fishing, and mothers teach their little girls to swim."

You didn't fill it. The river filled it. Like it gave you our farm.

The video faded and Nathan's countenance commanded the screens again.

"And then, there's the pit the Bible describes as Satan's domain. I heard some preachers talk about that when I was a little boy—it terrified me. So I asked the one person I trusted, if I was going to that pit. We were sitting on Grandma's porch. . . ."

An appreciative buzz rippled through the congregation. A man behind Clementine said, "It's going to be good one. His porch sermons are the best." Clementine opened her eyes, took some deep breaths, and squeezed Libby's hand. "I'm okay now," she whispered. "Thank you."

Nathan Flowers returned to the pulpit and opened his Bible. "Grandma opened her old dog-eared Bible, turned to Psalms 7:15, and read aloud to me: 'He made a pit, and digged it, and is fallen into the ditch which he made. His mischief shall return upon his own head, and his violent dealing shall come down upon his own pate.'"

Nathan Flowers patted the top of his head for emphasis.

"Grandma was very wise. She knew that a boy who beats the daylights out of other boys and tortures helpless animals just for fun was going to reap what he sowed. First time I got put in jail, I wasn't surprised. And once I got down to the pit I proved over and over that I belonged there. I was home!"

On the jumbo screens, the camera zoomed in on his hazel eyes, right on cue. They swept the auditorium and burned with intensity.

"You all know my story. There was no man in any jailhouse anywhere who was more deserving of being there than Nathan Flowers. But I was rescued from the pit by a young lady named Mary Kay Blankenship." He picked up his heavy Bible in one big hand, held it aloft, closed his eyes, and whispered, "Psalm 103:4: 'Who redeems your life from the pit, Who crowns you with loving kindness and compassion.'"

The screen cut away to Mary Kay Flowers sitting in the front row with their two children. Cool as a cucumber after saving a child's life, marveled Clementine. And incredibly telegenic.

Nathan came down from the stage and stood by his family, shaking his head as if he still couldn't believe his luck. He roamed up and down the aisles, pausing to look individuals in the eye, occasionally laying a pastoral hand on a shoulder. The cameras followed him every step of the way, so he was never out of sight on the screens.

"This morning you saw Mary Kay climb into a tower to rescue a child. Well, ten years ago she threw a ladder down to me in that pit I'd dug for myself. And I started climbing, rung by rung. Mary Kay taught me that I could learn in prison—she showed me the prison library, full of books and computers. Jailbirds call it 'The Education.' Some use it to learn the law to overturn their conviction. But Mary Kay taught me I had better things to learn—that getting out of jail was not the same as getting out of the pit. I could learn to read the Bible. I could learn to reckon numbers. I could learn to beat people at chess instead of with my fists. I could learn to be an engineer. I could even learn how to build a church from the ground up.

"So, I climbed. And I could hear her strong, sweet voice grow louder the higher I climbed. But you know what happened when I got to the top rung, trembling, my arms and legs numb from the effort? All I could feel was the pit pulling me back down. I teetered there. But Mary Kay reached down and cried, 'Climb! You can make it,' and gave my hand a tug."

The cameras cut away to Mary Kay again, in a close-up. She had tears in her eyes.

Clementine suddenly flashed back to their high school production of *The Music Man,* which, of necessity, had been an early practitioner of non-traditional casting since three times as many girls as boys auditioned. Libby had played the bloviating, sputtering Mayor Shinn—a delicious bit of foreshadowing of her political career—and repeatedly bellowed the line "That man is a spellbinder! I want his credentials!" Clementine was about to whisper that into Libby's ear but reconsidered when she saw the rapt expression on her friend's face.

"Later I went to Mary Kay and asked, 'How can I pay you back for saving me?' Mary Kay said, 'I didn't save you.' And I got all puffed up and thought, Why, that must mean I saved myself! Ain't I something! Except when my mind commenced to linger on it . . . I prayed. And I began to understand. I didn't save myself any more than Mary Kay saved me. *God* saved me. You know how? God *lent* me Mary Kay. I *borrowed* Mary Kay. And the reason I couldn't pay *her* back was I owed *God* for the loan."

A collective sigh of understanding floated up and over the congregation. Clementine saw heads nodding, smiles, as if the secret to the universe had just been revealed.

"Doing business with God is not the same as in the material world. Borrow money from the bank, you got to pay it back to the bank—with interest." Laughter from the congregation. "Borrow Uncle Willard's truck? Give it back when you're done, top up the gas." More laughter. "But God has a different business model. God sent His one and only Son into the world that we might live *through* Him. He *lent* us His son. We *borrowed* His son.

"And here's the mystery of it. God never asks us to pay Him back. We don't get a bill—even though He lent us His best—even though we kept Him long enough to make Him suffer for us—God never sends a bill.

"God lets *us* decide how to pay Him back. You know how? We pay back the next one in need. We pay our neighbor. We let God lend *us* out to pay back the next soul who needs help. In other works, my friends, we work off our debt by doing God's work."

Nathan Flowers swept his congregation with a gentle smile.

"Have you helped your neighbor today?"

For a second of stunned silence, Clementine Price thought they'd burst into applause like a theater audience. But this was still church, and their applause instead was a collective sigh and satisfied murmurs.

The screens flashed "Hymn 98."

Minister of Music Furman struck up the powerful introductory chords for "Throw Out the Lifeline."

The choir started with the first verse.

Throw out the lifeline.
Someone is drifting away.

Nathan Flowers sank into the chair behind his pulpit and cast his congregation the dead-tired smile of a man temporarily drained but determined to catch his breath. Clementine watched closely. He appeared to gain strength from the hymn, particularly when the congregation of six thousand rose as one and sang the chorus.

Libby leaned close to whisper, "What did you think?"

"That man is a spellbinder!"

Libby looked temporarily puzzled then stifled a laugh. "Well, maybe so, but he's no Harold Hill. He's got a lot more to offer than a sham marching band, too."

"He sure does. And I'm gonna get me some, too."

Libby's eyebrows arched in alarm.

"Not that, silly. Didn't I just tell you I'm booked up in that department? No, I mean he's got his own Vatican City here with money, infrastructure, and a devoted citizen army of twenty-two thousand who respond to personal stories. I'm going to give them a personal story about a flood—get them on our side in case the worst happens."

Libby reached smoothly into her bag, which she had kept pressed to her, and Clementine saw her phone blinking. Libby read a text in a glance, closed the bag, and whispered, "Wow."

"What?"

"Rolly got a DNA hit on the floater. White supremacist gangster from St. Louis. He and Duvall are headed up there now, hoping the St. Louis cops will help out. I'll text Mayor Killing to give them an intro. Here comes Mary Kay. Hon, we're on."

As Mary Kay Flowers walked them to the stage, Clementine said, "That was some pretty impressive climbing. I did rappelling for Air Assault Training. But we were *attached* to our rope by a D-ring. You were just holding on with your hands and bare feet—and no gloves!"

Mary Kay turned her palms face up. They were covered with red welts and blood was starting to ooze. "There goes my hand modeling career. But seriously, I've already asked Robby Bracken to incorporate safety training into our bell ringing program. This can't happen again, particularly when Hilltop's Tower Captain is also our Chief of Security."

Clementine dug a white handkerchief out of her pocket and pressed it into Mary Kay's hand. "So you don't soil your beautiful dress. By the way, I couldn't help noticing your necklace. At first I thought the dove was suspended by a rope—which would be so fitting for today—but I see now that it's a serpent. Yet there's no serpent with any of Hilltop's doves."

Mary Kay pressed the white cloth between her hands and answered in her soft drawl, "My husband is from the hill country where they have cottonmouths and copperheads and more kinds of rattlers than you can shake a stick at. Snakes are just about the only thing I've ever seen Nathan afraid of."

***

Nathan Flowers cast a warm smile at the singing congregation. Then he shut his ears to the music and let his eyes focus on the nearby pulpit so that their faces blurred. It was like watching them from outside through a rain-spattered window.

What do you see when you look at me? he wondered.

Could you ever imagine? My real grandma? What she did to me? What I did to her?

The last time he saw her was in her long-out-of-business Sarah's Sunrise Grill with buck racks hanging on the walls and cracked vinyl stools. It was the dead of winter in the mountain hollow with a cold fire smoking in a wood stove, blankets from Goodwill for warmth, candles for light. The parking lot was overgrown, pine trees were closing in on the lumber road. But he swore he could still smell chicken-fried steak, sausage gravy, and fried pies. Framed on the wall was the only hymn she ever sang, "Farther Along." The angriest hymn ever written:

While there are others living about us,
Never molested tho' in the wrong.
Then do we wonder why others prosper,
Living so wicked year after year.

She'd heard he had gotten out of jail, heard he was preaching and building a church in the Delta. She wanted money, asked in her sly way did he remember the colored hobo who drowned in the quarry. Wasn't it amazing they never found out? He'd known too well there was no paying her off. Once he started to, she would never go away, not for the money, but to antagonize him. When he appeared suddenly that night, she realized she had made a mistake threatening a man who wasn't a little boy anymore. A man who finally had something to lose.

"Don't kill me, Nathan."

"Why would I kill you?"

"All the terrible things I done to you."

"Only when you were drunk."

"I was drunk a lot."

He threw wood in the stove.

"No," she shouted. "That's my last firewood."

"I'll bring you more."

"Really?"

"A whole cord. I'll bring a truck in the morning."

"You got a truck?"

"Left it up the road." He had, in fact, come the same way he would leave, riding a muffled dirt bike on deer trails only a boy born in the hollow would know. "Need anything else?"

"Wouldn't mind more candles and blankets."

"I'll bring 'em with the wood."

"So, you're a holy roller now?"

"No, Grandma. I got bigger plans than holy rolling."

"Plans?"

"Remember the snake, Grandma?"

She looked away, pretended she didn't know.

"Not that snake you teased me with." *Teased*? There was a grandmotherly word. How about *tortured*. "Not that snake. The good snake. The snake you always told me about."

"Anaconda!" A toothless smile gladdened the old woman's face bright as a Walmart. "Anaconda was no ordinary snake. He was a snake and a half."

"He wasn't a real snake."

"He was a snake idea. A big snake idea."

"Tell me about him again, Grandma." He had closed his eyes and let the old woman's voice carry him back to black starry nights and country music from a car radio she had hooked to a 12-volt battery.

"Heck, I don't remember that long ago." But she did. She just wanted to be coaxed into the past, away from the frightening present with this ghost of a hated grandchild—hated child of a hated daughter.

"Tell me like you used to. Tell me about the anaconda."

It was a family legend, a story from her great-grandma Carey Winfield—kinfolk history that plugged a no-account child into great events.

"Back then, they got into the Civil War. Yankees agin' Confederates. There was an old Yankee general worked up the Anaconda Plan. He told President Lincoln: If you hold the Mississippi River you choke the Confederates."

"What was the general's name, Grandma?"

"General Scott. General *Winfield* Scott. My people are Winfields from way back in Virginia, you know. Before Arkansas. Long way, way back."

"Tell me about the Anaconda Plan."

"I already told you. General Winfield Scott he told President Lincoln you grab the Mississippi River, the Delta is yours—the en-tire South is yours—the fight is over."

"What happened?"

"It took 'em a goddamn long time to get around to listening to General Winfield. He was old, you know. Like me. And made a bunch of enemies. Like me. But in the end General Grant—General Ulysses S. Grant—he listened, and he did it. Grabbed hold of the Mississippi River from Cairo on down—Cairo to Bliss to Memphis to Vicksburg to Natchez to New Orleans—and set loose three hundred thousand coloreds. They got in the war on the Union side. General Grant and President Lincoln they used that old river to cut the Delta loose. Just like General Winfield told 'em to. Anaconda Plan, yes, sir. Without no Delta, the South was nothing. Hell, without no Delta, the whole damn country's nothing. You gonna tell me you don't remember that?"

"Oh I remember, Grandma. I remember like it was yesterday, and I thank you for it." Then he told her his plans for the Republic of

Alluvia—plans he had told no one—about a new nation of white landowners commanding the Mississippi River.

"Whites will have their own country, again. Like it used to be before the coloreds." This night in Grandma's shack was early on, but he was already working rooms full of rich men, and he had the big picture firmly in his head. Details kept evolving, but the basic concept only grew stronger. A Noah flood would split the United States, just like the Winfield Anaconda. "Alluvia will return the Delta to whites."

Grandma shook her head. "Don't know if white folks want to work hard farming, anymore."

Nathan Flowers barely heard her. The vicious old drunk had lost too many brain cells to understand that white supremacy could be a device, a tool to conscript no-account fools into armies of obedient haters. Tell them what they want to hear. Give them love or give them hate. All they wanted was something to believe. He repeated for her his best line for roping in money-bags Colson.

"We'll start over with a clean slate—just like Noah."

"Clean slate?" She stood up and shuffled to the door. She gazed out at the dark. He wondered if she would try to run. "You get rid of all those coloreds, there's gonna be a lot of dead on that 'clean slate.' You hate them that much?"

"I don't hate, Grandma. Not anymore. It's a just a waste of time and energy."

"Hell, Nathan, you talking about drowning thousands of people. You're acting like you was God."

She glared in his face, like she used to, and screamed, like she used to. "Noah didn't start the flood, you damn fool kid. God did. Noah didn't drown all those people and all those animals. God did. Noah at least managed to save a few."

"God told Noah to build the Ark."

"God took a hell of chance on one rickety boat. What if that damned boat sunk?"

Flowers didn't need her, but wanted her to understand that he had learned how real power worked and how to get it, how to be the strongest. He tried more code words. "God *saved our future*. That's what I'm doing, Gramma, saving our future, making a *new* future for *folks whose past got stolen from them*."

She had a way of cawing like a crow when she caught him off base, and she did it now, cawing like she'd won a prize. "Thought you just said you don't hate anybody."

"I don't. I'm just lining up people behind me."

Nathan Flowers picked up her wrinkled pillow. "It is written: 'God said unto Noah, the end of all flesh is come before me; for the earth is filled with violence through them; and behold, I will destroy them with the earth.'"

"How long you been aiming at this?"

"All my life, Grandma—training myself to be too strong to be broken."

"Suppose you think you gotta kill me, so I can't tell your plan."

His grandmother had pretended not to see him pick up the pillow. Now she looked him full in the face. "I am not ready to die."

He was not surprised how fiercely the old woman fought. Of course, he held back a little so he didn't break any bones the cops would notice. By the time Grandma finally stopped breathing, she would have clawed blood from his arms with her thick, yellow nails if he hadn't protected his skin with deerskin gloves and a long sleeve neoprene jacket under his shirt. The rest was easy. She wouldn't be the only drunken fool in the hollows whose stove set her shack on fire one winter night.

Sudden motion came his way. It yanked him back inside Hilltop.

Mary Kay was bringing Mayor Winters and the tall, good-looking acting commander of the Corps' Memphis District to the stage. Flowers reached into his back pocket to switch off his wireless mic, sprang to his feet, and crossed over to greet them while the hymn continued.

"Good morning, Mayor Winters. Major Price! Welcome to Hilltop."

They shook hands.

"It's a pleasure to be here, Reverend."

"I recall your predecessor, Colonel Garcia, mentioned that you are a hydraulic engineer. Gifted, he said. We are honored that you've agreed to say a few words."

"I promise very few," Clementine smiled back. "But speaking of engineering, I couldn't help but notice that you've clad your hillside with revetment mats."

Flowers said, "Overkill, perhaps. If I were protecting merely myself, I would not have gone to the expense. But as the number who worship here grew, it dawned on Mary Kay and me that their safety is our responsibility.

Not to mention the safety of thousands of potential refugees. We felt it was essential to protect the church from being undermined by scouring if a five-hundred-year flood ever crevassed the levee. When Colonel Garcia saw the mats, he expressed admiration that we 'built for the ages.'"

"It must have been a challenge getting them up the slope." Ordinarily, the mats were unrolled into the water from a barge.

"It was a challenge, indeed," Flowers admitted. "Have you heard how Colonel Garcia is faring in his new position?"

"I saw the colonel Friday. He was standing tall."

***

Clementine Price was used to public speaking but not in a close-up on a jumbo screen. She was relieved that Libby addressed the congregation first, so she could calibrate her own performance. Without a wireless microphone she would have to stay anchored to the pulpit; and she noted how Libby—experienced in TV news appearances—skillfully dialed back her volume and facial expressions for the camera as she thanked the Hilltop community for all the help they had pledged and went on to artfully press for more. The mayor closed with a laudatory introduction of Major Price, decorated veteran, West Point graduate, co-valedictorian of Bliss Consolidated High School, and commander of the Corps' Memphis District. She did not use the adjective "acting." But acting is exactly what Clementine intended to do, with a theatrical performance worthy of Nathan Flowers.

"Thank you, Mayor Winters, Reverend Flowers and Mrs. Flowers, Reverend Furman, and all of you for inviting us to share with you today. This is my first visit to Hilltop Fellowship and, quite frankly, I am amazed by what you have created here. But some of you may know that this is not my first visit to this *place*. I actually grew up on this very spot, in a little town called Tomato, which was swept away by the flood of 2008."

Parishioners gasped and edged forward in their seats.

"Yes, for four generations the Price family farmed ground in Tomato right next to the river, outside the levee. Or, as Reverend Flowers might say, we *borrowed* ground from the Mississippi River. But the river never let us forget it was our landlord. Our farm, our homes, our town, were flooded almost every year, and we lived with it. We'd clean up, dry out, and rebuild. In return, the river gave us the most fertile, rich soil on God's earth. But in 2008, the river called in its loan for good. And Tomato is no more."

She paused to look at Reverend Flowers, still seated onstage and listening intently.

"I'd be lying if I said that didn't make me sad. But nothing is forever on the river, and I'm glad that something new and powerful has risen in its place, something that is clearly built for the ages, a community of people who believe in helping their neighbors. And that's what I want to ask you to do today, because we are facing the possibility of a flood worse than 2008, than 2011, worse even than the great flood of 1927 that literally ripped this country apart.

"Has any one here ever been caught in a flood, or lost loved ones or your home in a flood?"

She heard murmurs of assent.

"Then you know, as I do, what it feels like to see your home torn up right in front of your eyes—your clothes, your family pictures, your child's favorite toys, your dishes and pots and pans, your tools, even your pets, swept away forever. You can be swept away too; did you know that just six inches of fast-moving water can knock you down, and one foot of water will sweep your vehicle away? When Tomato flooded, I saw it from overhead, flying my uncle's spray plane. I saw our house, the barns, our livestock, our tractors disappear in one awful glance back. The water would have swallowed my family too, if we had left one minute later. It looked like the hand of a giant brushing crumbs off a table."

She caught Mary Kay's wide eyes in the front row.

"A flood is a catastrophe in and of itself. And if you survive, you then experience a second, slow-burning catastrophe that's in many ways harder to recover from. It's not just all your personal property—including a change of clothes—that's been lost; all of your normal rituals are upended. You're bunking with relatives or even strangers or camping out in a motel. My family spent two weeks in the Motel 6—they took pity on us and didn't charge us for the second week—and then scattered to the wind. This is a family that had lived as next-door neighbors for four generations. We rarely see each other now. My father never went back to farming—there was no insurance, and he had no collateral for a loan—and he and Momma moved to an apartment in Bliss. One of my brothers is farming over near Dell, but another brother wasn't as resilient, he got hooked on opioids. And some of you probably know my Uncle Chance, my favorite uncle, who drives a van here at Hilltop."

Another murmur rippled through the congregation.

"Floods don't just damage property, they damage people. And people who've been flooded never really get over the fear that it will happen again. You know what is the most unhelpful thing you can say to someone who's survived a flood? 'You're lucky to be alive.' Just tell that to someone who's been waiting eighteen months to get an insurance check for half the value of their house or can't get a Social Security payment because all their identification was destroyed or who has to ride the city bus now because they lost their vehicle and can't afford to replace it. Flood survivors—and I can tell you, I am one—have to operate in 'fight or flight' mode for all that time. You get exhausted by that, and some people just end up broken."

Clementine paused. She was prepared to deliver a personal talk but wasn't prepared for the emotional wallop she felt herself.

"I want to say something else about flood preparation, from my perspective as an Army Corps officer. We do a lot of planning—just like Mayor Winters's administration is doing and like you've been doing here at Hilltop. Most of that planning is invisible to the public—as it should be. But these emergency shelters don't appear by magic from nowhere, the evacuation routes and procedures don't just spring into place; they've been thought through by public servants, first responders, and volunteers who may find *themselves* flooded out, stranded in those same shelters, and struggling with the same heartbreak as the people they're charged with helping. These folks are also likely to be underpaid and overworked, in addition to being traumatized by loss. That's where you can really help the most.

"Even if the worst happens, you will be safe here, on high ground. Hilltop has offered to shelter flood refugees from Bliss and elsewhere. I hope you have none, but you may have thousands. You will provide food and shelter, which they will need. They will also need your help to heal. You can help mend their broken hearts and spirits.

"There could be no finer way to help your neighbor."

Reverend Flowers leapt up to shake Clementine's hand. "That was powerful speaking, Major Price. Preaching from the heart. You've given me a lot to think about. Our congregation too."

"Well, Reverend, it's fair to say that it was your sermon that inspired me to speak from the heart."

The program listed the closing hymn as "Sunshine in My Soul," but Rev. Furman instead announced Hymn #1, pounding out the introduction to "Higher Ground." Clementine made her way off the stage as the congregation joined in. Mary Kay was waiting for her, eyes bright with passion.

"Anything you need, anything we can do, let me know. Here, I'm texting you my private cell number and Nathan's."

"Thank you. I'd like to inspect your dock. For that riverboat you've got. Tomorrow morning?"

"Just tell me what time." Mary Kay gave her an impulsive hug, and the two women raised their voices in the only hymn Clementine knew by heart.

Lord lift me up, and let me stand,
By faith on heaven's table land
A higher plane than I have found,
Lord plant my feet on higher ground.

19

The Floater

Day 34
Monday

Rolly Winters and Duvall McCoy hit pay dirt in St. Louis, thanks in part to a golden introduction from the mayor's office.

They had already learned from the Combined DNA Index System that their faceless floater's name was David Canning. St. Louis police detectives remembered him well, if not fondly, and recalled with great satisfaction that Canning had been sentenced to ten years at Potosi Correctional, Missouri's maximum-security prison.

"Good a place as any to hook up with Pure Dominion," said Duvall.

"And get made the Weatherman's bitch," said the St. Louis gang specialist.

"Weatherman?" asked Rolly. "You talking an eighty-year old student radical from the 1960s?"

"Not a radical. This guy was nuts for weather. Storm chaser. Tornado chaser. Knew everything about weather. Totally fixated on weather. So they called him the Weatherman."

"What's his real name?"

"Jack Payne."

"What's Payne in Potosi for?"

"Was. He got his conviction overturned."

"What was he in for?"

"Attempted triple murder of an African American family. Burned their house down. Sheer luck they got out in time."

"Where does the Weatherman live?"

"Disappeared."

Rolly and Duvall exchanged a skeptical look. Rolly said, "Skels like that tend not to disappear, unless someone does the world a favor and buries him in cement."

The detective said, "He came back to St. Louis from Potosi. Later, he vanished. No one who knew him ever saw him again."

"Maybe," Duvall ventured with little hope, "we can track him on his weather thing. Find racist rants on weather nut blogs."

"What do you want him for?" asked the gang specialist.

Duvall McCoy answered, "To tell us who fitted David Canning with the booby-trapped ankle monitor."

"Well, that sounds like the Weatherman."

"How so?"

"Payne's a major tech nerd. If he weren't so twisted, he'd have been a billionaire. The way he tried to kill the African American family, he called them on the phone, ranted at them, screaming insults. Then he set off a firebomb by remote control—like with a phone app? Forensics figured he engineered it himself. Wrote the code, the whole nine yards. The scumbag's a genius."

20

Built for the Ages

Day 34
Monday

There was steady traffic up and down Hilltop's steep driveway Monday morning, but nothing like yesterday's traffic jam. Clementine took the opportunity to pull onto the shoulder, shroud herself in the full-length raincoat she kept on her backseat, and inspect the revetment-clad slope. Any other builder would have dumped truckloads of rip rap stone and called it a day. These mats were the real McCoy, precisely laid concrete slabs linked with bi-directional stainless steel cables and copper-coated tie wire—what Libby had dubbed "chain mail."

Mary Kay Flowers greeted her at the front door of the parsonage wearing a sunshine-yellow dress and magenta ballet flats. She was mid-phone call, speaking into a headset and pantomiming to Clementine to follow her down the wide center hall lined with whimsically carved wooden benches and regional folk art. The house was ablaze with lights, in defiance of the perpetual wet darkness outside. A catering crew was setting up what appeared to be a tea party in an old-fashioned parlor. "I'll be right with you," Mary Kay silently mouthed, directing Clementine into a cypress-paneled study.

Clementine recognized the design hand of Steve Stevenson, who dabbled impressively in architecture and interior decorating: the pickled pine floors and woven scatter rugs, the clerestory windows and French doors opening onto a wraparound porch, and his signature Williamsburg color palette.

Steve's distressed, burnt ochre walls were barely visible under the collage of Nathan Flowers's diplomas, grip-and-grin photo ops with politicians and CEOs, and framed magazine covers. The Reverend had been declared *Southern Living's* "Person of the Year," *Time's* "The Face of the New Evangelism," and *People's* "Most Remarkable Redemption."

Clementine examined the mounted blueprints and engineering drawings for the Hilltop earthworks (odd that they didn't show the revetment she'd just inspected); skimmed the laminated front page of the *Commercial Appeal* from 2012 that headlined "Governor Commutes Sentence of Former Supremacist Turned Preacher;" and wondered why Flowers would have an engraved illustration of General Winfield Scott's Civil War Anaconda Plan.

She glanced down the hall. Mary Kay was still on the phone. Her own phone vibrated in her pocket. "Yes, Jesse."

"Major, I've got the Tiger Dams laid out and staked down, but the city's fire hydrants are for shit. Half we tested don't have enough pressure to douse a campfire."

"What do you advise, Jesse?"

"Let me think on it. I'll get back."

Clementine wandered impatiently, reading spines on the floor-to-ceiling bookshelves. As expected, there were biblical atlases, concordances, and dictionaries. Also dog-eared children's books, novels, and histories. She wasn't surprised to see John M. Barry's *Rising Tide* about the 1927 Mississippi flood; it was the book that had introduced her to James Eads back in grade school. She thumbed through it gingerly—its spine was crumbling from repeated readings—and smiled at the yellow highlights and margin notes penciled in neat block letters. Nathan had zeroed in on some of the same passages she had.

In the center of the study was an ornate oak refectory table that displayed an antique chess set the likes of which Clementine had never seen, with all the pieces carved and painted as famous Civil War figures. She did another double take at a fleet of bronze scale models of James Eads's Civil War ironclads arrayed in chronological order: *St. Louis, Cairo, Carondelet, Cincinnati, Louisville, Mound City,* and *Pittsburgh.* An ebony easel held a framed letter bearing James B. Eads's signature.

"Wow," said Clementine out loud. "Drive on!"

"Yes, that's Nathan's personal motto!"

Mary Kay had silently entered the room, carrying a tray with a porcelain coffeepot and two cups and saucers. "I found it at a rare bookstore in Nashville for our fifth wedding anniversary."

"I'm amazed it wasn't owned by the Smithsonian—Eads writing General Winfield Scott about ironclads. Scott's Anaconda strategy and Eads's gunboats won the Civil War."

"Nathan just idolizes Eads—he says what he designed and executed in the 1800s is still more innovative than anything that's been done since."

"Eads is my hero, too," said Clementine, accepting the coffee cup as Mary Kay gestured to the dainty matching cream pitcher and sugar bowl. "Black is fine, thank you. Where shall I meet Mr. Wells?" she asked, making a show of looking at her watch.

"I know how valuable your time is, Major Price," Mary Kay apologized. "He's en route from Bliss. Picking up cots from the Red Cross. All our drivers were already out."

Clementine resigned herself to the wait and tried to be gracious. "I'm curious—did Steve Stevenson design this house? It's so distinctive."

"You've got a good eye, Major. How do you know Steve?"

"We've been friends for years. You have some beautiful antiques here."

"Most of the conversation pieces—like that peculiar chess set—are gifts from supporters, and they're like wedding presents, you know?"

Clementine didn't know firsthand but smiled politely.

"They are more about the giver, who expects to see them when they visit. The refectory table came from home, when Mother and Daddy downsized from the big house on Pine Street to the First Methodist parsonage—we were on the same block as your Great-Aunt Martha."

Clementine softened. "Of course. When I stayed with her, she'd take me to First Methodist on Sunday morning. I remember your father's sermons really put the fear of the devil in me!"

Mary Kay laughed. "Daddy hasn't mellowed with age. He's still an old-fashioned fire and brimstone preacher—though these days he needs a couple of strong deacons to help him up to the pulpit."

"But I don't remember ever seeing you at the church. I'm sure Aunt Martha would have introduced me to a playmate my age."

"They sent me off to boarding school when I was nine. I was a big surprise to Mother, pregnant for the first and only time at age forty-two. They just didn't know what to do with me—and I'm afraid I didn't make it any easier! They chose Rabun Gap in Georgia, in the Blue Ridge Mountains. Do you know it? It's a Christian school with mandatory chapel attendance. I'm sure they thought it would cloister me from the evils of the world. But instead, it opened me up to all these wild new ideas. I mean, Rabun was teaching community service and environmental sustainability long before it was the fashion. We all worked on the school farm, we had our own recycling center and animal shelter, and everyone—including the faculty—volunteered at the local soup kitchen.

Plus, there was a serious circus training program! Which I loved. I got pretty good on the *corde lisse*."

"The suspended rope with all the gymnastic moves and poses? That explains your incredible rescue yesterday. How are your hands?"

Mary Kay held red calloused palms up to Clementine. "I'm a fast healer. Between you and me, the bell tower was no big deal—at Rabun Gap we used to hang upside down by one toe and twirl a baton."

Clementine laughed. "Quite a picture."

"I was very serious about it. When I was home for the summer, I got our yard man Enrique to hang my aerial rope from a big tree. I'd put on my spangled circus costume and practice my arabesques and upside-down hangs and miracle splits and double foot ties and every kid in the neighborhood would come running—especially the boys—to see if I'd fall off and break my neck. I thought Daddy would have a stroke."

Clementine laughed again as she reached for her vibrating phone. "Excuse me. Yes, Jesse."

"Can the Corps requisition Bliss's fire trucks? If we had their pumpers standing by to fill the Tiger Dams . . ."

"I'll have Lieutenant Harpur take care of it." She pocketed her phone and turned back to Mary Kay. "Excuse me."

"Of course. Major Price, I was so moved by your talk about Tomato, and what your family went through. Did you feel the emotion coursing through the congregation? You really touched them."

Clementine nodded. "I surprised myself by talking about it. I don't, usually."

"I think it's important that our members know what was here before Hilltop was built. Do you have any photographs you'd be willing to share?"

"We lost all our family pictures in the flood."

"Of course. How thoughtless of me."

"But a dear friend gave me a collection of historic photos of Tomato; you're welcome to make copies. They're in my apartment in Memphis. Let me know the next time you come down."

"Thank you, I will." Mary Kay patted a waist-high stack of leather-bound albums next to the sofa. "As you can see, I'm the official archivist." She pulled out one that had CIRQUE embossed on the cover and flipped through images of a skimpily-clad teenaged Mary Kay suspended in a series of physically implausible contortions that would have thrilled a bondage freak.

"Aerialists learn to tolerate pain in places you didn't know could feel pain. Like between your toes." She shut the album and gestured for Clementine to sit down. "Anyway, Mother and Daddy were so afraid I was going to run away and join Barnum & Bailey that they were actually relieved when I shipped off to college at Oberlin and came home ranting about putting faith into action, instead of making a spectacle of myself climbing up and down a rope!"

"They must be very proud of you now."

"Well, yes. I think so. But it's complicated . . . all families are. Your family must be very proud of you too."

Clementine smiled. "Yes, but as you said, it's complicated. Speaking of families, how is my Uncle Chance doing?"

"Chance is a kind, gentle soul and very reliable. He never comes to church, though."

"I'm not surprised. Never was the church-going type."

"And you, Major Price? Have you accepted Jesus Christ as your personal savior?"

"I've gone to church all my life, but it's fair to say I'm more of a supporter than a believer. You know, I haven't laid eyes on Uncle Chance since . . . well, since the flood. I've tried to reach him over the years, but he's completely cut himself off from all of us."

"He was a pilot, wasn't he?" asked Mary Kay.

"A brilliant one. He taught me to fly, and that the best pilots have to be responsible grown-ups. He gave me his plane, you know. I still hear him talking to me when I do my preflight check. It was really Uncle Chance and Aunt Martha who showed me I could control my own destiny."

Mary Kay pulled out another album, labeled PINE STREET, and flipped through the pages. She placed it on Clementine's lap, and Clementine gasped. There stood Aunt Murtha and Uncle Fred, dressed to the nines, in front of the big brick house, with the fins of her white 1958 Cadillac Eldorado jutting into the frame.

"Oh, my Lord! What a picture. May I—"

"Of course. I'll send you a copy right away. I just adored your aunt—she had such style and confidence. Like you. I love the way you wear your hair—like she did. So elegant and old-fashioned. You must know, she thought you hung the moon. 'Keep your eye on my Clementine,' she'd say. 'She's going all the way.'"

Clementine felt her face go warm. She stared at the faded snapshot. "I think of her every day. I live with her furniture. Right before she died, she put everything she owned in storage, with instructions to hold it for me until I finally got a home of my own. I didn't even know about it. But she knew I needed something tangible from my past—something permanent that wouldn't get washed away."

Clementine closed the album, handed it back to Mary Kay, and turned away, blinking back tears. Her eye fell on a massive oak partners' desk in the corner, unusually configured so that the partners would be seated at right angles rather than directly across from one another. "Aunt Martha sure would have loved that desk! Is this where you and Reverend Flowers work together?"

"It was a gift from the Colsons, who were the most generous of Hilltop's early supporters," said Mary Kay, straightening up the already neatly-arranged forest of framed photos, piles of mail and papers, and two sleek laptops. "It's really over the top—you could send a couple of kids to college for what it cost, I'm sure. But Mrs. Colson said, 'I've seen how you two work as a team, and I want to encourage you to keep it up.' How could we say no?"

Clementine picked up a silver oval frame featuring a smiling Mary Kay in her wedding gown and a very sober young Nathan.

"He looks so serious."

"When I met Nathan, his teeth were so bad he wouldn't smile. It sounds shallow of me, but I just couldn't imagine an effective preacher who never smiled! One of Daddy's classmates at Vanderbilt is a top dentist in Memphis. Nathan has a high tolerance for pain, fortunately, so Dr. Stern just drilled away for hours at a time." She picked up another photo of herself and Nathan with newborn Gabe. "See? He went from being scary to downright handsome."

"Not to mention a heck of a preacher. You know, he doesn't sound at all like the hillbilly he says he was. Did you have a hand in that as well?"

Mary Kay laughed. "I'm no Henry Higgins, turning a cockney flower girl into a duchess. But I did find a speech therapist who could 'tune' Nathan's voice without completely neutralizing his accent. I love accents—they make us distinctive—but a preacher also has to be intelligible." She held up a seashell-framed photo of Nathan, herself, and the two children in swimsuits on a beach. "This is from our last vacation, in Cape Hatteras. Notice anything?"

Clementine considered. "Only that you're all very attractive people who could model for travel advertisements."

"It's what you *don't* see. When Nathan got out of prison he was covered with tattoos. I mean *covered*, head to toe. And not cute little mermaids and flowers—really stomach-turning white supremacist symbols and slogans. I'd seen a few on his arms but it wasn't until our honeymoon when I saw the whole *ensemble*, if you will. Let's just say I was grateful when he turned off the lights. I couldn't bear the thought that our future children—or any children—would have to look at that hatred, burned into the flesh of a man who was supposed to be a role model. So I found this group, Redemption Ink—don't you love the name?— a not-for-profit that removes hate-related tattoos. Again, it was a good thing Nathan has a high tolerance for pain. It took a long time."

"Were *you* ever scared of him?" ventured Clementine. "I mean, he was doing time for a pretty violent crime."

"I won't say I didn't have some concerns at first, and Lord knows Daddy and Mother were hysterical on the subject—their only daughter taking up with a dangerous convict! But Nathan and I had a vision—we knew that we wanted to create a better world for children like Nathan who'd grown up with no adult role models, nothing but anger and resentment and ignorance fueling raging hormones. When he proposed, I asked him if there was anything else about his past he wanted to tell me that might come back to haunt us, so we could start our married life clean. He looked me in the eye and said there was nothing other than what was in his long criminal record—which is on the Hilltop website, by the way, so that the world can see where he started—and that the old Nathan had died and been reborn. I believe him," she said simply. "I love him."

Andrew Wells knocked gently on the open door. "I'm so sorry to be late. Whenever you're ready, Major Price, we can go look at the ferry dock. It's pretty rough out there, so I hope you've brought your foul weather gear."

"Thank you, Andrew," said Mary Kay, draining the last of her coffee. "Major Price—"

"Please, call me Clementine. All my friends do."

"Clementine, then. You must excuse me—I've got to get ready for today's preschool tea party. I know that sounds frivolous, compared with what you're doing, but we try to maintain normalcy for these little ones who don't have much routine in their lives. Tea parties are a chance to teach table manners and basic social skills that, sadly, they don't see modeled anywhere else." She hugged Clementine warmly. "Call me after you've taken the tour with Andrew. And I'll visit with your Uncle Chance; I see him every morning."

***

It was raining so hard when Clementine stepped out Mary Kay's door that she could barely make out the tiny white electric Polaris GEM two-seater parked at the end of the front walk. She folded herself into the enclosed cab while Wells double-checked the vehicle's flatbed payload, stacked four feet high with shrink-wrapped flats of canned dog and cat food.

"I wonder Mr. Wells, do you happen to know if my Uncle Chance, Chance Price, one of your shuttle drivers, is on the property today?"

Wells keyed the Hilltop dispatcher on his walkie-talkie and asked for the GPS coordinates on Chance Price's van. "Negative, Major Price. Looks like he's covering Caruthersville, Missouri, this week. Do you want me to raise him on the radio?"

"Oh no, that's not necessary. I just thought if he was around . . ."

The silent vehicle seemed to amplify the sound of the rain inside the cab.

"I know you have a full schedule today, Major Price, but would you care to see what we're preparing for the evacuee shelter before we head down to the dock?"

Clementine checked her watch. Her adjutant, Second Lieutenant Terry Harpur, was covering the first responders drill at Stevenson Memorial Hospital, and they were meeting Jesse Corliss and his deputy Morris Gilliam at noon for an inch-by-inch inspection of the Bliss Bends cut-off. "I've got thirty-five minutes."

"I'll be quick." He stopped in front of an inflatable military AirBeam Shelter on the edge of a soggy soccer field. Dogs barked from within. A volunteer in a yellow slicker and orange "Hilltop Volunteer" safety vest hurried out and unloaded the flats of food. "We've just started to receive people's pets—we've got five more of these AirBeams standing by."

"What's your background, Mr. Wells? It seems like you've done this before."

"Guilty. I was a FEMA contractor during Katrina, which was a great lesson in how *not* to be effective. After that I worked for the Red Cross. I was in New Jersey when Hurricane Sandy struck. I sure hope I'm not attracting these disasters—but I've certainly seen best and worst practices in action." The Polaris rolled past the fitness center. "We can shelter five hundred in the gymnasium, and we've stockpiled cots, blankets, MREs, and water bottles in all of the storage areas. There are showers and bathrooms there, obviously, and we can also convert the library, chapel, community center, and if necessary, the main sanctuary into temporary shelters."

"How long is Hilltop prepared to house refugees? A flood of this magnitude could displace people for months, not weeks."

Wells turned onto a switchback path leading down to the riverside dock. "Hilltop can help for weeks, but not months. We're not FEMA or the Red Cross. We're a temporary port in the storm, not a permanent solution."

He stopped the vehicle on the dock's movable boarding gangway which extended over the rushing water. Clementine looked around in astonishment. The gangway was huge—much higher and larger than Hilltop's ferryboats would ever need, as were the pilings and mooring bollards.

"You guys really do build for the ages, as Reverend Flowers says."

She gestured at the new mainline levee, right on the edge of the water. It hugged the bend in the river from the dock to the slope of the plateau. There, it appeared to meld into the foundation of the church, which rose like medieval ramparts beside the raging water.

"The levee revetment continues up from the base of the levee to—how high is that?" asked Clementine. "Ten meters above the crown?"

"Yes, ten meters. It's true that Hilltop far exceeds the standards for its Base Flood Elevation. But as you know, a five-hundred-year BFE doesn't refer to a flood that will occur only once every five-hundred years—it means there's a one-in-five-hundred chance of a flood of that severity. And I imagine you know better than anyone how many one-hundred-year and even five-hundred-year floods there have been just in the last several years. With global warming, the weather is only going to get more extreme and unpredictable. I would argue that Reverend Flowers has planned wisely and well for an uncertain future."

"I wonder why he built so close to the edge instead of farther inland."

"The church was their first structure. The rest of the campus came later. I believe—just my own opinion, of course— that Reverend and Mrs. Flowers wanted to make Hilltop so visible that potential parishioners would see a church that would stand at the center of their lives."

"I can't deny they've done that." Clementine steadied herself against the wind and walked out to the edge of the gangway. Whitecaps were wetting the air with foam. "Certainly, a wharf of this size and elevation could dock that chartered riverboat Mrs. Flowers mentioned. Do you happen to know which vessel she was talking about?"

"This is not for general consumption, Major Price, but I believe Reverend Flowers is planning to employ Noah's Lucky Ark—the floating casino."

Clementine stared. "But the casino sits on a couple of stationary barges—it's not seaworthy under normal circumstances—much less with the river at flood stage."

"Three barges carry the Ark, actually. The biggest ever launched. Two hundred and fifty feet long and a hundred wide."

Clementine did not know the specifics; the Ark was part of the Tomato-Bliss stretch of river that Robert had shielded her from. "Size does not make them seaworthy."

"That is what's interesting about them. Because they are so big, they are equipped with Z-drive thrusters to help maneuver them. So, with a little help from a towboat, they are quite seaworthy and safe, since Z-drive provides full-power thrust in any direction and eliminates the need for rudders."

"Z-drive is a modern miracle," Clementine said, dryly. "It still doesn't make a barge safe to carry human beings in a flood. Even with a lot of help from a towboat."

"Of course, but one of Hilltop's members—a Hilltop founder, in fact—owns Mid-South Marine Transport. He has his biggest towboat and his most experienced captain and crew standing by."

Mid-South Marine, an old outfit that had been a force in river commerce since steamboat days, had recently been sold to a Chicago conglomerate, but to Clementine this still sounded insane. "Have the casino owners agreed to this?"

"Reverend Flowers can be very persuasive. I believe his pitch was that a good deed of such magnitude would bolster the Ark's reputation in the eyes of the community. Although between you and me, I suspect that once Reverend Flowers has gotten the Ark to move, he might be able to persuade the owners to move permanently—like, to another state. I know Mayor Winters would be glad to see it go."

"Who *are* the owners?"

Wells shrugged. "As you're probably aware, most casino boats are owned by a handful of big companies not from around here. Perhaps Las Vegas or Atlantic City or the tribal operations in Connecticut."

Clementine was still trying to wrap her head around the image of that neon-rimmed eyesore carrying five thousand desperate souls to safety. Would the slot machines be operating on the trip? The bar open for business? The exotic dancers? It was surreal.

"Major Price, don't be distracted by the fact that it's a gambling casino and all that implies. It's an ingenious implementation of a resource that can, for once, be a force for good. Let your engineer's mind think on it and I think you'll come to agree."

"Where would evacuees board?"

"I would imagine where the casino currently waits. Good roads to that location."

"Those roads could be underwater soon—Listen, this is not my bailiwick. To authorize or deny the use of the Ark as a rescue vessel is the Coast Guard's call."

"Indeed!" Wells smiled. "That is precisely what Coast Guard Sector Commander for the Lower Mississippi River, Admiral James Congdon, told Reverend and Mrs. Flowers at lunch Saturday in Memphis. The good admiral promised to escort it himself, in fact, should the need arise. And despite his advanced years, Admiral Congdon is a man to ride the river with."

Clementine said, "I'll have my deputy inform the Coast Guard of when the Ark access road can be expected to flood."

Wells looked at his watch. "Thank you for coming today, Major Price. I don't want you to be late for your next appointment."

Clementine climbed into the Polaris, her thoughts a blur. What in the world would James Eads think of *this*?

21

The Forty Acres Martyr Brigade

Day 34
Monday

If one African American man and a fistful of recruits hoping to found a separate black nation were fighting a lonely battle, it beat doing nothing while poverty, isolation, and hate turned children into slaves. Abdul Muqtadir—U.S. Army special forces veteran, ex-convict, and jailhouse convert to Islam—used to operate a tough-love summer camp that took in orphaned, abandoned, and homeless boys from East St. Louis. Like its brother camps serving the old river cities of Bliss, Cairo, Caruthersville, Cape Girardeau, and Memphis, his Camp Never-Too-Late scraped by on contributions from churches and mosques, private handouts (Abdul's father, in his case, a well-off Chicago dentist), and the Mississippi Valley Mayors' Initiative.

His goal was to send the children back to East St. Louis with a start on the steady habits and self-discipline that bred hope and success. But summers were short. There came a day when he saw one too many lost boys who he knew in his heart was lost forever. And he had to admit that his best efforts had no more effect than a finger in a dike.

Having failed at peaceful ways, he swore a blood oath to fight for an independent African American nation where "Black Lives Matter" would be law instead of a slogan. He recruited a few brave souls— a mix of U.S. Army vets and former gangbangers—to join him. He was a clear-eyed man; he knew he was forming a martyr's brigade. But he had a born-optimist's sense of humor and a soldier's grasp of history. American slaves set free had dreamed that President Abraham Lincoln would provide each family with forty acres of farmland and a mule to plow it. Abdul Muqtadir named his unit the Forty Acres Martyr Brigade.

Tonight, a night of thunder and cold rain, he mustered his black separatist militiamen in the Never-Too-Late boathouse thirty miles northwest of St. Louis. Armed with stun grenades, mace spray, throwing knives, bayonets, pistols, and army carbines, they were on edge and growing impatient as they paced around a high-speed skiff mounted on a trailer.

"Where is Brother I?" demanded pious Brother Shariq, an ambitious self-educated man who could wax erudite and talk trash in the same breath. "Blowing us off? Playing *you* for a sucker?"

"Brother I will get here when he gets here," said Abdul Muqtadir, who had no doubt that Shariq was itching to take over the brigade. Brother I—Ismail Muhammad—was a righteous believer with access to money and weapons. For tonight's operation, he had supplied the Forty Acres Martyrs Brigade with head-to-toe body armor, scrambled-channel headsets, and radio jammers.

"We got a timetable—"

"Brother I sets the time table. The man has never let us down, he's not about to start tonight."

"Who's running this outfit? You or Brother I?"

"Brother I pays the bills," Abdul Muqtadir answered mildly. "I am Commander." Provided they both came out of tonight alive, he planned to shoot Brother Shariq in the face before Shariq shot him in the back.

Brother I had caught wind of his recruiting—not surprisingly, as ex-army and ex-cons inhabited small worlds with few secrets. So did government agents. Brother I had made his move in a dark parking lot with a gun in his hand and a mask on his face. Then he handed Abdul the gun and offered to help Forty Acres with money and gear. It was hugely tempting. Weapons were expensive, money was hard to get. But Abdul Muqtadir had danced around him very carefully. After months of clandestine meetings, with Brother I always in his mask, Abdul said he was still was not convinced that Brother I wasn't running an FBI sting—and no, it wasn't the mask, it just seemed too easy.

"Pick a cop," said Brother I. "Any cop. Call me when you see him on TV." Abdul fingered a Ferguson officer who had hassled him. Twenty-four hours later, the cracker was gunned down in a drive-by while writing a ticket for a broken taillight.

Abdul Muqtadir saw Brother I from that moment on as the man who made his dream possible. When Forty Acres needed money, Brother I saw to it they got money. When they needed gear, they got gear. He'd even found them a farm back in the hills where Abdul Muqtadir could drill his fighters until they excelled at the kind of precision warfare the army had taught him in Iraq and Syria and Yemen.

The lookout slipped inside the boathouse.

"Brother I just pulled up in a truck with a hitch."

"Brother Shariq," Abdul Muqtadir ordered with a righteous grin, "Open the door!"

The twenty-year-old pickup that backed in sounded better than it looked. Brother I stepped down from the cab. He was masked, as always. Abdul Muqtadir had still never seen his face but knew him by his gait. The man glided, smooth as ball bearings.

***

Nathan Flowers greeted Abdul Muqtadir with a sharp salute and a bumped fist. He wore recon gloves to cover his pale hands. Water-based kohl eyeliner darkened the slivers of skin around his eyes that might flash through the mask's eye slits.

It was Bliss Metro Chief of Police Billy Bob Owen who had turned Flowers on to Abdul Muqtadir, though neither of the fools ever knew it. "So, this Abdul," Billy Bob laughed, "comes nosing around Bliss Marine asking for a boat-pilot job. Well, everybody starts laughing—Abdul, that boy's blacker than a sludged-up oil filter. Who ever heard of a Africoon river pilot?—Sorry, Reverend, I know you don't like that kind of talk, but I don't mean nothing un-Christian. At any rate, one thing led to another. Abdul decked four or five of 'em. They ran out of boys willing to go up against him, so they called their old friends at 911. By the time my officers managed to beat him down, I had him for resisting arrest, assaulting a peace officer, etcetera, and the judge saw fit to allot him five years in Varner. Funny thing was, turned out at the trial he really did know how to run a towboat. 'Course, by then it was *waaay* too late."

Tracking down Abdul had been a simple matter of asking the Varner prison bosses about him. They reported that the river pilot had been baptized Rufus Briggs, son of a Chicago dentist who had somehow escaped Arkansas Delta sharecropping. By the time Flowers went looking for him, his father had paid to get him paroled and Abdul was losing faith in his Never-Too-Late summer camp, but still hoped to change the world.

A thunderbolt turned the sky silver. Rain rattled the tin roof.

"Thank you for the cover, Allah," said Brother I. "Thank you for your well-timed storm."

That drew laughs from most of the fighters grouped around their skiff, but scowls from Brother Shariq, who thought that Allah could only be worshiped with a straight face.

Flowers checked his watch. "Load up!"

Eight powerful men jumped to obey, hoisting the boat trailer onto the hitch and stashing weapons in the boat, which Flowers had secretly registered, along with the truck and trailer, in the name of the blacks' camp. That would ignite a firestorm after the attack when the cops found the truck and boat trailer.

The cloudburst moved on, leaving in its wake steady rain.

"Listen close!"

Time for "Brother I" to get this crew pumped.

"You have sworn to fight for Forty Acres."

Nathan Flowers indicated Abdul Muqtadir, standing proudly with one hand on the boat's blunt bow. "And you have sworn to Allah to protect Abdul Muqtadir with your lives."

No way Flowers would waste the river pilot in a single operation.

"Paradise awaits. But first—*your lives here on Earth have greater value.* Do not spill seed. Do not waste. Do not die if you don't have to. Do not betray your oath, but do not squander it, either. Suicide is half-pint jive."

Nathan Flowers expected the confusion his deliberately mixed message had sown. He could see it on their faces, their eyes shifting to each other, wondering, thinking: *It's not suicide, it's martyrdom; it's going to meet God.* He said, "I'll make it simple. If you can do your job and protect Brother Abdul Muqtadir and escape, then do it. Save Brother Muqtadir and escape to fight again. If you can't get away from the cops, then head for Paradise and take as many as you can with you."

That was what they wanted to hear. To be as brave as they would have to be tonight—to attack, to fight to win, to sacrifice their lives to save their leader's life—they would shut their eyes to reason, logic, and truth. Flowers saw the clouds skid off their faces. Only one still looked skeptical—Brother Shariq, of course—who demanded, "When do we get our suicide vests?"

"I've issued body armor. You're not to be martyrs yet. Forty Acres needs you to fight again."

In answer, Shariq snatched up a rifle and quoted Henry Kissinger: "'A conventional army loses by not winning. A guerrilla army wins by not losing.' Except Brother I, here, he's got us doin' both—losing *and* not winning."

Abdul moved swiftly to intervene. That's all he needed—crazy Shariq blowing away their guns and money. But Brother I blocked Abdul smoothly and said to him, "Thank you my good friend. I'll talk sense to the brother."

"Sense!" Shariq yelled. "Who you think—"

Nathan Flowers counterpunched with a speech he delivered often to Alluvia's fighters. For this crew, all he had to change was skin colors and grievances. White to black. Fantasy history to hated history.

"We fight for a goal. We fight to make a new nation, our nation, a homeland for black America. We are taking Slave Ground back by the right of our sweat and our blood that built it."

Flowers had learned as a boy to survive by observing enemies the way a cat watched other cats. A raised tail said, I'm cool. A low tail said, I'm going to jump you. Brother Shariq was sending low tail signals, pretending he was trolling for followers, while gathering bone and muscle to strike. Flowers watched the stages of the attack unfold as if in slow motion.

Shariq moved in on him, leading with his shoulder even as he faced the others. "I want Paradise!" He punched the air with an Al Sharpton finger. "Losing life for the cause of God is the highest form of pure belief. I want Paradise." He wheeled suddenly on Flowers. "I know why you wear that mask. You're hiding an old man's face. You are too old a man for this fight, Brother I, too old, too slow, too—"

No one heard Shariq's last insult.

One moment they saw Shariq high-strutting at Brother I—Glock on his leg, rifle in his fist, toe-to-neck in body armor—dissing the shit out of him. The next, he had an old-fashioned, old-man's switchblade protruding from his throat like he'd grown a second sharp tongue with a mother-of-pearl handle.

The knife was out before his knees buckled him to the floor.

The man they knew as Brother I wiped his blade on the fallen man's vest.

"Brothers," he said, "get in the boat."

22

MV *Miss Josephine of Blytheville*

Day 34
Monday

Captain Ike Edwards—master of the long-haul towboat *Miss Josephine of Blytheville*— felt like a prisoner set free when he pushed fifteen super jumbo hopper barges out of the Chain of Rocks Canal six miles north of St. Louis. The dams and locks that made the steeply descending Upper Mississippi River navigable ("Schedule-screwing, pain-in-the-butt water elevators," Ike called them) were behind him at last, good fucking riddance.

The Middle and Lower Mississippi River flowed along flat land and didn't need locks. *Miss Josephine of Blytheville* would stop only once between here and the Gulf of Mexico to pick up fifteen more super jumbos at a staging area a few miles below St. Louis. From there to the Gulf, the unimpeded river could accommodate his entire 45,000-ton fleet (which happened to be carrying, Ike would tell anyone who would listen, more gravel and grain than a freight train six miles long, or thirty miles of trucks in a row) without having to break it up into smaller units to descend locks.

But first, they had to get past St. Louis.

Seven bridges crossed the river on an obstacle course of piers and archways. Each of *Miss Josephine's* barges was nearly as long as the distance between home plate and the outfield fences. When they were cabled together in a fleet five barges long and three wide, it felt like steering the entire ballpark.

The earliest hint of trouble was a strange buzz on the radio, jamming the signals.

"Shit," said Captain Ike. But it was no big deal. The radio would kick back in a minute or two. They were well underway. He'd already spoken with all the boats nearby, and he could see everything ahead on the AIS. Behind him was a "poison fleet" of ammonia barges, her captain hanging back to give him time to pull ahead.

Ike Edwards envied the poison captain's extra pay. The ammonia captain had to be hauling down five hundred a day, easy, maybe more. On the radio he had sounded like a ninety-year-old geezer. Trouble was, management liked geezers running their red-flag boats more than hard-working, hard-driving young fellows like Ike Edwards—trusted cautious geezers to be safer. Just wait 'til that geezer got hisself a heart attack one night while flanking down a chute; fall dead on the steering bars, tear the hulls open on the revetment, and spill ammonia clouds across fourteen counties and two states.

He checked again that the geezer was still laying back where he belonged and got a surprise. The radar showed a boat pulling alongside, flying fast—a little guy he couldn't see out the window. He craned his neck, but still couldn't see his lights.

Ike Edwards could not abide anything moving around him that he couldn't see. He called his mate on the handheld radio, to tell him eyeball that little son of a bitch. The handheld was jammed too.

"Shee-it!" He was puzzled by the continued radio failure, but more concerned that some damned fool was ranging alongside on too many six packs to know he was in danger. Shouldn't be out here in the first place, not at night with rain coming down like sheet steel and the river blasting along at damned near flood stage. He telephoned down to the galley two decks below to roust out the boys drinking coffee. "Git on deck. Check out the right side 'fore we run down some damned drunk."

He flipped on a search light. "*Damn!*" There he was, a black rubber skiff with a bunch onboard, coming in fast at an angle that was going to slam him right against *Miss Josephine's* steel hull. Ike let loose a deck-shaking bellow on the air horns to warn him off, then lost sight of the skiff as it slipped under where he could see.

"*Shit.*"

He turned on the make-up lights—the deck floods—so his crew could see any drunks thrown in the water. Might get lucky and pull one or two out. He was not expecting gunfire and when he heard the sharp reports he thought, *Goddamn.* Cables were popping, the tow was breaking up, and he'd be chasing loose barges all the way to St. Louis.

Then his work lights went out in showers of white sparks. It dawned on him that he still didn't know what was going on, but he had more trouble on his hands than trying to keep fifteen barges in the channel while not running down drunks.

Boots pounded up the stairs. More shots. A frightened yell. Sounded like the cook. A black-clad commando pushed open the wheelhouse door.

The towboat captain took him in in a swift glance. Masked. Flak vest. More guns and knives than the Tulsa Arms Show.

The commando shoved an automatic rifle with duct-taped double banana clips in Ike Edwards's face and said, "Don't touch a thing."

A man who had earned the right to be master of a nine thousand horsepower towboat pushing forty-five thousand tons of corn and sand on a river famous for destruction neither panicked nor frightened easily. Ike Edwards replied in the same calm, clear voice he would use to straighten out a deckhand.

"You bet, mister. Only if I don't touch anything, we are going to crash into an upbound tow, or a bridge pier, or a flood wall, or a levee—whichever comes first."

The commando said, "Now wouldn't that be a shame."

The towboat captain still didn't know what was going on. But if the hijacker didn't care what they ran into then it had to be a terrorist attack. Which meant this was going to get a lot worse than anyone could guess. Ike looked into the brown eyes peering through the ski mask, saw a sliver of dark skin, and thought to himself, Sonuvabitch is a nigger.

Drilled and disciplined, the Forty Acres Martyr Brigade took control of the wheelhouse and the engine room. They forced the crew at gunpoint to hoist the skiff up on deck. Within minutes of boarding, the fleet was theirs.

Five stories high in the wheelhouse, Abdul Muqtadir could see night-shrouded land to either side of the levees. Downriver gleamed St. Louis's Gateway Arch, the city's skyscrapers, and necklaces of bridge lights. Floodlights illuminated the fan-like pattern of the cables that supported the first bridge, the Stan Musial Veterans Memorial, a modern cable-stayed span. It presented little to run into as its pylons were so widely separated. But below the "Stan Span," the older bridges squeezed the channel with many piers.

Brother Naib ran up and reported they had nine crew handcuffed together in the lounge. "This dude makes ten," said Abdul, indicating the captain, whom he had permitted back at the sticks so he could control the direction of the tow. Brother I had told him eleven. "We're missing one. Find him before he calls the cops."

***

Rolly Winters and Duvall McCoy wrapped up a long and very fruitful day by buying drinks for a St. Louis police detective who had been generous with his informants. They hadn't found the Weatherman yet, but the white supremacist was no longer a needle in a haystack, having "gone to ground, big-time," as Duvall put it, in an abandoned missile silo somewhere on the Great Plains. There were probably a thousand of them scattered over many states, but Rolly considered it a big step in an intriguing direction. As always-hopeful Duvall put it, the tale was too weird to make up, and the informant had no reason to lie about Jack Payne shopping for empty underground silos before he disappeared.

Which raised fascinating questions: who gave him the dough to buy the thing and a lot more dough to renovate a hundred-foot hole in the ground into livable space? And what was the Weatherman doing down there? And why did whatever he was doing down there make him think it was a good idea to clamp an exploding monitor on his bitch's ankle? The detectives had left phone and email messages with real estate brokers they found on the internet who specialized in selling abandoned silos and with contractors who remodeled them into survivalist hideouts. Not surprisingly, none of these types picked up their phone on the first ring. A couple of hobbyists had websites, laying out in detail how they were fixing up theirs. So far, they hadn't called back either. Out at Home Depot, Duvall speculated.

The bar the detective had led them to was on the excursion steamboat *Rose of St. Louis,* a fading tourist trap tied to the landing below the Gateway Arch. Rain splashed the windows. Lights across the river in East St. Louis smeared red, green, blue, and white reflections on black water. Happy Hour started early and ended late, but they had the *Rose* to themselves. The cocktail waitress explained that the *Abraham Lincoln,* a new luxury passenger boat, and the *Stonewall Jackson* casino boat were docked at the long landing, too, siphoning off any customers who had braved the weather.

The St. Louis detective left with the waitress—she being the reason why, Rolly had already figured out, he had chosen the unlikely venue in the first place. Blind tired, he signaled the bartender for more beers. Loosen up for the night, Uber back to their hotel, and drive home to Bliss early in the morning. The silo hunt would continue as a computer job done at the office in between regular work. Except neither detective was ready to let it go, even if it meant repeating what they'd been asking all afternoon.

"We're talking about Jack Payne buying an empty hole in the ground."

"Deep hole," said Duvall. "First thing he'd need is an elevator."

"Plumbing and electricity before he could even start to make a place you'd want to live in."

Duvall said, "Maybe the Weatherman bought one with the nuclear rocket still inside it. Sold it to North Korea for the dough to install his elevator."

"Somebody gave him the money."

"What would the somebody get out of that?"

Rolly shrugged. "Free weather forecasts."

"Cheaper to watch the Weather Channel."

"Or check it out online."

Duvall said, "So what else does the somebody get for his money?"

"A guy who blows stuff up?"

"We got a million army vets who know how to blow stuff up a lot cheaper than buying a silo. You think maybe his bitch gave him the money . . . Except where would the bitch get the money?"

"Whoever paid for the silo must have written the government a check."

"Except we found that one real estate guy who sounded like he bought a bunch to flip."

Both detectives checked their phones for messages. Nothing yet.

Rolly hit a number in his contacts.

"Who you calling?"

"Clem Price."

"Right." They had heard that the Army Corps of Engineers had supervised the deactivations.

Clem answered, sounding totally wired. "Hey, Rol. Libby said you're in St. Louis."

Rolly made it quick. "Duvall and I are tracing a lamster in a converted ICBM missile silo. Would you happen to know any Corps officers who deactivated the old ones?"

Clem said, "Let me touch base with a couple of people. I'll call you back."

Duvall asked him, "She's going to get back to you in the middle of a flood?"

"She does what she says. You hungry?"

The menu was printed in a microscopic script, in keeping with the Rose of St. Louis's "Lost Nineteenth Century Riverboat Elegance" theme. Rolly put on his reading glasses, decided to believe that the "Down Home

Fresh Catfish Fry" had not arrived frozen on a truck, and passed his glasses to Duvall.

Duvall studied the menu top to bottom, returned Rolly's glasses, and pulled a baggie of peanuts from his pocket. The bartender came over to tell them they couldn't bring their own food. A cautionary glance from the huge guy and fire in the eye of the slightly smaller guy put him in mind of a drug enforcer and his pit bull.

"I'll bring you gentlemen a bowl."

***

Deckhand Tom Parker had hidden himself on *Miss Josephine of Blytheville's* starboard lead barge so he could have a private conversation with his girlfriend on his cell phone. Conversation hell, he thought miserably. It was a fight that had been going on too long.

It all had to do with work. The money was good, but you might as well be on a ship in the middle of the ocean for all the time you got ashore.

"Hon," he finally got a word in. "We fought like cats and dogs the whole two weeks I was home. Now you're bawling that I'm not home."

"I miss you," she wailed. "I hate you going off like this. A month. I don't know anybody but me that would put up with a boyfriend that leaves for a whole month."

"I gotta make a living."

"But you're so ornery when you come home."

"I'm *tired* when I come home. I been busting hump for thirty, forty days. Six hours on, six off, I don't get no sleep. Then they throw in overtime. I finally get home, I gotta to catch up on some sleep and get a drink, and all you want to do is drag me to the mall with your girlfriends. Goddamn, Mary Lou, can't you go to the mall when I'm on the boat? Then you and I could get some sleep and go out and party."

She put soft tones in her voice. "I take you to the mall to show you off, hon."

"I sleep maybe four hours a day. I want to get some sleep."

"Sleep?" The soft tones were gone, and so was the wailing. She was full bent screaming. "Sleep? All you want to do is fuck."

"Yeah, well that's the other thing we don't get much of out here—hold on. Something's up—just hold on a second. I'll call you right back." He thought he'd heard someone shooting, which obviously couldn't be. But it started up again. Maybe one of the guys looking for him, stomping around the gravel, sounded like shooting. He climbed up and looked back. The gravel humped on the barges stretched like a chain of identical hills for a quarter mile back to the boat. He saw a man coming forward with a flashlight. A string of vehicle headlights on the Missouri bank silhouetted him for a second. Billy saw the rifle slung over his back and realized that what sounded like shooting probably was.

His cell phone shrilled in his hand. "Mary Lou, I can't talk now." He cut her off and punched 911.

***

Both the St. Louis Metropolitan Police Department and the United States Coast Guard had invested Department of Homeland Security funds in high-speed attack boats that were faster and more heavily armed than the hijackers'. The Coast Guard even had a machine gun mounted on their bow. It was manned by a gray-haired war veteran who had survived a year of his youth in Iraq defending the Khawr Al Amaya offshore oil terminal from waterborne attack.

But the fighters who had hidden themselves on the towboat and the barges had the overwhelming advantage of firing down at the police and Coast Guard boats from a stable platform. And the Coast Guard and police gunners bouncing around on river turbulence were under strict orders not to disable the towboat until they had rounded up enough powerful tugs and towboats to stop the fleet from drifting out of control on the six-knot current. This was not proving easy on short notice. Nearby boats had to disengage from their own tows and secure them before they could help. Boats in the marinas were either unmanned or had their machinery in pieces while undergoing repairs.

The police and Coast Guard attempted to board *Miss Josephine of Blytheville.* The plan—radioed in shouts, warnings, orders, and screams—was to storm the wheelhouse, kill whoever had hijacked the nine-thousand-horsepower, 130-foot-long, forty-foot-wide towboat, and put a man on the sticks capable of steering fifteen super jumbo barges through the narrow channel under six bridges that spanned the flood-swollen river between St. Louis, Missouri, and East St. Louis, Illinois. Accurate gunfire drove them back, their boats burning and sinking.

Police marksmen swarmed over the ancient girders of the Merchants Railroad Bridge. But they were too late. The hijacked tow was already under it and gone. The barges passed under the McKinley Highway and Railroad Bridge a mile and a quarter downstream. Sharpshooters on it, who had to rake the darkened tow from behind, claimed to hit at least one hijacker.

Two miles ahead of the hijacked fleet lay the heart of St. Louis with the Gateway Arch soaring into the clouds and the city's tourist and gambling boats moored at its feet.

Defying the rain, a former Air Force Pave Hawk pilot who now flew for the aviation unit of the St. Louis County Police managed to get a helicopter aloft. Compared to the medium-lift Sikorsky he had flown for combat rescue, it was like riding a bicycle instead of a tank, and at this moment he missed his tank very much. His passengers, a four-man squad who'd been about to break down a drug dealer's back door when the call came, were more afraid of the flight than the gunfight they were headed for. The pilot, who was using skills he had forgotten to keep the craft airborne, feared crashing into the Arch. It was with great relief that he located the Mississippi River—a fat black line between the rain-defused glow of city lights—and oriented himself by the Eads and Poplar Street bridges bracketing the north and south legs of the Arch.

The dispatcher droned in his headset, telling him that whatever he saw moving had to be the hijacker because everything else had been directed ashore. A second later she amended that: there might be other craft still on the river including police launches. Then she came back and warned the police pilot that the Coast Guard had boats engaged, too. The pilot spotted a fleet of hopper barges—five barges long and three wide—pushed by a white towboat.

That was nobody's launch. It was bearing down on the Martin Luther King Bridge, the first of the two bridges that anchored the northern, upstream boundary of Gateway Arch Park. His passengers agreed in a hurried radio-headset huddle that their best bet was to drop onto the barges and fight their way back to the towboat. But skill and bravery had its limits, which were tested when a rifleman hidden on the barges sent three rounds in one side of the thin-skinned helicopter and out the other. More bullets rattling the rotors made believers of them all, and they veered away.

A SWAT sergeant, who had raced to the King bridge with a nylon rope when he caught a heads-up text on his way home from work, took advantage of the helicopter distraction to rappel down from the bridge. The last barges were passing under him. Forty feet down the rope, the SWAT sergeant dropped onto the roof of the towboat pilot house and blasted away with the only weapons he had with him, his nine and his ankle gun, a reliable little thirty-two his father had given him for his birthday. The armed men in night vision goggles were wearing body armor, he discovered, when bullets to their chests had no effect. He felled a hijacker with a head shot before he was cornered by the rest.

With nothing to lose, he jumped ten feet to the Texas deck roof and pegged his last shot at the center window in the wheelhouse. Glass flew, peppering Abdul Muqtadir who had just steered left toward the East St. Louis shore intending to blast a huge floating dry dock loose from its mooring. He fell back in the pilot's chair, pawing his face, terrified he'd been blinded. Blood was stinging his eyes.

"*Water!*"

It worked. He could see again. But in those moments, he had lost control of the fleet. He was fully aware that he was not an actual Mississippi River pilot—no master of the river's thousand secrets—but he was one hot boat handler. He had learned the skills and instincts while recovering from wounds in Kuwait as an inland waterway "army mariner," driving pusher tugs in the Port of Shuaybah. Fighting now to regain control before he crashed into an Eads Bridge pier, he gave up on the dry dock and veered toward his primary targets on the St. Louis side.

***

Rolly Winters's cell vibrated. He grabbed it, telling Duvall, "Silo or Libby."

Silo. Clementine Price apologizing. "Sorry, Rol. The Corps left nothing to convert. We deactivated silos for the START treaty. Pulled the launcher closure doors, buried them nine feet deep, and capped ventilator and elevator shafts with concrete, like the treaty called for."

Call-waiting beeped. It IDed the detective who had left with the waitress.

"Clem, what about the silos themselves?"

"Filled the shafts with dirt and gravel, per the treaty—Rol, I gotta go."

"You filled *all* of the shafts?"

"We worked mostly on military bases. You could focus on off-base sites."

He said to her, "Thank you, Clementine, thank you very much," and to the St. Louis detective, "Yo, my man, what's up?"

"*Get off that boat right now!* There're runaway barges coming down the river."

Rolly and Duvall herded the bartender, a cook, a busboy, and the boat's engineer down the gangway. The second they set foot on the Arch landing they saw barge lights bearing down on the Eads Bridge. The tow was veering right, toward the St. Louis side, and it looked like it was on a collision course with the bridge pier nearest the bank. But instead, the massive fleet brushed past on the inside and aimed square at the first of the riverboats tied to the landing—*Rose of St. Louis.*

The lead barges rammed into the *Rose* with a force that parted all the sternwheeler's mooring cables. Rolly and Duvall dragged the others down on the cobblestones and covered their heads as broken mooring wire flew through the air, shrieking like shrapnel.

***

From high up in *Miss Josephine's* wheelhouse, Abdul Muqtadir saw the big riverboat swing broadside to the powerful current. Listing sharply from water pouring through holes stove in her hull, she was swept downriver.

Yards ahead of the tow was a museum barge, a converted 300-foot jumbo. The lead barges hit it with a bell-like *clang*, sending it too into the current. With 25,000 tons of corn, sand, and gravel providing momentum, the hijacked fleet had barely slowed, and *Miss Josephine of Blytheville*'s propellers were still churning Full Ahead.

The barges swept the St. Louis river front like a giant plow scattering snowdrifts. They tore the remaining riverboat restaurants, bars, and museums from their moorings and thrust them adrift on the Mississippi. The last boat set loose was the towering *Abraham Lincoln.*

The Poplar Street Bridge, which carried Interstate 55 between the cities, spanned the river immediately downriver. The first boat broken loose—*Rose of St. Louis*—continued taking on water as it drifted downriver, and its main deck was submerged when it struck a pier of the Poplar Street Bridge sideways. The current held it in stasis, even as her hull buckled open and she sank to the bottom, leaving only her top deck and her immense fake smokestacks exposed. Into that deck slid the museum barge and the replica sternwheeler *Stonewall Jackson.* The pile-up waited for the *Abraham Lincoln* like a giant's catcher's mitt.

The palatial riverboat, drifting out of control—and riding almost too tall already to fit under the bridge—ramped up on the piled wreckage. Lifted that extra two feet, her smokestacks slammed into the bridge deck with a screech of twisting metal, their ornamental funnel mouths toppled onto the highway in the path of an SUV that veered into a semi, which jack-knifed, blocking all three city-bound lanes.

Her stacks were not fakes, and they did not shear, but merely bent, jammed under the deck of the bridge, holding the front end of the boat in place and allowing the current to whip the back around against the pier closest to the St. Louis side. The floodwater impounded by this sudden obstruction formed a wave that lifted her yet higher and the *Abraham Lincoln's* top deck wedged under the Poplar Street Bridge with a rumble heard across the city.

Miss Josephine of Blytheville swept by, her lead barges sinking as river water poured through the holes punched in their hulls. Police boats converged like sharks on a blue whale. The towboat backed its engines full astern, flanking, chewing up ten-foot waves that overturned the police boats. The reversing action caused the towboat and barges to swing sideways to the current. The sinking lead barges struck the stone piers of the Douglas MacArthur Bridge. The steel cables binding the barges together parted with explosive retorts. Loose wire screamed through the air. No longer supported by the rest of the fleet, the lead coal barges sank. The current scattered the rest. Two, still tangled in wire, crushed a Coast Guard launch steaming upriver with lights flashing and sirens blaring.

Fuel oil in the wreckage began to burn.

Miss Josephine of Blytheville stormed into the dark.

When Abdul Muqtadir looked back, the entire bridge was on fire. He wished to God he managed to hit the floating dry dock and pile it on, too. He consoled himself by imagining how many lost boys of East St. Louis were watching the flames light the rainy sky in his wake, and for this moment, at least, the Forty Acres Martyr Brigade was no longer fighting a lonely battle.

***

Nathan Flowers sipped a Coke in a Cheers airport tavern and watched the fire on CNN. In his gray business suit with his shirt collar open and a folded necktie dangling from his pocket he looked at home among the tired businessmen and weary manufacturers' reps toughing out the delays caused by heavy weather and lock-down security. But unlike his fellow travelers, who were riveted by the burning Poplar Street Bridge, the live interviews, and the repeated replays of earlier video, he was paying closer attention to the weather crawl. Tornadoes. More rain. Thunderstorms.

He looked at the others in the bar wondered, *What do you see when you look at me? Could you ever imagine?*

He looked back at the screen. The reporter was interviewing a cop who looked exactly like Brother Shariq, right down to the Al Sharpton finger poking the air like a bird bill.

Reporters kept repeating that the wreckage would break up at any minute, float away, and sink, extinguishing the flames. They interviewed firefighters who explained that as the flames consumed the boats and barges, the pile-up would grow smaller and shorter and slip out from under of the bridge. Nathan Flowers knew better; the fire grew so intense it melted steel. The effect was as if welders had fastened the disparate parts into one huge, red-hot dam.

The woman who commanded the St. Louis Coast Guard District explained her priorities to the reporters. While her sailors were helping law enforcement track down the hijacked towboat on the fog-bound river, the Coast Guard's first responsibility was to keep the channel open, which meant preventing the interstate bridge from falling in and blocking it, which meant fighting the fire with every boat she and the St. Louis Fire Department could muster. Yes, it certainly did look like a terrorist attack. Who else would deliberately ram a fleet of barges into a row of riverboats? Law enforcement was tracking the terrorists full-time.

Flowers's spirit kept rising. Every face in the Cheers looked grim. The weather crawl reported severe thunderstorm and tornado warnings for Iowa and Wisconsin. He covered his mouth to hide a smile when a funny thought struck him: it definitely looked like God was on his side.

His flight was finally called. National Guard troops were patrolling the airport corridors with assault weapons. He looked each soldier in the eye and gave a colonel's nod. Good job, son.

Security got tighter at the gate. Every passenger was frisked and wanded, every bag searched. A frail, middle-aged Arab American was escorted away. Flowers passed that gauntlet. But after he boarded, TSA agents came down the aisle, staring into every face. He watched them with an expression of mild curiosity. They stopped at his row, ordered the Hispanic sitting next to him out of his seat and marched him off. When the plane was finally airborne, hours late, he could see the fire casting an orange halo over the city.

The TVs in the airport where he disembarked reported that the Mississippi River had continued rising at St. Louis, fed by the late spring thunderstorms and cloudbursts that continued to lash the upper Midwest. Air trapped in the wrecked boats had kept them afloat. Now rising water lifted the wreckage hard against the undersides of the road decks.

He rented a motel room in the hills outside Rolla, Missouri, paying cash, and turned on the television. A local tragedy took precedence—an elderly couple had drowned trying to save their chicken flock from a flash flood. When they cut to St. Louis, the wreckage was still burning. The Missouri side of the Poplar Street Bridge would have to be torn down and rebuilt before the highway could be used again. The city's exhausted Mayor Killing said that commuters were facing years of traffic nightmares.

The White House issued a statement consoling the families of the dead and injured, thanking God and the quick actions of the St. Louis first responders that the death toll was not higher, and promising that a thorough investigation conducted by the Department of Homeland Security was already underway. The DHS Secretary opened a dead-of-night news conference upon arriving at St. Louis airport with his own questions: "Was it terrorists? We don't know, yet. Who else would do such a thing? If they were criminals, not terrorists, what did they want? We don't know yet."

A reporter shouted, "Reports indicate they were black."

"We don't know that."

"African Americans? Black Muslims?"

"We don't know."

"Are we talking about Muslim terrorists?"

"We don't know."

"Or are they just anti-white?"

"We don't know. We haven't caught any of them yet."

When the secretary was done talking, the reporters found no shortage of angry politicians who denounced the "vicious terrorist attack." Soon a spokeswoman for the DHS director assured reporters that the director, too, considered the attack on St. Louis a vicious terrorist attack.

"Black or Muslim?"

"We don't know."

Nathan Flowers turned off the TV and placed a burner cellphone on the night table.

The Republic of Alluvia maintained a huge advantage over the enemy. Homeland Security and the FBI and the CIA were obsessed with foreign terrorists. But Alluvia men were not terrorists and sure as hell weren't foreigners. They were builders.

Homeland Security's Countering-Violent-Extremism system focused on radical Islam, even though the savvier law enforcement agencies knew that United States citizens—militias, racist skinheads, neo-Nazis—were the real terrorist threat. But no one listened to the savvier agencies, and Alluvia wasn't even on their radar. Homeland Security was trying to prevent random attacks against innocent civilians. Let them. Alluvia had no interest in random attacks. None in violence without purpose.

Like his colonel-nods to the young soldiers—Good job.

A successful dry run. A feint to confuse. And a distraction—scapegoats who would draw self-righteous prosecutors like maggots to meat gone bad. How long before government agents were breaking down doors?

The burner pinged a text from Cedric Colson. "Heard about St. L. Hope you're safe." Which was code to ring Colson's burner. He did.

Colson yelled, "They beat us to it."

"No one beat us to anything."

"The blacks hit St. Louis before you even got started."

"They were *our* blacks. Why the emergency call? What's up?"

"*What's up?* You said you would need me every hour every day. I haven't heard a thing since we were at Pete Fleming's. Now you say we attacked St. Louis. Why don't you tell *me* what's up."

Flowers almost laughed. Once again, everyday craziness reared its head. With a flood about to split the continent and forge the American heartland into a powerful new nation, Cedric Colson had had his feelings hurt.

"Here's what's up. Four major attacks coordinated in rapid succession. You are watching the first on CNN. The second, far more consequential, will hit a hundred miles downriver. For our third and fourth attacks, we will strike further downriver on the fifth day. Eight hundred miles apart. Simultaneously."

"Where?

"You'll know when the targets are hit. Meantime, I do need you. Go to Washington."

"Washington? What for?"

"Alluvia needs her ambassador in Washington, DC, when our enemy sues for peace."

Flowers turned off the phone and closed his eyes. They will look back and kick themselves, he thought. *Why didn't we see it coming?*

"You can't see me coming," he whispered. "I have the greatest advantage of all. I am doing the unthinkable."

23

Jumped from Behind

Day 35
Tuesday

"You have a visitor, Major," whispered Clementine Price's adjutant.

Rushing into her Memphis District headquarters, mind reeling from the St. Louis reports, Clementine blanked completely at the sight of a lieutenant colonel seated in her office. He stood up and greeted her with a nervous smile. She had known him well, years ago, but his presence was so out of context that it took her a moment to place him.

"Tommy Chow? Where did you come from?"

"I just want you to know, this isn't my idea."

Chow had been Robert's adjutant when she first met them on The Boat. They had worked together three years before he transferred out. He was smart and a decent guy despite being an unabashed careerist. Last she had heard he was in Washington, vaulting rungs in the Army Office of Business Transformation.

"What do you mean?" she asked, even as the meaning of his presence struck with awful clarity.

"I mean my kids are finally happy in school, and my wife is finally happy in her latest new job, and the last thing I wanted was to get transferred back to fucking Memphis, excuse my French."

"As what?" she asked and held her breath.

"Co-Acting District Commanding Officer."

"Co? But you're senior to me."

"Captain Standfast informed me, quote, 'General Penn hopes that you and Major Price can work it out.' Which sounds to me like a direct order, with Penn-to-grams to follow."

"Jesus H., Tommy, we're bracing for a project flood."

"And God-knows-what from the St. Louis terrorists. I'll stay out of your way while I get up to speed."

Clementine Price wanted to close her office door and try to think up solutions. But whose office was it? Instead, she placed her hands on his shoulders and gave him an arms-length hug. "Oh, Tommy you look as miserable as I feel. I know it's not your fault. There's unbelievable stuff going down."

Lieutenant Harpur rushed in with a phone. "General Penn, Major."

Clementine Price took the phone and a deep breath. "Good morning, sir."

"Major Price, I want you to get up to St. Louis ASAP. You will assist Colonel Garcia in his capacity as wreck master."

"Yes, sir. In St. Louis? Colonel Garcia, sir? St. Louis?"

"That's where the wreckage is, young lady, and it's making a killer dam out of the Poplar Street Bridge. Captain Standfast reminded me that you and Colonel Garcia did a heck of a job last winter untangling the Memphis barge pile-up before it could take out the Harahan Bridge. Margaret—Captain Standfast—further reminded me that our St. Louis district commander Colonel Hardy is from New York City and served mostly in Europe. He wouldn't know a barge pile-up if his mother was part of it."

"Yes, sir."

"And tell Colonel Chow I expect him to cover for you while you're gone."

"Yes, sir."

"Make haste. There's not a moment to lose."

She told Tommy Chow what the general ordered and said, "I have to make a call before I fly to St. Louis." He took the hint, left the office, and closed the door behind him. Clementine telephoned a longtime colleague at Engineer Research and Development—an Army Corps officer who had in his youth pioneered new methods of anti-tank ditching.

"ERDC. Major Rubenoff speaking. How may I help you?" The demolition genius had helped her with an innovative design for the Birds Point fuse plug, riddling the levee with a precisely laid mile of polyethylene piping. Liquid explosives pumped into the pipes from barges would blow it open to release water into the floodway—without the excessive damage and huge rebuilding expenses suffered the last time it was demolished.

"Andy, it's Clementine. I just got off the phone with General Penn. The general pointed out that our Birds Point Fuse Plug Levee might take its own sweet time eroding if we get to project flood."

"He finally figured that out?"

"I heard him with my own ears."

"Does that mean we can load the pipes to blow the sucker?"

Clementine chose her words as carefully as Andy selected blasting agents. "General Penn did not authorize pumping, yet. But I'm thinking we should move the explosives nearer than Memphis in the event he decides to."

"Couldn't agree more. A lot nearer."

"Can you ship four barge loads to Caruthersville Harbor?"

"Long as the Coast Guard doesn't shut the river."

"Charter the fastest towboat you can, my friend. As the general said to me in a slightly different but related context, 'There isn't a moment to lose.'"

Now, if they had to blow the levee to relieve flood pressure on Cairo, Caruthersville, and Bliss, she could deliver the explosives in sixteen hours, a lot faster than a full day and a half. General Penn hadn't precisely ordered it, of course. But even with Tommy Chow sharing her office, she got off the phone feeling back in control of her district.

***

"There are no direct flights from Memphis to St. Louis, Major," reported Lieutenant Harpur, who was simultaneously searching travel sites and transcribing phone messages.

"I know that," snapped Clementine, scrolling through her phone to see which of today's appointments Harpur could cancel and which required a personal call from her. There was a text from Mary Kay with Uncle Chance's cell phone number, and one from Libby reporting that Rolly and Duvall were safe in St. Louis but stuck there with the city in lockdown.

"You'll have to fly to Dallas, layover for ninety minutes, and then fly to Lambert Field, an hour's drive to downtown St. Louis. You could be there in about six hours."

"Screw that," said Clementine. "I'll fly myself."

Snoopy could make it from DeWitt Spain general aviation airport to Birds Point in ninety minutes, where she could check out the fuse plug levee. From there, an hour crow's flight would get her to St. Louis's Downtown Airport—a six- or eight-minute taxi ride to the Poplar Street Bridge if the roads weren't blocked. She packed her running shoes in case those last four miles required making haste for General Penn on foot.

While she warmed the Air Tractor's engine, she plugged in her flight helmet Bluetooth and telephoned New Orleans District headquarters. Robert's deputy told her that he was already on a Southwest Airlines nonstop to St. Louis. He'd be waiting for her. She'd been dying to see him again, she thought with a grin. Not quite like this, but don't look a gift horse in the mouth.

She brought up a sectional chart on her iPad and checked for TV and radio towers, power lines, and water tanks. She knew the route by heart between Memphis and Cairo, and had flown upriver to St. Louis often, but she studied the sectional methodically. As always, she could hear in her head Uncle Chance warning that the obstruction a pilot failed to see was the one that did the killing.

Her weather app promised no thunderstorms—diminishing the likelihood of turbulence and wind shear—and three miles visibility. Rain showers would reduce that to a mile through the windshield. But staying well under twelve hundred feet to get double duty out of the trip by eyeballing her district's levees, she would encounter no aircraft flying much faster than her 120 mph. They'd have time to see and avoid each other.

She had to wait for an enormous airliner-size Embraer Lineage 1000 private jet to land. Then her turboprop was winding up with a rumbly growl and the runway was racing under the Air Tractor's big yellow wings. The nine-foot propeller whipped her airborne like a slingshot, and another grin tugged her lips despite the turmoil in her mind.

She followed the river north. Sensitive to the controls and in tune with the ship, she held one hand light on the control stick, her lanky frame draped in the cockpit with such fluid grace as if to appear almost languid. But her eyes were on the move, scanning the sky for weather and other craft, her instrument gauges for trouble, and the ground below for roads to land on in an emergency.

Bliss's steeples and downtown buildings raised their snaggletooth profile twenty-five minutes after she took off from Memphis. She altered course to the northwest over the flatlands of the St. Francis Basin. The Mississippi River, which veered northeast from the city, slipped off to her right. At the Missouri border, she would turn back to the river as was her habit when flying to Birds Point.

"What am I doing?" she asked aloud.

Hadn't she exorcised her Hilltop demons Sunday? And again yesterday, in the Flowers' parsonage? Hadn't the three-star general of the division just ordered not a moment to lose? Why couldn't she fly up the river and over the ghost of Tomato like any normal pilot?

She banked to the right, crossed over the city and the interstate connector bridge, and followed the straight chutes up the middle of the Bliss

Bends for the first time in ten years. When she saw a bunch of white pickup trucks on the levee she telephoned. "Good morning, Jesse. I thought that was you down there. How are you today?"

Jesse Corliss gave her a wave toward the sky. "Good morning, Major. Just fine. How are you?"

Had Jesse already caught wind of the sudden return of Lieutenant Colonel Chow? She stifled her impulse to admit to feeling extremely paranoid that General Penn was getting her out of his hair before she complained any more about what she had come to think of as the "Bliss Floodway."

"I'm 'just fine,' too, thank you, Jess. How's our levee?"

"Looks strong, so far, Major. More than holding its own. Where you headed?"

"St. Louis."

"What a mess."

"Drive on."

"You bet, Major. Drive on."

Ahead glowed Hilltop's golden dove. Part of her wanted to drop Snoopy's nose to a hundred feet, skim the baptismal lake, throttle up the engine, and buzz the damned steeple with a full-throated bellow. Another impulse best stifled. Then Clementine's mind played a funny trick. She was suddenly back inside Hilltop's Sanctuary, gripping the pulpit, feeling the eyes of six thousand people and hearing her own voice repeated by the microphone.

"Some of you may know that this is not my first visit to this place. I actually grew up on this very spot, in a little town called Tomato, which was swept away by the flood of 2008."

Six thousand people stared. She felt her face flush, felt the heat. Her heart raced. She ran out of words, and she heard Robert say, ever so gently, as he had on The Boat, "You have more reason than most to fear the flood." She was breathing hard, struggling to get air. The parishioner's faces turned black and she was in the old bookstore New Salvation Baptist Church pleading, "Be ready! Be ready to leave, and don't look back until you're safe."

The stall warning horn blared, shocking her back inside the airplane.

Her eyes swept her instruments.

Air Speed indicator 70 mph. Altimeter seven hundred feet and twirling down.

"Oh shit!" were the commonest last words heard on black box recordings of doomed aircraft.

24

The Skidding Turn

Day 35
Tuesday

If the plane slowed any more, she would lose control and Snoopy would fall out of the sky like a sandbag.

Where was the steeple? There! Ninety degrees right.

She had somehow put the plane into a skidding turn. She wasn't even aware she had turned at all, but somehow something in her had shoved the control stick and stomped the rudder pedals. Heavy hands and clumsy feet threw the plane into too tight a turn, so tight that it was skidding in on itself. The plane was stalling, its wing on the inside of the turn starved of the airflow needed to lift it. The thousand thoughts speeding through Clementine's mind fixed on one truth—half her airplane was no longer a flying machine, and both halves were starting to spin. Barely six hundred feet above the ground now, she would never recover from a spin before Snoopy smashed a nose first crater in the mud.

"*Never try to climb when you fall!*"

That was Uncle Chance drilling it into her for months before he let her touch the control stick. "Go down when you're going down."

It was the hardest thing for a pilot to remember. And, based on the body count, often impossible. Against all gut instinct to try to climb, in a stall you had to point the nose down.

"Some rich businessman at eight thousand feet, he's got time to sort himself out. Spraying, we got no time. Go down, Clementine. *Fall.* Fall faster. *Faster!*" Shaking her awake in the middle of the night, her mother watching anxiously over his shoulder, Chance telling her mother, "This child is not going to die because I didn't teach her right," then whirling back to her.

"You're stallin' you're fallin'! What do you do?"

"Go down, Uncle Chance."

"How?"

"Push the stick to release the backpressure."

"Good girl!"

She had pushed the stick without even thinking about it the instant she saw catastrophe in the altimeter. The Air Tractor dove, gathering speed as Clementine tried to build air under her wings in a race to fly again before she hit the ground. The crown of Hilltop's tall, new mainline levee seemed to fill the windshield. She nudged her rudder, aiming for the lower floodplain ground inside the levee, desperate to buy an extra twenty-five feet between life and death. She glimpsed the side of the levee, so close she could see blades of wet grass and rust on an access well cover.

Clementine Price felt her wings harden up. They grabbed a hold on solid air, recovered, become effective, and she gained control. She was level, flying again, flying not falling, skimming the ground as if she was spraying Roundup. She pulled back on the stick, cleared the levee, swooped over the tumbled surface of the Mississippi River, climbed back up to eight hundred feet, and filled her lungs with air.

"Thank you, Uncle Chance."

Gripping the control stick with both hands, she sucked in deep breaths to lower her heart rate. Her phone rang in her headset. She glanced at the cell in its Bluetooth bracket on the dash. Caller ID read, Hilltop. Reverend Flowers.

"My security chief just telephoned. Are you all right, Major Price?"

She tried to collect her spirit before she answered. "Good morning, Reverend."

"Major Price, are you all right?"

"Yes."

"My security chief saw a yellow plane he thought was yours almost crash on our land."

"It was mine, and I didn't crash. Thank the chief for his concern."

"Then why you were flying so low? What were you looking for?"

Looking for? I was crashing, she thought. She almost said that he was lucky she hadn't flown into his goddamned steeple. Instead: "Please convey my apologies if I frightened anyone. I've got to get off the phone, Reverend. Give my regards to Mrs. Flowers."

Flowers wouldn't let it go. "Why did you fly so low over our land? No wonder folks say the Corps acts like God Almighty."

His twenty-two thousand parishioners made him a major stakeholder in the Delta. Clementine took a deep breath and tried to put a

General-Penn-country-boy smile in her voice. "Well, you know, Reverend, folks fuss more about the Corps when the water is low than when it's rising. Thank you for calling. I do appreciate your concern. Goodbye."

What had set him off, she wondered? No matter. She had her own problems to deal with. Her heart was still pounding. *Why* had she nearly crashed her plane? At home or in her office, she would consider calling her life coach to run it by him.

Hilltop had vanished behind her. The steel mill slid under her wings. On the river, tows moved purposefully like pointing fingers, but fewer than usual. She saw a Coast Guard patrol boat, but none of the private motor yachts piloted by professional delivery captains shuttling them north for the summer. Not in flood conditions. She spotted a fleeting area, eight fleets of barges—several hundred 250-foot jumbos—moored across the river on the Tennessee bank. Sensible captains, she assumed, waiting to see what the river was planning next. Double as many as she had seen last week.

Her heart would not stop pounding. She checked her pulse: 180. She had to talk to someone to calm down. She palmed her phone and saw Mary Kay's text from this morning. She pressed the highlighted number. Uncle Chance picked up on the fourteenth ring.

"How'd you git this number, Clementine?"

"Uncle Chance, I almost died. You just saved my life."

"What are you talking about? Are you in the Air Tractor? Sounds like it."

"I lost control somehow. Stalled at seven hundred. Went down like an anvil."

"What'd you do?"

"What you taught me. Made my ship fall faster."

"Good girl."

Click.

"*Goddamn you, Uncle Chance!*"

She called Mary Kay. It went to voice mail and she left a message saying she'd spoken with Uncle Chance and thanked her. She scrolled through Favorites, desperate to connect with someone who would be happy she was alive. Not Libby, who had enough problems already on her mayoral plate. Not Robert, even if he wasn't on a plane. Whatever chances they had wouldn't be helped by a needy woman. Not Will, who shouldn't have to worry about his big sister's mental health. How about a pretend life-coaching session via imaginary Skype?

It wouldn't be her first. She had saved the army a fortune in fees. Snoopy's windshield doubled as a computer screen, and she had her make-believe Tom start with the real Tom's usual, "Good morning, Clementine. Anything you'd like to celebrate this week?"

"Well, I think I am celebrating not dying in a plane wreck of my own making."

"How did you happen to survive?"

"I put in the hours."

"I don't follow."

"I'm thirty-six years old. I learned to fly when I was fourteen. I've been flying that plane two-thirds of my entire life. So my muscles and subconscious knew what to do."

"Suggesting they chose to live?"

"Suggesting my Uncle Chance was a brilliant instructor. Or maybe I was rewarded for spending so much time in church last Sunday."

"What do you mean when you said, earlier, 'of my own making?'"

"I meant I kind of drifted into a sort of nightmare. If I didn't know better, I'd call it a kind of PTSDy kind of a thing."

"What makes you think it wasn't an actual Post Traumatic Stress Disorder episode?"

She felt herself bristle in indignation. "My friends with PTSD have every right to it with the things that happened to them in the war. I didn't suffer that kind of war."

"What goals do you want to set today?"

"I would like not to have another PTSD attack while flying my airplane. Or driving my Jeep. Or doing my job."

"How do you plan to achieve—"

"Forget it, Tom, this isn't working."

"What do you think set you off?"

"Seeing Hilltop. Right after watching the St. Louis attack on CNN. Did I mention I got stabbed in the back by General Penn?"

Imaginary Tom cut to the chase. "Is it possible that Hilltop is a 'trigger' that lights up the survival part of your brain?"

"More like a reminder."

"Of what, Clementine?"

"Of that goddamned flood."

Just before Caruthersville, halfway between Bliss and Cairo, she saw a sunshine-yellow shuttle bus parked all by itself on an empty stretch of a two-lane road on top of the levee. She descended for a close look, wondering whether it was the one Andrew Wells had told her Uncle Chance was driving. The church probably wouldn't send many so far upriver. She flew low over it. Puffs of steam from the driver side window drifted on the moist wind. It looked like whoever was inside was vaping. Chance had quit smoking decades ago. But he wouldn't be the first to give his lungs a break while re-embracing nicotine.

Yes, General Penn, I know you ordered ASAP, but all things considered this morning, I'm feeling unruly. But not so unruly that I'd want Chance Price to see me execute a sloppy landing.

She turned the plane around and descended to the levee—angling into the crosswind that she measured by the drift of the vaping steam and a lone tree bowing toward the water—touched the ground first on her upwind wheel, then her downwind wheel, then the tail. If four thousand pounds of airplane could float to the ground like a feather, then Snoopy had landed like one. She braked gently to a stop fifty feet from the bus.

It was Chance, all right, climbing down a little stiffly.

"Clementine!"

She thrilled to the old, familiar growl.

"Uncle Chance."

He looked a little older—not much, really, and quite healthy. He might be favoring his bum shoulder as if it had gone arthritic. But he did not seem diminished, as she often had wondered, by not flying. So that wasn't why he was dodging her. The anger she'd felt earlier came roaring back.

But what to say? They were staring at each other.

Chance spoke. "Heard you swapped out the radial. How's that turbo treating you?"

"Fuel costs more, maintenance less. Takes off like a rocket. And much smoother cruising. . . . Uncle Chance, why'd you disappear?"

"I don't know that I 'disappeared.'"

"No one knew where you were living. I always hoped I'd bump into you somewhere. How come I never saw you?"

"You kids had your own lives to make new. You didn't need some old relative who couldn't work anymore moving in with you, being a burden."

"I'm not 'you kids,'" she said fiercely. "I never was 'you kids' and you know it."

He looked away. Then he nodded. Her heart soared. And he said, "I know, hon. I know. You were different."

"Then why?"

He turned back to her, abruptly, eyes fixed on hers like they'd fix when he was teaching her something new. But he whispered so softly that she had to step closer to hear him. "You kids—you, especially you—reminded me too much of everything I lost."

"We all lost."

"I didn't want to be reminded. The flood took everything. And I don't mean our ground so much as how we could all live together because of the ground. You, *you,* would only have been confirmation of the . . . of the void. I could not abide it."

"But we—but I lost the farm, too, and then I lost you."

"I did not want to be reminded . . . Clementine, I am sorry."

She looked away. Another squall was churning the river, closing in on them. "I'm sorry, too," she said. It felt like he was still disappeared.

Chance said, "Why don't we get out of the rain?"

They climbed into the bus. She took the front passenger seat. He took the driver's seat and turned so he could face her. She asked, "So where did you live, before Hilltop?"

"Got me a room at the YMCA down in Vicksburg 'til they asked me to leave. Account of the drinking."

"Drinking? I never saw you drink more than half a beer."

"Never liked it. But down in Vicksburg I found I liked it. Dulled the pain. Even made me sociable. Found a friendly bar. Made friends with another drunk. A man I knew—actually, friend of your Uncle Chase. Another boat pilot. Captain Scruggs. Billy Scruggs—you might have met Billy on Chase's boat."

Clementine shook her head. "I don't remember any Captain Scruggs."

"Well, you were just a little girl then. Anyhow Billy and I were drinking buddies for a while."

"Where'd you go when they kicked you out of the Y?"

"Came back home. Up to Dell, at least. Rented a little shack from Mr. Stevenson. Helped out in his machine shop."

"Steve never told me."

"Mr. Stevenson knows how to keep a secret if he's asked."

"Were you still drinking?"

"Remember the Drift Inn, outside Dell?"

"Drove by it Thursday." A low, wood structure in a muddy parking lot notched out of a cotton field. Budweiser sailfish in the window. Tiny church across the road not much bigger than Chance's yellow bus with a sermon board that read, "I Was Guilty, But Jesus Dropped the Charges."

"I had my truck and used to meet Captain Scruggs there when he had his time off the river, starting one of his benders. Seeing the direction Billy Scruggs was headed, I commenced to thinking about my own drinking. That's when I met Mary Kay Flowers—the church had sent notice they wanted to buy my title to the patch of ground I had left in Tomato. She asked me all about myself and offered me a job driving a church bus, which came with free employee housing. I knew I couldn't drink while driving church folks, so I would have to quit. Went back to reading books; amazing how much time drinking eats up. The church has a fine library. So that's where I've settled in." He turned to look out the windshield at the Air Tractor. "I am glad you kept the plane, Clementine. . . . Where you headed? St. Louis?"

Startled, Clementine asked, "How'd you know?"

"If I had sunken barges and riverboats blocking my channel, I'd call the Army Corps gal who cleared the Harahan Bridge last winter."

"How'd you know that?"

"Read it in the paper. Watched it on the TV. Went online and downloaded the Corps report, account of you wrote it. . . . Hon, why are you crying?"

"You just made me very, very happy. Thank you."

Chance gave her the wink he used to give her when she was eight. "I admired your prose. You ever tire of the army, you should take a crack at writing novels."

"Uncle Chance?"

"What?"

"Can I ask you something?"

"What?"

"How come you never married?"

"Well . . . Hell, Clementine, when they passed out the good looks, I was standing behind the door. Ears like a mule. Nose like a horse. Who would marry me?"

Clementine was surprised. It had never occurred to her before that Chance wasn't as handsome as the other Price men.

"Well, Aunt Martha always said, 'Handsome is as handsome does.'"

"Besides, I had all the kids I'd ever need with your bunch. Kids don't know if you're good-looking or not. They just know if you're real or not. What about you?"

"What about me?"

"How come you never married?"

"Oh . . . Like you. I didn't need kids. Raised my brothers."

"And your mamma and daddy, too."

She laughed. "Them, too, I suppose. Also, I never found the right man. Well, that's not quite true. I found him, all right. But he's not available." She jumped up from her seat and stepped to the door. "Uncle Chance, I gotta go. General Penn ordered ASAP, but I couldn't resist when I saw your bus. I'm so glad I saw you. Do you mind if I give you a hug?"

"Go easy on the shoulder."

She hugged him carefully and pressed her cheek to his. If the empty years between hadn't been totally erased, they were when Chance warned, "Watch that crosswind taking off. If it corkscrews going round that cottonwood tree, you're going to want to drop your upwind wing."

***

North of Caruthersville Harbor, Clementine was struck as always by how desolate the river's banks were. Roads and structures grew even sparser, farmland gave way to forest and swamp. She could see back-flooding where the volume of river water was so great that it forced its way into bayous and up creeks and made lakes of marshes. More troubling was all the water in the fields. That was seepage through the levees and under them, which told her how thoroughly soaked they were and how weakened while the rising river kept pressing harder.

Thirty minutes after leaving Chance behind, she spotted the half-mile notch in the tree line that marked the bare earth of the Birds Point fuse levee. She hadn't time to land Snoopy on the gravel road below the crown and walk the fuse plug from end to end as she had last week. Fortunately, she was a spray pilot and Snoopy a spray plane, so it shouldn't be a big deal to fly the length and eyeball it couple of times from ten feet.

Executing the precision maneuver buoyed her—as had her landing for Chance—proof that she had not been overly spooked by the near crash. The inspection showed no vegetation; it was ready to melt. And she saw no seepage or boils inside, no signs it would let loose before the water actually overtopped it.

Immediately to the north she saw the Confluence, where the Ohio River met the Mississippi in a Y-shaped junction that doubled their breadth. Were the rivers not running so high, she would see two different colors of water where they joined. One blue, one gray. She had seen them sometimes run side by side for miles before they blended. But this morning as she flew across, the sea of water that stormed from the Confluence was brown from shore to distant shore.

She got disoriented trying to locate the Point, the sliver of southern Illinois below the highway bridges that spanned the Mississippi and the Ohio. It was the tip of Cairo's Fort Defiance Park. She could see Cairo itself, fuzzily through the rain. It huddled along the Ohio River, just a mile above the Confluence.

But where the heck was Fort Defiance Park? Where were the tall trees that bordered the park? Then she spotted their tops poking up from the high water that inundated the Point. Cairo—the city of two and a half thousand diminished yearly by population loss—looked tiny, isolated in the gray and brown storm-drenched cropland and endless miles of Illinois and Kentucky forest that spread east as far as she could see.

She continued up the Mississippi toward Cairo Regional Airport, which was way too small to have a manned control tower, and broadcast her presence to other planes on the Common Traffic Advisory Frequency—"Cairo traffic, Air Tractor N5440A on a left downwind for runway 20"—landed, topped up her tank at the self-service Jet-A pump, hit the Ladies, and took off for St. Louis.

***

Rolly Winters telephoned Bliss Metro Police Chief Owen at the hour Billy Bob usually visited his girlfriend and told his voice mail. "We're stuck in St. Louis, Chief. We'll get back as soon as we can find a way out of the city." Then he telephoned Libby. "Just told Billy Bob we can't get back. Bought Duvall and me another day to run down friends of your faceless, one-legged bigot."

"Are you sure you're safe there? Mayor Killing says he's got bad flooding."

"It's real bad in the Arch neighborhood and traffic's a mess, but we're holed up on high ground and doing fine as long as we got juice for our laptops."

***

Clementine Price said, "Wow," and slowed the Air Tractor to near stall speed.

The rain had thinned to drizzle, and the cloud cover was lifting. St. Louis's handful of skyscrapers, the Gateway Arch, and its many bridges looked almost crisp in the sharpening light. Traffic at a standstill blocked highway lanes. But Interstate 55, which crossed the river on the Poplar Street Bridge, was eerily empty.

The bridge's road deck was littered with smashed cars and trucks. The wreckage of a gigantic riverboat jammed underneath blocked half the river's flow, raising it so high that water was spilling over levees into streets. That would be the *Abraham Lincoln.* This morning, CNN had shown the bus parked by the Arch submerged to its wheel wells. The water had since risen above its windows.

Three powerful towboats—seven-thousand-horsepower, triple-screw Z-drives—were hauling on cables hooked to the *Abraham Lincoln*, trying to pull it loose. Behind the boats jetted foamy streaks of white prop wash.

Her cell phone rang. Robert.

"Welcome to St. Louis, Major Price."

"Thank you, sir. How long have they been hauling on that?"

"Since before I got here. They have to stop every fifteen minutes when their engines overheat."

"From here it does not look like all their pulling is going to work."

She flew over the bridge, pulled a crop duster's 180, and headed back. From upstream, the wreckage looked like three or four enormous boats tangled into a single obstruction had welded to the bridge.

Across the river, moored on the East St. Louis side, was a four-hundred-foot floating dry dock that Clementine recognized as having recently transited through her district from its Indiana shipyard builder. Ironically, it was in St. Louis to raise the *Abraham Lincoln* to repair hull damage, and she saw that the catastrophe could have been far worse. Had the terrorists managed to crash that slab-sided monster into the bridge too, they would have blocked both sides of the river. Had they not thought of it, or had that part of their plan gone wrong?

A police helicopter buzzed her, suddenly enormous in her side window.

"Call you back, Colonel. I have a cop on my tail."

She heard angry shouting on the VHF radio. "Yellow Air Tractor, get the hell out of here. You're violating restricted airspace. Land your goddamned airplane and report to police headquarters."

Concentrating on the trouble below, she keyed her VHF.

"Officer, you are cursing at United States Army Corps of Engineers Major Clementine Price. I take my orders from Lieutenant-General Clinton Penn, Commander of the Mississippi Valley Division. The general has instructed me to clear the wreckage flooding St. Louis ASAP. Out."

She circled back toward the MacArthur Bridge, an old truss span just below Poplar Street. The towboats had stopped to cool their engines. Their prop wash ceased roiling the current, and she saw that the water immediately downstream from the wrecks was quite slack, though flanked, of course, by raging torrents generated where the river passed either side of the jam. She felt her eye drawn up the river. In the distance, she saw the clean, elegant sweep of the bridge that James Buchanan Eads had built in 1874.

Every St. Louis bridge built since looked ordinary by comparison, even the cable-stayed "Stan Span." But the Eads Bridge, the first to span the river, was only one product of his genius. Back before he built his bridge, before he launched his gun boats, James Buchanan Eads had earned his Captain title salvaging sunken steamboats with his diving bell and clearing the Mississippi's channels of "snags" like the wrecks jammed under the Poplar Street Bridge.

"What would you do, Captain Eads?"

25

Eads's Eyes

Day 35
Tuesday

The *Abraham Lincoln* was the only bit of the wreckage still recognizable as a boat. It stood so high on the water that its smokestacks were jammed against the bridge deck. That told Clementine Price that it was squatting on the solidly crushed remains of the casino sternwheeler *Stonewall Jackson,* a museum barge, the excursion steamboat *Rose of St. Louis,* and who knew how many sunken coal, sand, and corn barges. Thanks to Eads, she had a good idea what *they* were resting on.

Her best bet was to try to observe the wreckage through Eads's eyes. She gave the river more spray pilot passes. These closer wave-top sweeps revealed that what had appeared to be slack water immediately downstream of the wrecks was actually much stiller. Between the torrents flanking it, the water shielded from the current by the wrecks was as calm and flat as a mill pond. A picture of how James Buchanan Eads would try to pry the wrecks loose from the bridge took shape in her mind.

She swooped low again. With twenty-first century technology and horsepower, she could do in a day what would have taken him weeks in the 1850s. In theory. Good thing that General Penn had sent Robert to St. Louis, too. Many stubborn minds would have to be convinced to take the risk Eads would take. Full colonels changed minds a lot quicker than lowly majors.

"Uh, ma'am? Major?" The helicopter cop was back on the VHF. Whoever he had radioed for advice knew how the world worked in the Mississippi Valley.

"Go ahead, officer."

"Dispatch says I should give you a fly-over after you land. I can hover and give you a closer look."

"Thanks, I've seen enough. But maybe you could give me a lift over the traffic from Downtown Airport back to the bridge."

"Yes, ma'am. I can do that."

She climbed to fifteen hundred feet and radioed Downtown tower control for permission to land. Before she entered the traffic pattern, she called Robert's cell. "Powerwash."

Robert got it instantly. He barked a "ha!" of a laugh. "What's the channel bottom?"

"Ordinarily, a slurry of mud and sand. Right now, packed harder by the wrecks—hopefully not too hard."

"How deep is the water?"

"We're at flood stage, probably fifty feet."

"What will we powerwash with?"

"Remember the treasure hunter we collared?"

He did, of course. No one forgot a rogue salvage operation to recover artifacts from a Civil War gunboat conducted at night by a famous novelist who thought he could skate by without Corps permits. "He used a prop wash diverter to blast away the mud."

"They called it a 'mailbox.' We've got to build a bunch and fix 'em on a Z-drive boat."

Robert said, "I'll put Colonel Hardy right on it. He knows that the fastest way to get you and me out of St. Louis is to help us clear this bridge."

***

It was the Corps at its best, Clementine Price thought proudly—free-thinking engineers and can-do contractors teaming up to make the unlikely possible. The floating dry dock at East St. Louis flooded its ballast tanks to sink beneath the surface. The biggest Z-drive towboat crossed the river and maneuvered inside the dock and over its submerged cradle. The dock regained buoyancy by emptying its ballast tanks and lifted the 160-foot towboat out of the water. At the same time, a pipe fabricator the St. Louis District had used for years worked up the mailboxes, cutting and welding ten-foot diameter tubing into gigantic ninety-degree hollow elbows. These right-angle tubes would be the nozzles attached to the thruster shrouds that would divert the towboat's prop wash straight down to the bottom of the river.

Even Colonel Hardy got his nose back in joint when he turned out to have a background in aeronautical thrust vectoring flight control nozzles to make fighter aircraft more dynamic. TVFC might seem a far cry from scouring mud and sand under wrecked riverboats. But a nozzle was a nozzle, and they captured Hardy's whole-hearted engagement at the expense of having to listen to nonstop bloviation about fluid dynamic steering, effective vectoring angle, throat diameter, and exit area.

The only naysayer was the Z-drive towboat captain Kenny Pike who, Hardy assured Garcia, was the best boat handler on the river by far. The tobacco chewing Captain Pike did not cotton to folks drilling holes in his nozzle shrouds to bolt on the mailboxes, and that was only his first complaint. Emphasizing his displeasure with streams of rust-colored juice aimed in the general direction of the river, he pointed out that in their single-minded haste, they had forgotten to consider how he would drive his boat with all his prop wash aimed down.

Garcia assured him that the third diverter was a spare in case one was damaged during installation. The captain said that he would only allow one diverter attached to his boat and stomped off.

Garcia took Clementine aside. "We need this guy and his crew. You want to try your wiles on him?"

"Wiles? Which wiles would those be?"

"Whatever gets job done."

Clementine found Captain Pike at the back of the dry dock. He was standing under the towboat's stern, arms crossed, glowering at the elbows, which were twice as tall as Clementine. A front-end loader was standing by to hoist them. "Cap," she said, "you don't look happy."

He strode to the edge and spat in the water. Clementine followed closely.

Kenny Pike looked up at the tall major. "Ma'am," he said, "if your scheme works and the wrecks cut loose, they'll be riding a sixteen mile per hour wave of backed-up water. How do I get out of their way?"

"We're installing lasers to measure their movement. We'll watch 'em like hawks and warn you in time to skedaddle."

"Only way I can count on skedaddling is if you divert only my middle prop and leave me my outboard propellers to drive the boat."

Clementine Prince shook her head. She needed to nozzle both outboard props for maximum scouring power. "You'll have your middle propeller to drive the boat. Are you telling me that a man of your experience can't dance her around the river on one Steerprop thruster?"

"What happens when it sucks up a rope or a log? Anyone ever tell you Steerprops shut down automatically?"

"We'll have two boats stationed to hip up beside you in case you ingest debris. They'll maintain your position while the divers clear your drive." She named the boats the Corps had hired, piloted by St. Louis men he knew well.

"Fine for you to say, little lady, but me and my boys will be the ones in the way when fourteen barges and three steamboats cut loose."

"So will Colonel Garcia," said Clementine. "Right beside you in your pilothouse. And so will I."

"I will not abide a woman on my boat during such a risky operation."

Clementine Price said, quietly, "No problem. I will have the United States Army requisition your boat and run it myself."

The captain smirked. "I'd pay money to watch that stunt."

"My uncle was Captain Chase Price."

The smirk wavered little. "Chase Price who ran *Delta Clementine*?"

"Named for my great-grandmother."

"The old-timers always said Chase Price was a man to ride the river with."

"I grew up on that boat." She multiplied that exaggeration with the claim, "Uncle Chase taught me the sticks." (True. On clear sunny days when the river was calm, and no tows shared the channel.)

"Say, when did your uncle pass over?"

"Uncle Chase died twelve years ago."

Captain Pike seized on the hole in her story. "I doubt old Chase ever drove a modern Z-drive."

"Your steering and propulsion controls are electronic. A baboon can drive it—even a lady baboon," she added with a smile. It didn't move him.

He spat. "Go ahead, requisition it. It's not my boat. It's the company's boat."

The major's smile went out like a light. Her expression put the towboat captain in mind of the view from his wheelhouse in an ice storm. She said, "You can explain to the company why the army exercised emergency authority to seize it. Tell 'em they'll get it back after we've finished our job and they've adhered to prescribed procedures, completed their filing and certification, and met all our admin requirements."

"Well, now, let's not go off half-cocked, little la—Major. Heck, I didn't intend my remark about a woman the way it might have sounded."

"Thank you, Cap. I will take that as a yes."

She marched back to Garcia and saluted. "Mission accomplished. Neanderthal wiled."

***

"What do you have for me?" asked Nathan Flowers. He had on the same nylon ski mask he had worn for the Martyr Brigade, but there was no need for recon gloves and kohl eyeliner with this bunch.

"Shot Caller," said Maguire, who had blond, blue-eyed good looks, a long-sleeve Kevlar ballistic vest under his hoodie, and a boyish smile that Flowers didn't believe. But he was of a new breed that Flowers was recruiting—no visible prison tats, which made them more useful outside in civilization. Newly freed from Potosi Correctional, he was angling to make himself boss of the White Boys, a St. Louis chapter of Pure Dominion. "You're going to love this."

Sudden riches were making the gang cocky. Methamphetamine and heroin sales were going strong, and fentanyl knockoffs were booming beyond expectation. They had slaughtered their rivals in St. Louis's suburban towns and had paid cash for a farm in the Ozarks outside Rolla, a two-hour drive from the city. With 128 acres on a rugged plateau, miles from the nearest neighbor who didn't hate the police, they had the privacy to modify weapons, practice shooting, hop up cars and trucks, and stabilize their leadership.

"Show me," said Nathan Flowers.

"Let's just say we took your basic idea and juiced it up."

Flowers had found them trapped indoors by the rain, which had turned the place into a muddy junkyard. They were getting bored with being cooped up, the kind of bored that bred risky behavior.

He said, "I ordered you to attack the 'Love Your Neighbor Rally' at Gateway Arch Landing."

"Yeah, yeah, yeah, we know. Shit-libs, Black Savages, and Jews are gonna demonstrate at Gateway Arch Landing."

"Big turnout," chimed in Benson, the current boss who seemed to have no clue that young Maguire would soon slit his throat.

"It's on Facebook," said Maguire. "The 'Love Your Neighbor Rally.' 'Terrorists can't scare us, we're diverse.'"

"They're bitching about genocide," said Benson.

"But it's the White Man who's getting genocided," said Maguire.

"That is why I ordered you to attack them," said Nathan Flowers. "Where are you going with this?" He listened closely to distinguish the jerks who would go along with anything, from the fools who hatched the scheme.

"Prius repellent!" several chorused.

"Smokers!"

"Rolling coal."

This sounded interesting, maybe a cut above the average jail-brains big idea. Smokers, or rolling coal, were trucks with their engines fiddled to spew thick, black smoke—a farm boy and hillbilly middle finger to environmental regulations.

"Show me."

They led him proudly out of the farmhouse and through the mud to the barn where they had installed tall chrome smokestacks on four diesel pickups.

They started a Ram Dodge that was nearest an open door and engaged the smoke switch that flooded the fuel injectors with excess diesel. Black smoke shot from its stacks. In the seconds it took them to shut it off, an oily cloud filled the pitched ceiling.

"Then what?" Nathan Flowers asked Maguire.

"We circle the demonstration. Rolling coal. The TV cameras go nuts, Shot Caller. Everyone whips out their phones. Selfies, Instagram, Facebook. Our message goes viral."

"Which message?"

Maguire answered in headlines. "White Pride takes action. Diversity demos getting rolled on look like assholes."

"Then what?"

"We got the brass to say the fourteen words," Maguire said, and recited the White pride creed: "We must secure the existence of our people and a future for white children."

"Then what?"

Maguire's smile got brighter. "We line up the vehicles, side by side. Real tight. All four are blowing smoke. Like a wall of smoke. Every camera locks on it. Every shit-lib face looks our way. Every savage. Every Jew. Livestreaming to Facebook. Then we stomp the gas and blast right through the middle of 'em at fifty miles an hour."

Not bad, thought Nathan Flowers. A modern-day equivalent of an old-fashioned massacre. He was impressed. Maguire was a natural showman. In jail, showmen were mistrusted and had to waste energy dealing with suspicions they were bluffing. But in the outside world, showmen called the tune.

Some of the White Boys had the brains to gauge their shot caller's reaction. They were watching him carefully, trying to read an expression they couldn't see under his mask.

"How do you get away?"

"Scatter in the confusion, dump the trucks—they're all stolen—and hook up with cars we have waiting."

Their getaway plan sucked, but that wasn't his problem. If they believed they'd all get away, they wouldn't hesitate. And since they knew nothing about his flood, any captured by the cops would only add to the confusion he had started with the St. Louis barge attack.

He was about to say, "Go for it," when a burner phone vibrated in his pocket. He glanced at a text from a woman he had spying on the Justice Department's Counterterrorism Section.

TOUGH LOVE BUSTS.

That changed everything. The Feds were breaking down black doors, just like he set them up to, even quicker than he had hoped. All attention must shift to his scapegoats. He put the phone back in his pocket and said to Maguire, "No."

"No. What no? What do you mean no?"

"Cancel it."

"What? Why?"

"Call it off."

"We're all set, man. The guys are pumped."

"Call it off."

"You afraid?"

More than the question, Maguire's tone caught every ear in the barn. They knew they had heard a major challenge and the result would be interesting.

Nathan Flowers spoke mildly. "I'm going to ask you to apologize."

"Apologize? What, are you out of your fucking mind? No fucking way."

Flowers watched the young dude's eyes, while his own eyes went to slow-motion mode. The attack unfolded in stages. He waited for the exact right moment to reach into his pocket. The gangbanger raised Kevlar protected arms to block him. Flowers whipped out the burner phone.

"I won't ask again."

"Give me one good reason—"

Flowers asked Maguire, "Inside you're known as 'Captain,' right?"

"Damn right."

Flowers dialed from memory. At Potosi Correction, a contraband cell phone vibrated. Flowers heard it picked up on the first ring. He waited, picturing in his mind how his man found a safe place to talk, a shallow corner out of sight of the security cameras with a couple of his people standing watch. "Hey pal, what's up?"

Flowers pivoted the phone so Maguire could hear both ends of the call.

"I got a bitch here calls himself Captain."

"His cousin's in my car."

"Thought so," said Flowers. His man's "car" was the prison unit he bossed. "Do we know anybody at South Central?"

Maguire's smile, which was growing tight, vanished.

Flowers said, "Captain's little brother just got to South Central."

"No problem. We own South Central."

"Now this Captain, himself, the way he's acting will end up back in Potosi any day."

"We'll make him a party."

"I'll keep you posted, if the bitch doesn't straighten out. Good to hear your voice, Boss."

"You, too, Shot Caller."

Flowers cut the connection, ripped out the battery and ground the phone under his boot. To Maguire he said, "It pays to remember the system. You've got your cousin to protect in Potosi. And your little brother to protect in South Central. And your own sorry ass next time they lock you up."

"Shot Caller," said Maguire, "I'm sorry."

"You have every reason to be."

"Okay, man. I said I'm sorry."

"What was that?"

"I said I'm sorry. I apologize."

"Smart move, you little prick."

Flowers landed a lightning fist on Maguire's nose. Blood sprayed.

Maguire wiped his face and shook off the pain. Then he whipped up his fists and rose on the balls of his feet like a prize fighter. He was two inches taller than Nathan Flowers, fifteen years younger, and considerably broader. Body blows would bounce off his ballistic vest. "You son of a bitch, you had no call to do that."

Flowers asked, "Are you sure you want to fight your shot caller?"

"You're the one that's gonna apologize."

"You are you even stupider than I thought. Here, take your best shot." Flowers stepped closer, hands at his side. "Come on, jail-brains! Do it."

Maguire threw two punches, a lightning-fast combination. Flowers slipped the first over his shoulder with reptilian speed and sidestepped the second. In the millisecond before Maguire could raise his hands to guard his face, Nathan Flowers unleashed three jackhammer blows. The bigger man fell with a groan, eyes glazed, cheekbone shattered.

26

No Lady

Day 35
Tuesday

Captain Billy Scruggs, unexpectedly ashore in Bliss, Arkansas, steadied himself on a pillar outside the Stevenson Memorial Hospital Emergency Room, belched loud enough to draw the attention of the security guard, and peered uncertainly into the rain.

He had passed the city hundreds of times on the river. He had landed a thousand barges at the steel mill above the Bliss Basin, and as many or more at the old mill below South End. He had delivered turbines to the new power plant—even took back a turbine they busted installing upside down. But this was the first time he had actually set foot on the city's streets. Even when backing down mid-channel, powering against the current to hold the tow stationary while he took fuel and fresh meat from Bliss Marine, about all a man saw from the wheelhouse was flood walls, levees, railroad tracks, and the ass end of factories and warehouses. Billy Boy, he thought, as another belch of secondhand Jack Daniels sweetened his throat, get used to a new perspective.

So far he didn't like it much. Main Street looked like they'd run low on paint years ago. Some of the storefronts were empty. When he asked the emergency room nurses where he could find a place to sleep, they recommended motels out on the highway, unless he was fixing to spend $250 for fancy sheets in the Hunnicutt House. Should he find a cab to drive him out to the motels or walk to a bar? That was all he needed, get stuck in some motel without a drink. It wasn't that he needed a drink right this very minute. But what about when he did?

He had to admit, getting suspended—getting kicked off his boat—felt like a doozy of a turning point. A hairpin bend in the channel was more like it. He wasn't saying he didn't deserve it. A man could not run a boat drunk. Aside from the standard zero-tolerance no-drinking rule, truth was you just weren't up to the surprises the river threw at you.

Well, now. Boozing got him here, and he might as well admit a drink was what he wanted. The nurses told him they had AA meetings in the churches. Trouble was, if he started wandering around in the rain looking for one, he'd end up getting mugged by some meth head on a dark street. 'Course, the meth heads wouldn't care if the skinny old white guy was headed to AA or a wino bar. That thought provoked an unexpected smile. It stung sharply as it opened his cut lip. He'd fallen in the gutter. An ambulance going by brought him in for tests. The nurses knew an alkie when they saw one, and after confirming he hadn't broken any bones—and failing to persuade him to talk a counselor—cut him loose.

Billy knew the one-day-at-a-time story better than most folks. For Captain Scruggs, "one day at a time" had always meant getting through every day and night of a thirty-day trick, waiting for his own time—miles from the river—when he could hole up with a case of Jack, get drunk, and stay drunk. When the waiting got hard, or the company suddenly stretched his thirty days to forty, he would daydream himself into an escape reverie, recalling the warm glow of preparation. He had a cabin in the Missouri hills he rented from a mule breeder. Buy the Jack. Stock on up on food—simple stuff, loaf of bread and sandwich meat for the first week, cans after that.

The mule breeder would want his rent. It struck him forcefully that next time he pulled that stunt it was going to be house bourbon. No way he could afford to pay for a case of Jack Daniels. No job. Mortgage payments on his ex-wife's house. Alimony. Child support. How long before he'd be buying by the pint? He peered into the rain and wondered where to go.

An old black Lincoln town car with Illinois plates pulled up. The window slid down on a scrawny guy about his age, with bony fingers wrapped round the steering wheel and his face drawn tight across his skull. "Captain Scruggs."

"I know you?"

"Climb in."

"What for?"

"You want a job?"

"What kind of job?"

"*Delta Lady* lost her captain."

Scruggs swallowed to hold down another belch. He had last seen *Delta Lady* making Vicksburg bridges northbound. She was a big old five-decker and, at eleven thousand horsepower, no lady. "I'm suspended."

"We'll deal with that."

Horseshit, thought Billy. Never heard of the United States Coast Guard winking at booze. But looking on the bright side, there were a lot of towboats—at least fifteen hundred working the river and hundreds more—maybe a thousand more—on the tributaries. And the Coast Guard was shorthanded, running worn-out boats, tied in knots with Maritime Transportation Security Act paperwork, and bracing for eighteen rivers to flood. He might skate by if he didn't do anything to draw attention.

"You coming or not?"

Billy Scruggs thought of a cheap motel out on the highway, thought of leaving an AA meeting on a dark, wet night, thought of lying on a sagging bed watching a bottle go light, and climbed into the car.

"Where is she?"

"Down at the mill."

The man drove, not bothering to introduce himself, through the streets of the old city, past a Greyhound terminal with plywood windows and an old Woolworth's the coloreds had turned into a church. "Sinners Are Welcome," said the board outside. Probably meant the coloreds had AA meetings, too. When the car stopped for a light, he heard the choir singing. Old ladies crossed the street, carrying fat black Bibles and dragging little boys by the hand.

Cop-light-flashing detours sent them in circles. The levee was leaking, closing streets. They drove past some bars. A lot of bars. And a lot of churches. Storefront churches for the coloreds. A couple of storefront mosques fortified with roll-down window gates for the Muslims.

The street flooding shunted them through an old cotton warehouse district. Some of the red brick loft buildings were covered in scaffolding. Here and there, tall windows gleamed golden light, and he could see young white couples hurrying through the rain carrying bottles of wine and flowers, like they were visiting for supper. The old Fords and Toyotas he'd seen parked on the streets gave way to Audis and BMWs, fancy Jap and Korean cars, and snazzy-looking electrics. After the loft district came tree-lined streets. The coloreds had a large brick church on the edge of that neighborhood, an old one they must have bought from the whites. They were fixing it up; scaffolds climbed the steeple.

Down the side streets he could see houses with porches set back from the sidewalk. The white church was Baptist and built of stone, with an illuminated notice board that asked, "Where Will You Spend Eternity—Smoking or Non-smoking?"

Further along Main rose an even bigger Methodist church. AA meetings there, too, he'd been told by the nurses. But a man would have to be mighty desperate to throw himself at the mercy of the Methodists.

The neighborhood changed again. They drove past a housing project, past gangs of teenagers smoking in the rain. Suddenly the kids all broke into a run, like the start of a riot or something. A big touring bus rounded the corner. It was towing a bright red Jeep and had the name Shakur emblazoned on the sides.

"What the hell is that all about?"

"Rip rap singer," the driver grunted, speeding up.

Rip rap? The only rip rap Scruggs knew was rock the Corps spread on the bank to stop towboat wake wash eroding the levee. Cheaper than revetment. "What's rip rap singing?"

"The coloreds got a hard on for it."

"You mean hip hop. Not just the coloreds, I had a boy who liked it."

"I'd say that's your problem."

The car splashed through a puddle, drenching an old man begging at a traffic light. How old? Not much older than he was, just looked a little worse, at least for the moment. The silent, bony, hollow-eyed driver pulled onto a levee road and headed downriver. It got darker and foggier. Billy Scruggs shivered, cold, tired, hung over, and aching from his fall. All of a sudden he wondered if the driver was recruiting for the Devil. Billy, he told himself, that sort of thinking comes from seeing so many churches all at once.

Lights in the old Bliss Steel loomed through the rain. Back in business after the new mill shut them down for a while, buildings sprawled and hulked over the flat lands below the Bliss Basin. Second thoughts crowded in on Billy Scruggs. He'd been twenty-eight days on his last boat before he cracked when they told him he had to work an extra week. He had been bracing to get past that week—probably would have too, except all of sudden he had had to tie her off at Bliss Marine so the chief could change out a busted cylinder head. Thought he'd take a walk, stretch his legs. Hit the first bar he found and had a few shots. Enough to trip in the gutter, enough to fall down and cut his face, but nowhere near enough to get a two-week bender out of his system.

"How long 'fore your captain's replacement takes over?"

"You're it."

"Goddamn. How long?"

"They're working twenty-ones."

"Goddamn," he said again. Three weeks. He could not go another three weeks.

Then he saw her tied off at a jetty, and he murmured to himself, very quietly, "Shoot."

"Something the matter?" asked the driver.

"No, sir, there is nothin' the matter. That's a fine-looking old boat is all. What happened to the captain?"

"Killed."

"What? How?"

"He was arguing with me on the cell phone, apparently he didn't look where he was going. Fell in the river."

"When?"

"Last night. Gone in the dark."

"The hell you say . . . surprised I didn't hear no talk on the radio."

"Well, maybe you were busy drinking."

Fact was, the only talk on the radio concerned the St. Louis terrorists. "How'd you come to find me?"

The driver stopped the car and gave him a flat stare. "They said at Bliss Marine that your boat left for St. Louis without you. Let's go." He climbed out of the car. Billy Scruggs followed him down a rickety boardwalk and out on the jetty.

"They say why?"

"We'll discuss that in a minute."

One look at the *Delta Lady*'s crew told Billy Scruggs more about himself than he wanted to know. A boatload of losers, hard men who'd seen their best days too long ago to recall. He was clearly not the only one the Devil's recruiter had pulled out of the gutter. Odd thing how she was such a big, strong boat. You'd expect crew like these with their mottled skin and missing teeth on some two-bit operation one step ahead of the sheriff. The

Delta Lady didn't look none too clean and shiny, but nothing about her was two-bit.

The driver beckoned the mate, a short, powerful man wearing a cut-off vest despite the rain. His head was shaved, he had a White Pride tattoo on his bare arm. The mate fixed Billy Scruggs with a cold stare while the fellow who had driven him here pointed at the towing winch and asked, "Ever seen a man get his hand caught in the cable?"

"What do you mean?"

"I mean when the drum is turning, taking up a tow wire and the tow wire is wrapping around the drum have you ever seen a man get his hand crushed by the wire wrapping around the drum?"

Billy Scruggs had seen many bloody injuries on the river—a parting line whipped off a man's leg; barges pulverizing hands against a lock wall like mashed beets; an exploding breaker box frying an engineer's face into well-done steak—but never that one. "No," he said.

"But you could imagine such a thing?"

"If a man weren't careful."

The driver said, "The hand that picks up a glass or a bottle of liquor while you're working on this boat will end up crushed in that drum."

"What did you say to me?"

"You heard me, Captain. We need you sober, and sober you'll be."

He was mostly grateful to be rescued and had no desire to question a stroke of luck that had vaulted him off that sagging motel bed back into the wheelhouse, but there was shit a man didn't take. "I don't cotton to being threatened."

The driver laughed. He turned to the mate. The mate threw his head back, opened a mouth of jagged yellow teeth and laughed, too. Scruggs spotted a red blood drop tattooed on his throat, a mark of the Ku Klux Klan, and under his eye, tattooed tear drops, which signified the man had killed someone. (Three someones, one for each tear.)

"Maybe we're just pulling your leg," said the driver. "Maybe we're not. The point is we got a job to do and we don't want you fucking it up."

"Who the hell are you?"

"General manager of this company is who the hell I am. Down from Chicago."

"You got a name?"

"Minden—And your mate's Joey. Now listen up, here's your orders. Soon as they're done loading that steel, you're going to run them barges upriver and moor 'em ten miles past the bridge. You'll see a fleeting area above Mile 815, Tennessee side."

Billy counted thirty barges in the fleet. Big 290-footers, carpeting six acres of river. "Up? Don't steel go down?"

"That steel's going up."

"But finished steel goes to the Gulf."

The driver, the general manager, whoever the hell Minden was, laughed again. "The way I see it, someday if fellas like you and me save our pennies so we can buy the company's boat, then we can put the steel where we want. 'Til then, we run it where management tells us to run it. Any more questions, Captain Scruggs?"

"Yup." Billy Scruggs looked the mate up and down. "Where's my relief pilot?"

"You're lookin' at him."

"Joey got his ticket?"

"Joey knows the boat."

"Does he know the river?"

"That's your job," said Joey. "Anytime it's gets complicated, I wake you up and you're back on the sticks."

Scruggs ignored Joey and stared the general manager in the eye. "I won't run a boat with the mate over me."

"The mate'll run the crew. You run the boat. Isn't that right, Joey?"

"Yes, sir," said Joey. "You run the boat, Captain. I'll keep the boys in line. And steer for you when it's safe for you to rest."

Scruggs returned a curt nod. He could still taste the Jack in his throat. His head ached. So he couldn't count on his relief pilot when the going got tough. Fact was, he'd rather have a relief pilot who knew he didn't know the river instead of pretending he did. And for better or worse, he was back on the river counting days, again. Probably where he belonged. Getting paid for doing rehab.

"I'll take me a look at her."

He peered into the doghouse—the rigging locker and workshop forward on the weather deck—and found it orderly enough. He checked out the galley. None too clean, with the linoleum deck in need of a mop last month. The off-watch men hunched over their phones in the crew lounge didn't bother looking up when he stuck his head in. Didn't appear to be grieving much for their drowned captain, either.

Back on the weather deck he said, "Joey, jump down to the engine room. Tell the chief to crank up his mains and come see me in the wheel-house. I'll run her out to the channel see what she can do. Meantime, you get your people swamping the grease off these decks 'fore somebody else takes a header."

The general manager handed Scruggs a cell phone. "Hang onto this. Keep it charged and on twenty-four-seven in case I issue new orders."

"What's wrong with the radio?"

The general manager looked exasperated. He turned to the mate. "You know something, Joey?"

"What's that, Mr. Minden?"

"I'm beginning to wonder whether they kicked Captain Scruggs off his boat not for drinking whiskey but for asking too goddamned many questions."

27

Operation Powerwash

Day 35–36
Tuesday–Wednesday

"Drive on!" Major Clementine Price ordered at midnight, and Operation St. Louis Powerwash jumped into high gear. She and Robert Garcia watched from the back of the Z-boat wheelhouse for results from their jury-rigged thrust vectoring nozzles. They wore transponders clipped to their life jackets, so rescuers could find them if the whole mess suddenly let loose and they were thrown into the black water. At more immediate risk were the Corps' civilian divers on the main deck below, poised to jump in the water to clear the Z-drives if they ingested debris.

Floodlit bright as day, the wreckage jammed under the Poplar Street Bridge loomed only a few meters behind the straining towboat. Her engines thundered, gouging giant whirlpools on either side. The deck was shaking, the windows rattled. The middle engine held her in place by backing against the nearly still current. Propellers driven by the left and right engines blasted prop wash at the riverbed.

Clementine's eyes flickered between two monitors. One displayed three-dimensional depth-finder images of the riverbed; the other screen showed the laser rangefinders that would warn them when the fire-blackened heap of wrecked boats and barges began to move. Captain Eads, she wondered, are we kidding ourselves? Robert is terrific to take a chance on our theories, but what if the bottom is harder here, or the weight of the wrecks has compacted it like concrete?

So far the heap hadn't budged. In the event it did, towboats were standing by to snag chunks before they crashed into the MacArthur Bridge, just a quarter mile downstream. Twice the engines overheated, and Captain Pike had to throttle back and wait for them to cool. The third time they had to wait, Clementine and Robert stepped out on the wheelhouse's rear platform. Clementine made sure the door was closed behind them.

"Is General Penn losing it?" she asked.

"General Penn is sharper than I've ever seen him."

"Dumping you and me on poor Hardy?"

Robert's handsome features set in his most neutral expression. "General Penn rises to challenges. Stress brings out his best."

"Not to mention ordering us out of our own districts during an emergency?"

"He ordered his engineer officers best qualified by training and experience to respond to a unique catastrophe," the Cuban Sphinx replied blandly. Then he surprised Clementine with a smile and a whisper that warmed her heart, "Not to mention playing matchmaker, my darling Clementine."

They went back in when the engines roared to speed.

A second later, the laser monitor flashed red.

"What moved?" asked Garcia.

"The whole damn thing," said Pike, lunging to throttle back the nozzles and full forward his only drive thruster.

"*No!*" the lunatics who had commandeered his boat chorused.

"Wait a moment," the colonel added firmly, and the lady major said, "Cap, you're doing great. I'll give you the heads up in time to skedaddle."

The Z-drive captain looked at his depth finder, which the Corps gearheads had monkeyed with. It flashed red, too.

"Stand by, Cap," the major called, "We're outta here in a minute."

The numbers showed the forty-five-foot river depth plunge to fifty-five and just as quickly sixty-five. The image of the mud bottom directly below the bridge shifted abruptly and the bottom edge of the compacted wrecks appeared to hang over a void. Pike heard the major say to the colonel, "It's working. See that excavation? The current accelerated. The river's flowing under the wrecks—Go now, Cap! *Punch her!*"

She didn't have to ask him twice. Kenny Pike killed the diverter nozzles and powered ahead with his middle prop. If his boat was a living, breathing animal it would leap with a howl at the sight of fire-blackened riverboats and barges jumping it with all four feet. But it was doing less leaping than shuffling on a single propeller.

The *Abraham Lincoln* hurtled after it, riding a surge of abruptly released river water. Three times as long as Pike's Z-drive, it was so tall that its shadow blotted out the work lights. He muttered his first prayer since Sunday school. Damned if the Lord didn't lend a hand. Instead of crushing them, the *Lincoln* toppled on its side, generating a huge wave that shoved the towboat out of its way.

A dozen towboats stationed in the short stretch of river between the two bridges converged on the drifting wreckage. Deck hands risked their lives hooking up lines, and by the time the invisible sun lightened the clouds, the first stage of chaos was under control. As wreck master and wreck master's deputy, Colonel Garcia and Major Price oversaw a very long morning of dragging floating wrecks to shore, raising sunken ones from the bottom, and clearing snags from the channel.

General Penn addressed the media at noon.

"The channel is clear. The impounded floodwaters have commenced to draining. We have a long way to go, and the U.S. Army Corps of Engineers is proud of the officers who led the effort, the troops who are working in dangerous conditions, and our civilian contractors who proved once again that nothing beats free enterprise."

When the cameras were off, General Penn turned to Clementine and Robert. "You two sure tore up the town. The mayor says they'll erect an Army Corps statue under the Arch. Good job, Colonel Garcia. You too, Major Price. You make quite a team."

Garcia said, "Thank you, sir."

"Thank you, sir," said Clementine.

Robert added, "Actually, sir, I did little more than hold Major Price's coat."

Whatever Penn answered was drowned out by a helicopter with the Corps' castle logo and three Lieutenant-General stars on its tailboom. It swooped onto the landing. Captain Standfast jumped down and ran to Penn's side with a smart salute. "Helicopter standing by, General."

"I'm off to Cairo," said Penn.

Clementine's self-preservation antenna locked tight onto "Cairo." The fate of the little city was entwined with her Birds Point fuse levee. "Excuse me, General. What can I do to help in Cairo?"

"You've got your hands full here, Major Price—Colonel Hardy!"

"Yes, sir," said the St. Louis District commander.

"Keep these two as long as you need."

Hardy saluted. "Thank you, sir."

They stood at attention until Penn had clambered into his helicopter, at which point Colonel Hardy said without a glimmer of a smile, "If the sun sets on either of you in my district, I'll have you shot."

Garcia said, "I would do the same in your position."

Clementine asked, "Would the colonel permit me to catch a few hours sleep before I fly my plane?"

"Just enough to take off safely."

In their taxi, Robert said, "Told you the general made the right decision."

She was still wondering what Penn was up to in Cairo. Thank God she'd gotten a good look at the Birds Point fuse levee and knew he wouldn't find problems there.

The cab dropped them at a Comfort Inn a mile from the Downtown Airport. They registered separately for two rooms and she went directly to hers. Robert stopped to pocket muffins, fruit, and yogurt from the all-day breakfast bar and presented them with a flourish when he knocked on her door.

"Showers first," said Clementine, peeling a proffered banana and toasting him with it.

"We'll save time and water if we shower together."

"Conserving natural resources is a Corps mission, Colonel."

Noble environmental aspirations notwithstanding, the longer-than-strictly-necessary shower transitioned into an energetic bath, with so much water sloshed onto the floor that they used all but one of the ample supply of towels to swab it up.

With the immediate needs of cleanliness and desire sated, Clementine slowly combed out her wet hair and Robert indulged in a leisurely shave, provocatively clad in their last dry towel—a skimpy one at that. Perched on the edge of the tub, Clementine observed her Latin Lover with the avidity of a traveling salesman at a strip club.

Robert took his time, filling the sink with hot water, putting a fresh blade into his safety razor, lathering up with Barbisol, then exploring each section of his face with his fingers before touching it with his blade. Sometimes he stroked up, sometimes down, and sometimes he would stop halfway through an area and reverse direction. He caught Clementine's eye in the mirror and said "Finding the grain. So I shave with it, not against it."

That would explain the incredible smoothness of his cheeks, she thought. He's mapping his face the way a general maps battleground terrain. Or, the way he has mapped every square inch of my body.

Clementine kept watching, mesmerized as his shiny, sculpted features emerged inch by inch from behind the foamy white cloud. But when he completed the final stroke and patted his face with after-shave—the mildly spicy scent she knew only as *Eau de Robert*—she was suddenly struck by overwhelming sadness. The ordinary intimacies that punctuate a shared life together would never be a part of their relationship. She did not know what he ate for breakfast, or how he laid out his clothes in the morning. She would never be able to hold his hand in public or brush a stray eyelash off his cheek. She could never refer to "us" except among themselves.

"Clementine?" He must have caught a glimpse of her despair. She tried to smile but it turned into a yawn. They had both been awake, wired, and working flat out for more than thirty-six hours. "I'm just tired. It's been a long couple of days."

Sliding between clean cool sheets, entwined in each other's arms, they fell asleep instantly.

Three hours later, Robert Garcia opened his eyes. He had no intention of hurrying out of town—General Penn had provided a bulletproof excuse for them this time, and God only knew when they could next be alone together. He closed his eyes and thought back to the morning she'd walked into his life—nervous, brave, obviously hurting but determined to conceal it. Not at all his type; he liked his women dark-haired with full breasts and hips and not too tall. But then he looked into her pale blue eyes, framed beneath her crisp salute. And once he heard that tuneful honey-dipped drawl spinning yarns about Tomato and Eads and cement shoes, he was a goner. How on Earth did they keep their hands off each other for ten years?

And now what? Would their love affair prevent her from finding a man she could build a life and a family with? She had always insisted she didn't want children of her own, but she'd never said she didn't want a husband. And Clementine deserved more than a part-time lover—even a faithful one. Retreating out-of-town for a "romantic getaway" sounded less sordid than sneaking away for a "dirty weekend," but it was no different. What if, God forbid, they were discovered? He could rebuild a new life outside the army but he could not bear the thought of torpedoing her career. And why was it that he couldn't even contemplate the concept of divorce, even in his own mind? Was he using Rita and the kids as an excuse for him not being man enough to make a difficult decision?

He rolled over and reached for Clementine. The sheets were still warm, but her side of the bed was empty. He sat up, trying to orient himself in the unfamiliar dark room. Clementine, stark naked, was standing outside the bathroom door. She opened it, but did not go in. Instead, backlit by the fluorescent lights, she turned around and opened the closet door. Her eyes were open and she moved with purpose, but Robert immediately recognized a sleepwalker. His younger brother had sleepwalked nearly every night the first year they came to the United States from Cuba, and he knew not to shake her awake lest she panic and fight back.

He got out of bed and shadowed her. She went methodically to each of the windows in their corner room, parted the curtains, and cranked open the casements as wide as they would go. Rain splashed her but she kept moving. She then opened the front door wide, hesitating a moment before stepping forward as if to continue her rounds in the parking lot. Robert got out in front to block her and slammed the metal door with a bang, which jolted her awake.

Clementine stood stock still and blinked for several minutes, gradually registering that she was naked, Robert was naked, and they were in a motel room with all the windows open.

"Clementine, darling," he said tenderly. "You were sleepwalking." He approached her slowly, put one arm around her shoulder while securing the chain lock on the door with his free hand, and guided her back to the bed. He sat down on the edge, searching her face. Clementine started to shiver, and he tucked her under the covers and slid in beside her, holding her close.

"You're safe now, you're here with me." She was still trembling, and he stroked her hair and held her tighter. "Do you remember what you were dreaming about? You went all around the room and opened all the doors and windows."

Robert had never seen her look so sad, but she spoke without emotion. "I was opening the doors and windows to let the water flow through." She searched his face. "Otherwise the flood will knock the house off of its footings."

He nodded. *I understand.*

"I must dream that a lot," she continued in the same hollow voice. "I sometimes wake up in my apartment, freezing, with all the windows open. The front door too. I was always baffled how that had happened. I guess I didn't want to know. . . ."

"My darling Clementine, what can I do to help you?"

"When I first met you, you gave me a card. Of people who can treat PTSD. I didn't call any of them, but I kept the card. I could never throw away anything you gave me. So I guess you can help me to help myself."

"Of course."

"One other thing?"

"Anything, darling."

"Just make sure I don't leave this bed without you."

28

The St. Louis Lockdown Blues

Day 36
Wednesday

"The Bliss Metro Hate Crime Unit is living high on the hog," said Rolly Winters.

Uninterrupted by competing cases, admin chores, office politics, and a meddling police chief, the detectives were closing in on the Weatherman's underground silo faster than they would have if the terrorist attack hadn't stranded them in St. Louis.

"We are living so high on the hog," Duvall McCoy agreed, "we can reach out and scratch his ears."

Their otherwise-budget downtown hotel had lightning fast Wi-Fi for their laptops. Rolly's subscription to NordVPN linked them securely through the Bliss Police intranet to databases around the country. And Duvall had located barbecue joints close enough for SkipTheDishes.com to deliver it hot: breakfast from Bogart's, which served early; lunch and supper from Sugarfire and Pappy's; and a 2 a.m. infusion from Mike Lipskin's late night jazz club to carry them over to breakfast. The barbecue was about what you'd expect in a city so far north—a small sacrifice when every instinct told them they had stumbled onto something bigger than one supremacist bigot criminal blowing another supremacist bigot criminal's leg off.

Chief Owen texted complaining that Rolly Winters and Duvall McCoy should display more initiative to get home to Bliss. No way. Not with this rare opportunity to hole up shielded by chaos that Billy Bob couldn't penetrate. Not when there was nothing part-time about a hate-crime squad running damn near twenty-four-seven.

Years of soldiering and policing had so heightened their ability to run on food in place of sleep that hotel security marveled at the ceaseless deliveries of ribs and burnt ends, brisket, wings, and bottled water. By a relentless process of elimination, they homed in on a stretch of western Missouri 250 miles west of St. Louis that was riddled with abandoned, sold, and renovated silos.

Trouble was, much of it was inside the perimeter fences of Whiteman Air Force Base. And since the 509th Bomb Wing flew B-2 Spirit bombers to terrorist bases in North Africa and the Middle East, drop-in visits would not be encouraged, even by special ops vets. Besides, Clem had said the Corps had filled them all in anyway.

"We know tons of guys there," said Duvall. "Everybody ends up at Whiteman."

"Mike Coligny," said Rolly.

"The lunatic Black Hawk driver," said Duvall.

Coligny was a tiger pilot, the sort who could fly you into the worst place you could imagine, but always come back to get you when the job was done or things got worse. He had a war record to get any normal soldier elected president and would have made general long ago if he hadn't been busted so often for flying under bridges and barnstorming skyscrapers. Rolly and Duvall had served with him in the Libyan desert before 9/11.

Rolly texted Coligny a secure VPN address. Coligny texted back and they were soon talking on a safe line. "Still enjoying the cop business?"

"Believe it. I get to sleep in my own bed. With the mayor. Except at the moment, I'm in St. Louis."

"The river attack?"

"No. I'm looking for a supremacist who turned a decommissioned missile silo into a hideout. It was probably one of Whiteman's."

"Thought they were all filled in."

"Apparently not."

"Must be on private property. Outside Whiteman's perimeter. Say, ever hear from that lunatic Duvall?"

"Right here with me," said Rolly.

"How's he doing?"

"Still fangs out."

Then Coligny said what Rolly was hoping to hear. "Want me to nose around for you?"

***

Clementine Price filed an instrument flight plan for eight thousand feet to Memphis and took off in a steady drizzle with Robert strapped into the jump seat. It was dusk, yet not too dark to celebrate a deeply satisfying sight below in Gateway Park. The river waters had receded enough that a heavy-duty wrecker was towing away the bus that had stalled there.

When she reached altitude, she handed him her spare headset so they could talk.

"General Penn was right," said Robert. "We make quite a team."

"Roger that." She flashed him a thousand-watt smile, then got serious. Part of a pilot's preflight was to preflight herself. She was not at her best on so little sleep. And she hadn't told him about her near crash over Hilltop and was not about to now, in the air. "Robert, don't hesitate to be a backseat driver on this trip. I've only had a few hours of sleep—thank you—and visibility will degrade as we head south. I wouldn't mind an extra set of eyes on the radar for thunder cells and other planes."

"Aye aye, Captain. I am delighted to, once again, put myself entirely in your capable hands." He leaned in and did a dirty-old-man eyebrow waggle.

Yes, let's keep it light, she thought. Enough drama for one day. "Speaking of salvage operations, did I ever tell you how my Uncle Chase rescued a team of mules in his towboat?"

"I am prepared to enjoy the in-flight entertainment."

"So, Uncle Chase gets a call from the ferry captain up in Cottonwood Point, in Missouri, who was loading a horse trailer carrying two prize diving mules, when the hitch broke and the trailer slid into the river."

"Stop! *Diving mules*?"

"You've never seen them? It used to be a big attraction at county fairs and rodeos. These mules would climb up a thirty-foot ramp and then dive into a little round pool of water about six feet deep."

"What did the ASPCA have to say about that?"

"It's been banned most places now, but when I was little it was still going on. Anyway, these very valuable animals are floating down the river. Uncle Chase is going to try to head them off at Tomato. By the time he spotted them, their trailer had broken apart in all the bends and they were swimming on their own."

She felt Robert's skeptical gaze and met his eyes. "Mules are excellent swimmers. Google it if you don't believe me. Any rate, one of them managed to struggle out onto the Arkansas side, where my brother Abram was able to catch it. But its mate swam to the Tennessee shore at the wildlife refuge where it would surely get lost—it's all swamp and hardwood forest, bears, wolves, snakes, and more snakes. Problem was, if they tried to chase after it, the mule would panic and run farther into the woods. You want to know how Uncle Chase saved it?"

"I am all ears."

"It's actually very romantic."

"Convince me."

"Just let me get around this thunderstorm first." Clementine stepped on a rudder pedal and nudged the control stick. Then she tilted her radar antenna to check that heavy rain wasn't attenuating the beam. They watched the screen and nodded mutual agreement when their new course would clear the cell by twenty miles.

"So, Uncle Chase had worked with mules as a child, on the farm. He knew that teams of mules bond, often for life. He figured the only way to lure the Tennessee mule back to Arkansas was to show him his teammate. So Abram led the Arkansas mule onto the towboat, and they chugged across to the Tennessee side. But the Tennessee mule wasn't on the shore anymore. Fortunately, Abram had a way with animals. He got the Arkansas mule to talking—whinnying and wailing and hee-hawing."

Clementine demonstrated her childhood repertoire of mule vocalizations that left Robert gasping with laughter.

"Dang if the lost mule didn't come wandering out and start talking to its teammate! Uncle Chase hipped up to the bank and set a plank for the mule to board. And it walked right onto the deck and nuzzled its mate, and they stood there with their necks and heads together the whole way back."

"You know the moral of that story, don't you Clementine?" Robert leaned in to look directly into her face. "Some creatures are meant to be a team." He sat back. "Maybe we should resign our commissions and start a salvage business."

That set off daydreams that lasted until Memphis, when she taxied to the private aviation hangar. A silver Chevy Suburban was waiting on the apron, lights on and wipers beating.

Robert cursed under his breath. "Looks like I have a welcoming committee. I texted Rita that I'd catch a ride with you to Memphis and head back to New Orleans in the morning, so I could at least see the kids for a few hours." The children were finishing up their school term in Tennessee before the family joined him in New Orleans. "Do you feel up to coming over to say hello?"

"Tell them I have to put away my plane."

Robert jumped down with his deployment bag. He touched his patrol cap in a comradely salute and trudged through the rain toward the SUV, which flashed its lights and opened a rear door. Clementine signaled the hangar attendant who rolled out on the lawn tractor to tow Snoopy inside.

She got home wiped out but too wired to fall asleep and a little afraid of waking up to open doors and windows. She showered, replied to messages, and turned on the TV. The Weather Channel forecast good news. No more thunderstorms, at least for a while. But Noah ticked off the thirty-sixth consecutive day of rain.

CNN showed the oft-repeated loop of the *Abraham Lincoln* breaking loose from the Poplar Street Bridge, careening after Captain Pike's Z-drive, and captured by a pair of towboats, which shepherded the sinking hulk between the MacArthur Bridge abutments. General Penn was interviewed, again, sounding simultaneously grave, avuncular, and optimistic. "The immediate crisis is over. It's time for the clean-up to begin, and for law enforcement to run down the miscreants." She was reaching to turn it off when the loop was interrupted by breaking news.

"FBI agents raided Black Muslim tough-love boot camps up and down the Mississippi Valley early this morning. Suspects were rounded up in St. Louis, Cairo, Bliss, and Memphis. Agents seized weapons and explosives."

Thank God, she thought. They caught the sons of bitches before they attacked again.

She boiled water for chamomile tea and decided instead of counting sheep she'd count how many years before Robert's children grew up and left home, leaving him free to get a divorce. Candace was the youngest at eleven. Clementine felt a pang of guilt for not going over to say hello to the child who idolized her. Ten years 'til she reached her legal maturity. That would make Clementine forty-six and Robert, ohmygod, sixty-one. Did she really want to spend her prime years on hold, having to accept crumbs while his wife and children devoured the whole delicious pie? Could they be secret lovers for ten years and not get caught? They'd already spent ten years pretending not to be in love. But it was risky to play a long game in a world where catastrophe lurked around every corner. As Aunt Martha used to say, "A bird in the hand is worth two in the bush." Don't count on a future that may never come. She fell asleep pretending Robert was the pillow she was hugging.

You're safe. You're safe with me.

29

Tough Love Tested

Day 37
Thursday

Clementine Price was on her first cup of coffee, fielding apocalyptic texts about multiple flood crests from Will's WhetherChannel science student friends, and toggling between terrorism stories on CNN and Weather Channel warnings of high water on the Mississippi's tributaries when an extremely upset Libby Winters telephoned about the camp arrests.

"It's insane."

"I was just watching the news. It sounds like they rolled up some pretty bad apples."

Libby said, "I don't know about the other raids. But I know our people. They arrested ten Bliss Hills camp counselors."

"What were these camp counselors doing with weapons?"

"Weapons?" Libby echoed, scornfully. "Do you call skeet guns weapons?"

"Skeet guns?"

"For shooting clay pigeons. The counselors' practice is to wean children off their street weapons with sport shooting. The kids make plenty of noise, but no one dies. They also get healthy food, regular hours, and tutoring in reading, math, religion, and art in a loving atmosphere—for the first time in their lives—which those men have provided for the past *nine years*."

"But it's not summer yet. What were they doing in the camp?"

"*Painting the damn dining hall!*" Libby yelled.

"CNN said that the FBI confiscated bomb-making material."

"They were hoping to plant the vegetable garden if the rain stopped. The FBI confiscated their fertilizer."

"Libby, are you sure?"

"Of course," she snapped. "Billy Bob Owen checked it out for me. He's no friend of the black community, and hates Muslims on principle, but even he admits they're just ordinary folks rousted out of their beds and thrown in jail for no reason."

"All I can say is, it comes as news to me," said Clementine.

"Can you help?"

"How?"

"You're a major in the army, Clem. You serve in the Mississippi Valley Division. The Corps has been part and parcel of the Delta for over a hundred years. Tell the media the FBI went off half-cocked and you're requesting an immediate investigation."

"I cannot do that—as much as I want to."

"And then tell them that you apologize to the falsely accused black camp counselors in the name of the United States government."

"No one would listen and I would be transferred out of here so fast my head would spin."

"And would it be possible at the same time to ask the Justice Department to apologize for leaking twenty-year-old criminal court records to smear the camp counselors who long ago found a religion—which happened to be Islam—that saved them. Men who dedicated their lives to helping children of all faiths and colors less fortunate than you and me?"

"Libby, I would if I could."

"These people have nothing left. Their work. Their reputations. The good they do. Their freedom. All ripped from them."

"Maybe I can talk to Senator Garfield."

"I already tried. He won't take my calls."

"Then I doubt he'll take mine. Libby—"

"Clem, I'm desperate."

Clementine Price said the only thing she could: "I will be there in two hours."

Her pilot's weather app and the TV threatened hellacious wind and lightning. She drove her Jeep and filled in Tommy Chow on the phone. He was freaking out as it dawned on him that even though a Memphis District command was the last thing he wanted, if the district suffered major flooding on his "co-watch" it would look catastrophic on his service record. She calmed him down as best she could. And she promised to check out the latest with their people watching in Bliss, Caruthersville, and Birds Point, while thinking to herself maybe they should split responsibility for the district: give Tommy Memphis and West Memphis while she covered everything from Bliss north—her old "home place" as it were. Next, she spoke with her (their) district's Public Affairs Office chief who reported that a joint FBI-Deputy Assistant Attorney General press conference was scheduled at Bliss City Hall.

Senator Garfield's office would not put her through to him, as she had feared; he knew, of course, that she and Libby were close. She continued working the phone the length of the drive, polling civilian contractors about the levees, and making an appointment with one of the therapists on Robert's list.

"Nothing for two weeks."

"No rush, two weeks will be fine."

She dialed Robert's burner phone. He picked up on the first ring.

"Robert, I just wanted you to know that I've booked my first session with one of your PTSD people."

"I'm so glad. There's no shame in this, Clementine. I've gone through it myself, you know."

"No, I didn't know."

"There was no reason to mention it. I didn't sleepwalk like you, but I had nightmares, to the extent I dreaded going to sleep. From time to time, I go in for a tune-up. And now, when I fall asleep, I dream of you."

"I fell asleep last night dreaming of you, too."

When she got to Bliss, a crowd of gray-haired protestors was demonstrating outside the city hall, waving hand-lettered signs decrying false arrests. Reverend Eddie was there with a contingent from his New Salvation Baptist Church. So was Libby's mother, stone-faced. Clementine waded into the crowd to give her a hug, told her she had come to see Libby, and ran inside.

Libby had shut the door to her private office. Libby's chief of staff, Sharon, said, "Don't bother knocking, Major Price. Just go in. She needs a friend real bad."

Clementine pushed through the door and closed it behind her. Libby was standing behind her desk, staring at a monitor. Tears were streaming down her cheeks. Clementine stepped beside her and slung an arm around her shoulder and saw that Libby was watching a TV loop of the middle-aged camp counselors handcuffed to each other and stumbling off a corrections bus.

Libby said, "You want to know why my heart is broken, Clem?"

"That's why I'm here."

"These men try to fill the void when families disappear. When families disappear, kids see no one but other kids as lost as they are. Don't you see, most everything that happened to black people in the last five hundred years messed with their families? Africans captured by slave traders broke up their family. Dragged across the ocean, made slaves, broke up the family. Slaves found God, made new families. Slave auctions broke up families. Finally get their freedom, finally get a chance to plow their own ground, here come the night riders. Folks run for their lives. Break up their families. Imagine if horsemen galloped up to your door in the middle of the night swinging whips and rifles, wouldn't you light out for the North?

"So we make our 'Great Migration.' But when we land in the North, we're smack in the face of white immigrant working class hatred. Made it hard to find a place to live, breaking up families. But people keep on trying to make a family, trying to hold it together. Along comes World War Two. Steady factory work. Finally start to get settled in the cities after the war. Make families. Now they build the interstate highways right through their front door. *Tore apart every black community in every city in the country.* 'Well hell, where we going to build this thing? White man's neighborhood? The white man don't want no six-lane highway on his front lawn.' Neighborhoods cut in half, cut in threes and fours, housing knocked down, broke up families. In comes dope. Alcohol. Along comes heroin. And here come the riots.

"Every time you break something it becomes weaker. It is a miracle how many black families survived at all. Some even flourished. But it's a *tragedy* how many have been scattered to the wind. Half the black children in this rich country are growing up poor. How many of them, do you suppose, don't have families?"

"Libby, I—"

"Had no idea? Heck, not every black woman and man is living poor. Half of us are doing okay, some even better than okay. Until one night we get pulled over by a white cop. Clementine, if my husband—my beautiful man—the chief of homicide of the Bliss Metropolitan Police and a war veteran with medals and scars he got sending God knows how many terrorists to hook up early with Allah's virgins—if Rolly gets pulled over by a cracker highway patrol officer, his life is in danger! Don't you get it? Rolly can get killed tomorrow by a white cop who's either poorly trained or racist, or both. I want to ask you Clem, can you imagine waiting at home wondering if tonight's the night your man will be shot by the police?"

"No, Libby."

"Can you imagine trying to teach your children—two rambunctious little boys—how to survive being questioned by the police? *Rolly, Jr. and Kevin are the sons of a police officer*! But what does a white cop see? Nothing but troublemaking black kids."

Libby stared at Clementine. Her eyes filled with helpless tears.

Clementine said, "I've done what I can, so far."

"What? What have you done?"

"Garfield would not take my call. Since Garfield's a member of Hilltop, I telephoned Reverend Flowers. But he's on the road."

Libby said, "He never calls back when he's ministering to prisoners."

"I called Mary Kay Flowers."

"What can she do?"

"I'm betting that Senator Garfield will return her call."

"Dammit, I should have thought of that."

"You've got a lot going on, Libby. Let's hope Mary Kay can help us."

Sharon stuck her head in. "Press conference starting."

Clementine saw immediately that Libby was right, and the demonstrators had good reason to be angry. The FBI and the Deputy AG had fallen back on the sorriest of PR tactics: send a woman or an old guy to explain bad news. Today they had sent both, and the media smelled blood.

The questions flew. The designated woman stood there answering as stoically as a grade-school teacher who had failed to meet PTA expectations.

"Were these arrests prompted by the St. Louis barge-jacking?"

"No, sir. We already had—"

"Was the fact that those alleged barge-jackers towed their attack boat with a tough-love boot-camp pickup truck a factor in these raids?"

"No, ma'am. We had credible—"

"Was the collapse of a flood levee on the Ohio River a factor in these raids?"

Libby looked at Clementine.

"No big deal. County levee breached by backwater."

"Ma'am," answered the FBI agent. "We had credible-sounding—"

"Was—"

"We had credible information from numerous sources indicating—"

Clementine whispered, "This sounds as bad as you said."

"The Bliss Hills Muslims are good men," Libby repeated.

Sharon leaned around her to say, "A fact that will do squat to spring them."

Suddenly a relative who had somehow slipped past security yelled, "You won't even let 'em have a lawyer. Not that they can 'ford it."

The AG's woman shouted, "We'll conclude with a joint statement from Mayor Libby Winters and the Reverend Eddie Parker, pastor of the New Salvation Baptist Church. Mayor Winters and Reverend Parker."

Libby spoke first, her voice grave.

"To the Black Muslim community of Bliss and the families of the dedicated men of the Bliss Hills Boot Camp, I ask that you be patient, and pray that *our brothers* will soon be released. To the Attorney General, I say that Homeland Security benefits us all so long as we remember that hardworking peace officers can make mistakes. The presumption of innocence is the right of every American citizen, and when you take it away from one, you take it from all."

Reverend Eddie had barely opened his mouth when there was another commotion at the door. The cops surged toward it, then just as suddenly stepped back. In swept Hilltop Outreach Minister Reverend Mary Kay Flowers accompanied by her father, the patrician Reverend Keeler T. Blankenship, pastor of Bliss First Methodist. Mary Kay shot Clementine a thumbs-up, marched straight to the stage, and bounded up the steps.

"The Hilltop Fellowship will put up half the bail for these gentlemen who dedicate their lives to helping children less fortunate than we are."

With that, Mary Kay Flowers began to preach. Clementine Price saw that Reverend Eddie and Reverend Blankenship suddenly had the same expression of astonished admiration on their very different faces.

"In the Christian faith we say, 'Let those who are without sin cast the first stone.' Our Muslim neighbors say, 'Allah forgives those who repent.' And today all of us here in Bliss say, 'Let us bond together to help our neighbors in need.' Hilltop Fellowship has established a legal defense fund for our Muslim brothers and contributions are being accepted as of this moment. So, let us all return peacefully to our homes and workplaces and pray that our arrested brothers are well treated and out on bail before the day is ended. Remember what our Lord told Moses to demand of Pharaoh: '*Let my people go.*'"

30

The Double-Crest Guarantee

Day 37
Thursday

United States Air Force rules and regulations left no wiggle room. Air Force helicopters were not to be flown on joy rides; not even old crates stripped of rockets and cannon and held in the sky by wheezing turbines ten thousand hours past their depot rebuild date. Guests were not welcome; not even veterans of Air Force special-tactics outfits, no matter how long they had served, no matter how decorated. But, as Rolly Winters and Duvall McCoy knew from long experience, if you ever want a tiger pilot to do something he shouldn't do, order him *not* to do it.

Besides, it was for a good cause. With Mike Coligny flying, they eyeballed more abandoned missile silos in two hours than they'd have found in two weeks driving cars and off-road vehicles on the rugged stream-and-creek-riven hills of western Missouri. Some were easily spotted by the junk scattered around them, rusting doors in hillsides, sagging chain-link fences, heaps of scrap metal and concrete. Others, almost obliterated, were nearly invisible in the rain.

The silo enclosures—typically two fenced acres—had in common a driveway running to a county road. Theorizing that even hermits and survivalists ran out of groceries now and then, they examined these links between roads and junk piles for parked trucks or SUVs and tire tracks indicating recent use. But as Coligny descended for closer looks at site after site, all they saw were the fading signs of a two- and three-decades-old past.

Rolly thanked his old friend for his patience. Coligny—who limped from numerous crashes, bore rakish scars on his face, and was milder of manner than his service record would suggest—assured Rolly that silo hunting was more fun than transporting senior officers to VIP functions, which he had been assigned to thanks to his latest demotion. Mike's flight engineer, a bright, young shifty-eyed kid who probably reminded Coligny of his misspent youth, agreed.

***

"Now's your chance," the Weatherman told the Shot Caller. "Guaranteed. Multiple storms will swamp the Ohio Valley and the Upper Mississippi Valley. Flood crests will descend both rivers simultaneously. The timing is perfect for them to meet at the Confluence." He tapped his monitor where the Mississippi and Ohio Rivers joined at Fort Defiance Park, just below Cairo, Illinois. "The double crest will blast down the Mississippi River like a million bulldozers."

"The Weather Channel agrees with you on the Ohio Valley," said the Shot Caller. "But not the Upper Mississippi."

The Weatherman cast a scornful glance at the flat-screen displaying the Weather Channel's Noah cartoon, stalled by no rain predicted for St. Louis at day thirty-nine. Then he pointed one by one at the rest of his monitors: at the graphic displays of rain cores, storm cells, and rainfall reports; at Network Control cloud-to-ground and intra-cloud lightning flashes.

"I don't care what they say on the Weather Channel. Simultaneous flood crests will join at Cairo, at the Confluence. If for some reason the Birds Point fuse levee doesn't melt . . ."

Nathan interrupted "Assume it doesn't."

The Weatherman paused, thinking that the Shot Caller knew something no one else did about Birds Point. "Right. If Birds Point doesn't melt, then Cairo, Bliss, and Memphis are toast."

"Except the National Weather Service agrees with the Weather Channel."

It struck the Weatherman that he had never before heard the Shot Caller sound as if he doubted himself. He was dressed in his usual sales-commission-slave costume of sport coat and necktie. His black mask covered his forehead and his nose and lips. All very much as he always was. But he had remained in the elevator when he arrived, and he was still there, with one hand on the ascent rope like a rocket poised to launch out the silo straight to Russia.

The Weatherman asked, "Have I ever been wrong?"

"Too bad about your bitch."

The Weatherman took a deep breath, half-expecting the Shot Caller to draw a knife, stride across the silo floor, and slit his throat from ear to ear. "Sorry, Shot Caller. I meant wrong about the weather."

"Understand, when I start this moving, I can't stop it if your flood does not materialize."

The Weatherman said, flatly, "The combination will drive the Mississippi out of its banks. Guaranteed!"

"How many monkey-brain jailbirds are doing time for guaranteed, sure-thing convenience store stick-ups?"

"There will be no stopping this double-crest flood," said the Weatherman. "And more crests will follow the double."

The Shot Caller said, "The attack will be in plain sight. It will be like throwing the first punch. Once I start, the Army Corps of Engineers and the Coast Guard and the cops will be watching to see what I do next."

"Guaranteed flood!" the Weatherman repeated. "I'll bet my life on it."

"That *I* guarantee," said the Shot Caller. "Don't you understand, Weatherman? The more ground we capture, the more we need the flood to defend it. The government can't counterattack during a flood. A flood gives us the time to defend ourselves, and the government the time to hesitate and hesitate until it's too late to stop us."

He tugged the rope. The wooden car rose. The Weatherman listened to it creaking up the shaft and wondered would he ever see the Shot Caller again. Next year in Jerusalem, he thought with a smile. Jerusalem, Alluvia, all the same: if things won't be better in the future, at least they'll be different.

His eyes flickered to the screens. New data streaming in made him grin with pleasure. He was still right. He was absolutely right. He was more right than ever. If Alluvia needed double flood crests, triples, quadruples, rampaging down the Mississippi, then Alluvia was made in the shade. Especially if for some reason the Birds Point fuse levee didn't melt. He cocked his ear. The car was creaking, again, lowering slowly back down the shaft.

Back so soon? To apologize for doubting my forecast.

That's okay, Shot Caller. I forgive you.

The Weatherman rubbed his nose. Funny smell coming down the shaft. Like fertilizer. Then he smelled diesel. Not truck exhaust, but raw diesel fuel. And now he smelled acrid smoke, like a burning fuse. Nitrogen fertilizer. Diesel. Ignition. He stood up. But at the bottom of a reinforced-concrete cylinder buried fifteen stories underground there was nowhere to run from an ANFO bomb.

***

Mike Coligny's Hawk was swooping down on the fifteenth or sixteenth silo site when a shout from Duvall suddenly erupted in their headsets. The driveway was the usual quarter mile straight line to a paved road. But Duvall had spotted a thin track running at a right angle toward a distant tree line.

"Off-road bike!"

Coligny dropped the old machine to the ground and touched his skids beside the path as lightly as a falling leaf. Rolly and Duvall piled out. It was a motorbike trail, a narrow line of flattened grass and puddled rainwater. Tire marks looked fresh in the mud. They traced it back to the chain-link fence and through a gate hanging open. Two hundred feet across the littered enclosure stood the silo doors.

They had seen some sites with the doors shut, and others where scavengers had carted off the doors, leaving a gaping hole in the ground. These were still in place, but hinged wide open, exposing the missile maw. Duvall started toward it. Rolly, constrained by some mysterious instinct that he couldn't explain until later when he remembered the dirt bike tracks, grabbed his arm.

"What?"

"Wait!"

"Goddammit Rolly, sometimes you're like a timid old man on a cane."

Rolly tightened his grip so Duvall got the message. "Only 'cause my knees hurt."

The ground shook.

Rolly Winters and Duvall McCoy fell flat and covered their heads.

A tongue of flame shot from the silo's mouth.

They felt as much as heard explosions far below the face of the earth.

Smoke lit by flame spewed in the air.

"I think we found it," said Duvall. "One minute late."

Rolly eyed the pillar of smoke. The rain and a thermal inversion flattened it into a mushroom-shaped cloud that stank of burnt electronics and melting plastic. "Glad we weren't a minute early."

But Duvall was right. Barring an amazing coincidence, they had found the Weatherman's hideout. "Next question: who bought it for him?"

In actual fact, the Bliss Metro hate-crime squad was less interested in talking to the supremacist roasting down below than to whoever had paid the bills to install him down there. And now that they had zeroed in on a single two-acre plot of real estate, locating that bill-paying bigot had gotten a whole lot easier.

"Except . . ." said Rolly, and they began ping-ponging thoughts.

"Based on what St. Louis told us about the tech genius . . ."

"And the job he did on that ankle monitor . . ."

"The Weatherman was the last guy I'd figure to blow up himself up."

"By accident."

"Suicide?"

"Snuff job."

They whirled in unison, ran to the helicopter at surprising speed for big middle-aged men, and scrambled aboard. "Dirt bike in the woods, Mike. Go! Go! Go!"

Mike blasted off the ground and slung the machine over the woods, which grew along both sides of a creek. The trees were only partially leafed out and patches of ground were visible. They spotted where the path from the enclosure hooked downhill and followed the turns in the creek bed. They traced the path almost to the county road before they lost it in the dark.

"Sonofabitch was right here."

31

A Brand New World

Day 38
Friday

Mary Kay Flowers parked her blue rubber boots, yellow poncho, and red umbrella in the designated racks and bins in New Salvation Baptist Church's entryway and slipped silently into the sanctuary, where the Friday night youth service was already underway. Reverend Eddie was observing from the back row and waved her over with a smile.

"Your Saline Solution is the talk of the town, at least in church circles," whispered Mary Kay. "I'm sure I'm not the first to invite them to guest preach."

"Not the first," said Reverend Eddie with unmistakable pride. "But Hilltop would certainly be the largest flock they've ever ministered to; and after you stepped in to bail out the tough-love counselors, Hilltop goes to the front of the line."

Reverend Eddie's son Morris and his rappers were on the stage, writing rhymes on a big whiteboard as fast as the teenaged congregation could shout them out. When the board was full, Morris held up his hand for quiet, as they all studied the list of possible lyrics. He turned to the girl with the grill and spangled hat first. "Daneesha, you start." She was ready with her rap:

Outside that fancy locked gate lay a bum,
All day he'd wait, just for a crumb,
But that rich man only threw him shade,
Wouldn't share a dime of all the money he'd made.

The sanctuary erupted in whoops, snaps, and fist bumps.

"The parable of Lazarus?" Mary Kay ventured.

Reverend Eddie grinned. "You got it, Sister Flowers. Of course, most of these youngsters never heard of Lazarus before tonight. So when we make the video, each rap starts with one of them reading the original story from the Bible. Once they've gotten the source from scripture, they're welcome to get creative 'til the cows come home."

Morris was frantically signaling his father, pointing to an empty tripod in the center aisle. "Looks like tonight I'm the cameraman again," said Reverend Eddie with mock exasperation. "'Cause I got the key to the AV closet. Would you excuse me?"

Reverend Eddie disappeared through the rear doors while Mary Kay grabbed a few minutes of video with her iPhone to send to her youth minister. She was consulting Hilltop's master calendar for the first available Guest Youth Preacher slot when Reverend Eddie returned. "Mrs. Flowers, there's someone from Hilltop come to fetch you—says it's important."

She felt a whisper of a kiss on the back of her neck and closed her eyes.

"Nathan, what are you doing here? I thought you were in Cape Girardeau."

"And let you celebrate our anniversary alone?" He encircled her from behind, and placed in her hand a bouquet of camellias, lilacs, and lily of the valley.

"My wedding bouquet? Nathan, where did you get these? None of these are in bloom now."

"I plan ahead. Reverend Eddie, would you excuse us? We have a reservation at the Hunnicutt House, and I wouldn't want them to give away our table."

The Hunnicutt House was Bliss's most luxurious boutique hotel, with a farm-to-table restaurant that drew foodies from all over the mid-South and beyond. By some miracle, the grand Victorian showplace had not been razed when Bliss's downtown was carved up by the interstate spur and slabs of brutalist high-rise public housing. It was now the crown jewel in Bliss's increasingly gentrified Old District. Its oversized windows cast a golden glow, making the raindrops sparkle like cut crystal.

On their way through the ornate lobby to the restaurant, Nathan paused at the front desk. "Reverend and Mrs. Flowers," he said. "Our luggage is in the car, if you'd be so kind as to have it taken to our room while we have dinner." He pressed a five dollar bill into the bellman's hand, along with the car key. He took Mary Kay's bouquet from her and passed it across to the concierge. "And could you please have this put in a vase in our suite?"

"Well, you are full of surprises tonight, aren't you?" Mary Kay laughed.

The maître d' led them through the plushly upholstered dining room to a corner table tucked into an alcove and seated them at right angles, with Mary Kay on the right, just like they sat when they worked together at their partners desk. On the table was a half-bottle of Veuve Clicquot—a gesture more than a promise, as Nathan rarely consumed more than a few sips of beer, preferring to keep his wits about him at all times, and Mary Kay drank alcohol so infrequently that a half a glass of champagne would put her to sleep.

To her surprise however, tonight that half-bottle was emptied, and another ordered. They feasted on each other, laughing, flirting, touching hands and faces, and pressing knees together under the table. The dining room emptied, but they kept talking and touching.

"I have to tell you something, darling," Nathan took both of her hands in his. "I was fixing to share some big plans with you tonight, plans about our mission to make a better world."

Mary Kay raised her eyebrows but said nothing.

"But you know how important it is for me to plan everything out, to check and double check before I say it out loud."

"I know you can't stand uncertainty, Nathan. That's one of the things I love about you; you don't make promises you can't honor."

"So, you understand then. Darling, you're going to be so excited when I tell you; it's an opportunity to take our vision to a higher level." Nathan's eyes were bright, almost feverish, and Mary Kay could feel his pulse quicken as he tightened his grip on her hands. She suddenly felt dizzy.

"Well, I'll be all ears when you're ready to tell me," she said, looking at the empty Veuve bottle upside down in its silver cooler. "Meanwhile, I think this champagne has gone to my head, and I'm eager to see what other surprises you have planned for tonight."

She squeezed his hand and stood up experimentally, relieved to have her sense of balance mostly intact. Nathan jumped up and grabbed her arm, walking her briskly out of the dining room toward the lobby elevator.

May Kay swayed against him as they waited. "Could you just give me a hint?"

The elevator dinged and the doors opened. The car was empty. Nathan pulled her close, nearly taking her breath away. "Darling, it's a bigger arena—a brand new world."

32

Don't Go Near the River

Day 38
Friday

Late that night, the old mill that housed Bliss Alloy Steel below South End finally finished loading Captain Billy Scruggs's barges. When his crew got done making tow and had all thirty barges cabled into one big fleet, he took it off the wharf and headed upstream.

It was black as a root cellar, and highwater eddies were growing strong. Strong enough to drag even the powerful *Delta Lady* into the path of a down-bound tow if Billy Scruggs let them. The wind was picking up too, shouldering hard against the barges, shrieking around the wheelhouse. He poked at the dark with the searchlights, but the fog was thick, despite the wind. Swooping and swirling, it reflected the searchlights like a mirror, blinding his eyes.

The radar showed him the arch of the interstate connector bridge.

The AIS Monitor promised no other tows were occupying the channel.

The radio confirmed no one else was fixing to make the bridge.

He ordered a deckhand to take a handheld radio forward and stand on the bow of the lead barge to talk the fleet between the piers. He could see on the radar the long truss of the channel span. But when he looked out the window for the bridge lights, he could not see the greens that marked the sailing line down the middle of the channel or the red on its piers. They were five hundred feet apart. The tow was the better part of three hundred feet wide. And both below and above the bridge, stone jetties stretched into the channel, waiting to grab anyone who looked the other way.

The deckhand radioed that the head of the tow was getting mighty tight with the starboard channel pier. Scruggs felt he was still an easy distance off. He had never hit a bridge yet and did not intend to start tonight; they made the absolute worst accidents imaginable because the first hit was just the beginning. The current took you sideways and every barge in your fleet ended up smashing into piers, tangling around abutments, or sinking on jetties.

He managed to make the bridge without bumping anything. He radioed the deckhand to check the sounders and the lights and come back to the boat. The radar showed the channel clear of tows ahead, but the truth was, he couldn't say he would be disappointed to land the fleet before the night got any worse.

He continued on up past Hilltop and the new steel mill to Mile 815. They had established quite a fleeting area on the Tennessee side, apparently waiting out a Coast Guard decision to close the river above St. Louis. He passed ten fleets tied off, several hundred barges hunkered against the bank like alligators drowsing, except there weren't no sun to drowse in, just sheets of rain and curtains of fog; no self-respecting alligator would have been caught dead there. It had thickened into a real shutout fog before the radar and the sounders found him a nice quiet stretch of mud bank.

There he landed, nudging the head of the tow in softly, and letting the powerful current swing the rest of the fleet alongside. Losers or not, the *Delta Lady*'s deckhands got tied off without incident. Billy Scruggs stood up from the sticks and tried to stretch the kinks out of his back.

"I've had just about as much fun as I can stand tonight," he told Joey, who had watched him close the whole time. Before the thug could answer, the general manager's cell phone went off in Billy's pocket. He fumbled it out, searched for the talk button while it rang and rang like a lonely bird. Finally, he found the damned thing and said, "Hello?"

"What you have to do now is cut loose and deadhead back down to the casino barge."

"Now?"

"You seen her. She's on that jetty just below the bridge. Noah's Ark."

"I seen her." Big critter heads sticking out of fake windows.

"Well get on down there."

"What happens when I get there?"

"Tie off and wait for orders."

***

"Colonel Chow this is Major Price. Is it okay if I call you Tommy and you call me Clementine?"

"What the hell time is it?"

"0200."

"Jesus, Clementine."

"I heard you were bunking in the office. I figured you might be up."

"Up for a huge fight with my wife on the phone. What's happening?"

"At the moment, Cairo and Bliss are in a lot more danger than Memphis."

Tommy Chow was a lot blunter than he would be with most officers, but they had known each other and worked together a long time; or maybe he was still amped up from battling his spouse. He said, "That's a relief. I'd rather the army blame me for Bliss than Memphis."

"That's why I'm calling. I've got your back in Bliss, Hilltop, Caruthersville, and Cairo. You can concentrate on protecting the cities of Memphis and West Memphis, which are in less danger, for the moment at least. Worst case, I'll get the blame for a PR disaster in Bliss or the Hilltop megachurch with twenty-two thousand parishioners."

"Clementine. No offense, but I can't believe you're doing this out of the kindness of your heart."

"Between you and me, Tommy, Bliss and Hilltop and even Cairo are closer to my heart than Memphis. This was my home."

"What do you want in return?"

"The Boat."

"The Boat? What do you want The Boat for?"

"I'm strung along hundreds of miles of river. I need a mobile HQ and a visible presence to rally my people. And if the levee is breached, God help us, I need to respond fast with men and machines."

"Okay, you'll have The Boat in Bliss by noon."

She said, "Thank you, Tommy. Please ask the captain to prepare a stateroom for my adjutant."

She telephoned Lieutenant Harpur at home, got the machine, hung up, and dialed repeatedly until the young officer woke up. "Terry, The Boat is leaving for Bliss. Get aboard. Arrange accommodations for staff. I'll catch up."

She got off the phone with de facto command of the district from Bliss to Cairo.

***

"You could shoot moose down there."

The co-manager of the Noah's Lucky Ark Casino mourning the dearth of customers was Big Al Striker.

"You ever wonder why we have no mooses sticking their heads out our windows?" The co-manager lamenting the lack of moose heads was Holly Green, Big Al's bean pole of a partner.

"They don't have moose in the Bible," Big Al told Holly.

"Want to bet?" said Holly.

"No, I don't want to bet," said Big Al, who was learning the hard way that Holly only bet on sure things.

From the security overlook behind one-way glass, they had an unobstructed view of the Ark's red and yellow gaming hall. Splendiferous lights blinked and shimmered, the ceiling changed colors at programmed intervals, and video screens promoted triple payoffs. But the "Down Home" free buffet was mostly untouched, and the three-acre expanse of game tables, slot machines, blackjack, craps, roulette, poker, and Spanish 21 was occupied mostly by bored dealers, yawning cashiers, and anxious cocktail hostesses.

"Speaking of betting . . ." Holly Green opened a narrow hand, palm up. He was a slow-talking, twenty-eight-year-old Texas con man, all drawls and smiles. "Ah believe our wager was for one thousand dollars. And Ah further believe that we agreed to take the measure of our business the third week of May."

As Holly had predicted—and Al had said would never happen—the rain was finally playing hell with the gambling business. For a long time the customers kept coming despite the weather. Big Al Striker had a simple explanation. "Gamblers gamble. What the hell else are they going to do with themselves?"

The answer, feared by casinos, was they could gamble on the internet. But since last harvest, when the rains had started, through Christmas and Easter, the Noah's Lucky Ark parking lot was full most nights and traffic backed up to the interstate connector on weekends. So Big Al had accepted a thousand-dollar side bet from his co-manager that business would drop off if it kept raining into May. Rain they had agreed to define as seven inches a week.

He shouldn't have taken the bet. Should have remembered—like he just had about the moose—that Holly Green was no gambler. Holly was a hustler, which meant he must have known something. A thousand bucks was a lot of money. It wasn't like he owned the casino. Nor was this Atlantic City or Vegas, where you could get very rich just running one. The competition was hell. Every pissant town on the Mississippi had a casino barge. And they were scrambling for small fry—mill hands and Walmart clerks. To make matters worse, the people he and Holly were working for were not the type you stole from. It was like they had learned security from the Russian Secret Service.

Holly demanded Al pay him in green. "Green for Green," he drawled and smiled.

Big Al wrote a personal check to cover his withdrawal from petty cash and pressed twenty fifties in Holly's hand. Holly counted them twice.

"All right, goddammit. Tell me how you did it."

"Suppose Ah got lucky."

"You didn't get lucky. You knew something. What did you know?"

Holly Green weighed the question a long, slow moment. Then he said, "Oh, hell, Ah don't suppose it'll matter to tell you the secret, now that Ah took your money." Another big, lazy smile reminded Al Striker why he hated con men. All such grifters really wanted was to hurt somebody. Still, he wanted to know the secret. But just as Holly opened his mouth to explain, the room moved.

Not a lot, but enough to tell Al that something enormous had bumped into the barge.

"What the hell was that?"

Down in the hall, employees and the few customers were looking around, wondering. Al and Holly exchanged an anxious glance. Out-of-control runaway tows had crashed into more than one casino parked beside the river long before the St. Louis attack; the next bump might tear them off the bank. They hurried to the door that led to a second-level deck, suddenly reminded that while land-bound gambling "boats" satisfied a legal nicety, Noah's Lucky Ark was afloat without engines in swift-flowing water.

They opened the heavy, water-tight door.

Black diesel smoke thundered in.

Al felt real terror and turned to run back indoors.

Holly stuck his head out and yelled, "What in hell are you boys up to?"

A huge towboat was pressing its push knees against the barge, snorting smoke and grinding engines. A bunch who looked like motorcycle gangsters and dope smugglers jumped onto the Noah's Lucky Ark Casino. They dragged ropes onto the barge's narrow side deck. A middle-aged alkie leaned out the boat's wheelhouse window with a walkie-talkie.

Holly Green yelled again. "What's up boys?"

A half-naked, tattooed, skinhead weightlifter shouted, "Tying off."

"What for?"

"Orders."

"You're on private property."

"Owner's orders."

"Why?"

"Get out of my face, man."

Just then a pair of the casino security men who operated out of the off-limits hold came up on deck. To the gambler's and con man's amazement, they shook hands with the skinhead. "It's okay, Mr. Striker," one of them called up. "You all can go back inside now."

"What's going on?" asked Al.

"I said you all can go back in. Now, sir."

Al and Holly retreated indoors. A drink suddenly seemed like a very good idea. Courvoisier, Al's latest kick. Holly had his usual white wine spritzer, heavy on the bubbles, maintaining his edge.

"You think the owners sold out?" Al asked.

"Who knows?"

"Anyone tell you they're moving the barge?"

"Hell no."

"You sure?"

"If they did, I would have told you."

Al sipped a while, thinking. Fact was, no one from the absentee corporation that owned the casino ever told them anything. They just collected the money. Nor did the close-mouthed bastards listen to their advice. He and Holly were just glorified errand boys.

"What do you think?" he asked Holly.

Holly Green wondered if this had anything to do with the below-decks space of the barge, which the owners had made strictly off limits to the casino managers. And wondered, not for the first time, if it was worth risking a broken head to steal a look. Except they had placed their security office at the only entrance.

Al asked him again what he thought.

Holly changed the subject, "You were wondering how Ah knew?"

"Yeah?"

"How Ah knew business would drop off?"

"How'd you know?"

"It's not the rain keeping away the customers."

"Yeah, what is it?"

"The flood. The customers believe that it's going to flood and they're voting with their feet."

"They got no way of predicting that."

The slow-talking Texan merely smiled. "It don't take a soothsayer to tune in the Weather Channel. And Ah've noticed something about folks born around here. Something deep in their bones says don't go near the river."

33

THE FUSE LEVEE

Day 39
Saturday

Clementine's brother Will telephoned late in the afternoon with a chilling report of WhetherChannel hacker readings lifted from the National Weather Service experimental sensors. The students had been calling data right all week and she believed their latest warning enough to get to the Birds Point fuse levee as fast as she could. Before her yellow Air Tractor was airborne, the NWS and the Weather Channel were in agreement: multiple crests were marching down the Ohio River and the Upper Mississippi; timing was the only question; and the timing kept advancing as storms bred flash floods.

Racing upriver, she got a call from Chief Engineer Jesse Corliss.

"He's back," said Corliss, and Clementine knew that could mean only one thing: General Penn was headed for Cairo again.

"Bless you, Jesse. I'm already on my way to Birds Point. How's our fuse levee?"

"Looked good this morning. The river ought to start topping it around midnight, maybe a little earlier depending on the crests."

"I'll overfly it and get another look. Jesse?"

"Yes, ma'am."

"I have The Boat at Bliss. I'd like you go aboard with your people."

"I'm supposed to meet Lieutenant Colonel Chow in Memphis."

"I'll deal with Tommy. See Lieutenant Harpur for your accommodations."

She telephoned Chow, persuaded him to give her their chief engineer until the crests had passed Bliss, and flew straight up the river at eight thousand feet, right over Bliss and right over Hilltop. A tall, dense cumulonimbus cloud she had been tracking since before Bliss suddenly grew a mean-looking anvil top. Towering over Caruthersville, it forced her off course. She flew west of the monster, deep into Missouri airspace, battered by turbulence and blinded by lightning. Twice she tried to cut back toward Birds Point. Twice it blocked her. The delay would cost her dearly.

Dusk would be closing in soon. The best she could hope would be to skim the fuse levee with her landing lights.

***

Off Birds Point, just below Cairo, the Ohio River and the Mississippi united in an oceanic expanse so immense that river, alluvial plain, marsh, empty forest, and the flat sky itself merged in seamless, timeless desolation. All that moved in the wind-blown rain, other than brown water rolling between low banks at a relentless seven miles per hour, was a tall cottonwood tree waving the inverted pyramid of its widespread crown like a horseman's cloak, and three red workboats with the white stripes and letter "H" of the J. B. Hanley Levee Maintenance Company on their stacks.

They jetted black diesel smoke into the rain, racing their engines to hold deck barges against the current. Maneuvering at the water's edge, their pilots allowed boats and barges to slip backwards, foot by foot, while deckhands sprayed the Birds Point fuse levee with high-pressure nozzles linked to a revolving mixer. With every revolution of the tanks, the trademarked brand-name ROUNDUP scrolled by.

If it seemed inefficient and environmentally dubious to spray herbicide in the rain, no one along this remote section of the river, which looked and felt to be a hundred miles from anywhere, was watching from either the Missouri or the Kentucky banks. A Coast Guard river-buoy tender came along, slowed down so as not to disturb the operation with its wake, traded radio greetings with the Hanley pilots, and steamed on. Brush clearing was routine fuse levee maintenance. Deciding when to apply herbicides—not to mention whether poison was better than chopping weeds—was up to the EPA.

Besides, the Coast Guard boys had their hands full chasing channel markers torn from their moorings by high water, and J. B. Hanley & Sons had been doing river work since 1923, five years before President Calvin Coolidge signed the first federal flood control law. Hanley had grown with the flood control system, like the ever-rising levees, winning its share of bids when the Army Corps of Engineers called for "soil excavation, dredging, rock placing, clearing, and grubbing." Their bright red workboats and sturdy black barges had been a reassuring presence for generations.

John Brown III, the last Hanley to ramrod the outfit, had sold out to a Chicago corporation for a price that suggested they had more money than sense and retired to Florida. By then, the whole damned business had changed. Bids entered for contracts in his grandfather's day were sealed by a handshake over a jelly jar of corn liquor. Now they were solicited and entered online. And the Corps enforced Small Business Administration diversity initiatives: J. B. Hanley—which once enjoyed a lucrative sideline towing "Love Barge" brothels down from St. Louis—now served as a "joint venture mentor" to women- and minority-owned businesses; a black man driving an eight-row cotton picker was still a very rare sight in the Delta, but who would notice that a federal project engineer directing the spray operation from the lead towboat was African American?

Abdul Muqtadir—who had made a clean sweep of the Gateway Arch Landing at the helm of *Miss Josephine of Blytheville*—wore a red Hanley hard hat, a red company storm slicker, and a pen pack bristling from the pocket of his pressed khaki shirt. Horn-rimmed glasses streaming rainwater—the blessed rain, Allah's gift—made a large man seem less imposing. His photo ID security badge read "Rufus Briggs."

As fog thickened on the water and dusk darkened the sky, one of the nozzle men suddenly shut down his sprayer, ran to the back of the deck barge, and cupped his hands to shout up to Abdul Muqtadir the same question he had asked twice already. No doctor could undo multiple concussions. Not the kind Usama had received when he jackrolled six cops while blazing on angel dust. He probably hadn't even felt the nightsticks back then. But they haunted his brain. Like an old boxer staggered by punches he'd taken in his youth, Usama was lucky to find his shoes in the morning.

"'Splain, again," he shouted. "Why are we making this levee stronger when we want to make it weaker?"

"Just keep on spraying. I'll fill you in at supper."

"That's not Roundup in them tanks, Abdul. That's gunite. Gunite's liquid cement. White folks make swimming pools out of it. When it dries it's gonna be hard as a rock. That's gonna make the levee stronger. Not weaker."

"I'll tell you at supper."

Suddenly, both men looked up at the fog-muffled buzz of a small airplane. It was approaching low overhead, very low. They watched anxiously, hoping the sky was too dark for the pilot to see them. It roared right over their heads, whipped around, and came back. Muqtadir reached inside the wheelhouse for a compact bullpup assault rifle. They saw the glow of landing lights pounce toward them.

No hobby pilot was flying that low at night, in the rain and fog. Muqtadir set the rifle's fire selector lever to burst mode, so a single squeeze of the trigger would fire multiple rounds.

The lights passed over again, diffused by the fog, and soared off. Again they zeroed in, lower, trying to pierce the murk. Again, they left. At last the noise faded upriver.

Muqtadir released his breath. "'Splain again?" asked Usama.

"Get back to work spraying, Usama—and don't forget to lay it thicker on the access well covers. You remember well covers?"

"Yeah, Abdul, I remember. Spray well covers thicker. Twelve full inches. A whoooole foot. But look how fast it's drying. Why we making it stronger, Abdul?"

Book Three

Outside the Levee

34

Failure to Maintain Situational Awareness

Day 39
Saturday

Clementine Price landed at Cairo Airport and secured her plane with tie-downs in case the wind got worse. The St. Louis terrorist attack was seared in all minds, and General Penn had a full MP platoon deployed for Cairo area security, plus a fireteam at the airport. Clementine ordered up a ride to the city in a Humvee with a box-fed machine gun on the roof.

She spotted four more fireteams guarding the route to Cairo's floodwall. Soldiers with pistols and pump shotguns manned checkpoints and roadblocks. Team leaders had grenade launchers attached to their carbines, and if it weren't so dark, she would most certainly glimpse snipers training night-fighting scopes from the parapets of abandoned buildings.

Her ride stopped beside a bunch of Corps trucks and SUVs gathered at the foot of the twenty-foot concrete flood wall. The wall was ablaze in work lights. General Penn himself strode atop the rampart, his camouflage slicker beating in the wind.

"Clamber up those rungs," he bellowed down to Clementine. "Don't mind that shaking. They'll hold you."

The steel rungs vibrated like tuning forks, so violent was the thrust of the water the wall was holding back. Her head cleared the top, and Clementine suddenly met the Ohio River eye to eye. This was less than a mile above the Confluence, and one look told her that the Ohio was tripling the Mississippi's volume. Visible in the lights was convulsive motion, a lurching surface exploding in eddies and counter currents. The wind had raised big waves. The water was studded with dirty whitecaps, the air thick and cold.

General Penn pulled her up the last rungs with a firm handshake.

He looked like a different man outdoors, a born field officer who preferred the sky to a ceiling and far more rugged than the public relations front man Clementine had always suspected was his main strength. His cheeks glowed red, his eyes were bright, and he seemed ten years younger and immensely vigorous. Clementine could not recall seeing a happier man so caught up in the moment with the exception of Reverend Nathan Flowers strutting on his Hilltop stage. But she glimpsed doubt deep in Penn's eyes, as if he were wondering what might happen next, and she was reminded instead of an Afghan warlord barricaded in his fiefdom.

Margaret Standfast was at Penn's side, her round cheeks as ruddy as his. A row of whirlpools roared by like locomotives. The massive wall trembled under their feet.

General Penn swept his arm across the raging water. "Welcome to Cairo, Major Price."

"Thank you, sir."

"Good thing you got here. I'm considering extreme measures. The forecast is hellacious. Cloudbursts up and down the whole system. Sustained precipitation throughout. We've got more than two hundred gauges above flood stage already or plumb disappeared. In all my years I've never seen so many highwater gauges washed away. We've got soil soaked, levees weakened, and streams brimful. Did you notice all the water in the fields? That's seepage. Water's coming through the levees and under them, which tells you how thoroughly soaked they are. They're weakened when they get that wet—while the rising river presses harder and harder."

"Yes, sir," said Clementine. Was General Penn confusing her with some other officer who didn't happen to be a hydraulic engineer and hadn't served ten years in the Memphis District? She wondered again, as she had asked Robert, was the general losing it?

Penn wheeled back to the rumbling expanse and bellowed with the bodacious pride of a NASCAR sponsor, "Look at that sucker go! He's discharging two million cubic feet per second. You do the numbers. That's 7.48 gallons per cubic foot. Fifteen million gallons every blink of your eye. But we've still got the capacity to carry another million cubic feet per second before we let her overtop at the floodway to save Cairo."

No, he wasn't confused about her. He was excited. But not by the river. It was the Army Corps of Engineers' systems General Clinton Penn was really cheering. Suddenly he sobered. "However, there's a strong possibility of a double flood crest forming at the Confluence."

"Yes, sir. Very strong. I'd say 100 percent. That's why I'm here."

Penn said, "I'm reconsidering my initial decision to allow a 'natural' floodway levee overflow. How long will it take to deliver explosives from Memphis to the Birds Point levee fuse plug?"

"They would be thirty-six hours from Memphis, sir."

"What do you mean 'would be?'"

"I already moved four barges upriver to Caruthersville. Twenty hours closer."

Penn stared. "Against my orders?"

"No, sir. Your orders not to pump explosives into the blasting pipes were obeyed."

"What prompted you to move the barges?"

"We studied Desert Shield and Desert Storm at West Point, General. I was put in mind of the forward "log bases" where General Pagonis cached tank fuel in the desert before the battle."

"Good job. But sixteen hours is still a long time."

"In actual fact, sir, I ordered the barges forward again last night—when I saw the new forecast. They're en route. Less than five hours away. We can start pumping at first light."

There was another long silence. Penn's jaw worked. His eyes narrowed. Suddenly, he spoke. Loudly. "Major Price?"

"Yes, sir?"

"I believe I am beginning to like you."

This is what it was like to be the fair-haired Robert, she thought. Her mouth went dry. Her senior rater was about to give the selection board an officer evaluation report that could earn her the permanent command of the Memphis District.

Captain Standfast rushed up with her phone. "General!" Her face was a ghastly shade in the harsh work lights. Her eyes were wild with shock.

Clementine guessed that the flood crests had accelerated. But it was worse.

"Sabotage!"

"Sabotage? What are you talking about?"

"Gunite. Liquid cement."

"I know what gunite is. What the devil are you talking about, Margaret?"

"On the fuse plug levee. It's coated with gunite, sir. It can't erode."

"*Major Price!*"

"Sir!"

"When did you last examine the fuse plug levee?"

"Four days, ago sir, I flew low over it on my way to St. Louis. Everything was as it should be. My chief engineer checked it on foot this morning."

"Why didn't you inspect it this afternoon on your way here?"

"I tried, sir. It was too dark to see from the aircraft."

"Didn't it occur to you to skim it with your landing lights?"

"I made three passes, sir. The fog acted like a mirror. I couldn't see a thing."

"Major Price! How long until those explosives arrive?"

Clementine's head was spinning. This terrorist attack was more sophisticated and would be far more deadly than St. Louis if it funneled multiple flood crests straight down the river to Bliss.

"How long?"

"Five hours, sir. But if the fuse plug is really covered with gunite it will take hours to even find the pumping manifolds and open the access wells." If the Bliss levees held, the latest rain forecasts for the river basins below Memphis—the White, Arkansas, and Yazoo—would force Penn to open the Atchafalaya Floodway.

Penn said, "The city of Cairo will be inundated before your people can pump explosives into the blasting pipes."

"I recommend we evacuate Cairo, sir."

"I had the foresight to order that this afternoon."

"I meant our people, sir. I'm afraid Cairo will be underwater by morning."

"Just in time for the TV cameras." General Penn's face contorted with rage. His voice grew so soft he was almost whispering. "Failure to maintain situational awareness is negligence, Major Price."

"Sir, I—"

"It is negligence because in war failure to maintain situational awareness equals defeat. We're at war with the river, Major Price. And now, we're losing. Dismissed!"

He turned away, shouting for his helicopter.

Captain Standfast stepped closer to Clementine.

"Get out of here before he relieves you. I've seen him do it. Go! And keep your head down."

35

THE FIRST LADY

Day 39
Saturday

Nathan Flowers eavesdropped outside the parsonage study.

"Chapter Two," Mary Kay read in her silky warm drawl. "'In Which Pooh Goes Visiting and Gets Into a Tight Place.'"

He had heard this one so many times he could recite it himself. Mary Kay was using their favorite Winnie the Pooh tale to teach Gabriel and Cora to read.

"Who's this?" he heard Mary Kay ask.

"Rabbit," chorused the children.

"What does Rabbit say to Pooh?"

Nathan edged into the doorway to savor the tableau of domestic harmony. Mary Kay was nestled on the big leather sofa, a child draped under each arm, bare feet propped on the coffee table, as Gabe and Cora's tiny fingers poked at the pages spread out on her lap and haltingly tested the words out loud. Nathan had dreamed big, but he had never imagined his new world would include this beautiful, intelligent, capable woman. He would have to explain his plans to Mary Kay very carefully; he must launch the Republic of Alluvia with her and the fruit of their loins at his side.

Mary Kay raised her eyes and met Nathan's. "Cora and Gabe are going night-night as soon as Pooh gets pulled out of Rabbit's hole."

Nathan scooped up both children in a bear hug and hoisted them into his arms. "They know how the story ends, darling. I'll put them to bed tonight. You just stay here and relax for a few minutes. I've got something important to talk to you about."

***

"My beautiful wife, you're about to become the First Lady of a new nation."

Mary Kay's big green eyes got bigger. "Nathan, are you planning to run for office? You know how strongly I feel that politics and religion don't mix."

Nathan smiled. "I'm not running for office."

"Good. Leave Caesar's to Caesar, while we preach the good news."

Nathan said, "But it's fair to say I will shortly *assume* office."

"I'm not following you, sweetheart."

Nathan took her hand and led her to their partners' desk. "Let me show you." He opened his laptop and waited a moment for the facial recognition security to unlock it, then slid it to the corner of the desk so they could both see the screen. Nathan scooted his chair close to Mary Kay's and double-clicked the icon for FalconView Commander. The program opened with a trumpet fanfare and full screen image of the Alluvian flag: white silhouettes of a barge fleet, a cotton boll, and an ear of corn on a blood red background.

"That's our flag, darling. And our motto: 'Pure Blood, Pure Faith, Pure Power.'"

Mary Kay stared at the image. He waited for her reaction, but she said nothing. The light of the screen reflecting from below made her look slightly pale.

Nathan clicked through to his map of the United States. A scarlet funnel-shaped swath stretched down the middle third between the Canadian border and the Gulf of Mexico, west to Wyoming, and east to Pennsylvania. "Our new nation is called Alluvia. The Republic of Alluvia. It occupies 1.2 million square miles in the heart of North America. We will control the most fertile cropland, the most powerful and essential river system, and our population of righteous, pure-blooded Christians will restore the polluted environment, and the degraded morality that has poisoned our country. It is prophesied in the Bible, Mary Kay. God told Noah 'I will cause it to rain upon the earth forty days and forty nights; and every living substance that I have made will I destroy from off the face of the earth.'"

Mary Kay stared silently at the map for several minutes. "Nathan, are you telling me you are part of a group that wants to overthrow the government?"

"Not to overthrow. To secede."

"And you believe that God has instructed you to do this, like Noah?"

"Yes, now you see! Like Noah."

"And that's God's reason for the extreme weather we're having—to achieve this goal?"

"Yes! I am the divinely inspired leader of a movement to secede from the toxic, tainted society that the United States has become. Alluvia will divide and then isolate what used to be the USA into an East Coast and West Coast. We will control the majority of the continent's food and commodity production, ports, waterways, and transportation hubs. Our enemies will be forced to reckon with us."

He tapped the keyboard and a 3D map appeared that modeled weather systems across the nation in the next twenty-four hours.

"'And behold, I do bring a flood of waters upon the earth.'"

He gently turned Mary Kay's face to his and looked into her eyes. "'But with *thee* will I establish my covenant; and thou shalt come into the ark, *thou*, and thy sons, and thy wife.' This place, my love—our creation, Hilltop—is our ark, where we and our followers will shelter from the flood."

Nathan cycled through infrastructure maps to help her understand—levees, bridges, highways—marked up with arrows, line drawings, and color-coded symbols, which shifted position or disappeared as he scrolled along a timeline at the bottom of the screen. He smiled at Mary Kay. "Of course, the Lord helps those who help themselves. God has filled the bathtub to the brim, but even He needs a final assist for it to overflow and wash away mankind's crimes. I have assembled a mighty army in His service, and you can see here how we will bring to completion what God has started." As he scrubbed through the timeline, vast sections of the map turned blue, and the word "Inundated" flashed.

Mary Kay turned away from the screen and looked him in the face. "Nathan, I don't understand. This seems like some kind of apocalyptic video game. Who is in this army you're talking about?"

"Many of our members and most generous donors. And many dedicated soldiers I recruited in our missionary work."

"In prisons?"

"Where better to find fierce warriors?"

"White supremacists?"

"God works in mysterious ways. These men are loyal and obedient to the cause. The means is justified by the end."

Mary Kay took his face in her hands and her eyes bored into his. "You're telling me that God has commanded you to escalate the damage from an existing natural disaster so that millions of people will be killed in order for a new 'pure' nation to be born?"

Nathan took her hands from his face and held them firmly. "There may be some casualties, as in any war, but those who are Christians will have their reward in heaven hastened. Any survivors who are not pure will be humanely deported from Alluvia and compensated for their property."

"Nathan, do you hate black people?"

"I used to, back when I was a kid. No-accounts with nothing *need* someone to look down on in order to raise their estimation of themselves. Later, in prison, the blacks and whites stuck to their own kind in order to stay alive. Self-segregation was a matter of survival, not ideology."

"I'm asking, Nathan. Do you hate black people?"

"After I met you, and met Jesus Christ on a personal level, I learned to see beyond color, beyond creed, beyond . . ."

"For God's sake, Nathan, answer me! Do you hate black people?"

"No, sugar, *I* don't. But there are plenty of white people who do—even after all this time, after centuries of so-called 'racial progress.' The United States of America is never going to get past its original sin of slavery. The best way—the only way—forward is to wipe the slate clean, like God did with Noah, and to found a new nation, untainted by the past, and united by our purity of blood and purpose."

"What purpose?"

"There will be no racism or discrimination in Alluvia, darling. Just peace and prosperity, defended by an army of volunteer warriors—*my* army—who will protect our people, our pristine forests, rivers, and farms from anything or anyone who would poison its purity."

Nathan stood and kissed the top of her head.

"It's a lot to think about, I know, sweetheart. I must lead my troops now, and I promised Gabe and Cora I'd come say good night first."

He left Mary Kay sitting at their partner desk and took the stairs two at a time up to the children's room. He had never felt more alive and powerful. Both Gabe and Cora had already fallen asleep in their beds. He tucked the blankets to their chins. "You are the future," he whispered to Cora.

On the wall facing their beds, Mary Kay had painted a huge rainbow.

All is fore-ordained, he thought. He perched on the edge of Gabe's tiny bed and whispered to his son. "'And God spake unto Noah, and to his sons with him, saying, behold, I establish my covenant with you, and with your seed after you. I do set my bow in the cloud, and it shall be for a token of a covenant between me and the earth. Be ye fruitful, and multiply; bring forth abundantly in the earth, and multiply therein.'"

Mary Kay was still at their desk when he returned to the library. She was staring out the rain-splattered window. "You get a good night's sleep, sugar. We've got big days ahead." He snapped his laptop closed and slipped it into a waterproof nylon gym bag. "Next time I see you and our beautiful children will be when we christen the new nation that you will lead with me for the Glory of God."

Flowers kissed her again, went out the back door, and sprinted down the hillside to the riverside dock, where a powerful boat would speed him to war.

36

"A Colored Runnin' 'Round Loose"

Day 39
Saturday

Black-skinned and on foot at night, Abdul Muqtadir was as vulnerable as a molting crab waiting for its soft shell to harden—an automatic stop-and-frisk target if the state police saw him alone in the dark or somebody punched 911. "There's a colored runnin' 'round loose on the highway, Sheriff, thought you'd want to know."

He had made it most of the way from Birds Point, Missouri, to the Desha County safe house in southeast Arkansas that Brother I had directed him to. But things hadn't gone all to Brother I's plan—a driver fell asleep and wrecked the car—and he found himself alone on an empty two-lane highway. But he was getting close. The Google map on his dying phone showed the farm road he was looking for dead ahead. He started running for it to get off this damned highway.

Headlights blazed and he ran harder, racing them to the farm road.

He saw he'd never beat them. He jumped off the pavement into the roadside ditch where he crouched in cold water up to his knees until the car passed. He climbed out of the ditch, stopped when he reached the farm road to pour water out of his boots, and commenced the long walk to a distant light, crunching gravel and counting utility poles. Fifty to a mile. After a hundred he came to the light, a single lamp on the last pole. He stopped in the shadows and studied tumbled barns, shotgun shacks, two tall trees, and a low, shingled house set off at one side. It was an abandoned home place, an old-fashioned cotton farm worked by field hands, like the one his father and grandfather had been born on.

Abdul knew their stories by heart. His eye was drawn to the commissary, a one-story company store that sold canned groceries and rice and beans on credit, just like they used to tell. In the years between his father and grandfather being born, time had stopped. They had grown up the same, three decades apart. Payday Saturday night, they'd told him, a boy would sneak out of bed to watch the dancing and drinking.

Saturday night someone who won in the crap game out back might buy him a hard candy. Or a Baby Ruth bar. Around midnight, out came the knives and razors. Men shouting. Women screaming. Someone yanking his arm. "What you doing out here so late? You run home now 'fore I tell your Momma."

He inhaled the scent of mud clay and thought of the white folks' farm in sunshine. Rows of cotton as far as you could see, said Granddaddy. Garden plots in front of black folks' shacks. Twice a year they had to move the shared outhouse in back. A white picket fence around the farmer's house. Saturday night the farmer's wife answered the door with a .45 on her hip.

Headlights came down the dirt road. He edged deep in shadow.

A pickup truck, a big one with a crew cab, pulled up. When it stopped under the light, he saw the bumper stickers.

Don't Care How They Do It Up North
Welcome to America . . . Now Speak English
I'm not a racist. Racism is a crime. And crime is for niggers.

A cracker in a John Deere cap climbed out, cupped his hands, and turned a slow circle on his heels shouting into the dark. "Don't care if you believe it or not, but Brother I sent me to drive you to Louisiana. So if you're out there, come into the light. You're safe. Just me."

He opened the truck's doors to show it was empty. "Y'all out there?"

Abdul Muqtadir glided into the light, ready to kill the motherfucker with his bare hands if he pulled a gun.

The cracker said, "Climb in back. There's a cooler with Coke and sandwiches—no pork in 'em, don't you worry, Brother I made that damned clear—and a blanket to hide under in case I get pulled over, which I don't expect. If I am, the story is we're spelling each other driving to the oil fields. Got the papers to show we got jobs waiting. Me a roustabout, you a cook."

"Where are we going?"

"Louisiana."

"Where in Louisiana?"

"Vidalia. Hundred miles down Route 65 and over on 425."

River Mile 361, thought the last surviving member of the Martyr Brigade. "Why are you doing this?"

"Money, what did you think? Get in the truck."

"Why did Brother I hire you?"

"I was born and raised in Vidalia, and the sheriff's my uncle. The cops won't bother me. You're safe with me. Long as you get in the goddamned truck."

37

Operation Anaconda

Day 40
Sunday

Clementine Price tasted salt in her first sip of coffee from the sweat that soaked her army tee shirt and glued it to her skin. Her hair, pulled tight into a messy topknot, was matted to her skull. She had arrived home at 3 a.m. vibrating with anxiety after the debacle at Bird's Point, gave up trying to sleep at 5 a.m., and ran down to her building's fitness center to burn off the tension with back-to-back high-intensity workouts. Six-thirty found her with plenty of time for multiple replays of last night's disaster.

She avoided looking at her phone, where she expected a division headquarters directive demoting her to Tommy Chow's deputy or worse. Instead, she sifted through the pile of mail that had accumulated on her counter. The volume of Pablo Neruda poems had arrived, and there was a fat manila envelope from Robert containing travel brochures touting Romantic Getaways for Couples: a secluded cabin on Table Rock Lake in the Missouri Ozarks, a private cottage in a vineyard in Missouri Wine Country, and a loft-style suite in a barn at a bed-and-breakfast in Oxford, Mississippi. She slipped them inside the book of poetry and pondered calling Robert to tell him what had happened at Birds Point. But she was still too embarrassed and confused and angry.

The doorman buzzed. "Major Price, you have a visitor. A Mrs. Flowers."

She answered, "Send her up," thinking that Mary Kay had chosen a weirdly early time to drop by to see the Tomato photographs she had offered to share. She pulled on a hoodie and started turning on lights in the still-dark apartment. She let Mary Kay in with a quick smile and led her down the dim hallway. "The pictures are in here. Follow me."

Flipping on the lights in the guest room, she finally noticed that Mary Kay's hair and clothes were damp, and that she wasn't wearing her usual boots, poncho, and umbrella ensemble. Her face was ashen, with dark circles under reddened eyes. She seemed to have trouble keeping her balance.

"Are you all right?"

Mary Kay shook her head, and Clementine led her to a chair.

"I've been awake all night. Nathan has either lost his mind—which I pray is the case—or he is a monster. A monster I helped create." She was rubbing her hands obsessively, as if trying to wash them.

Had Nathan lost his mind? Clementine wondered. Or had Mary Kay?

"Why do you think that?" Clementine asked, in the neutral tones of her life coach.

"He told me about this plan to . . . to destroy the country with a flood, a flood he will make worse than the one that's already coming."

"Why would he do that?"

"To found a new nation. An all-white nation called Alluvia. He said his followers are members of our church. It sounds insane, doesn't it?"

It would sound, thought Clementine, totally insane—a sick fantasy—except for St. Louis and last night's sabotage of the Birds Point fuse levee.

Mary Kay said, "But what if he's not insane and this is real? That means anyone connected to Hilltop—like Chief Owen, or Senator Garfield, or Mr. Colson, or even Andrew Wells—could be involved. I don't know who I can trust. Except you."

"This weather is freaking out a lot of people, Mary Kay. Maybe Nathan had a temporary meltdown, like a paranoid hallucination."

Mary Kay gripped Clementine's arm and dug in her fingernails. "He *showed* me his plan. A *military* plan, on his laptop. You have to tell me if it's a fantasy or not."

"How can I do that?" Clementine was now deeply concerned about this frightened woman she had come to think of as a friend. Gently she asked, even though she had seen Mary Kay arrive empty-handed, "Did you bring his laptop?"

"How could I? He took it with him."

"Well, I'm not sure—"

Mary Kay cut her off, impatiently. "I uploaded it to the cloud."

Even more gently, Clementine asked, "He allowed you to copy it?"

"I uploaded it when he left the room to say good night to the children."

Clementine exhaled. "Talk about presence of mind. I wouldn't have thought to do that."

"Yes, you would. Can you download it and look? You're an army officer. You can understand it."

Mary Kay typed her password into Clementine's computer and the download began. It was a large file and Clementine filled the time by walking Mary Kay to the kitchen and pouring coffee. She gave her hoodie to Mary Kay, who was starting to shiver, and double-clicked the new folder on her desktop.

"I'll be," said Clementine quietly. "He's using FalconView Commander."

"What does that mean?"

"FalconView Commander is the latest upgrade of a software program for battlefield planning. Military commanders use it to manage warfare with real time situational awareness. It's got 3D maps for a first-person view of the area—so you can 'go there before you go there'—satellite images, elevations, overlays like weather—Nathan's got river conditions, too—databases, intelligence, and timelines to simulate the action. Essentially it's a high-tech toolbox for going to war."

"Look at it. Please." Mary Kay paced around the room rubbing her hands together. Clementine watched Nathan's slideshow preview of "Operation Anaconda." It began with a map of the Republic of Alluvia that slashed the length and breadth of the Mississippi Valley like a gaping wound down the middle of the United States from Minnesota to the Gulf of Mexico.

The slideshow was a sales pitch built around Alluvia's national motto—Pure Blood, Pure Faith, Pure Power. Thinking Flowers was clearly nuts, she ran the entire simulation. Was this nothing more than the half-baked war game of a charismatic con man who fell for his own fantasy? If it was more—if Alluvia could break away—how could Nathan hope to counter the full force of a U.S. government determined to take it back?

"Is it real?" asked Mary Kay.

"It could be," Clementine said carefully. She went to the timeline feature and scrolled backwards. On the date of the St. Louis terrorist attack, NATO tactical-mission symbols representing "AMBUSH" and "DESTROY" were located at the Arch landing and the Poplar Street Bridge.

"He got St. Louis right."

Mary Kay paced faster. "But he could have programmed it in afterwards, couldn't he? From the media reports."

"He wouldn't be the first armchair general to use FalconView like a video game."

She scrolled ahead to Saturday, yesterday, and zeroed in on Cairo. The Birds Point fuse levee was overlaid with symbol for "BLOCK" with a chemical attack icon. As of this morning, General Penn had kept the gunite sabotage from the media.

"The only way he could know about Birds Point was to be the saboteur."

St. Louis. Birds Point. Back-to-back attacks many miles apart. And he had implied to Mary Kay that he was just getting started.

"What's next?" asked Mary Kay.

Clementine dragged the cursor to today, Sunday. Two targets pulsed red. Five hundred miles apart. Two cities: New Orleans, Louisiana and, she saw with a sinking heart, Bliss, Arkansas.

Today. Sunday. An attack within hours. Or already underway.

Clementine jumped up and corralled the pacing woman with firm hands on her shoulders. "Mary Kay, Nathan has not lost his mind. This is a credible plan for waging war. If it weren't so evil, I would call it masterful."

Mary Kay twisted away from her, whirled in a distracted circle. "What can I do?"

"You did it already. You came to the right person." Clementine's mind was racing. She had to move on this. The clock was ticking. She steered Mary Kay toward the door. "I will do everything I can to stop it. Right now you need to go home, where you'll be safe from any flood—Wait! If he came back to Hilltop, are you afraid Nathan would hurt you?"

"No. That I know. He would not hurt me. Or his children."

"Contact me the instant you hear from him. Are you all right to drive? Do you want to rest here for a couple of hours?"

Mary Kay gathered herself and stood. "It's Sunday. Nathan's gone. I have to preach."

"Mary Kay, you're in no shape to stand up in front of six thousand people."

"I will preach what I must preach."

"But if you don't know who to trust at Hilltop, how can you attack Nathan from the pulpit? His people will stop you."

Mary Kay's chin rose, and her eyes flashed. "I have more important things to preach than attacking the father of my children."

"Where are they, right now?"

"Downstairs in the car."

"Alone? You should have brought them up."

"They're not alone, they're with your Uncle Chance."

"Chance is here? Come on, I'll ride down with you."

The elevator was still stopped on Clementine's floor, and the two women rushed in.

"He drove me," said Mary Kay, as they watched the floor numbers descend. It was the longest elevator ride of Clementine's life. "Remember, he doesn't go to our church? I knew I could trust him." The thinnest imaginable smile lit Mary Kay's face and she was suddenly as strong as the woman who climbed the bell rope. "What a driver. I swear the car barely touched the ground. We'll be back to Hilltop in ninety minutes."

The elevator doors parted and they raced through the lobby. Chance was standing outside the car, vaping in the rain. He palmed his vape pen and gave Clementine an awkward hug.

"Look out for yourself, Clementine."

Back in her apartment, Clementine raced through "Operation Anaconda" again to make sure she wasn't hallucinating herself or stuck in a nightmare she could wake up from. It was all too real, and it was already underway. But she understood why Flowers had risked showing it to Mary Kay. Behind all the fancy graphics, it was very sketchy. Crucial details were missing. Now she was the one shivering; St. Louis had been a dress rehearsal.

She ran the program again. This time Nation Flowers's map of Alluvia bleeding down the middle of the continent stopped her breath. She saw a terrible thing she had missed earlier. The Mississippi River had moved west.

It reminded her of an image she knew like the back of her hand. She ran with her laptop into the living room and held it beside the Mississippi River Meander plate of central Louisiana.

"He's going after our Old River Control Structure."

Nathan Flowers intended to demolish the Corps' Old River Control Structure at the Atchafalaya Floodway. The Mississippi River would be swallowed by the Atchafalaya and New Orleans would disappear into the Gulf of Mexico. She checked her watch and sent a text to Engineering and Research Development Major Andy Rubenoff.

HYPOTHETICAL TERRORISTS ATTACK OLD RIVER CONTROL STRUCTURE. HOW?

This early Sunday morning, the Corps' explosives expert might still be awake, winding down from his Saturday night piano bar gig. Andy texted back instantly.

BARGE BOMB. FERTILIZER & DIESEL & BARGES. LOTSA BARGES.

She stared at her phone. Who would believe her?

General Penn would never take her call. Even if he would, was his command infiltrated by Captain Standfast, who she had seen at Hilltop? The same unanswerable question applied to the Bliss police. Everybody knew Chief Billy Bob Owen was a bigot, but was he also a secret agent for Alluvia? What about the civilian contractors she had seen at the church?

Who could she recruit to fight back without orders from superiors? Who would sacrifice their career to act like lightning? She punched her phone.

"Robert!"

"My darling. What a surprise to hear from you so early. Are you all—"

"Are you ready to go back into combat?"

Robert listened without interruption. Then he said, "I have two questions."

"Quickly!"

"How can a career officer, a creature of institutional rules and hierarchy, believe she can stop Nathan Flowers by going rogue?"

"I wouldn't go rogue if I had two days to convince our superiors. But we don't even have one day, Robert. We have *hours*."

"Question two: "I got a heads up that General Penn is returning to headquarters. Vicksburg is a lot closer to Old River. How long do you think we can stay under the general's radar?"

"Long enough, I hope. Please be careful Robert. I love you."

She hung up and dialed again.

Libby said, "Good morning, Clem, you're up—"

"Evacuate Bliss. But ask everyone strong enough to stay and hump sandbags. Where's Rolly?"

"Already at headquarters. It's all-hands-on-deck in case of flooding."

"It's no longer 'in case.' It's guaranteed. Evacuate."

She dialed Rolly. Rolly listened and said, "Attack two cities at the same time five hundred miles away from each other? Clem, the guy's fantasizing."

"He's got FalconView Commander. I'll send you his file."

"Any nutcase can buy FalconView and play war games."

Rolly put her on speaker for Duvall McCoy, and she could tell by the tone of their voices that neither was convinced.

Duvall said, “Any nutcase. They love that stuff. The 3D maps. NATO symbology. Real-time situational—”

“I know that, you guys. But look what’s already happened. St. Louis. Birds Point. Back-to-back attacks miles apart. His data is deep, deep stuff. I’ve never seen such sophisticated weather forecasts.”

“Weather?” said Rolly Winters.

“Weather?” echoed Duvall McCoy.

Clementine said, “I’ll be in Bliss in an hour. Pick me up at the airport. Armed.”

“You got it.”

“In a helicopter.”

“I don’t know if we can—”

“We have hours, Rolly. Only hours.”

Duvall said, “We’ll get a helicopter.”

“Drive on!”

38

Deployed

Day 40

With Noah's Lucky Ark Casino barge tied to the riverbank in the middle of nowhere, their cell phones unable to raise a signal, and the security guards busy doing something out on deck, Big Al Striker and Holly Green went their separate ways. Big Al to the bar. Holly looking for an edge.

He and Al were the last casino employees onboard, not counting the guards. Bartenders, cocktail waitresses, dealers, and kitchen staff had all been dismissed when the barge left Bliss. And yet, even though he saw no new faces among the security men, Holly had the funniest feeling there were a lot more people still aboard. He went down to the main deck, to the security office. No one there, not even the thug who was always guarding the door.

"Hello, hello!" he called repeatedly, and when no one answered he opened the door to the hold, called three more innocent-sounding hellos, and started down the steel steps and along a dim corridor that led to a lighted area. Because it was a barge, he expected to smell oil and paint. Instead, he smelled the river, like he was up on deck with the wind and rain blowing in his face. He rounded the corner and saw to his astonishment the pale early morning light through a huge hole in the side of the barge.

The river was coming right inside.

But not flooding the barge, he realized. Bulkheads contained the water, creating a slip, in which floated rubber boats with huge outboard engines. Like a secret marina, he thought, a hidden harbor.

In the dark distance, past the slip, he saw a dozen men dressed in black combat gear rounding a corner. He slid behind a pillar. These were not security guys. These were soldiers. Got it, Holly Green said to himself. That's why we weren't allowed down here. These fighters have been living here.

He sensed somebody behind him.

He whirled with an innocent smile, a smile that explained how he had stumbled down here by accident and how he hadn't seen any boats, hadn't seen any soldiers wearing quadruple-lightning-bolt insignia on their arms like Nazis, hadn't seen—he felt a explosion of noise and pain in his head. A black hole opened up where he had never seen one before and down in the middle of the black hole was a pinpoint of light—a revelation that his last thought on Earth would be, Man did I read this one wrong.

***

Up in the casino, at the empty bar, Big Al Striker poured another cold one.

Best thing about being a gambling man, he always said. If you don't care what time of day it is, even morning wasn't too early to have a drink. He looked up and saw someone coming his way across the darkened gaming floor. One of the security guards, he assumed, but when the man came around the final row of slot machines, Al recognized the alkie he'd seen sticking his head out the wheelhouse of the towboat that had bumped alongside last night. He looked older, up close. The huge bolt cutter he was carrying looked like it weighed more than he did.

"Howdy," Al said. "What's that for?"

"Thought the bar might be locked up."

"Nope. Wide open. What do you want, pal? It's on me."

"I don't mind paying."

"No bartender, no hostess. Your money's no good here. What do you want?"

"JD."

"Help yourself."

"You mean just go back there and pour?"

"Well, it's not going to pour itself."

The alkie looked at him. Scruffy, unshaven, haunted eyes. But he had a touch of class about him, Al noticed. Even as his eyes swept hungrily over the bottles, he paused to extend his hand and introduce himself. "Billy Scruggs."

"Please to meet you, Mr. Scruggs. Or should I say, 'Captain' Scruggs?"

"Billy's okay."

"Al Striker. Friends call me Big Al. You *are* the boat captain, aren't you?"

"Yup."

"Any idea where we're going?"

"Nope."

"Not a clue?"

"I'll know when they tell me. . . . Well, I'm going to go pour that drink." He hurried around the bar, found a glass, and picked up the nearest Jack Daniels.

"*Captain Scruggs!*"

Billy Scruggs froze. For a second he felt like he could see himself like he was looking down from the ceiling—through one of them damn surveillance cameras, probably—standing there with a glass in one hand and bottle in the other hand and his skin going white as the blood rushed out of his face. Slowly he turned, expecting the Devil's recruiter fixing to crush his hand. Instead, he saw a huge, tattooed skinhead with an ugly gleam in his eye.

"That's me," said Scruggs.

"Put that bottle down. They want you in the wheelhouse." Which sounded better than the main deck where the winch was. Sounded like they wanted him to drive the boat. Hope so, he thought. They ain't going to maim the hand that drives the boat. I got two hands as long as they let me drive the boat.

***

Abdul Muqtadir reckoned that Vidalia, Louisiana, hadn't been much of a town even before half of it was underwater, even taking into account a pair of four-thousand-foot truss bridges that crossed the river to Natchez on the Mississippi side. The driver who Brother I had paid to smuggle him to Louisiana pulled off the levee road into a mostly flooded sand pit with cranes and front-loaders half submerged and a loading dock that barely cleared the surface of the river.

"Here you go."

"There's nobody here."

"I'm guessing they're sending a boat. Maybe that one."

Abdul Muqtadir was already watching the four-decker backing down mid-river with a fleet of sand and gravel barges. A jon boat with an oversize outboard cut loose from it and headed for the dock. He stepped out of the truck.

"I'm outta here," said the driver and drove away quickly.

Abdul hurried to the dock, splashing through mud and ankle-deep water.

The jon boat came in fast. The guy driving reached to help him aboard and handed him a life jacket, which he was glad of, the river running the way it was. They made it out to the channel without capsizing, tied the jon boat alongside—instead of hoisting it aboard with the deck crane—and the towboat headed downriver riding the current at fourteen miles per hour.

The off-watch crew in the galley were a reminder that Brother I had some mighty strange contacts. Typical of the river, they were all white. Less typical—much less—all reeked of the jailhouse. And every one of the convicts was inked with white supremacist prison gang tats.

No surprise, he got no friendly greetings. But no one threatened to mess with him after the mate, who was built lean as a knife fighter, announced, "Anybody got a problem with the nigger, you take it up with me."

They gave him his own cabin where a bullpup rifle and body armor were laid out on the berth. As much as he was dying for his first full hour of uninterrupted sleep since St. Louis, he went up to the wheelhouse, where he saw strange things. The towboat had a lot of long fueling hoses coiled on deck. A deckhand was working on the lead barge, some four hundred yards ahead of the boat. Abdul picked up binoculars from their rack by the steering sticks and eyed the barges through the powerful glasses. The deckhand was smoothing sand with a long-handled rake. Here and there on other barges, he saw funny streaks under the sand.

The mate watched him study the barges but said nothing.

The streaks, Abdul realized, were not streaks, but stretches of canopy exposed where the sand had slid off. Someone had gone to a lot of trouble to make covered barges look like sand barges. Under the sand was the waterproof cover needed to protect dry cargoes of corn, wheat, soybeans, or fertilizer.

"Where's the captain?" Abdul asked.

"You're it."

"Who drove us here?"

"Fellow who just went ashore."

"Is he coming back?"

"No."

"Who's my relief pilot?"

"You won't need relief. We're only going thirty miles."

Abdul would bet money that under those sand-covered barge canopies was fertilizer. "When did you take fuel?"

"Yesterday at Natchez."

"What does she hold? Sixty thousand gallons?"

"About."

"I see," said Abdul Muqtadir.

"What do you see?" asked the mate.

Abdul ignored him. He saw fifteen fertilizer barges disguised to look like sand barges. He saw the extra fueling hoses, a lot more than the boat needed to take diesel while backing midstream. He glanced at the chart. With the current running hard, the Old River Control Structure was a three- to four-hour run downstream.

Abdul had to hand it to Brother I: the man thought big, bigger than anything he could ever have imagined. He had turned the barge fleet into a gigantic bomb of nitrate fertilizer and diesel fuel. A monster bomb, big enough to demolish the Old River Control Structure. Goodbye Mr. Mississippi. Goodbye Baton Rouge. Goodbye Port of South Louisiana. And goodbye New Orleans. Which explained why they had gone to such trouble to deliver him all the way down here from Cairo. Brother I was smart enough to know that steering the bomb into the structure was not a job they could trust to a mate or deckhand who had occasionally steered in prime conditions. The river was running at flood stage, and God knew who might try to stop them. It would require slick driving to make the hairpin bend at Jefferson Point, and slicker still to steer the bomb. They needed a real boat handler—a man on the sticks to ride the river with.

***

Nathan Flowers drove a nearly invisible speck of a boat at remarkable speed against the current to reconnoiter his battleground in the Bliss Bends Basin. His custom inboard RIB, the fastest on the Mississippi River, was worth every Cedric Colson penny. It was agile, dodging disaster with fingertip movements of the wheel. Digital camouflage—hand-painted to mimic flood-stage browns and grays—made its reinforced hull disappear into rain and waves.

But as seaworthy as the boat was, he barely made it under the interstate connector bridge. The water was even rougher where sandbars shallowed the bottom, and the powerful current exploded like surf against the channel piers. He had studied the bridge a thousand times. The stone channel piers that supported the main span trestle were as rugged as the base of a skyscraper. An A-bomb wouldn't move them, much less the runaway barge fleet they were designed to withstand.

But the tall, slim columns that carried the highway approach ramps on both sides of the river had caught Flowers's interest years ago—his predatory eye drawn to weakness. There was no shipping channel outside the natural levee where, for most of the year, the low ground was marsh and backwater. Even now, with the water so high, no tow pilot would stray that far from the channel. So those approach columns had been constructed to meet highway specs. Unlike the massive channel piers, the outer columns were only strong enough to hold the road.

He continued racing north, upriver, and soon passed Hilltop, which he observed with a cool eye without slowing. Built for the ages, his church would withstand everything he was about to unleash. Down on the water, the boats at the ferry dock had lights off. No surprise there. The water was too wild. He looked back for a glimpse of the causeway. Yellow vans and Bliss city buses were inching among the parishioners' cars and pickups coming for Sunday services. He had forgotten to tell Mary Kay who should preach in his absence. She would work it out. She always did. She might even preach a service or two herself—give them a hint of the new world coming.

He passed the steel mill and angled across the river toward the Tennessee side. As soon as he passed the swamps, he saw the first of the barge fleets tied along the bank. Hopper barges bearing sand, coal, gravel, grain—heavy but "safe" cargoes that the overburdened Coast Guard would inspect only if they had time after they had scrutinized ammonia, chemicals, gas, and petroleum. He passed another fleet and another and another. Two hundred barges at least.

Flowers roared by seven moored barge fleets in all, drawing curious looks from the few crew braving the rain. He could see in the distance the bright loom of the Noah's Lucky Ark casino. He slowed alongside. The sally port opened for him. He paused before he entered, gazed up the river, and inhaled the wind. For a second, he swore he could smell the flood crests hurtling down from the Confluence where the crazy ground-stomping giant was born.

He nosed his boat out of the current and inside the Ark's enclosed docking pen—a secret boathouse inside the barge—that was surrounded by bulkheads that rose above the water line. Engines echoing, he wove among the attack boats hidden in the steel cave, tied a line to a ladder, and cut his motors. The fresh silence was broken by the deep rumble of the river. He scaled the ladder two rungs at a time and leapt onto the catwalk overlooking the boat pen.

There were three men in each boat, a driver and two fighters. For all except Joey, this was the first time they had seen Nathan Flowers's face. Judging by their expressions, whether they recognized the famous megachurch preacher was less compelling than a sensation of hardly believing it was finally going to happen. It was time, as Brother I would shout, to get them pumped.

"Today is the day," he called down. "We fight today, with God's blessing. Tomorrow we build our Republic of Alluvia."

Ideally, he would send them into action focused and serene. But Flowers saw that they could not be serene when fifty million gallons of water hurtled by with every syllable he uttered. Bold and hardened by prison and the streets, undaunted by fears that struck most men down, they had survived their lives by fighting. No challenge ever went unchallenged, every insult was returned in blood. But their eyes widened with dread at the immensity of the river. He circled the catwalk to stand between them and their nemesis and raised a mighty voice.

"Our flood will scour the land. Our flood will purify the land. Our flood will sanctify the land. When our flood chases the black man from the land, white men will come from across America. Rising out of the cities. Up from the prisons. To seize the land. And hold our ground forever. *Alluvia!*"

Their eyes kept drifting toward the river. At last, Flowers realized that they didn't need a sermon, they needed practical details they could carry into combat.

"Shaped charges?" he shouted over the roar.

The fighters assigned to scatter the barge fleets tapped the miniature explosives packs Velcro-ed to their sleeves like old-fashioned 35mm film canisters.

"Highway Patrol radios?"

The commando team that would ambush the Tennessee Highway Patrol when it responded to 911 calls from the fleeting area had radios tuned to the troopers' frequency.

"Stun grenades? . . . Tasers? . . . Don't damage any wheelhouse 'til we're done with the towboats. But if any towboat cuts loose of its barges, you'll RPG 'em."

The rocket-propelled grenadiers saluted him with their weapons.

"Rifle?" To defend Noah's Lucky Ark.

"Rifle and tripod up on the roof," a marksman answered.

"Remember. You dam the sides of the bridge. I'll dam the middle."

39

DRIVE ON!

Day 40

Bliss Municipal Airport was as deserted as the muddy cropland that crowded around the concrete runway. The single, short landing strip was slick with rain and wreathed in mist, and the only aircraft Clementine Price could see were a couple of Cessnas and an old Mooney M20 tied down in front of the maintenance hangar. She telephoned Rolly Winters before she began her approach, guessing that a black and white SUV with a number on the roof was his.

"Where's your helicopter?"

"Turbine issues and thunderstorms."

"ETA?"

"Soon."

Instead of wasting time on the ground, she banked toward the city to eyeball damage from the flood crests that had roared past Birds Point. Bliss's back levee, raised six feet by a fresh crown of water-filled Tiger Dams, looked like a long orange snake. It hadn't been tested yet, as the mainline levee had withstood the first crest. But higher slow-moving crests were predicted to arrive mid-afternoon. She saw people sandbagging the Old District levee—hundreds of volunteers filling bags and carrying them up to Levee Street. The water had risen to the first row of sandbags.

She spotted The Boat. Motor vessel *Mississippi V* was plowing up mid-channel, battling the current and trailing a frothy brown wake. She hailed the pilot on the VHF.

"Is that Captain McCargo?"

"Yes, ma'am."

Good. Zelvert McCargo was the best. "Zelvert, what I want you to do is moor up at Hilltop's ferry dock."

"Yes, ma'am. Hilltop Ferry Dock."

The 240-foot-long, fifty-foot-high five-decker craft looming even taller than Hilltop's campus plateau would make Nathan Flowers or whoever he left there to cover for him think twice. Her smile darkened as quickly as it crossed her lips. *What am I thinking? Wake up! I'm not thinking.* That would be a viral image on every social media screen on the planet—a heavily armed gang of white supremacists capturing the Army Corps of Engineers' symbolic headquarters.

"*Captain McCargo!*"

"Yes, ma'am."

"I am countermanding my earlier order. Do *not* tie up at Hilltop. Stand off! Repeat, do not moor at Hilltop. Stand off in the channel. Acknowledge."

"Don't tie off at Hilltop, ma'am. Back down in the channel."

"Let no one board you."

"What was that ma'am?"

"I want security on deck."

"Yes, ma'am."

"Armed."

Silence. "Security" on The Boat typically meant helping dignitaries who'd had a few get safely down the gangway.

"I want The Boat protected. And defended if attacked. Do you copy?"

"Attacked? Yes, Major. Security on deck, armed."

"I want your security officer observing from the pilot house. Do you copy?"

"Yes, ma'am."

"No one boards without my authorization."

"Yes, ma'am. Umm, what if a contractor . . ."

"Call me for authorization."

"Yes, Major."

Think. Think like Nathan Flowers. Most of the people on The Boat were civilians. None had signed on to go to war. "Zelvert, who's your security officer?"

"Uhh—Second Lieutenant Pickett, ma'am."

"Get Lieutenant Pickett up in the pilot house. Tell him to radio me—No! *Phone* me. Phone." Flowers's people could have heard every word on the open channel VHF radio. *Think like Flowers.* She texted Zelvert her mobile number.

She flew over the interstate connector bridge. Fog was thickening. She continued upriver, noting how the crest had flooded the backwaters on the Tennessee side. She telephoned Rolly again.

"On their way, Clem. Just a little turbine trouble. ETA fifteen minutes."

At Hilltop, the megachurch parking lots were packed. Refugees? Or Sunday services? Otherwise, things looked normal. Innocent. As always. She continued flying upriver past the steel mill and cut across to inspect the fleeting area on the Tennessee bank. More barges than ever. And above them, an incongruous site. An enormous old towboat was pushing the Noah's Lucky Ark casino.

She swooped down low enough to read its name, then hailed it on the VHF, fearing that some well-meaning fools were intending to board refugees despite her warnings and a stern follow-up she had arranged with her counterpart at the Coast Guard, which should have put the kibosh on that dangerous fantasy.

"*Delta Lady,* this Major Clementine Price, Army Corps of Engineers, Memphis District. Morning, Captain, do you read me?"

She repeated the call twice.

"Major Price, this is *Delta Lady*. That you overhead, ma'am?"

"Captain, where are you headed with the Ark?"

"Just moving her below the fleets, Major. We wasn't happy with our hold on the bank up above."

"Are you headed down to Bliss?"

"Bliss? Good Lord, no, ma'am. Just hunkering down like the rest of these fellows and praying the crests don't get higher."

"Who's onboard the Ark?"

"Two man riding crew."

"Good luck."

"Thank you, Major. You too."

She put Snoopy in a 180 and raced back down the river.

Lieutenant Pickett telephoned. He sounded fourteen years old.

"Lieutenant Pickett, you stood wheelhouse watch in New Orleans last week, when Colonel Garcia and I visited the chartroom?"

"Yes, Major."

"Good. We have a situation, Lieutenant Pickett. No one. I repeat, no one, is allowed aboard The Boat with the exception of army officers and soldiers. Do you understand?"

"Yes, ma'am."

"What's your armament?"

"Light, ma'am. Sidearms. Shotgun for snakes and gators. One rifle with grenade launcher."

"Have you qualified with it?"

"Yes, ma'am."

"Where?"

"Yemen, ma'am."

Clementine Price exhaled with relief. "You'll do fine, Lieutenant Pickett. Call for anything you need."

"Is there anything else you want me to know, ma'am?"

"Know this: a flood could be the least of our troubles. The St. Louis terrorists are back in business. You're my eyes and ears on The Boat. Keep me posted."

She telephoned her adjutant. "Lieutenant Harpur, are you armed?"

Brief silence greeted her question. "I can be, ma'am."

"Make it so. Get up to the wheelhouse, assist Lieutenant Pickett with security, and call me when in doubt."

"Ma'am?"

"What?"

"Is it like St. Louis?"

"Worse. Is Mr. Corliss aboard?"

"Yes, ma'am. He's got a whole bunch with him."

"Fill him in and tell him I am glad he is standing by."

Downriver below Hilltop, the rain and mist got denser. When she passed over the interstate connector bridge, the center span arch appeared to be floating on fog. The water was so high that the river had spread far outside the Corps' navigation chute. Waves were splashing the tall, slim piers that supported the highway approach ramps. Where ordinarily was low marsh ground and backwater ponds, the water had risen two or three meters above their pile caps.

***

"Have you helped your neighbor today?"

The Reverend Mary Kay Blankenship Flowers smiled serenely at the half-empty sanctuary. Burton Furman—the only Hilltop minister she could trust—had followed her instructions to "vamp 'til ready" and kept the music rolling until she arrived for the first service of the day. She'd fixed her hair as best she could in a car hurtling along at 100 mph, donned a choir robe over her disheveled clothes, and clipped Nathan's wireless microphone to her collar. The volunteer who made Nathan HD-camera ready every Sunday—a professional makeup artist—was kind enough not to inquire why Mary Kay's face was splotchy and hollow-eyed while he did his best with lipstick, mascara, powder, and a heavy layer of concealer. Gabe and Cora were sitting in the front row with Chance Price. This was going to be the high-wire act of her life, without a net.

"I'm not surprised to see that many of our neighbors stayed home this morning—with God's sky storming and His river rising. I'm sure it's not lost on any one here that today marks forty days and forty nights of torrential rain. Y'all might expect a preacher to turn for today's sermon to God's Judgment Day as told in the seventh chapter of Genesis—the story of Noah and the flood."

Nervous laughter, a few uneasy smiles from the congregation, but mostly tension. Tension is good, thought Mary Kay. It's related to "attention," as her father used to remind her.

"But instead, I'd like to share Jesus's words from the New Testament, from the seventh chapter of Matthew: 'And the rain descended, and the floods came, and the winds blew, and beat upon that house; and it fell not: for it was founded upon a rock.'

"Jesus was a man of words *and* action, and he expected his followers not only to listen, but to *do*. Those of us who are here right now, in our house founded upon the rock of our faith, are safe in our sanctuary. 'Sanctuary' means 'holy place,' but it also means 'refuge.' Hilltop is a place of refuge for us and for all of our neighbors."

Strangers were filtering into the auditorium—frightened families clutching suitcases and plastic bags, holding small children; old people on walkers and some in wheelchairs. Black and brown and white faces. Another busload of refugees had arrived.

She nodded to Burton to resume the music, left the pulpit, and strode up the wide aisle. "Welcome to Hilltop. You are safe here."

The jumbo-screen cameras followed her, and her mic amplified every word as she shook hands with the newcomers, asked their names, and where they were from.

"We have many visitors from Bliss today. And I expect there will be more as the river rises. We are glad to see you. Please introduce yourself to your neighbors around you."

Mary Kay signaled the ushers to seat the refugees among members. The congregation started to relax, as people shook hands awkwardly at first, then warmly. Pleasantries were exchanged. She watched and waited until the pleasantries bloomed into full-blown conversations and the auditorium was buzzing. Now that they were comfortable, they were ready to be led. Mary Kay nodded to Burton, who struck a closing cadence that silenced the crowd. She began to prowl the aisles, as she had taught Nathan to do.

"Some of you recall last Sunday Major Clementine Price asking that we comfort those who become victims of the flood. And I see that happening right now, with the kind welcome our members are offering. We will hold you in our hearts and keep listening.

"But this flood has just begun, and I believe that God is asking more of us. He is asking who will resist the waters. *Who will resist the waters?* Isn't there another way to help our neighbors?"

She returned to the pulpit and waited for a response. None came.

"I'm speaking now to our most fortunate parishioners—who are strong and healthy and able-bodied. You have seen that our causeway is filled with Hilltop vans and Bliss city buses delivering people here to safety. As each vehicle arrives, I am asking the strong, the healthy, the able-bodied to help the old folks and children off kindly but quickly. Because those vans and buses have to turn right around and go back and rescue more citizens.

"But God is asking, why are they going back empty?"

She paused and bored into the crowd with fierce green eyes.

"God is asking, who will resist the waters?

"If you're able-bodied enough to shovel sand, God is asking, have you helped your neighbor today?

"If you're healthy enough to hold a canvas bag while someone fills it, God is asking, have you helped your neighbor today?

"If your back is strong enough to lift an eighty-pound sandbag and stack it on another, God is asking, have you helped your neighbor today?

"God is asking, who will resist the waters? Who will be in that long line of vans and buses going *back* to Bliss to sandbag our neighbors' levees?"

She saw heads swiveling around to exchange glances. Heads began to nod, yes, I will.

She had some of them now. Start with *an*ticipation and lead them to *par*ticipation, her father always said.

"I see some of you hesitating. Those of you who haven't yet joined our outreach ministry may not be familiar with Bliss—which is where I grew up and where my parents still live. You may have been led to believe—mistakenly—that historic old river city is nothing but poor people—poor *black and brown* people—housing projects, *immigrants*, even criminals. But even if that *were* the case, they are still God's children, just as we are. Jesus said, 'Ask, and it shall be given you; seek, and ye shall find; knock, and it shall be opened unto you.'

"Our neighbors in Bliss are asking. Today. They are knocking on our door. Today. They need your loving welcome. Today. And as you help them out of the vehicles, look into each person's face and look in your own heart. Ask yourself if there is any difference between her and your favorite aunt, between him and your beloved granddaddy, or your brother, or the neighbor you've been friends with since grade school? Their skin may be a different color, they may speak a different language, they may not have grown up in comfort. But they are God's children. 'Therefore all things whatsoever you would that men should do to you, do you even so to them.'"

She stripped off her choir robe and spread her arms.

"Mr. Chance Price will drive the next van back to Bliss. I will ride in the front seat. We've got room for more."

Mary Kay Flowers whispered to Reverend Burton Furman to preach the same sermon at the rest of the day's services. He nodded and hugged her hard. Mary Kay collected her children and marched up the aisle, Chance Price hurrying after her, as the music minister struck up "Higher Ground." At the auditorium exit, she turned around and beckoned her parishioners to follow. The jumbo screens proclaimed

I want to scale the utmost height,
And catch a gleam of glory bright.

40

The Cavalry

Day 40

"*Find out where your enemy is. Get at him as soon as you can.*"
General Ulysses S. Grant sent cavalry roving the wilderness to find his enemy.

Colonel Robert Garcia was his own cavalry, flying over the Old River Structure—the "valve" that protected the Mississippi River from General Penn's Atchafalaya "seductress"—on a Louisiana National Guard helicopter. The powerful machine, so recently upgraded it smelled of paint, was operated by Aviation Regiment reservists who one hour earlier had been on weekend search-and-rescue training exercises. Garcia had a pilot and copilot, crew chiefs to nurse the turbines and run the hoist, the hottest search radar and forward-looking infrared the army could buy, and an MP fire team cradling weapons in the open doors—young soldiers so fresh-faced they could have been his sons had he married earlier.

If Clementine was right, he understood more about Nathan Flowers's objective than Grant knew about those of the Confederates. Flowers could destroy either the navigation lock, or the dam, or the hydro-power plant, or one of the flow-control structures. Garcia was betting he would hit the zipper-tooth flow-control gates, but all six elements were in close proximity and readily monitored from the air despite the teeming rain.

Garcia had another advantage: he commanded the terrain. The Corps imposed an exclusion zone above the Old River Control Structure where barges were forbidden to moor. It was a safety precaution as barges commonly broke loose, and the Atchafalaya River pulled so hard on the waters of the Mississippi that it could suck runaways into the outflow and damage the structures grievously. He had sentries down on the water—the fast New Orleans District picket boat that ordinarily patrolled the vital structure and enforced its exclusion zone—and a second, improvised picket—a towboat that he had Shanghai-ed when he spotted it deadheading to Baton Rouge Harbor. He had deployed MP fire teams on each.

"*Strike hard and keep moving on.*" Garcia was looking forward to that Ulysses Grant directive the instant he spotted Nathan Flowers. But so far, this was less the combat Clementine had promised than a standard assets-management job—positioning men and machines and standing by.

Should he call in reinforcements, just to be on the safe side?

Reinforcements could turn messy. It had been relatively uncomplicated to recruit a helicopter by calling in a favor from an ambitious National Guard assistant adjutant. But going through channels made every act official. Asses longed to be covered. And bold requests scared cautious officers into demurring, "Not in my lane."

Besides, he had the exclusion zone wired. Flowers could not get past his picket boats and under his helicopter. The Old River Structure was safe. Except why did he keep thinking about his grandfather? Could Flowers attack elsewhere? Could he pull a Nazi end run around the Maginot Line? Or, like Castro's communists, behind Grandfather's front gate? *Abuelito, where is my kitchen door?*

He studied the chart on the copilot's navigation monitor.

"Head up to Jefferson Point."

The Corps had built a rock channel jetty in a hairpin bend where the Mississippi made a U-turn around Jefferson Point. The line of rocks thrust a barrier partway across the river. Like shunting highway traffic from three lanes into one, the jetty directed water toward the Louisiana side of the bend. Extending his exclusion zone to that U-turn would widen his Maginot Line by ten miles. Better than reinforcements.

He radioed the picket boat. "Follow me up to Jefferson Point. Boarding party, stand by."

"We can't make your speed, sir."

"Do your best. And keep a sharp watch for the jetty. The rocks will be completely submerged by high water. The marker may be washed away."

He texted Clementine.

COVERED

***

Clementine Price landed at Bliss Municipal and stopped on the taxiway.

An ancient Black Hawk helicopter lumbered down beside her, smoke pouring from its left turbine cowling. Rolly Winters and Duvall McCoy scrambled aboard it, armed with grenade launchers, carbines, Kevlar helmets, bulletproof vests, radio headsets, and chest mics—surplus U.S. military gear transferred to the Metro Police SWAT arsenal.

Clementine grabbed her iPad from the Air Tractor and vaulted into the helicopter. She pulled on the helmet and headset waiting on the copilot seat and told the aging hotshot driving, "Here's your terrain."

Her iPad displayed the sectional chart on which she had highlighted cell phone towers, power plant and steel mill smokestacks, high tension wires, and the ramps and tall center arch of the interstate connector bridge. Her phone rang a call and bonged a text alert simultaneously.

Robert's COVERED was the best news she had read this morning.

Her phone IDed her brother, who had texted earlier that he was sandbagging the Bliss levee. "Will, I can't talk. You okay?"

"Momma and Daddy won't evacuate."

"What, are they crazy? Libby ordered everyone over forty to evacuate."

"You talk to them."

"Momma—"

"Your daddy and I are not going to any motel, ever again."

"You can live with me in Memphis. Top floor. One hundred twenty feet above the river."

Her father said, "I won't be cooped up in some skyscraper," and her mother said, "Why would I want to live in Memphis?"

"Momma! Put Will back on the phone—Right now!—Will, call Uncle Chance."

Mike Coligny spooled the turbines up to speed.

Another text bonged. Lieutenant Harpur.

RUNAWAY BARGES

Clem texted back.

STOP THEM

All they needed was a loose barge smashing a weakened levee.

A gust of wind shook the helicopter. She saw half the short runway disappear in a rain squall. "Radar still working on this crate?"

"Got us around two thunderstorms and a tornado," said Coligny and cracked a helicopter-pilot joke she had heard before. "Don't worry, Major. If the weather gets too bad for instrument flight rules, we'll fly visual."

"Head upriver."

Coligny lifted off and climbed swiftly. Buffeted by a sudden crosswind, he swung north to dodge a fast-moving thunder cell. The airport vanished under them as another squall knocked visibility down to a hundred feet. Eyes on the radar, Coligny oriented himself by the interstate connector bridge.

Clementine looked back into the low cabin to give Rolly and Duvall a grateful thumbs-up. Although their elderly helicopter—festooned with battle decals from wars fought before she entered West Point and pillaged of weapons—was days from being dismantled for spare parts, their pilot was the real deal—hands smooth on the collective and cyclic levers, feet tapping the rudder pedals light as Fred Astaire, and every obstacle on the sectional chart stored in 3D memory.

He swung south and tried again to make the river. The squall raced to Tennessee and suddenly Clem could see all of Bliss from the edge of the ocean-flat cotton fields to the downtown crowded along the river. Immediately under them stood the orange-rimmed back levee. They were over the Old District in moments. People were lined up to escape on the yellow church vans and city buses that crept away toward Hilltop. Police cars blocked flooded streets. Levee Street teemed with sandbaggers.

Lieutenant Harpur texted. MORE BARGES ADRIFT

Clem texted back. RADIO HELP TOWBOATS. I AM ON MY WAY.

The Black Hawk's right turbine suddenly shrieked like a frightened animal.

"*Put her down, Mike!*" the flight engineer shouted. "*Down, down, down!*"

Coligny dropped the big machine out of the sky, muttering, "Where the fuck?"

Clementine, with one spray-pilot eye always on the ground, pointed toward Levee Street which offered an unimpeded approach from the river side—at the risk of plunging in the water—and stood high above Bliss's First Street and thus separate from city rooftops. But Levee Street was swarming with sandbaggers, who were stacking them at the water's edge. A fire department pumper pulled into a spot they could have landed on. The helicopter was shuddering, buffeted by hellacious wind, so close to the ground Clementine could see people's faces.

"Where . . . ?"

She spotted a hook and ladder truck moving slowly past the sandbaggers, a quarter mile further downstream. But the stricken machine was too low, now. It would never make it that far.

"There!" She pointed at an open patch behind a yellow Hilltop bus.

"Thank you, ma'am."

She heard Rolly in the headset ask Duvall, "You okay?"

"Me? Fixing to blow up stuff and shoot bad guys? I'm flying high. You're the one who keeps saying don't re-up."

"I'll say it again," Rolly growled. "You done your bit. Don't re-up."

***

Red raincoat billowing in the wind, Mayor Libby Winters strode up and down the steep levee calling, "I am so proud of you, I am so proud of you," to the teenage boys and girls who had formed human chains to pass sandbags from First Street up the slope to Levee Street on the top. She had been stopping every few moments to spell an exhausted teenager or over-ambitious weekend warrior.

"Hey Libby!" Steve Stevenson hailed her from his Chevy Silverado. Behind him trailed a caravan of dump trucks: "I've got two thousand more tons of sand made up at the quarry. You just give a holler."

"I'm hollering. They need it at the back levee, to shore up the Tiger Dams."

Libby Winters charged back up the slope to Levee Street. Mary Kay Flowers had arrived in a Hilltop van driven by Chance Price. Young and not so young men and women piled out of the van, grabbed sandbags from Bliss kids struggling up the slope, and ran the bags across the street to the water's edge. On the first trip in, Mary Kay's children had been with her in the van. Libby asked, "Where are Gabe and Cora?"

"At the first responders' unit, on the top floor of the hospital. Your boys marched straight up to welcome them."

Sandbaggers suddenly looked up, covered their heads, and ran for their lives. A helicopter was falling out of the rain.

Mike Coligny's crippled Black Hawk dropped on Levee Street swinging like a pendulum bob. It swept a row of sandbags into the river, lurched over the water, pivoted back, and settled softly inches from the edge. His flight engineer shut the engines and crossed himself.

"Give me five minutes." He clambered out the door, scaled the maintenance steps, and started banging on the turbine cowling. Coligny, Rolly, and Duvall scrambled to hold lights, pass tools, and scavenge parts.

Clementine telephoned The Boat. The banging got too loud to hear. "I'll call you back." She jumped down to the street. Down below on First, she saw Libby's mayoral Suburban, police cars and ambulances, and a row of Stevenson Sand & Stone dump trucks. From high in the air, the human chains of sandbaggers had looked like orderly worker ants. Here she saw them shambling from exhaustion and shooting fearful glances at the brown water grabbing at the sandbags. She jumped up on the fire truck bumper to see the length of the narrow Levee Street to the other red fire truck in the distance. In between them, thousands labored. But, capped with sandbags stacked helter-skelter, the levee looked fragile, as if all that held the river back was a frayed rope. It was all too easy to imagine the fire trucks, the sandbags, and the people stacking them, suddenly underwater.

Clementine called The Boat again.

"We are doing what we can, ma'am," reported an admirably cool Lieutenant Harpur. "We snagged two barges, and we're chasing another."

"How many are there?"

"Fifteen on the radar, Major."

Fifteen! "Get towboats down from the fleeting area. I will be there soon."

Libby Winters came up the slope shouting encouragement. She spotted Clementine. "Clem, can you believe this! Reverend Eddie got the Saline Solution rapping for volunteers from the projects, and Mary Kay must have brought a thousand folks down from Hilltop." She lowered her voice. "How bad is it?"

"The evacuation looks amazing from the air. Tons of vehicles. And the lines of people are getting shorter."

"Clem. How bad is it?"

"Where are Kevin and Rolly Jr.?"

"The first responders' floor with Mother June. . . . Clem?"

"I'll know better when we get that chopper flying again."

Libby turned around to look at the helicopter and registered for the first time that that was Rolly, *her husband*, hauling himself up and down the maintenance steps, bulkier than usual in his bulletproof vest, thigh holster, and Kevlar helmet. And that her husband was therefore going into battle alongside her best friend.

"Clem." She kept her voice low and as steady as she could manage. "Rolly texted me that he and Duvall were heading out to back you up on 'a situation.' He didn't say what." Libby looked Clementine up and down. She noticed her hair was shoved up under her patrol cap, not in its usual Victory Roll. She took in the Sig Sauer pistol holstered on her leg, which she'd never seen Clementine wear. "Who are you going to war against?"

Clementine glanced over at the helicopter, which now mirrored the rhythm of the human chain of sandbaggers; Rolly seemed to have decided to spare his creaky knees at the expense of his back. Duvall was now the step-climber with Rolly hoisting tools and spare parts up to his partner. Five minutes to fix the turbine had stretched to ten.

"Libby, please trust me that the less I say the better. But Rolly and Duvall are essential to this operation."

Libby now looked ten years older and an inch shorter. "Clem, Rolly is *my* hero but he's not a *super*hero. He turns fifty next month and is celebrating with a double knee replacement. He's got high blood pressure and two young sons." Her eyes filled. "He's my life."

Clementine gripped Libby's shoulders and looked into her crumpled face. "I swear to you I will do everything to bring all my people home alive and in one piece."

Libby nodded, wiped her face, and returned to the chain of sandbaggers. Clementine ran back to the chopper. "Five more minutes," promised Coligny.

With nothing to do but wait, Clementine joined the sandbaggers. The kids around her who had been going since dawn looked numb with fatigue. But they kept humping the bags, driven by fear. They had seen enough of the wind-whipped river to believe it could top the levee and rampage through the streets. The wind blew harder, building waves that pounded like surf. It seemed all of Nature was on Nathan Flowers's side.

Lieutenant Pickett called from The Boat. "Radio chatter, Major. Tennessee Highway Patrol engaged in a shootout at the fleeting area."

"It's started. I'll be there as soon as I can. Keep me posted."

She hung up, debating whether she should try to alert General Penn, but still wary of Captain Margaret Standfast.

"*Clementine!*"

She whirled to the old, familiar growl behind her.

"Uncle Chance." She hugged him hard.

He flinched. "I put your Momma and Daddy on the bus."

"Thank you."

"They always was a pair of damned fools."

Really still himself, she thought, cantankerous, caring, and brave. Her second father. And—forgive me Daddy—first in her heart.

"Gotta go, Hon. Driving Mrs. Flowers back for more volunteers."

Clementine reached for him, again. "I want to kiss your cheek, good-bye. Just in case . . . today doesn't work out."

Chance assessed her with a piercing glance. "Mary Kay gave me a fair picture of what's going on with Reverend Flowers." He took Clementine's face in his hands. "Mary Kay turned to the right gal for help," he said, and touched her cheek with dry lips.

She felt her heart soar. "Uncle Chance, I believe that is the first time you have ever kissed me."

"I guess I was always more a head patter than a kisser."

"You said Mary Kay's in the van? I have to talk to her." They hurried around the fire truck. Chance squeezed past sandbags between the van and the water to climb behind the wheel. Mary Kay lowered the front passenger window. She looked, Clementine thought, equal parts determined and haunted.

"I've heard nothing from Nathan."

"I just heard from Louisiana. We got there in time to stop him."

That brought a glint of victory to Mary Kay's eyes. "Thank God."

Clementine said, "I thank *you*—Mary Kay, do you have any clue what he'll do next?"

Her question erased the triumph from Mary Kay's face. She looked bleak and afraid. "All I know is that he will have a plan. Nathan always has plans and back-up plans. There is no stopping him. He's a chess player, he thinks far, far ahead. It's how he survived prison. It's how he did this—this vicious insanity. I'm sorry, Clementine. I wish I could tell you more. Chance, let's go! We've got old folks to pick up."

"Wait." Clementine put her hand on Mary Kay's arm. "Do you mean he has an actual plan when something stops him? Or will it be off the cuff?"

Mary Kay looked proud to understand him in a fuller way. "It could *seem to be* off the cuff, because it will be something you never would imagine. A complete surprise no one could think of."

Clementine felt a hard jolt under her feet. The levee trembled as if a silent explosive had detonated nearby. Still holding the window ledge, she ducked back from the van, instinctively. The street under it rippled like Jell-O.

"Get out of the vehicle!" roared Chance.

"Jump!" Clementine yelled. "Both of you! Jump out!"

She lunged for Mary Kay's door.

Chance Price popped Mary Kay's seatbelt, then fumbled for his.

The asphalt cracked under Clementine's feet.

She locked disbelieving eyes with Mary Kay. But she knew exactly what was happening. It was a slough slide. Deep underwater, weakened by seepage, the edge of the levee was collapsing. The face of its steep slope—a thin slice—was separating from the main body and skidding to the bottom of the river. Most of the levee would hold—there would be no breach—at least for now. The catastrophe was restricted to the narrow sliver of Levee Street under the church van. With no foundation to support it, the roadbed tilted toward the water.

The van tilted with the street before Mary Kay Flowers and Chance Price could get their doors open. Clementine held tight to the door as if to stop the van from falling. She felt the vehicle pulling her off the crumbling street and clung harder. Only primitive physical instinct saved her from a fatal attempt to do the impossible. Her hand opened reflexively, and the van tumbled into the water.

It landed upright, a miracle.

Quick-thinking firemen threw ropes and wrestled a ladder off their truck and extended it into the river. Three men held it. A fourth scrambled out on the rungs. The current racing at ten miles per hour—faster than a woman could walk—swept the van toward the ladder.

Clementine Price had already whirled back from the crumbling pavement. In case they couldn't reach the van, she sprinted past the fire truck shouting to the driver, "Radio your truck downstream to put out their ladders."

She was running full speed toward that fire truck, a quarter mile downriver, when she heard a collective groan from the sandbaggers. She looked over her shoulder just as the current whipped the church van past the first truck's ladder. Her only hope to save Chance and Mary Kay before the van sank was the ropes and ladders on the second truck. But ten miles an hour was a mile in six minutes. A quarter mile in ninety seconds. Fifteen feet for every second it took Clementine to reach it.

The sandbaggers mobbed the street, crowding against the barrier they had stacked, straining to see what was happening in the river. She lost speed dodging around them. "Disperse!" she shouted. "Disperse!" Then screamed, "*Get out of my way!*"

Some scrambled aside. But clumps of people froze where they stood, gaping at the sight of a tall woman in camouflage battle dress running full out and shouting at the top of her lungs.

"Disperse! Move! Let me through."

Without breaking stride, she jerked the pistol from her thigh holster and fired shots in the air. The crowds scattered, ducking heads and throwing themselves flat on the street. She jumped over them and ran faster. The fireman on the distant hook and ladder truck looked toward the gunfire. They had been watching, gaping, just like the sandbaggers. The radio had not gotten through. Now they saw her running, saw the van racing the current almost as fast as she could run, and flew into action. They pivoted the power ladder out and down over the water like a gangway.

She looked back again. The water was up to the van's windows. But Chance would wait until the water was deep enough inside the vehicle to reduce the outside water pressure enough that the doors could open—a maneuver that demanded a cool willingness to hope that the right moment came before they drowned.

She reached the hook and ladder truck 150 feet ahead of the van just as the firemen were lowering the truck's stability pods that would counterbalance the weight of the horizontal ladder and people on it. Clementine brushed past the man about to mount it.

"Hey, where—"

"I'm sixty pounds lighter than you. Give me that rope!"

She caught the coil he lobbed to her and ran out on the rungs. The van was less than a hundred feet upstream, slowing, but still on course along the edge of the levee. Was it moving more slowly because it was sinking deep in the water? No, it was beginning to turn, whirling in the grip of an eddy. The whirlpool was slowing the van but sucking it under at the same time.

Clementine braced herself at the ladder three feet above the racing water, tied on one end and prepared to throw the rope. The van was drawing near, spinning faster, whirling in the eddy. It flipped on its side, passenger window in the air, driver's window underwater. The van was sinking. Clementine saw Mary Kay's head pop from the window, then her shoulders. There she seemed caught. Ten feet away, Clementine glimpsed Chance's hand push her from the vehicle. Suddenly she was swimming, the current pulling her past the ladder. Clementine shouted and threw the rope.

It splashed between Mary Kay's hands. She grabbed it and Clementine fought to pull her against the current as Mary Kay hauled herself along the rope, hand over hand, until she was so close Clementine could see her green eyes as if they were talking across a table. The fire in them was dim, the effect of cold water or shock, or, Clementine feared, despair that she had committed a sin that she believed could never be forgiven. "Hold on, Mary Kay. Don't give up."

"Where's Chance?" Mary Kay cried. "Did he get out?"

"I don't know," shouted Clementine. "Give me your hand."

"I am sorry," said Mary Kay, "I am so, so sorry."

"No! Hold on, Mary Kay!"

Mary Kay let go of the rope.

The river took her under.

When Clementine sprang upright on the ladder to see where she went, her eyes fixed in horror on the yellow-brown glow deep underwater of the headlights of the church van sinking with Chance trapped inside.

41

Martyrs

Day 40

Robert Garcia's helicopter hovered over the hairpin bend at the Jefferson Point jetty, where the mainline levee on the Louisiana side of the U-turn was most vulnerable. The long rock barrier was entirely submerged. But quiet water upstream of it, and roiled current below, clearly marked the line the rocks cut halfway across the river.

Through the rain he could see the lakes and bayous that speckled the wildlife reserve between the Mississippi River and the Atchafalaya River, where the Mississippi often flooded low-lying ground in the spring. The river had already spread past its natural banks and inundated the floodplain all the way to the Louisiana levee. Judging by trees submerged to their crowns, the water was easily deep enough to float loaded barges.

"Here comes another barge fleet, Colonel."

"I see him."

"Sand barges, sir."

The tow was coming downriver, moving fast on the current and hugging the Louisiana side. He studied it in the binoculars.

"Pilot. Get over him. Soldiers, cover the wheelhouse and that guy on the lead barge. What's that he's holding?" he asked the copilot who was eyeing a screen with powerful optics. "Is that a rifle?"

"Looks like a rake, Colonel."

"Rake?"

"Like he's smoothing the sand. Want me to get them on the radio, sir?"

"Get closer." If the barge fleet did not turn with the channel when it reached the U-turn in the river, and if it was, as Clementine feared, a fertilizer bomb, it was on a course to land a direct hit on the mainline levee. His Black Hawk closed the distance. A rigid inflatable jon boat was hipped up alongside the towboat, bouncing violently, instead of hoisted on deck. Getaway boat?

Garcia's phone blared a Penn-to-gram bugle call in his helmet speaker.

He'd been expecting one sooner. That he had actually had four full hours to improvise his defense of the Control Structure could be chalked up to the disasters Penn was fielding at Cairo and Birds Point. But as he had reminded Clementine, the general's radar was formidable because nothing happened in the division that one of his hundreds of officers or thousands of civilian employees didn't soon tip him to. The Penn-to-gram was a classic.

REPORT

The general picked up on the first ring. "What is going on in Louisiana, Colonel Garcia?"

"I have deployed a helicopter, two picket boats, and an MP platoon to guard the Old River Control structures from terrorist attack."

"Is this an exercise?"

"No, sir."

"Are you responding to a specific attack?"

"The strong possibility of one, sir."

"Why wasn't intelligence about this attack forwarded to me immediately?"

Garcia saw the flag on the tall jack staff at the bow of the center lead barge flap sideways. The wind had shifted violently. He swiveled the phone mic from his lips and spoke into his helmet mic. "Pilot! What are those white streaks on the lead barges?"

They looked like snow or ice had frozen on the sand, which of course it hadn't in the rain. To General Penn he said, "Time was of the essence, sir. I could not wait on orders."

"You are way out of line, Colonel Garcia."

"No, sir. I've kept you out of the loop."

"What in blue blazes is that supposed to mean?"

"If I am wrong, sir, it won't come back at you."

Robert Garcia had just admitted to General Penn that he had laid his entire career on the line. Would Penn acknowledge initiative and turn a blind eye to the breach of discipline while he scoped out Garcia's motive? Or would Penn bust him on the spot?

He swiveled the phone mic from his mouth again. "Pilot! Right on top of him. Soldiers, ready weapons."

"How did you learn of this?" Penn demanded.

"A source best left nameless, sir," Garcia replied, asking for a deaf ear along with a blind eye.

"Colonel Garcia," said Penn, "land that machine and report to me at Vicksburg."

Garcia looked down through the open door. The Black Hawk descended rapidly over the lead barges. Its rotor wash blasted clouds of wet sand, and the streaks widened into patches of white canvas where the sand had been blown off.

"Are you trained in fast-rope rappelling?" he asked the soldier next to him.

"Not yet, sir. But the chief can lower me on the hoist."

"General," Garcia spoke into his phone, "I've got something strange here."

"Not as strange as you not acknowledging my direct order."

A bullet twanged off the titanium edge of a rotor blade. Another penetrated the blade itself and blew a big hole that made the flight controls vibrate.

Garcia spied a rifleman leaning out a wheelhouse window. "Shoot that man!"

The gun leapt to the MP's shoulder.

"General," Garcia told Penn, "they're shooting at my helicopter. I am returning fire."

Clinton Penn's answer was swift, smooth, and for-the-record. "No officer in my command needs permission to return fire."

A face filled the soldier's sights. Young and unseasoned, he hesitated for a split-second. The shooter ducked down, and the moment was lost. Garcia started to order the pilot to land on the towboat's wheelhouse roof, but a tall light staff, spinning radars, a spotlight, and radio antennas made a thicket of obstacles.

Garcia did not like the jack staff flag blowing one way and another. A sudden shift to tailwind would make the helicopter lose lift at a crucial moment. And the air was very humid, which also attenuated lift. He glanced at the pilot's cyclic control lever. On it, covered so it wouldn't be hit accidentally, was a switch to shear the hoist line to drop the load to save his ship from crashing.

"Crew chief! Hoist line. Soldier, give me your weapon."

"Sir, you can't—"

He took the kid's carbine, set the fire mode to burst, and stepped to the hoist. The crew chief, a grizzled vet near Garcia's age, looked at him like he was out of his mind. Garcia said, "I'd prefer to fast rope, but I haven't done it in years."

"Let the boys do it, Colonel."

"I've had my children already. They haven't." Which was better for unit morale than stating the fact that when they landed on the towboat, they wouldn't have a clue who to shoot first.

"Pilot, come in high over the top of him and down fast as you can. Soldiers, give me covering fire—semi-automatic, single shots. Keep them inside, but don't spray the windows. I don't want to find the controls shot up. Cease fire when I launch." He raked them with cold eyes. "Direct order: Do not follow me." All he needed was getting shot accidentally in the back. "Pilot—go!"

Pushing the Back Hawk to the edge of its capability, the pilot executed a skilled break turn, crossed over the towboat at a high banking angle and dropped into a hover fifty feet above the wheelhouse. The MPs opened fire. Garcia went out the door with one foot on the hoist line hook, his right hand on the line, his left gripping the carbine.

The wind, which was blowing hard over the barges and ricocheting an updraft off the flat-fronted four-story deckhouse, suddenly spun on a dime 180 degrees behind the helicopter. Garcia heard the Black Hawk's rotation rate drop. He felt the big machine falter in the air, its rotors losing lift. He was forty feet above the roof when the hoist line shook in his hand. A sharp noise and a sudden sense of floating told him that the pilot had been forced to hit the shear-switch to save his ship. Then he was falling. Radar, light staff, aerials, and searchlights on the wheelhouse roof lunged for him like crooked teeth.

Garcia let go the severed line, kicked loose of the hook, and pressed his knees and ankles together, hoping to execute the parachute landing fall he'd learned thirty years ago at Fort Benning jump school. A successful PLF required landing flat on his feet and rolling sideways to distribute the impact up ankles, calf, thigh, and back. Worst case, shattered femurs and tibia healed faster than crushed vertebrae. Break a leg to save your spine.

He crashed to the wheelhouse roof, dodging the searchlight by inches. A radar antenna blocked his sideways roll. His ballistic vest saved his ribs where he smashed the antenna off its mount, and his helmet kept him from cracking his skull on the light staff pivot. He ended his landing flat on his back, breathless with pain. His jump school instructor would be proud. He had broken his leg instead of his back.

He heard a noise like tearing cloth—a suppressed bullpup assault rifle firing at full automatic. No way he could stand, much less run. But his rifle was still in his hand. He rolled to the edge of the roof, slid over it, tumbled past the windows, landed in a new explosion of pain on the open deck behind the wheelhouse, and waited for them to come to him. Emboldened by their body armor, two men made that mistake and charged out the door. Garcia cut them down with head shots and dragged himself inside the wheelhouse. No surprise it was bullet-riddled despite his instructions. He could only pray the controls were intact. A tattooed skinhead came at him swinging a fire ax. Garcia shot him. Before the bullpup could start blasting again, he rolled over broken glass to get behind an instrument console and took cover there, flat on the floor.

He looked up toward the pilot's chair and got a huge surprise.

The terrorist seated between the sticks, driving the boat, was African American, like the rumored black pilot who destroyed the St. Louis waterfront with *Miss Josephine of Blytheville*. He was dressed in full combat gear and wore it like a proud career soldier. They leveled their weapons simultaneously. Their eyes locked and a weird thought threaded through Garcia's mind. Brother warriors in a Mexican Standoff.

If they both died who would steer the towboat?

"You're not a white supremacist."

Abdul Muqtadir glanced at the fallen skinhead and the bodies heaped outside the wing door. "Found out they were too late." He still couldn't figure out how Brother I fit in with the whites. Though he had a grim feeling—without proof, and no knowledge why—that the man who made his black-separatist dream possible had set up the whole thing.

Robert Garcia figured the man had to be confused, at the very least, and very likely conflicted. Maybe he could reason with him. Garcia let his rifle slip from his hands. It clattered on the linoleum deck. "What do you say we defuse their bomb before it blows the levee?"

"Too late," said the black terrorist. "That skinhead you shot knew his stuff. Fuses are burning. Two minutes after we hit the levee, you are going to Kingdom Come and I am hooking up with Allah."

Quite a sense of humor, thought Garcia, for a man willing to kill so many innocents. But the terrorist could drive the towboat a million times better than he could. He tried again. "What's your name? I'm Robert Garcia, Colonel, U.S. Army Corps of Engineers."

"Abdul Muqtadir," the terrorist answered and echoed Garcia's introduction with a mocking smile, "Jihadist, Forty Acres Martyr Brigade."

"Abdul, I know how to defuse the bomb before it drowns ten thousand Cajuns in the Atchafalaya Floodway."

"No way, Colonel."

"Any luck, I can do it without you and me getting killed."

"I already told you. You and I are going out in a martyr-inspiring blaze of glory."

Garcia blinked to clear his eyes. The pain was dragging him down. The engine vibrations that rattled the floor were agony. His eyes closed. When he forced them open, Abdul Muqtadir had turned to the windscreen. He was watching ahead of the fleet, like he knew Garcia was done for. He might be right. Garcia gathered breath in his lungs to call out, "Who is your 'Powerful'?"

Abdul did not take his eyes from the river. "Say what?"

"Your Muslim name, 'Abdul Muqtadir,' translates to mean, 'Slave of the Powerful.' Who are you slaving for?"

"Sounds like the army made you take a counterterrorism course."

"I aced it," said Garcia. "Did your 'Powerful' tell you to steer your barges into the mainline levee?"

Abdul Muqtadir turned in his chair and glared down at Garcia. The colonel had the look of those one-in-a-hundred officers a soldier could trust. Such an officer should understand who he slaved for, and he answered, "I 'slave' for lost children. I 'slave' for a nation where Black Lives Matter will be a law that people love. Who's *your* 'Powerful,' Colonel? Who do *you* slave for? You're Cuban, aren't you?"

"*American*-Cuban."

"Who are *you* 'slaving' for?" He swung the bullpup toward Garcia, wondering why he hadn't shot him already.

Garcia looked him in the eye. "I swore an oath to defend the United States Constitution against all enemies, foreign and domestic." He saw that the soldiers' vow had resonated with Abdul Muqtadir as he had hoped it might.

"I swore the same, once," Abdul replied, slowly. "Except the enlisted man's version included obeying officers."

Garcia forced a comradely smile. "If you obey my order to ram this bomb into the rock jetty in the middle of the river instead of the levee, we will save thousands of innocent people from drowning."

Abdul Muqtadir was in no mood to smile back. "I stuck to my oath longer than I should have."

Robert Garcia knew then and there that it was up to him to steer the boat. He collected his spirit and whispered harshly, "We all try to keep hope alive."

Abdul heard a dying man clutching at platitudes. The colonel was no longer a threat, and he looked ahead to focus total attention on the bend in the river.

Garcia summoned the strength to stifle an agonized groan. He rolled silently onto his left side. He unholstered the pistol he had shielded with his body and fired it twice.

Abdul Muqtadir heard the first shot. *The Cuban suckered me.* He knew he would never hear the second.

Robert Garcia crawled across the wheelhouse, climbed over Abdul Muqtadir's body, hauled himself up to the pilot's chair with trembling arms and fell backwards into it. Through the rain-streaked and bullet-pocked windshield he saw the fleet stretch a thousand feet ahead, longer than most ships. He couldn't see the bend in the river. He thought he had lost sight of it in the rain. Then he realized, his vision was fading. He was sliding away, escaping the pain. He dragged himself back to consciousness and laid his hands on the sticks.

Clementine, I wish you were here. I am way outside my wheelhouse.

Thank God, what he had to do was simple. No need to mess with flanking rudders, he thought. He wasn't slowing down or going backwards. No need for throttles. He wanted every bit of speed he could get out of her. All he had to do was turn left before he hit the bend.

He knew which sticks to move to turn her two main rudders. Except, when he nudged them, nothing happened. The fleet kept rushing straight at the bend where the bomb would explode against the mainline levee. He pushed them harder. Nothing.

He was wrong about the flanking rudders. He needed to reverse the left propeller and move the left flanking rudders to force the barge fleet to turn. He puzzled them out. Slow as molasses, the lead barges swung a little bit toward mid-channel. There it hesitated, and he felt the current draw it back toward the hairpin bend in the river.

Ahead he saw the white marker with black stripes that warned of the jetty.

Garcia battled the sticks to veer out of the channel. He had to turn far to the left—left toward Jefferson Point—as far as he could get from the mainline Louisiana levee—and ram the floating bomb head-on into the jetty, which would sink the fleet. But the strong current kept pulling him toward the levee.

The wind shifted again, suddenly. He felt it shoving the right side of the fleet. He saw the jack staff at the head of the tow swing slowly left. The wind was helping, like a huge hand adding force to his efforts with the sticks and the throttles and the flanking rudders. He saw the jack staff sweep past the black-striped marker. Ahead was smooth water and ahead of the smooth water was the roiled surface that marked the submerged line of rocks.

The fleet hurtled straight at them.

The lead barges struck with an oddly silent shudder that tore out their bottoms.

Garcia exulted. The barges were sinking fast. He had pulled it off. The fleet had struck far outside the channel, a full half mile from the levee. Even if the water rushing into the fertilizer barges did not disable the bomb before it exploded, at this distance the levee was safe. Which was more than he could say for himself on a towboat, still cabled to the sinking fleet, drifting toward the rocks.

***

Clementine Price blinked away tears as the Black Hawk rose from Levee Street. From above, she told herself, she would see a miracle—the Hilltop van floating on the river. Air trapped inside would have made it buoyant when it escaped the eddy that dragged it under temporarily. She would spot its yellow roof. Uncle Chance was tough. His bum shoulder would have slowed him down, but he would have overridden the pain to worm out an open window. When the Black Hawk gained enough altitude for her to see him, there he would be, safe on the roof.

Already Clementine could see the rush of men and machines dumping rock and gravel and sandbags where the levee had sloughed. She craned her head to follow the current downstream. He would be floating past South End or even the steel mill.

"Jesus," Mike Coligny yelled over the turbine howls. "Look at them."

Clem twisted around to look ahead. The helicopter had climbed so high she could see way upstream, beyond the interstate connector bridge.

Rolly said, "Gotta be a hundred of them."

An armada of runaway jumbo barges covered the river from bank to bank. At least a hundred were racing on the powerful current, hurtling toward the bridge.

42

The Dam

Day 40

Something was wrong with the bridge.

Clementine Price stared in confusion. She cleared the tears from her eyes and forced her mind to focus on what had changed. Confusion turned to disbelief. The arch that spanned the channel stood as always. So did the road deck suspended from it. But there was a gap in the highway ramp that approached the Arch from the Arkansas side. A section of that roadway had disappeared. And there were empty places in the orderly row of concrete columns that supported the approach.

A runaway barge plowed into a column next to that empty space. It leaned drunkenly, and another section of roadbed broke loose and crashed into the river, landing on top of sinking barges. The stricken barges and the fallen road sections heaped up a junk island that extended from near the shore to a point a third of the way across, blocking the river. White water splashed over the island like mountain rapids. But upstream, behind the barrier, the trapped water pooled to form a giant lake.

Clementine looked across the river. As she feared, a mirror image of the destruction was repeating on the opposite bank. Barges slammed into ramp columns. Columns collapsed. The barges sank. The roadway fell—carrying with it a yellow Hilltop van that must be packed with flood victims from Tennessee—and a second lake rose so swiftly that it instantly submerged the van. She heard Rolly in her headset.

"He's damming the river."

"Pulling another St. Louis," said Duvall.

"It won't work here," said Clementine. "Most of the water will continue draining down the main channel."

The Bliss Bends cutoff—the chute the Corps had dredged down the middle—was deep and broad, a full 500-feet wide between the interstate connector channel piers. It seemed an odd miscalculation by Nathan Flowers. Clementine peered down through the rain. What had she missed? Nothing within their ring of visibility. She looked at the radar.

"What's that?" she asked Coligny.

"Something big," said the pilot.

"Go!"

Coligny pushed his cyclic lever and the Black Hawk shot upriver.

"Lower."

Loose barges drifted under them. Then a shape formed mid-channel. The Boat? she wondered, but it was even larger than the Corps' towboat.

Out of the rain came Noah's Lucky Ark.

***

The huge casino barge was following the runaways down the middle of the Bliss Bends chute. Pushed by the *Delta Lady* towboat Clem had radioed earlier from her Air Tractor, the triple-unit barge looked to be making seven or eight mph. Add ten mph of flood current and the monster was flying. It would make the bridge in twenty minutes.

"Clem," Rolly said sharply. "How long is that thing?"

"Longer than the channel is wide—Mike, get closer."

"Hold on," said Duvall. "Is that a fifty on the roof?"

Clem said, "We can't let the Ark block the channel under the bridge."

Rolly scoped the Noah's Ark with the binoculars. "Sally port in the side. For their attack boats."

"The roof," said Duvall. "Check out the fifty."

Rolly passed the glasses to Duvall. "Clem, he's got a heavy weapon on a tripod."

Clementine said, "The river is discharging 25 million gallons of water per second. If he dams the channel, the river will fill the Bliss Basin in a flash."

"Fifty on a tripod," said Duvall. "Piece of cake to put an armor-piercing round through Mike's windscreen."

Mike Coligny whipped the machine sideways like a dragonfly. A half mile away he hovered so low to the river that the rotors beat clouds of spray.

Clementine said, "The water that Flowers dams up will top the mainline levee in twenty places."

They looked at her. They knew that, of course, and Clementine Price was suddenly and acutely aware that these brave veterans who had flown unquestioningly to her aid were middle-aged guys who had started the day at ordinary breakfast tables. She had to focus every breath in her body to rally them. She had to drive empty hope for Chance from her heart and give her all to them. They didn't need a sermon; they needed a picture they would never forget.

"Nathan Flowers is twenty minutes from damming the river. We're the only people who can stop him. If we don't, an ocean of water three stories deep, forty *miles* wide and forty long will drown the Delta. *One million acres.* Farms, factories, towns, suburbs, the entire city of Bliss, will drown before people can back down their driveways."

"Affirmative," said Rolly. "We're with you, Clem."

"First the .50," said Duvall.

"We need a plan," said Rolly and they huddled with Mike.

Clementine telephoned Tommy Chow in Memphis. "Tommy, Bliss is under terrorist attack. They are damming the river with a logjam of sunken barges, like St. Louis times ten. I am trying stop them before they divert flood crests over the levees. If I fail, it's your turn. Send everything you've got."

"But the flood crests are bad already."

Clementine shouted, "He's going to make them worse."

Tommy Chow asked, "How big is your force?"

"Me and two Bliss cops who served in special-tactics."

"I'll clear it with General Penn and get right back to you."

"No. Help first, Penn second, or innocent people will drown. Gotta go, my people are heading out."

Rolly Winters and Duvall McCoy clipped onto tie-down rings and opened the doors.

Clementine Price had served enough years as an officer to know when to observe closely from the copilot chair and keep her mouth shut while the specialists did their job. Mike Coligny held the Black Hawk low to the water and attacked the towboat from behind. Noah's Lucky Ark was three stories high, and *Delta Lady* five. Her taller deckhouse blocked the roof gun's line of fire.

When Coligny closed to two hundred meters, fighters in black battle dress stepped onto the wing behind the wheelhouse and opened fire with assault rifles. Coligny slewed the Black Hawk sideways presenting the target to Rolly Winters's carbine. The fighters fell and the Black Hawk flashed past the towboat, raced alongside the barge past elephant, cow, rabbit, and lion heads and popped up suddenly in a dead-steady hover.

Duvall McCoy was ready and shot the marksman on the roof. Coligny spun the helicopter 180 degrees. A second marksman ran to the gun. Rolly Winters disabled it with a long burst that sent parts flying.

Coligny climbed to a thousand feet.

Rolly and Duvall reloaded. Rolly said, "Clem. We're going down. Soon as we clear out the rest of them Mike will drop you on the roof of the Ark. You make your way to the wheelhouse to drive the boat."

Clementine unbuckled, climbed out of her chair and duck-walked under the low ceiling to Rolly in the open door. "That will take too long. I'm coming with you."

"Major," said Rolly. "I'm sure you can handle yourself, but even if we believed that you singlehandedly blew away Osama Bin Laden and let the Navy SEALs take the credit, you haven't drilled with me and Duvall. So you've got to do what I say or one of us'll end up shooting the rest of us by mistake."

"I'll stay out of your way. I will not fire my weapon. I will stand by to steer the boat."

Rolly and Duvall exchanged a look. "Here's what we'll do for you and this is final. You stay on the Hawk until we clear the wheelhouse. Then Mike drops you directly on the wheelhouse roof. You come down the ladder and you're at the sticks. Okay?"

"Yes, sir."

"And if you hear us say take cover, you hit the deck in extreme fetal. Leave the heroics to the pros."

The headwind generated by the Ark's speed suddenly shifted to a crosswind. Mike Coligny was ready for it, and for the tailwind that followed, and swooped in as if heading for an easy landing on the Ark's broad, uncluttered roof. Gunmen swarmed. Rolly and Duvall shot them. Mike jumped the big machine up and over *Delta Lady's* wheelhouse. Rolly and Duvall bailed onto the roof and disappeared over the side, firing short, controlled salvos.

Clementine heard a warning horn. Lights flashed and she made a fast decision to jump for the towboat while she could. Just as she unbuckled, a sudden loss of lift staggered the Black Hawk. Coligny pulled up on the collective stick to recover stability, but the faltering turbines could not provide enough power.

"Brace!" he yelled and tried to slow the rotors before they hit. The helicopter fell on its side. The rotor blades shattered against the steel deck house. The torque of the spinning blades' impact whirled the 14,000-pound aircraft off the roof. It fell on the wing deck behind the wheelhouse, crushing a gunman, toppled down onto the next deck and rolled across it, slamming to a stop against *Delta Lady's* exhaust stacks. Clementine felt herself propelled across the cabin and out the door.

Thank God for the helmet, she thought, as she tried to tuck into a ball. Everything seemed to slow. It was like almost stalling again, except this time for real. Her mind fixed on a hundred images—Snoopy falling to the Hilltop levee, a vivid replay of the ground growing large, so close she could see blades of wet grass and rust on an access well cover, Nathan Flowers losing his cool about the Corps acting like God Almighty. *What were you looking for? What were you looking for?*

What was I looking for? What were you hiding?

Something you never would think of. A complete surprise.

She was thrown between the *Delta Lady's* stacks and landed against the soft tube of an inflatable jon boat hanging in its deck crane. It bounced her face first against the outboard motor and she came to a stop, head spinning and feeling around for something to wipe the blood from her eyes.

Coligny and the flight engineer strapped into their seats were unscathed. They scrambled out of the wreck to look for Clementine Price, found her climbing out of the jon boat with blood on her face and a pistol in her hand, then hit the deck and covered their heads when gunfire erupted. The pattern of fire, the measured, disciplined sounds of Rolly Winters and Duvall McCoy at war stopped abruptly, as if everyone had died at once.

43

The Innocent

Day 40

Nathan Flowers could not recall a quieter place than the high, wide wheelhouse of the *Delta Lady* after the helicopter crashed and the shooting stopped. It was like waking up in an Ozark holler in the middle of the night without a soul or a machine for miles around.

The spell didn't last long. He felt the engines grinding under the deck and heard the labored breathing of a man dying. He saw Joey stagger in from the wing with his arm and shoulder crushed as if they had been flattened by a steam roller. His eyes rolled into the back of his head, his legs sagged, and he fell face first.

Nathan Flowers drew the pistol from his thigh holster. "Captain Scruggs!" He pressed the gun barrel to Scruggs's forehead. "Will you steer the barge where I tell you to?"

Captain Scruggs said, "It don't look to me like I have much choice."

"Do you see the left channel pier?"

"Yep."

"Hit it."

Billy Scruggs could see the highway sections that had fallen on the Arkansas side, and another sagging above the water on the Tennessee side. Apparently, the madman with the pistol was under the misimpression that the channel pier was as fragile as a highway column and Scruggs felt no compunction to tell him the truth. He'd hit the pier like he was told and hope for things to get better.

Flowers felt the powerful towboat regain control of the casino barges. But five seconds later, a massive eddy seized them. Scruggs muttered, "Rat's ass son of a bitch." Flowers watched him work the steering levers like Hilltop's pansy organist nailing his notes. The barge straightened up on the pier again.

Suddenly Scruggs reversed the engines. The propellers shook the boat and rattled the windows. "What are you doing?" Nathan demanded.

"Flanking . . . backing down. Current's shooting so fast, only way I can control her."

The bridge was getting near and Flowers could see the city beyond it. The levee seemed to be topped with ice. But it was the sandbags they tried to waterproof with white sheets of polyethylene. The sandbags put him in mind of how sandbags had led him to first meet Mary Kay. She would be all right as long as she stayed at Hilltop. But if he knew her, and he surely did, she would probably be leading a contingent to Bliss to "help their neighbors."

He pictured her beautiful face and hoped she would stay safe at the church. Suddenly a terrible hesitation pounded at his heart. He had to brace himself for the question burning in her eyes. "What about our church?"

"All I did with that church was stick my finger in the dike. The flood's going to make people's lives new. Neighbors helping their own kind. Whites pulling together. Blacks helping themselves where they belong. We must secure the existence of our people and a future for white children."

"*Drop it! Drop it! Drop it!*"

He couldn't believe his eyes. A wiry black man he recognized as Bliss Metro police detective Duvall McCoy burst into the wheelhouse with an assault rifle. Rolly Winters, the mayor's husband, crashed through a door on the other side, yelling, "Drop it, Flowers. Drop it."

Major Clementine Price came up through the inside door with blood on her face and a pistol in her hand and suddenly all three were aiming weapons at his head.

Nathan Flowers looked ahead of the huge Noah's Ark. His dam of sinking barges and fallen road was piled at both sides of the bridge. Only one last stretch of open water remained for the river to escape, the middle five hundred feet between the channel piers. He looked at Clementine Price and her blacks fixing to blow his head off. He looked down at the skinny little man struggling with throttles and rudder sticks. The towboat captain was concentrating so hard on controlling the boat he had paid no attention to the yelling.

Flowers had the strangest thought. He, of all people, was in the arms of God.

He dropped his weapon and raised his hands.

Major Price called, "Captain? Are you able to make that bridge?"

"That is my intention," said Billy Scruggs.

Winters said, "Flowers, what you're going to do now is slowly turn around and lay flat on the deck."

Nathan Flowers turned slowly. He lowered his right hand as if to steady himself as he knelt.

"No!" shouted Clementine Price.

Before any of them could fire, Flowers's left hand fell like an ax on the back of Billy Scruggs's neck.

44

The Runaway

Day 40

The riverboat captain's startled cry was cut short by the roar of guns. Powerful rounds pounded Nathan Flowers's body armor. The blunt force hurled him backwards, breath slammed out of his lungs, his arm pivoting upward after chopping Scruggs's neck, jerked high toward the wheelhouse ceiling. Out the door—get out the door, he thought. Cradling his head, he rolled down a flight of steel stairs, and flopped on the deck like a dead man. The huge boat lurched violently, jerked to the left by the mass of the Ark swinging toward the Tennessee shore.

Clementine Price jumped over the skinny towboat captain who had collapsed like a handful of twigs and was staring at the ceiling as if paralyzed—innocent as a sleeping child. The controls were the old-fashioned pre-electronic variety—two sets of rudder levers, one over the other, the short on top, the long on the bottom, and two throttles, the left marked PORT, the right STARBOARD. The boat rattled and shook like a Jeep skidding out of control on a gravel road. It was so big, thought Clementine, that when it turned it seemed as if it were actually pitching and rolling in place while the whole world turned around it. But it was in fact moving and moving fast—closing in on the tangle of sunken barges and fallen ramps that blocked both sides of the rampaging river—and the instant she touched the steering levers she knew that the river was in complete control. Uncle Chase said that steering a tow on a river at flood stage was like riding a barn over a waterfall, but to her it felt like flying Snoopy into the air wake of a 747.

She hauled the throttles back, felt them engage Reverse. She kept pulling back until she had both propellers spinning backwards at full speed. Nothing happened, except the deck shook harder. Momentum and the current were still in charge.

Somehow she had to get the boat going straight down the middle. If she got caught crosswise, she would block the whole bridge, exactly as Nathan Flowers had intended.

"She's swinging right, Clem." That was Rolly standing behind her.

"I got it . . . I think." She eased off the engines, backed the left again, until she thought she could feel the water going over the rudders and see the Ark start to straighten. At the moment she had it lined straight down the channel, a whirlpool a thousand feet across—what Uncle Chase used to call a "rat's ass son of a bitch eddy"— gripped Noah's Lucky Ark and the thrashing towboat and spun the entire unit 90 degrees. Clementine frantically swung the rudder levers and tried every trick she could dream up with the throttles. But nothing she did shook the barges and *Delta Lady* loose from the Mississippi River, which was hurling them sideways at the bridge.

Clementine had done the math. Only five hundred feet separated the channel piers. The barges alone were more than seven hundred feet, and the towboat added another one hundred fifty. She could still feel the giant propellers blasting water over the rudders. Every law of physics said they should turn. But the river in flood played by different rules, and the barge was out of control.

She felt something at her ankle and glanced down. The old captain was staring up at her, tugging her cuff with his fingers. "*Wait.*"

"What? What did you say?"

Billy Scruggs tried to gather air in his lungs to make himself heard. He couldn't move more than one hand and it burned like hell to talk. He wondered if he might live longer if he didn't speak. Thing was, he could feel it all happening through the deck. Flat on his back, he could see things the girl on the sticks couldn't dream.

"Wait. *Ease up*. Wait for it. Wait for the bar. Slack water. Wait."

Clementine throttled back both engines.

"Something underneath?" Rolly asked Clementine.

"*He* thinks so."

Suddenly they slowed. She felt the change instantly. Something was stopping them. The raging water had smoothed, slightly. The muddy white caps flattened.

"Port ahead," whispered Scruggs. He was running out of air. "Starboard back."

She powered the port engine full ahead and pulled the starboard throttle to full back and worked the rudders. The barge swung, straightened up parallel with the river, centering on the channel between the bridge piers.

"Drive!" Captain Billy Scruggs gasped with what he knew was his last breath. "Punch her! Give her all you got!"

Clementine was already shoving the starboard throttle.

As the front of Noah's Lucky Ark slipped between the piers, the smooth water exploded into wild motion again, grabbing the tow and shaking it so hard that Clementine knew that whatever she did with the rudder levers had no effect on controlling their course. The bridge blotted the sky. Partway under it, the rearmost barge struck a glancing blow that resounded like thunder and sent the tow caroming and scraping along the massive pier.

Suddenly they hung up.

The water rose behind them, crashed over the back of the towboat, and submerged the main deck. Clementine felt *Delta Lady* stagger under the weight. The boat was falling backwards, sinking.

Clementine whispered, half to herself, half to Rolly and Duvall, "She squats when I throttle forward. Maybe—" She threw both engines in reverse. "Lift? We're getting lift."

Slowly, the stern rose. She could feel the towboat struggling to break free of the water. They hurtled through the piers and under the road deck. Clem looked up. She saw the sky. It was bleak with rain, but it was beautiful. They were clear, the bridge behind them, the channel wide, the torrent racing down it.

Duvall McCoy bounded down the stairs to look for Nathan Flowers's body.

Clementine radioed Bliss Marine. "This is Major Price on *Delta Lady.* We need a pilot and engineer ASAP and towboats to assist landing the Ark."

"I'm putting a pilot and engineer in our fastest jon boat, ma'am. Two five-deckers right behind him."

Duvall McCoy radioed Rolly Winters. "Sonofabitch is gone. I'm tracking blood to the front of the boat. Looks like he jumped on the Ark."

"How much blood?"

"Not enough to slow him down."

Rolly spotted Duvall on the main deck. He was vaulting from the towboat's push knee onto the Ark, pivoting off one hand with his rifle in the other. Rolly stormed after him.

Duvall McCoy spotted a bloody handprint on a door, pushed it open and charged inside and across a service corridor and through a second door which opened on the casino's main gambling hall—a space big enough to store airplanes—that he had visited several times while investigating whether drowned gamblers were suicides who had intentionally jumped in the Mississippi River or homicides thrown in by loan sharks. It was empty and cold and smelled like fried food. The lights were off, except for battery backups, the video screens blank, the slot machines dark and silent. The blackjack, craps, roulette, and poker tables made an obstacle course of a hundred round and square shadows, each of which could conceal an armed man hiding.

If Flowers was in here, the way to find out was to draw fire.

Duvall raced among the tables, weaving a zigzag path, primed to fire back and counting on superior speed, skill, reflexes, and training to kill Nathan Flowers before Flowers killed him. It worked like a charm. The sonofabitch stood up behind a roulette table a hundred feet away and took deliberate aim with a rifle similar to Duvall's.

Thank you, Reverend. *Now you're mine.*

Duvall exploded into motion. Running hard, he went airborne. He somersaulted over a table, hit the deck rolling, and sprang upright, fifty feet closer to Flowers than a heartbeat ago. Flowers opened fire. Bullets passed well behind Duvall who was now close enough to hit him with a rock, much less a weapon he had trained with for fifteen years. He touched his trigger. In the same instant, he jerked the muzzle up at the ceiling.

A tall, bald drunk waving a bottle had reeled up from the shadows between him and Flowers, wide-eyed with terror. In that crazy millisecond, Duvall recognized Big Al Striker, the manager of Noah's Lucky Ark Casino, whom he had interviewed several times. He had almost killed the poor fool. Nathan Flowers fired another burst. Duvall McCoy was no longer running, but a stationary target at point blank range. Bullets kicked his legs out from under him.

Rolly Winters ran toward the gunfire, hurled himself through doors and into the gambling hall. "Duvall! Detective McCoy!"

"Over here, sir," called a voice.

He recognized Al Striker. The casino manager was pointing fearfully at the floor. Rolly rounded a faro table. Duvall was sprawled on his back with his left leg twisted behind him.

Rolly knelt with his infantry first aid kit and pulled open the body armor fasteners. The vest had deformed where it had stopped two rounds, creating hopefully superficial wounds. But Duvall had also taken a round below the vest. Blood pulsed from his upper thigh. The femoral artery was damned near impossible to tourniquet that close to the groin.

"Duvall?"

"I'm cool. I'm cool." His voice was thin with shock, piping like a little boy's. "Get that sonofabitch!"

There was no way on God's earth Rolly Winters would leave him to die. Until he got Duvall stabilized and into the hands of a medic, Nathan Flowers was someone else's war.

***

"I got her, ma'am." The relief pilot clapped hands on the sticks and held *Delta Lady* still as a rock mid-channel.

Clementine Price bolted from the wheelhouse, down to the main deck and forward to the push knees and onto Noah's Lucky Ark. Rolly Winters had spotted a sally port in the side of the Ark barge. A planner like Nathan Flowers would have an escape boat.

She drew her pistol and followed a stairway to a utility passage. At the end was a desk set up like a checkpoint to guard another flight of stairs. She was pounding down the steps when she heard the rumble of powerful boat engines starting up. She landed beside a well dock just as Nathan Flowers drove an inboard RIB built for speed out the sally port and swerved up the river.

The only other boat in the well dock was a bullet-riddled RIB with a dead man slumped over the helm. She jumped in, wrestled the body over the side, and started the outboards. Both ran despite the boat being shot up, and the hard lower hull wasn't damaged. But an air tube gunnel had been punctured. Partially flattened, the gunnel would not keep the boat afloat if Clementine encountered big waves, which made it no match for Nathan Flowers's inboard.

She drove out the sally port, glimpsed Flowers flying up the river, and raced after him, only to lose sight of him in the rain when he lengthened his lead. As she passed the levee that had sloughed, she saw it was crumbling. The river was chewing pavement and earth out from under Levee Street. Sandbags were sliding into the water as fast as people could throw them. Trucks and bulldozers charged the break. But when she looked back, the sandbaggers were running for their lives. The levee dissolved and the Mississippi River rushed into the city.

***

"Didn't Nathan pick an awful time to disappear?" said Reverend Keeler Blankenship. "I fear that his born-again prison inmates get more of his attention than Mary Kay."

Lois Blankenship was praying that their daughter, who was still not answering her phone, would at least return a text. The elderly couple had been about to board the last bus in sight, which had been packed, standing room only, when a terrified girl from the South End projects ran up with a passel of kids. They had repeated what they had told their deacons earlier: "You go, we'll take the next." But no more buses had come, and they had taken shelter in the nearest church, Reverend Eddie Parker's New Salvation Baptist in the old Barnes & Noble that used to be Goldsmiths. The lights were on, but everyone had gone. Mrs. Blankenship finished praying for Mary Kay and opened her eyes.

"Keeler!" she said in a choir mistress's strong voice. "Do you recognize what we're sitting on? Our old pews! Reverend Eddie took them in a pickup truck when we installed the new ones."

The floor shook. Suddenly the rumbling in the street was louder than the sand and fire trucks racing toward the levee. They shuffled down the aisle to look out the glass doors.

"My God."

Water tumbled up Main Street. It climbed the roofs of cars and in seconds it was up the steps and pressing the doors. Automobiles floated past, spinning on currents. A police cruiser with two men inside crashed against the steps. A tall wave whisked it away. The next bore an old truck from the Greyhound parking lot that shook the building to its foundation. The doors bowed inward.

The elderly couple retreated. The doors burst open and the water filled the foyer in a flash and poured up the aisle, knocking pews loose from the floor. Before they could think, they were in water to their knees. They struggled toward the stairs that led to the second floor. The water leapt to their chests, freezing cold.

"It's time."

Mary Kay's mother took her husband's hand. They turned as one to face the flood.

***

Clementine telephoned Lieutenant Pickett on The Boat. "Nathan Flowers is headed your way in a fast inboard RIB. Do not let him get to Hilltop. . . . Yes, the Reverend. Direct order: stop him. And look out he doesn't kill you."

Robert had stopped him at the Old River Structure.

Rolly, Duvall, Mike, and Clementine had stopped him at the bridge.

But there was more to Anaconda. Nathan Flowers was not done.

She continued after him, pushing the crippled boat as fast she dared.

Mary Kay had warned her on the levee. Nathan always has plans and back-up plans. He's a chess player, he thinks far, far ahead. It will be a surprise.

She flashed again to Snoopy stalling over Hilltop and Flowers losing his cool when she almost crashed. *What were you looking for?*

What were you hiding?

It could seem off the cuff. Because it will be something you never would think of. A complete surprise.

She flashed again on the rusted access well cover.

Blowing up his own levee would be unthinkable. A complete surprise.

45

Ready When You Are, Shot Caller

Day 40

The monkey brains had staked out Hilltop's ferry dock with patrol boats and the biggest motor vessel on the Mississippi River and radar, just as Nathan Flowers had anticipated. But the idiots' patrol boats were underpowered RIBs manned by desk clerks, *Mississippi V* could barely get out of its own way, and there was no way their radar could differentiate his camouflaged inboard from the waves, flood debris, and their own vessels that corrugated the surface of the rain-swept the river.

He sped tight to the Tennessee shore, drove past Hilltop—invisible across the river—then cut across the mile-wide torrent, and down along the Arkansas mainline levee. No surprise the morons weren't smart enough to watch Hilltop's half-built LNG dock. Though even if they had the brains to inspect the construction site, even if they drove a boat right inside the slack-water off-loading harbor, they would never know that one of the floating gas-storage tanks concealed inside it a mooring for his stealth boat.

Robby Bracken was waiting with a squad of black-clad Alluvian storm troopers.

"Ready when you are, Shot Caller."

***

Clementine Price telephoned her chief engineer from the damaged RIB, which was making slow progress in rough water. Driving with one hand, shielding her phone from rain and spray, and shouting to be heard, she said, "Jesse! Up at the north end of Hilltop, where the river bends left, I saw what looked like an access-well cover in the mainline levee. Would it exist for any reason other than loading explosives?"

"Could be from two years back. Hilltop licensed a natural gas wildcatter, and we issued a permit for exploratory drilling."

Clementine heard this with a sinking heart. The Corps regulated all subsurface work within three hundred feet of the levee centerline. Flowers would have used the phony gas-drilling permit as cover for the men and machines boring holes for explosives piping. The location was particularly vulnerable on the outside of a bend that took the full force of the river.

"I'll be there soon, Jess."

She telephoned Lieutenant Pickett.

"Recruit a squad of volunteers to go ashore at Hilltop."

Through the rain, she could finally make out the glow of the golden dove on the steeple and, moments later, the tall, square loom of The Boat under it. The big towboat was backing its engines against the current to hold a position a quarter mile off the levee. Suddenly Clementine saw motion flicker from the Arkansas side—a small craft veering toward her. She pocketed her phone and drew her pistol.

A second boat swooped from her right, dark and fast.

The first was suddenly close enough to see three men with rifles in a blue and white Supreme S202 water-ski boat. What the—?

"Major Price! Major Price, is that you?"

She recognized two long-serving civil engineers, brothers, and one of their sons, who was a permit manager in the Memphis District Regulatory Branch. They had hunting rifles slung over their life jackets.

"Heard you sent The Boat here. Figured we'd lend a hand."

The craft nearing from the right was a beat-up Phoenix bass boat driven by a retired geologist, a courtly old gentleman who had overseen the district's earthquake response plan. "Are you all right, Major? Your face is cut."

"Tip top, Mr. Griswold. Thank you for coming."

A huge, open-water, deep-V hull aluminum boat flying a Ducks Unlimited flag roared between them, nearly swamping old Griswold. Big-bellied Lester Gill stood at the steering console, one foot propped on a bungee-corded heap of bird guns and deer rifles shrewdly wrapped in life preservers.

"Clementine! Your boat's all shot to pieces."

"Thanks for the weapons, Lester."

She threw a line to a deckhand and scrambled onto *Mississippi V*, ordering, "Help them aboard—guns first," and bounded up the four flights of stairs outside the wheelhouse. More volunteers in small craft were converging on the Corps' motor vessel—a flotilla of jon boats, fishing boats, ski boats, and duck-hunting boats.

She burst into the wheelhouse calling to Captain McCargo, "Cap, take her up to the north end of Hilltop."

"You got it, Major"

Lieutenant Pickett and Lieutenant Harpur saluted.

Pickett reported, "I have more volunteers than guns, ma'am."

"Choose your six best to come with us. Lieutenant Harpur, station the rest on deck with guns to cover us and fire axes to keep boarders off The Boat."

She grabbed Zelvert McCargo's binoculars and focused on the distant levee. She saw no one moving on it. But, of course, Flowers would have pumped his liquid explosives before he started his Anaconda attack, probably stored in a phony natural gas tank. Sweeping the surrounding area through the glasses, she called to the pilot, "Zelvert, when you get there, nose into the ferry dock. Back out as soon as we're off."

"Yes, ma'am."

"What we're going to do is—"

Jagged plumes of mud shot up from the levee like shattered earthenware.

Long before sound waves carried the dull thump of the synchronized explosions, she knew she was too late to storm Hilltop with Pickett's volunteers. Nathan Flowers had blown a two-hundred-meter hole in the levee before she could stop him and opened the old Tomato floodplain to the full might of the Mississippi.

"Lieutenant Harpur, bring me Jesse Corliss."

In the moments her chief engineer took to get to the wheelhouse, the river doubled the levee crevasse with the force of its water. Instead of turning at the bend, it now blasted straight into Hilltop's baptismal lake and was threatening to fill the square mile of low ground inside the levees.

"Worst case, Jess? Now what happens?"

Corliss—a short, unkempt, rotund man with a direct gaze and a harsh voice that carried—answered Clementine in the manner she expected of the just-the-facts-ma'am engineer. "The river fills the old Tomato floodplain like a bathtub. When the bathtub overflows, the water takes out the mainline levee to the west. After that, there's nothing to stop it from inundating the Delta."

"But what about Hilltop's own levee along the river? Why doesn't the water top it too, right back into the river?"

"Can't."

"Why?"

"Picture the levels in descending order." He pointed at Mary Kay's golden dove glowing high in the sky. "Top level is the church and campus way up on the plateau; then the new Hilltop levee; then, next down, the original mainline levee; then the Mississippi River, itself, cresting at flood stage; and down at the bottom the old Tomato floodplain, where your farm used to be."

"But why is Hilltop's levee higher than the mainline levee?"

"Flowers wanted it built higher. I told him and Senator Garfield that he didn't have to build higher than the existing mainline levee to meet our specs. I also told him that in a thousand-year flood, Hilltop would be sitting by itself surrounded by water—which is what we're about to see today. He told me, 'If that happens, we'll provide sanctuary.' Couldn't argue with that. Same thing with that crazy revetment up the side of the church."

"So, inside our levee and his levee is a bathtub?"

"What I just said."

"Okay. Let's pull the plug and drain it."

"I don't follow you, Clementine."

Clementine telephoned Andrew Wells who answered instantly, "I was hoping you would call, Major Price. I'm in the machine shed. What can I do to help you?"

"Convince me whose side you're on," Clementine said coldly.

Wells answered without hesitating. "I've never been allowed in the church cellar. Now that I know what Reverend Flowers is up to, I suspect he hid his fighters down there."

"Thank you. Now what I want, very quickly, is for you to lead everyone out of the church. Shelter them in other campus buildings, far as you can from the church."

"But they feel safe in the church."

"The church won't stay safe. Do you have any Tiger Dams on the property?"

"Of course."

"Enough to top the entire mainline levee?"

"More than enough. Reverend Flowers always plans—planned—for the worst."

"Are any of your machines still above the water?"

"All back hoes, front loaders, and bulldozers are parked high and dry in the plateau machine shop. Like I said, Reverend—"

"The Corps has just requisitioned them. We'll be there soon."

She hung up and said to Jesse Corliss, "We will drain the bathtub back into the river."

"How?" demanded Jesse Corliss.

"Tiger Dam the mainline levee so it's higher than Flowers's, then excavate a crevasse in Flowers's levee."

"We'll never dig one big enough in time."

"Next to the church foundation."

"No, no, no. That'll taken even longer. The church is like an anchor for his levee. It's not going anywhere. Don't you see? That's why he revetted the foundation."

"Strip the revetment! Tear it off! Expose the foundation. The river will finish the job, scour under it!"

Corliss grinned. "Clementine—Major—you'd make a hell of an engineer."

"I *am* an engineer. Get your people in gear."

Corliss was already dialing his phone. "I mean a *civil* engineer, not some highfalutin officer."

Clementine gave the pilot and her lieutenants new orders.

The Boat circled back and headed downriver.

Lieutenant Pickett deployed riflemen on the wheelhouse roof, fifty feet above the water.

Lieutenant Harpur stationed hunters and target shooters with shotguns and pistols on the weather deck behind the push knees.

Jesse Corliss's workmen, augmented by the youngest and strongest of the volunteers who had come by boat, gathered behind them ready to sprint to Hilltop's machine shop. The Boat's crew stood by with grappling hooks and rigging. Corliss himself bossed a work gang armed with bright orange Morse-Starrett hydraulic cutters that could slice through stainless steel revetment cables in thirty seconds.

"Ready when you are, Major."

Gunfire rained down from the church, shattering wheelhouse glass and ricocheting off steel.

46

Nathan's Levee

Day 40

Prone on the wheelhouse roof and arrayed up and down the outside stairs, deer hunters and target shooters fired back. A black-clad Alluvian storm trooper tumbled from the bell tower, bounced off the levee, and splashed into the river. A Corps lawyer cried out, clutching a face peppered with glass.

"How you holding up, Cap?" Clementine Price asked Zelvert McCargo, who was aiming The Boat at the intersection of the church foundation and the Hilltop levee.

"Told you already, Major," drawled the pilot. "No need to make yourself a target standing beside me. You ought to hunker down before both of us get shot."

"Appreciate the sentiment," said Clementine, continuing the banter to give each other courage, "but I am obliged to keep track of what's going on."

"—Hang on, now, we're going to hit."

He blew his horns to warn their people to hold on and backed engines violently. The Boat shuddered, slowed, and rammed its push knees tight against the levee. Alluvian storm troopers charged firing assault rifles. Flowers's fighters could not know Clementine's strategy, but they were blocking the route to Hilltop's machine shops.

Sheltering behind a push knee, Lieutenant Pickett fired his grenade launcher. The explosion in their midst slammed four to the ground and panicked others. Some dropped their weapons as they scattered.

Lieutenant Terry Harpur leaped from behind the other push knee, ran along the levee and scooped up fallen rifles. She bolted back to The Boat, then ran back for ammunition. The Hilltop bell ringer Robby Bracken charged her.

"Die you stupid black bitch!"

Lieutenant Harpur drew her pistol, eyed her attacker down the barrel, and saw it would never pierce his body armor. She lowered her weapon and shot both his feet.

Bracken went down with a howl.

"I'm black," said Harpur, crouching to pick up the fallen storm trooper's pistols and spare magazines. "And I've been called a bitch by better men than you. But I'm not so stupid I'd forget my Kevlar boots." She galloped back to The Boat. Bracken sat up, pulled a long-barrel pistol, and took deliberate aim. A Corps of Engineers permit-appeals clerk on the wheelhouse roof shot first.

Bullpup rifles opened up somewhere in the steeple, sweeping the wheelhouse with a rattle like hail. At that same instant, Clementine saw a second wave of Alluvia storm troopers burst from the main doors. Where the hell was Tommy Chow? It was an hour since she had asked for help. She telephoned again.

"Almost to Bliss," he answered, sounding pumped by his unexpected "promotion" from desk commander to field officer. "Marching to the sound of guns."

"Who?'

"Squad of the most unpleasant MPs you've ever seen jammed into a Black Hawk."

Her heart sank. Twelve soldiers. "Only one squad?"

Tommy said, "Plenty for a holding action. Soon as General Penn gets wind of this—which can't be long—the entire United States Army will invade."

"They can't invade a flood!"

Even as she shouted in despair, Clementine Price realized that was Nathan Flowers's final fallback plan—a desperate gamble that with millions of refugees flooded off tens of thousands of square miles of the Delta, cooler heads would say, Wait. Don't rush. Don't make it worse. Giving Nathan's forces time to dig in.

She forced herself to settle down and speak calmly.

"Tommy, only we can stop his flood. There's a ton of gunmen blocking the machines we need ASAP, and my people are pinned down on The Boat. Ask your pilot for his ETA to Mile 806 and tell him that I've cleared civilians from the church."

"ETA five minutes."

"We'll be ready," said Clementine Price.

***

"What in hell is on that church steeple?" asked Tommy Chow's Black Hawk copilot.

"Flag," said the pilot.

The rain was blowing hard sideways, and he was gauging the wind's direction from the long red banner flying just beneath the lighted dove.

The church and its campus of outbuildings looked like an island in the middle of the river. Brown water surrounded it on all sides and its only connection to the Delta ground inside the mainline levee was a narrow causeway blockaded by wrecked cars and trucks. The Corps' towboat was spewing angry white prop wash to press against the levee under the church.

The helicopter halved the distance. The left door gunner eyed the flag over his swivel mount. It was decorated with white images of a Mississippi River barge fleet, cotton, and corn. Under them, stark white block print proclaimed the motto "Pure Blood, Pure Faith, Pure Power."

"These people insane?"

"Grenade launcher!" warned the copilot. "Bell tower!"

The Black Hawk roared over The Boat, guns spraying Hilltop's bell tower.

Clementine Price heard church bells clang in a weird cacophony of ricocheting bronze and lead. From her vantage in the wheelhouse, eye-level with the plateau, she saw the helicopter land hard and fast in front of the church, gunners peppering Hilltop's front doors. Army MPs spilled out of the machine, moving with an aggressive synchronicity that told her Tommy Chow had delivered a unit that had seen action.

The Black Hawk roared back up into the sky.

The lead MP fire team drove Flowers's storm troopers into the church. But once safe inside the stone walls, the Alluvian fighters returned heavy fire. Chow's outnumbered MPs took cover and fired back.

The helicopter swooped at the tower. Its guns raked it again, and again the bells rang. Three MPs sprinted toward the campus. They drew fire from gunmen blocking the route to the machines and they, too, were forced to take cover.

The shooting intensified.

Tommy Chow, dressed in a bright, clean combat uniform and waving a pistol, stood up and hailed Clementine over the short stretch of water between the plateau and The Boat.

"Get down, Tommy!" she shouted. Bullets pocked the mud around him. Tommy fell. He started to sit up. "Stay down, you idiot."

"Ma'am, we should step inside," said Lieutenant Pickett, eyeing the bell tower and moving closer as if to shield her. His head snapped back before Clementine heard the shot.

"Sniper!"

She dragged Pickett under cover of the steel roof. Not that it would help. The bullet had shattered the back of his skull. But it hadn't touched his face and he still looked as young and innocent as her brother Will. He had served in the Yemen wars and came home to this. And all she could do to thank him would be to call on his mother and father to tell them what a man he would have become. And that if he hadn't saved her, he would still be alive?

"Captain McCargo! Push knees, tight in."

She vaulted down the outside steps to the weather deck where heavy equipment operators in hard hats and safety-harness nylon lines coiled over their shoulders crouched behind the push knees. Zelvert McCargo shoved The Boat hard against the levee.

"Come on!"

Clementine was first onto the levee. Equipment operators exchanged looks—*Is she nuts?*—and clambered after her. The MPs sprang into action. Half ran alongside, shooting at anything that moved. Half chased storm troopers back into the church and this time, followed them inside before they take up defensive positions. Clementine and the equipment operators bolted across the campus to the machine shed.

Andrew Wells rolled the steel doors open. He had already started the machines. The Corps boys piled onto them. Wheeled backhoes roared out, belching blue smoke. Yellow bulldozers thundered after them, tracks clanking.

The backhoes sped down the Hilltop levee to its juncture with the church foundation. Here the levee was narrowed by the river outside and the flooded low ground within. They planted their stabilizer pods, extended their booms, sank toothed buckets into the levee, tore the ground, and scattered it into the racing river.

The Black Hawk made another pass at the bell tower, which proved definitive. The shooting died down. MPs secured prisoners. Lieutenant Harpur, who had picked up an assault rifle somewhere, escorted Clementine back to her vantage point in The Boat's wheelhouse.

Far across the flooded baptismal lake and low ground that had once been her home place, Clementine could see her people extending orange, water-filled Tiger Dams along the old mainline levee, raising it higher even as the backhoes tried to lower Hilltop's levee to release the trapped "bathtub water" back into the Mississippi River.

She was in a three-way race—the ever-rising water pushed inside the levees by the river versus the raising of the mainline levee with Tiger Dams versus the demolition of Nathan Flowers's levee. Their first success was catastrophic for Jesse Corliss's son, the backhoe operator who achieved it. Jesse Jr.'s was the lead machine, and it was chewing the ground ferociously when the bathtub water suddenly exploded through the crown he had weakened. That water scoured a channel that spilled into the river with such force that it widened and deepened the breach too quickly for the young man to lift his stabilizer pads, much less drive his machine to safety. A two-foot channel was suddenly four feet across and just as suddenly, twenty feet wide. His backhoe sank in a torrent of liquid mud that swept it into the river like a Styrofoam cup. Jesse Jr.'s lifeline, tied to a parked bulldozer, yanked him off the backhoe. Men grabbed it and pulled him in, bloody and barely able to stand. The next machine trundled forward to fill the gap. Before it could lower its pads, Jesse Corliss Sr. stomped after it, strapping on a harness line, and climbed aboard shouting to give him the controls. When the young operator resisted, the chief engineer tossed him to the ground, seized the joystick, planted his pads, and resumed digging. The water scoured the drainage channel deeper. Corliss's machine flipped into it.

Heart in her throat, Clementine Price saw her chief engineer try to scramble free as it was swept out from under him. He was saved by his harness. But he landed hard in the mud with his neck at a terrible angle. Grim-faced assistants carried him away. The operator he had replaced climbed on another machine and continued the attack.

The artificial crevasse grew to a one-hundred-foot gap in the levee, then two hundred. But the water escaping still did not equal the quantity the river was driving into the Hilltop bathtub so the water inside kept rising. Corliss's deputy radioed from the mainline levee that it was topping the crown in gaps where they hadn't finished filling the Tiger Dams.

Clementine Price looked at the sky. Still raining, of course, but darker. The day was getting away from them. This would only get only worse at night and there were more flood crests coming. "Zelvert," she said, quietly. "It's your turn."

Captain Zelvert McCargo nosed the giant towboat against the levee that underpinned the church at the point where flexible chain mail revetment mats prevented Nathan Flowers's foundation from being scoured away by the escaping floodwater. Jesse Corliss's roustabouts muscled hydraulic cable cutters onto the mats and battled rushing mud and water to slice laboriously through the stainless-steel cables that linked the slabs of concrete that formed the mats. Deckhands slung grappling hooks and cranked The Boat's powerful winches to rip the slabs apart.

Time and again, roustabouts were plucked from the torrent by their safety harnesses. But they kept slicing links. More mats pulled apart. The new channel grew wider as floodwater rushed back into the river. The water scoured the ground beside the church and burrowed under it. Cellar walls were exposed. The breach spread. The outflow swelled in volume and speed. The scouring deepened. The river swept away the ground beneath the cellar, exposing a hodgepodge of naked steel pilings.

When her people on the mainline levee reported that the water that had been threatening to top even the Tiger Dams had begun to recede, Clementine Price knew victory. The revetted plateau was no longer shunting floodwater toward the Delta. Most of it was flowing back into the Mississippi River. And with Flowers's barge dam at the bridge a failure, those raging waters would keep going down the river. Bliss was spared from total inundation.

She stepped out of The Boat's wheelhouse and stood alone on the wing. The Mississippi River was running wild. The entire Hilltop sanctuary and its steeple and bell tower tottered beside it on rickety stilts.

"Nathan Flowers," Clementine Price whispered aloud, "you borrowed my home place too long. We're calling in the loan."

47

The Cottonmouth

Day 40

Robert Garcia heard a helicopter taking off and another landing. Things grew quiet and he heard the earnest reservists young enough to be his sons whispering. This evidence that he was not blown to smithereens proved, as he had hoped, that wet fertilizer would not explode. The fact that he could not move his arms or legs was panic-inducing until he realized he was strapped tight into a Stokes litter, which meant the reservists and the helicopter crew had risked their lives to lift him off a sinking towboat. It occurred to him that he had littered the Jefferson Point jetty with sunken barges. Clearing them would be an ideal first salvage job.

"He's mumbling again. Same thing, over and over."

"'Clementine salvage. Clementine salvage.'"

"Poor guy's hallucinating."

The Stokes litter shook hard, shooting eye-popping bolts of pain down both his legs. Garcia saw the whispering soldiers leap to their feet, saluting at rigid chin-up, chest-out, shoulders-back attention.

"Sir!"

"General! Sir!"

"He's not hallucinating," roared Lieutenant-General Clinton Penn. "The damned fool's in love."

***

The first responders' refuge on the top floor of Stevenson Memorial Hospital was strangely quiet for how crowded it was: firefighters, police officers, medics, and rescue workers—some bandaged, some staring with hollow eyes at images they couldn't unsee. Clergy moved among them, whispering. A nurse lowered the blinds on the destruction below the windows.

Rolly Winters, slumped on a bench with his eyes closed, felt a firm hand on his shoulder. He rose in a rush and crushed Libby in his arms. They held each other in long, silent gratitude and could not let go until at last, Rolly pulled back to look at her face. "I saw Mary Kay's van fall in the river and I thought what if that were you in the 'Mayor-mobile.'"

"I thought the same when I saw Duvall on the stretcher—any word?"

"The surgeons weren't making any promises. But Duvall was wide awake and fighting-mad at himself for letting Flowers get the drop on him. So I'm just banking on the fact he's never been an easy man to kill. Levee still holding?"

"For now. But the Old District was hit hard. Probably our place too, I don't know for sure. Thank God most folks evacuated. But we lost six kids from River View and eight from South End—including Daneesha, Lord have mercy, from the Saline Solution—all of them volunteers."

"Sandbagging?"

"Where it breached. And Reverend and Mrs. Blankenship drowned inside Reverend Eddie's church. They must have taken shelter there after the last bus left."

Rolly shook his head. "At least they didn't know about Mary Kay. Poor Clem, she looked like she wanted to die."

"Uncle Chance was her hero. . . . Have you seen the boys yet?"

"I was waiting for you. Didn't want to stagger in there looking like death."

The children's area was curtained off. Holding hands, they slipped quietly through it. Across the room, they saw Kevin and Rolly Jr. next to Mother June. She was reading a story to little Gabriel and Cora Flowers.

The boys rocketed into Rolly and Libby's arms.

They held them and whispered with them, assuring them everything would be fine, no their house was still there, maybe some water in the cellar. Where's the Black Panther? Uncle Duvall is having a little nap. Sometimes even Black Panthers get sleepy. Then Libby Winters said to their sons, "You guys go and play with those Legos. Your Daddy and I have to talk."

They slouched off reluctantly, glancing back. Libby waited until they had settled down with the blocks. Her gaze shifted to Mother June reading to Gabe and Cora. "Rol?"

"What?"

"Rol?"

Rolly Winters's jaw set. "Yes, dear?"

"Rol? Their mother and their grandparents are all dead. And God knows what will become of their father."

"Their father is a monster. His seed is in them."

"Rol? They're innocents."

"A fucking white supremacist."

"Their mother was the finest woman on God's earth."

"They are tainted."

"They are tainted," Libby agreed. "No one around here will touch them. Do you want them to be in the arms of Social Services?"

"They are white and beautiful. They'll be adopted in a heartbeat."

"They'll be sold to the highest bidder."

Rolly Winters lumbered toward the children. They looked up. He stared down at them. Their skin was so white it almost hurt to look at them, like staring at the sun.

Rolly glanced back at Libby. She was wearing that expression that said, Rolly I'd never ask you to do anything you didn't want to. He looked down at the kids.

Gabriel stood and stuck out his hand. Cora smiled.

Rolly Winters spoke to them in the chocolate voice he used to turn suspects, the voice that promised, everything will work out fine as soon as you tell me your troubles. "Gabriel? Cora? How'd you like to come live with the mayor?"

Their little faces showed him it was too big a question to take in all at once. He squatted down on creaking knees, scooped one in each arm, and carried them to Libby.

Gabe asked, "Mayor? Why are you crying?"

"I'm so proud of my husband."

***

Tommy Chow's helicopter had just lifted off with another load of the wounded, including Tommy, when Clementine Price got a call from a news producer contact who covered the Delta for CNN. "Major, I have a camera crew in Bliss and I'm—"

"What's the situation?"

"Well, as I'm sure you know . . ." The news producer paused, trying to lead her to fill in the space. Silent, in her command post in the wheelhouse, Clementine focused on the outflow scouring the ground under the church.

". . . they secured the levee and confined the flooding to parts of the Old District."

"Yes," said Clementine, thinking, *Thank God, thank God, thank God.*

"But what's the story about gunfire on the river and the Black Hawk helicopter that crashed on a towboat that was pushing the Lucky Ark casino barge?"

"The story's at Mile 806," said Clementine. "Bring your camera crew as fast you can get here. . . . *Lieutenant Harpur!* Raise The Boat's biggest American flag. And the Corps flag. The humongous ones they fly when General Penn's aboard."

A Penn-to-gram bugle blew.

REPORT

Too late to stop her now. She telephoned General Penn.

"Major Price reporting, sir."

"I want you to know that Colonel Garcia was medevacked, alive, to University Medical Center, New Orleans."

"Sir, how bad is he?"

"They're operating on severely broken legs."

Oh, Robert! But better, a million times better, than gunshot wounds. Full-metal- jacket bullets swerved before exit. Ballistic shock waves surged to the brain. "Thank you, sir. Thank you for telling me."

"You will need to compile classified after-action reviews with Colonel Garcia *the instant you complete operations."*

"Yes, sir.

"Captain Standfast will deliver you to the hospital in my helicopter," said the general, adding dryly, "I understand 'yours' could do with a depot re-build."

"Thank you, sir, I—"

She saw a bright orange Coast Guard RIB racing downriver toward Bliss. But the sailor at the helm was the only one onboard and he wasn't wearing an orange foul-weather slicker, both of which were odd. Had Nathan Flowers had once again planned ahead?

"Sir, I must complete —"

"Drive on, Major Price."

Clementine ran down to the main deck. None of the boats tied alongside were RIBs. She chose the civilian engineers' blue and white twenty-foot Supreme S202 water-ski boat for its rough-water, deep-V hull and big engine, jumped in, and cast off lines. But it was no match for the Coast Guard boat in such heavy water, and she saw she would never catch up.

She dialed the telephone number Mary Kay Flowers had given her for Nathan.

He sounded vaguely annoyed, like a man interrupted at a solitary lunch. "What is it, Major Price?"

"I have eight boats coming up river to capture you," she lied. "And helicopters overhead. Stop where you are and raise your hands in the air."

"Your one helicopter just flew to Bliss, and it's getting late, the light is failing."

"I won't let you kill any more innocent people. You've killed enough already, including your own wife."

"That's a lie. She's safe at Hilltop."

"I saw her drown."

"You're lying."

"I looked into her eyes. She was almost out of the water, then she let go."

"I don't believe you."

"I saw her surrender. Like she couldn't live with herself."

"No!"

"She was with my Uncle Chance. They both drowned, trying to save people from your flood."

"No!"

"Mary Kay died believing that she had created a monster. But you were always a monster, Nathan. She just gave you a place in the world."

"She loved me."

"She loved the man she believed you were. Not the man you really are."

"She loved me," he said again, and his boat veered abruptly toward the Tennessee side.

She cut left too, to intercept him. It was futile. His faster boat had him over the submerged natural levee and into the flooded Tennessee bottomland hardwood forest while she was still four hundred meters out in the river. When she finally did get among the half-submerged trees, he was nowhere to be seen. She steered inland, weaving among the tree trunks, deeper and deeper into swamps she knew from her childhood. Here, directly across the river from Tomato, was where they had rescued the diving mule.

She knew where to find solid ground above the floodwater, which meant going half a mile deeper into the flooded woodland. She shut her engine, abruptly, and listened for his over the rattle of rain on the forest canopy. There! A steady murmur. She started up again, followed for what felt like a quarter mile. She shut down and listened. Still there, ahead of her. Again, she followed and shut down. He was still moving, heading straight in. Having lived for years at Hilltop, he too would know where the floodwaters stopped at higher ground.

When next she listened, she heard a loud grinding. It sounded like he was backing his engine in reverse or gunning the boat onto the shore. She started her engine and went slowly, quietly, toward the sound.

A sudden glimpse of orange. There was his boat, beached on a mud bank. He had gone ashore. She cut her engine again, let the ski boat drift, and stepped off when it touched bottom, looping a line around a shrub. Then she entered into a dark understory shaded by tall, close-growing trees. Eight steps in, she froze. A huge blacksnake was climbing down a rough-grooved sweet gum. That it was not a poisonous rattler or cottonmouth rendered the purposeful length of scaly muscle no less riveting.

She stood dead still, watching the snake and listening for Flowers to splash through puddles or snap branches. She heard only the rain beating leaves and the faraway noise of boats and helicopters buzzing around Hilltop. Flowers made no noise, and it struck Clementine forcibly that she was not the only country child in the swamp. Nathan Flowers was a backwoods boy like she was a backwoods girl.

The snake oozed back up the tree and she rushed deeper into the woods, pausing repeatedly to listen. But Flowers was either moving as silently as she was, or standing as absolutely still. The light grew stronger. Overhead, the canopy parted as she came to a patch of backwater, deepened by the rampaging river. It had surrounded three sides of a point of ground, creating a miniature peninsula not much bigger than a suburban barbecue patio. A single oak tree stood in the middle, spreading branches over it. She stood and watched it. Were the branches thick enough to conceal him?

She backed up to a gum tree, shot a glance over her shoulder to make sure no snakes were climbing it, and pressed her spine against the bark. She studied the oak tree on the peninsula and drew her pistol. The branches seemed to be moving. It took a moment to see why. She shivered violently. The tree was alive with long blacksnakes that had climbed above the flood. Senses on highest alert, she felt a sudden change in the air. The rain stopped falling on her face and a shadow filled the sky. He heard my boat, she thought. He heard me following him. Suddenly Nathan Flowers was above her, plummeting from the gum tree.

The blocked rain and his shadow were just enough warning to get out from under some of his weight and he fell only partly on her. One of his boots connected with her forearm. Her pistol went flying. A gloved fist landed on her face and down she went into the mud, even as she slipped some of the force of the blow over her shoulder and kicked him hard in the stomach.

She vaulted to her feet. He was up as fast and all over her. She was taller, quick, and strong. Flowers looked shocked when she threw a punch that bloodied his nose. But he was stronger, heavier, and faster, a born fighter landing body blows that hurt and a rock-hard fist to her temple that sent white flashes storming before her eyes. A small, cool, detached section of her mind took voice and told her that if she weren't so strengthened by grief and rage that he would have overwhelmed her already. The flood he had made worse had killed Uncle Chance. The flood he had made worse had crevassed the levee at Bliss. God only knew how badly Robert was hurt. Who on Earth could calculate the hopes for a better world lost when Mary Kay drowned?

They rolled into the backwater and Flowers got on top of her and forced her head under. The small, detached voice whispered, I'm fighting out of my class. I'm drowning. I know what drowning is. I've drowned before. I gave in to the power of the river. I said a prayer to the river as I went down to the bottom. I am out of air. The river wasn't ready to drown me yet, but Nathan Flowers is.

She let herself go. She stopped fighting. Her body went limp. Flowers eased his grip and she kneed him in the balls with all her might. He doubled over, grunting.

She scrambled out from under him and lunged to the bank.

"Oh, no, honey, you're not going anywhere."

Flower seized her ankle and dragged her back into the water.

He reached for her throat with his other powerful hand and had begun to squeeze when Clementine saw his eyes widen with fear. They locked on a poisonous cottonmouth slithering down the bank. Threatened when it saw them, the snake opened its jaws to frighten them with its ghastly white mouth. Snakes, Mary Kay had told her, were the only thing Nathan feared.

They terrified Clementine too, but she moved as fast as she had ever moved in her life, grabbed the cottonmouth's thick body behind its head with both hands, and thrust the powerfully writhing creature in Nathan Flowers's face.

Flowers shrieked like a frightened child and scrambled out of the water onto the peninsula. Clementine Price flung the snake away, sucked life-giving air into her lungs, and watched him climbing with superhuman strength into the oak tree where the blacksnakes had retreated. He got ten feet up and suddenly screamed in terror, fell to the ground, crawled back into the water, swam the few meters to the opposite shore and pulled himself up on the bank where the cottonmouth was waiting in a deadly coil.

Flowers kicked frantically. The snake struck his chest, smearing his ballistic vest with venom, levered up on its tail as if seeking softer tissue, and struck again. Flowers gave a cry of pain. He staggered back clutching his cheek. He pulled his hands away and stared at the blood in disbelief. Clementine saw two puncture wounds side by side, where the fangs had entered.

Flowers turned and ran, which Clementine knew was a fatal mistake. Snake bite treatment was basic first aid to care for your people in the field. First rule: carry the victim. Running, even walking, makes the venom go faster to the heart.

You probably don't have a heart, she thought. But you're a force of nature. What if you're strong enough to power through the poison? There are people who can. Somewhere out there you will find a road. You will hitchhike. You will kill the driver for his car.

"Wait!"

She sprinted ahead and blocked his path.

Nathan Flowers bared his teeth. "Don't try to stop me. You won't get lucky twice."

She went up on the balls of her feet and threw quick jabs. He danced too, laying back, watching her moves, gauging her style, smirking to remind her that she was outclassed. She connected nicely on his cheekbone and tried another shot at his nose, but he had seen that one before, slapped it aside, and attacked.

She had to stay out of his clinch.

At the Academy, she had learned to beat better boxers by using her long reach to control a match. But his arms were almost as long. And punching it out with a convict who had survived half his life in prison was not a match, but a free-for-all that favored the stronger, heavier fighter.

She had to keep moving. Exertion would speed the venom to his heart. Keep jabbing, in and out, in and out, circle, make him move. Was his face getting red? He seemed to be sweating, but that could be the rain.

He lunged repeatedly, trying to get close, astonishingly quick. She struggled to keep out of his grasp and felt herself tiring. It was getting hard to hold her guard high.

Flowers blinked his eyes and rubbed at them. Was his vision blurring? She took a chance and got close enough to hit him hard. It snapped his head back. He recovered and suddenly charged, straining to close his hands around her neck. She jabbed again and again and again until she was gasping for air.

Flowers threw a body punch that caught her by surprise. It was a long, hard left that powered out from behind his torso with incredible speed and gained energy with every inch it traveled. She twisted to her left to save her breast. The impact was devastating. His fist smashed into the side of her rib cage. It knocked the breath from her lungs, and she felt pain so sharp that she knew he had broken her ribs. She could only hope it hadn't driven bone splinters through her lung. She could not lift her right arm, and she was suddenly afraid.

Flowers charged again. Clementine saw in his expression that he was putting everything he had into a final, all-out, killing attack. But her fear paralyzed her. She had nothing left to fight him with. He had ruined her body and broken her heart. He had killed an old man she had loved her whole life. He had killed a woman who would have been her friend forever. Falling back, pivoting her hopeless right side away from his rush, she cocked her left arm and tried to gather strength to launch a punch through the pain from the only thing she had left—rage and grief. It felt like she was shoving her arm in a fire. In her mind, she repeated: You killed Chance. You killed Chance. You killed Chance. She stopped backing up and swung her fist. She aimed for his nose, again. He turned his face, and the full force of her blow struck his temple.

Staggering, Nathan Flowers shambled past her, his fists falling. He whirled around to face Clementine Price. He was breathing hard, his face projecting an iron will. He started to raise his guard, but he couldn't lift his fists higher than his waist. Red-faced, perspiring, rubbing his eyes, gasping for air, Nathan Flowers sank to his knees.

"She did love me."

"Who could ever love you?"

His eyes widened, flicking toward motion. The cottonmouth was climbing out of the water.

"*Grandma . . . don't, please don't.*"

Book Four

Nature is Patient

Six Months Later

Seen from the river, Hilltop Church appeared to teeter on forty-foot stilts fixing to topple into the water. Lieutenant Colonel Clementine Price, now Commander of the Army Corps' Memphis District, had watched it warily from MV *Mississippi V* while supervising the repair of the levee that Nathan Flowers had blown. She was not about to let an 18,000-square-foot building collapse on top of a multi-million-dollar public works project on her watch. Despite assurances from Andrew Wells—who had stayed on as Hilltop's operations manager and self-appointed institutional memory—that Nathan Flowers had built for the ages, she made her contractors stabilize it with cable and turnbuckles. The spiderweb of rigging that guyed the stilts reminded her of a safety net in a circus.

Which reminded her of Mary Kay.

Mary Kay's illuminated dove and the bullet-scarred bronze tower bells had been taken down and stored in the gymnasium. The crowd gathered on this brisk fall day under crystal blue skies at the inland edge of Hilltop's high, flat campus saw only the front of the sanctuary in the distance. It was an optical illusion, like a stage set, so the church appeared to sit on solid ground—a more reassuring view, thought Clementine, for a dedication ceremony and "barn raising."

Below the campus, where Hilltop's pristine lake had been filled by mud and debris from Flowers's unleashed Mississippi, a volunteer brigade of earth moving machines—skidders, bulldozers, forklifts, tractors, and big red Stevenson Sand & Gravel dump trucks—stood ready to dig a new borrow pit to restore the sanctuary's foundation.

It was obvious to Clementine that the owner/operators of these machines, with the notable exception of Steve Stevenson, were of far more modest means than the millionaire landowners and equipment dealers who had pitched in for the church's original barn raising. Even though most of Hilltop's 22,000 members had been totally unaware of Nathan Flowers's Alluvia plot, the Hilltop "brand" had tanked. Innocent members resigned in revulsion. Those who remained were still grieving, still gripped by anger, depression, and guilt.

But today was the day to turn the page to acceptance and hope, which is why Clementine was there on the speakers' dais, along with a Who's Who of the Delta—motivated less by love for the megachurch, she suspected, than by respect and admiration for Mary Kay Flowers.

Mary Kay's children were on the laps of their new parents, Mayor Libby Whitcomb Winters and Bliss's new Chief of Police Rolly Winters. They clung like cockleburs. Gabe looked like a tiny marionette perched on Rolly's knee, his small pale hands clutching the big brown one that steadied him. Cora kept one arm so tightly around Libby's neck that Clementine wondered how her friend could breathe. If preschoolers could exhibit shell shock, this was it. Directly behind them sat the rest of the Winters family: Rolly Jr., Kevin, Mother June, and "Uncle" Duvall McCoy—now Chief of Homicide, a cane at his side—ready with relief laps and hugs.

Clementine was seated next to the recently promoted Major General Robert Garcia, crutches at *his* side, just in from headquarters in Vicksburg where he was stationed as General Penn's Deputy Commander for River Security and Counterterrorism. Robert was immaculate in his dress blues, with a fresh row of glittering decorations and handsomer than ever. Thinner, though, with gray hairs flecking his temples.

"Fifty-one-year-old bones knit more slowly," he had told her gamely when she went to visit him in rehab a month after the attack and was unable to conceal her dismay at how battered he was—though certainly improved since they had compiled their after-action review in the hospital. She had brought him an anthology of war poetry. Clementine had discovered in her own PTSD therapy that it was perversely healing to read about other experiences of loss.

They were flanked at the last minute by General Penn and Senator Garfield, who had arrived dramatically on The Boat, flying all flags. Clementine gave a warm smile to Steve Stevenson, who was occupying a swath of prime real estate in the front row. Steve, for some reason, winked.

Across the dais on the other side of the pulpit sat Hilltop's new Pastoral Council. Wary of putting their faith in a single charismatic leader again, the megachurch's lay leaders had assembled a roundtable of local

Protestant, Catholic, Jewish, Muslim, Buddhist, and Unitarian clergy who took turns leading services in the circus tent erected on the campus green.

The Interdenominational United Nations of Worship concept was certainly appealing as an antidote to a preacher who was a secret white supremacist. But Libby had confided to Clementine that it wasn't all kumbaya, peace, and brotherhood. While the old Hilltop was the embodiment of Mary Kay's singular vision of Christianity, Hilltop 2.0 had to accommodate many visions. And crucially, it no longer had a bottomless bank account. Alluvia's financial backers had been exposed, shunned, and ruined. Who wanted to be linked in a Google search with a notorious racist and charlatan? Still, Libby held out hope that the new Hilltop could keep at least some of Mary Kay's ideals alive. After the physical and emotional carnage of a flood and a home-grown terrorist attack, her church had more neighbors than ever who needed help.

Reverend Eddie Parker had drawn the long straw to deliver the invocation on behalf of the Pastoral Council. He read from First Corinthians 3:16–17, in measured tones several notches below his usual rating on Libby's Sanctified Spectrum.

"'Know you not that *you* are the temple of God, and that the Spirit of God dwelleth in *you*? If any man defile the temple of God, him shall God destroy; for the temple of God is holy, which temple *you* are.'

Reverend Eddie closed his Bible and looked up. "Brothers and sisters, I want to say something else about temples. Today I learned that the legacy of a heroic Christian lady dear to every heart in our community—our own Reverend Mary Kay Blankenship Flowers—will live on in a memorial chapel to be erected right here, on this re-sanctified ground. From that chapel the mighty tower bells of her church will ring out, and her great golden dove will once again glow like a lighthouse in a storm—thanks to the generosity of Mr. and Mrs. Cedric Colson." Reverend Parker gave a smile and a nod to the expensively attired couple in the front row. Colson rose from his chair as if to speak but Reverend Eddie had already turned to the choir. "And now, Reverend Furman, would you lead us in a song of praise?"

The Minister of Music's sixty-voice chorus had shrunk to a chamber choir of sixteen, and outdoors he had no piano or orchestra. But no one was disappointed in their spine-tinging a capella rendition of "How Firm a Foundation."

It was the perfect lead-in for General Penn, who marched straight to the pulpit, seized the microphone, and launched a stemwinder extolling the bravery of his officers Major General Garcia and Lieutenant Colonel Price. Clementine wondered—again—Has General Penn lost it? Did this grieving, disoriented audience really want to hear a graphic, blow-by-blow account of combat with an enemy who they used to trust? An enemy who they called Reverend? "*Crawling on his belly, blind with pain from breaking both his legs jumping forty feet out of a helicopter—General Garcia persisted!*"

Oohs and aahs, gasps of awe.

Penn pounded the pulpit and glared at the unnamed Enemy. "*Not just hand-to-hand combat, but psychological warfare! Colonel Price knew the Enemy feared snakes, but first she had to vanquish her own fear of those infernal reptiles . . .*"

Clementine shifted her gaze to the river sparkling benignly in the sun. It was running low, even for fall. Fixing for a drought? From flood to drought in six months? Why not? The river did what it wanted.

"*. . . Picked up the big old cottonmouth with her bare hands! Coulda killed her with one venomous bite—but she conquered that serpent and wielded it like a righteous sword!*"

Whoops and hollers, even some Amens.

General Penn knew what he was doing, Clementine realized. He was rallying his troops, giving them heroes they could believe in again, heroes in the flesh, right in front of their eyes, heroes who would fight to the death for them. The Corps had their backs, the Corps would help rebuild their church, and General Penn's army would shield them from the evils of mankind and of nature.

Only a fool would try to follow Penn's act, and Reverend Eddie, the consummate showman, knew to drop the curtain *now*. He bounced to the pulpit, pumped General Penn's hand, and shouted "Brothers and Sisters! Let's go dig ourselves a borrow pit!"

Clementine had no intention of watching the barn raising. No fire ants were going to march on her naked body. Her therapist had explained that trigger warnings need to be recognized and acknowledged, not invited in and given a seat at the dinner table. And she was hoping for a few moments alone with Robert before he had to go back to Vicksburg.

Steve Stevenson was waiting when Robert finally crutched his way off the platform. He shook Robert's hand vigorously. "Land sakes, Colonel—I mean, General. I had no idea what a *warrior* you are!"

Robert smiled. "But as you can see, I'm not indestructible. I certainly do appreciate the offer of your guest cottage tonight."

Steve ignored Clementine's slack-jawed stare. "We just finished work on it last week. Needs to be test driven now by an actual guest. I sure hope you'll find it cozy and comfortable. One level, no steps."

"Excellent. I recall your email mentioned something about providing transportation out there?"

"Clementine knows the way. I'm off to Little Rock. Got me some lobbying to do at the State House. Clementine, be sure and take a look at the pecan grove out back." He waddled off, laughing his big laugh.

Robert turned to Clementine, who was shaking her head with a smile.

"He is a sly one," she said. "Looks like I'm your car service." She picked up Robert's deployment bag. "And your roommate." She glanced again at the river and put his bag back down. "Could you wait a few minutes? There's something I have to see."

Clementine scrambled down the steep slope and picked her way to where the Mississippi lapped the stones. It looked a hair lower than yesterday, ambling peaceably, not a madhouse current in sight—only a baby whirlpool that rose from nowhere and spread soft ripples on the surface. The reflected sunlight was blinding. She cocked her dress cap to shield her eyes and knelt to touch the water. It snatched her fingers and pulled hard.

***

Mary Kay's grave was beside her parents' in the churchyard behind the First Methodist Church of Bliss. Interment had to be postponed after their funerals, amid grisly reports of floating coffins rising up from waterlogged cemeteries. But the practical and prosperous Methodists had an ornate, climate-controlled marble sarcophagus for those who departed in the winter when the ground was frozen, and First Methodist's first family had slumbered in private dignity until their final resting places were dry.

Clementine placed a bright red bucket of giant sunflowers next to Mary Kay's headstone, which was engraved with a dove in flight and inscribed:

Mary Kay Blankenship Flowers
1982–2018
Beloved Daughter, Wife, Mother, Minister

Robert lowered himself on his crutches to kneel. He closed his eyes in prayer and crossed himself, then struggled upright without assistance. They stood side by side in companionable silence, listening to the wind and the groans of the ancient burr oak that shaded the churchyard with its thinning scarlet canopy. Blue jays squawked and dive-bombed for acorns that dropped whenever a gust loosened a fresh sheaf of papery leaves.

"I'm surprised to see the name Flowers there," Robert said finally.

"That was the decision of the First Methodist congregation, and it was a brave one, I think. It would have been so tempting to erase her history with Nathan. 'Flowers' will be a cursed name in these parts for generations to come. But it was *with* Nathan that she was at her most powerful and effective. Think of all the good she accomplished as Mrs. Flowers—as his life partner."

"Do you think she really didn't know about his dark side?"

Clementine paused. She had thought about this a lot. "Yes, I do. And I don't mean that she turned a blind eye. I think it was impossible for her to imagine."

"*'And what I assume you shall assume,'*" Robert quoted. "*'For every atom belonging to me as good belongs to you.'*"

Clementine squeezed his arm. She was grateful she didn't have to hide her tears from him. He brushed them off her cheek.

"Let's go. I'll show you my Aunt Martha's old house on the way. It's just up the street."

***

Clementine took the back roads to Steve's place, avoiding Dell's main drag in case some old busybody happened to spot her Jeep and its handsome cargo. Robert rode in the back, with his cast propped up across the seat, but he was still visible—and unmistakable in his uniform.

"Looks like a lot of farmers will be getting their crops out of the post office this year," she observed.

No one had put a crop in this year. By the time the fields were dry enough to run machines on it, it was too late to plant. Hundreds of thousands of acres had lain fallow, absorbing the rich alluvial sludge delivered by the overflowing tributaries and distributaries. Clementine had never seen it so lush—usually by this time of year the fields were parched and brown, furrowed with gigantic tire treads from the pickers.

Today it was as if God had dropped a green silk handkerchief flecked with red and gold over the endless flatlands. Songbirds darted about, gorging themselves on seed heads of black-eyed Susans, pokeweed, and goldenrod—the wildflowers she remembered from childhood. Since there had been no crops planted, there had been no pesticides, no herbicides, no exfoliants applied. Nature had come roaring back. That's right, Captain Eads, she thought. Nature is patient. Drive on!

Steve's new guest house was screened from the road by a stand of cypress trees, and last week, when he invited Clementine to be his inaugural guest, he gave her the garage door opener so she could stash her Jeep inside. "Shelter from the storm," he'd said airily. And prying eyes too.

Knowing Steve, she expected the cottage to be worthy of a spread in *Southern Living*, and it did not disappoint. It was not just well-stocked—it was *curated*. In the refrigerator was a fresh-killed, fresh-dressed heirloom chicken from his own flock, a dozen fresh eggs, even bottles of Robert's favorite Picpoul wine. The counter was heaped with fruits and vegetables from his garden, fresh-ground coffee, a plate of his favorite pecan rolls, and, displayed on an antique cake stand, Miss Maudie's Bourbon Pecan Pie.

"Pecans!" said Clementine. "He told us to check out the pecan grove."

The day had gotten warmer and they left their jackets inside and rolled up their shirtsleeves. Robert crutched his way gingerly along the pea gravel paths that wound toward the main house, past a peach orchard (no peach crop this year, Clementine thought, but she had a lifetime of the pickled Elberta peaches Steve sent her every August), a formal rose garden (finally in bloom, Steve had exulted), and the pecan grove that stood between Steve's house and the livestock barns and pens. Dragonflies zoomed past their heads, and flycatchers swooped into clouds of gnats.

At a distance, it looked like the pecan leaves had turned gold already. Then one of the leaves fluttered and flew to another branch. Monarch butterflies! Thousands of them, draping every branch in every tree with necklaces of stained glass. Clementine felt the tears come again, for the second time today. "Steve called this a wonder of the world."

They wandered in, observing the fragile creatures up close at eye level.

"Like jewels."

"Illuminated manuscripts."

A butterfly landed on Robert's crutch. He pretended to be a tree until it flew away. He caught Clementine's eyes just as the low sun lit them like aquamarines and impulsively kissed her. She kissed him back. For a long time.

"I feel like Adam and Eve in the Garden of Eden," said Robert, coming up for air.

"Watch out for serpents," said Clementine. A mosquito whined in her ear. "And skeeters." The sun was sliding off the horizon. They'd been out a long time. The crickets were warming up and the wood thrush—the last bird to say good night—was starting his silvery song.

"Time to go indoors," she said, pointing to a pair of bats circling above. "Mr. and Mrs. Bat are going to have supper and so should we."

Clementine considered herself a competent cook, but Robert was an artist, even hopping around on crutches. They dined on a screened porch overlooking a pond, with bullfrogs interrupting their conversation, and katydids and barn owls offering a running commentary. The harvest moon was so bright they didn't notice when the candles burned out.

Robert kissed her hand. "Thank you again you for the book of poems. I'd forgotten how much poetry meant to me. At school, the Jesuits made us memorize poems—in Latin. I can still recite them."

Of course, my Latin Lover speaks Latin! she thought. Aloud, she said, "I'm listening."

"This is by Virgil—it was in the book you gave me, translated into English. *Omnia vincit amor; et nos cedamus amori.*"

"Which means?"

"Love conquers all things; let us too surrender to love."

"Yes, let's." Clementine stood and passed Robert his crutches. "I never studied Latin, but I learned a few phrases from Aunt Martha."

She led the way to the bedroom and opened the drapes. Moonlight streamed in. She recited:

"'*Carpe diem*
When you see 'im,
Looking at you
With that gle-am.'

"In other words, my beautiful Colonel—my brave General—Drive on!"

"Thank you, ma'am," said Robert Garcia. "I intend to take you up on that. But first may I ask a question?"

"Anything, Robert."

"This afternoon, when you asked me to wait, I saw you climb down to the water. Were you saying goodbye to your farm?"

"No. I was just saying 'Hey' to an old friend."

"You still love that river, don't you?"

Clementine Price thought hard before she answered. "I can't love what I can't trust. But I do admire it."

THE END

ACKNOWLEDGMENTS

If we ever collaborate on a thriller set in Heaven, Hell, or Infinity, we will research the same way we explored the vast and mysterious Mississippi River: consult the best guidebooks we can find. For *Forty Days and Forty Nights*, we are indebted to many:

Old Glory by Jonathan Raban, who voyaged the length of the Mississippi River in a very small motor boat and chronicled his unlikely survival mile by elucidating mile and character by fascinating character.

Rising Tide: The Great Mississippi Flood of 1927 and How It Changed America by John Barry, presents a river unimaginably powerful and dedicated to destruction. Barry details the history and engineering techniques of the Army Corps of Engineers and the man who invented most of those methods, James B. Eads. John Barry also writes rainstorms better than anyone in the business.

John McPhee's "Atchafalaya" essay from his *Control of Nature* renders the Mississippi's might and capriciousness thoroughly believable, while his account of the immense mechanics of the Old River Control Structure is a model for speaking plainly to the laity.

Mark Twain's *The Adventures of Huckleberry Finn* and his definitive Mississippi River pilot memoir *Old Times on the Mississippi* are packed with journalistic detail.

Personal Memoirs of U. S. Grant, published by Mark Twain in 1885, still tells us much about our river, our army, and our nation.

Florence Dorsey's *Road to the Sea: The Story of James B. Eads and the Mississippi River* portrays the great engineer's personal life and times, which dovetail intriguingly with Ulysses Grant's.

Joy J. Jackson's *Where the River Runs Deep: The Story of a Mississippi River Pilot* pictures the life of river-piloting in the first two-thirds of the twentieth century.

The U.S. Army Corps of Engineers publishes many, many online articles about every aspect of the Mississippi River: flood control;

navigation; wetlands and wildlife preservation; construction of levees, dams, and weirs; and dredging channels and harbors.

The *Brown Water News* section of the *Professional Mariner Journal* contains the latest on barges, towboats, and river navigation, including clear-eyed accounts of groundings, sinkings, collisions, and fires.

Stick and Rudder: An Explanation of the Art of Flying by Wolfgang Langewiesche is required reading for anyone who wants to fly a small plane, much less write about it.

After the books, people were kind to us and generous with their time and knowledge.

We thank LTC Heidi Demarest of the U.S. Military Academy at West Point for aligning us with army customs.

Our good friend "Eddie the Cop," NYPD First Grade Detective Edward Thomas, has always cast an exacting eye and ear on our depictions of police work.

We learned about helicopters from Kenneth Pike and Alasdair Lyon and the National Helicopter Museum in Stratford, Connecticut.

We learned about airplanes from Mike Coligny, Master Instructor Emeritus, Justin's grade school mate.

Our old friend Walter Kisly taught us the finer points of executing a parachute landing fall.

Tom DiGiovanni explained how a life coach is not like a shrink, not like a therapist, and not at all like a bossy wife.

We were able to observe unusually closely the intricacies of Mississippi Delta cotton farming from planting to ginning to land management during frequent visits with Amber's cousin Steve Stevens. Thanks to Steve's tire-size Rolodex, people of all walks of life welcomed us into their lives, their homes, and their churches.

Once we were writing, we received meticulous and imaginative editorial readings from Deborah Schneider, Mary Gay Shipley, and Rod Lorenzen, and, ultimately, Devon E. Lord and her colleagues at the University of Louisiana at Lafayette Press–including an extraordinarily insightful "Anonymous Reader."

Four special friends were immensely helpful:

Clyde Lynds turned figments of hopeful images into arresting cover art.

Henry Morrison suggested an overview to help readers see what our huge canvas really looked like. That inspired the "blimp trip," which we hope helped readers. It certainly helped us.

Claiborne Hancock, as always, opened doors locked to ordinary mortals.

And Julia Reidhead led two reserved writers out of the desert of reticence, dragged them up onto the pulpit, and encouraged them to preach the good news of strong feelings and visible emotion—starting at River Mile 806.

Amber Edwards & Justin Scott
March 11, 2021